The Compounders

To Belynda,
My #1 stalker fan!
Thanks for everything you do.

Much love,
Julie Trettel

THE
COMPOUNDERS
BOOK ONE

JULIE TRETTEL

Kamel Press

Please visit
www.JulieTrettel.com
to see more from this author!

Please visit
www.KamelPress.com
to see more great books!

ISBN-13:   978-1-62487-080-4 - Paperback

                978-1-62487-081-1 - eBook

Library of Congress Control Number: 2015956668

Published in the USA.

This book is dedicated to:

My wonderful husband, James. Without you, The Compounders, would still be just another story running through my head. Thank you for your love, patience, and encouragement.

I also need to thank God for the many blessings bestowed upon me. With Him all things are possible.

A special thanks to my dear friend, Angie Tubbs for being a sounding board and honest critic at all hours through this whole process. Love you girl!

And finally some shout outs to Roman, Hope, Bethany, Kathryn, Mom, Aunt Deanie, Kari, and Kermit for believing in me and supporting me every step of the way.

Prologue

"HOLLY JENKINS, if you can't pay attention for more than two seconds, I'll be forced to issue you a writing assignment for the weekend." Mrs. Lamay was miffed.

And so was Holly.

Seven years living underground, and I still have homework on weekends! Holly thought. *Her lesson is so boring today. How does she expect me to pay attention? She's lucky I didn't fall asleep!* Holly couldn't refrain from rolling her eyes.

"That's it, Holly, you will write an essay on the history of this bunker, and it's due Monday."

"But I was paying attention!" She protested aloud. *The history of the bunker? Who cares? Nobody but those who live here will ever care about that. I'm quite certain that normal teens across America are going to parties and movies, hanging with friends, and going on dates. That's far more exciting than what's going on here. When mom finds out about this, the highlight of my Friday night will be writing the most boring history of the most boring people on the planet!*

* * * * *

"Holly, have you started writing your history paper? Remember, you have to have it ready to turn in to Mrs. Lamay on Monday morning!"

"Yes, mom. I'm working on it now."

Holly read the paper aloud to herself.

A History of the Bunker
by Holly Jenkins

They say there were no signs but, in hindsight, there always are. No one really believed it could happen here. No one except my father, Mike Jenkins. He did. He was what they once called a prepper, and people thought he was crazy.

They said 9/11 really changed him. With the nation at war and a country at odds over it, he stocked up on food, water, guns, ammo, first aid supplies, camping equipment, and more. My mother went along with it. . . learning survival skills and gardening tips.

When my brother, Charlie, was born, father worried even more about everything. Three months later, when mother turned up pregnant with me, father began to really fret and searched for a safe place where he could take his family if things turned bad. He found a small, rocky mountain in the hills of western Virginia. Two hundred and four acres of land that no one wanted. With its rocky cliffs and steep hills, no one would think to go up there.

At first, he built a tree house. Seriously! It was a small covered building up in the trees. Someone would have to know it was there to see it. Hidden high in the branches of a cluster of sturdy old oaks, it was just big enough for a double bed, a couple of pack 'n plays, and a small kitchen area. Later, Charlie and I spent years playing in that tree house.

When the new year rang in, I was just twelve days old. New Years always stressed my father out more than any other day. If someone was going to take down a grid or attack while our defenses were down, New Years was the night to do it with the greatest impact while the whole world got drunk and cared more about partying than what was actually happening.

Much to father's protest, mother refused to spend a cold, snowy New Years with two small children in that primitive tree house. So we remained in the city with bags packed and car loaded . . . just in case. When midnight came and went with not even a hiccup in electricity, mother chastised him as paranoid but continued to support him.

I was four years old when he began erecting the compound. It was a massive underground town built into the side of the mountain at the top of the hill. It took over two years to complete construction.

He outsourced the project to a company in Utah, figuring they lived far enough away to trust them with such a project. If the stuff hit the fan, the distance would be too far away for them to invade the compound. The fewer local people that knew what was going on up on that mountain, the better.

The bunker itself consisted of common areas and family wings called pods. There was everything we would need in life. Everyone pitched in and had jobs that helped around the compound . . . even the kids. Father wanted as normal a life as possible for his family, no matter what happened outside the walls of the sanctuary, so he created a small town inside the bunker to ensure we missed nothing in life.

There was a large community room complete with several couches, a pool table, a big screen TV, and a huge video library. Just to the side of the community room and to the right was the dining room and kitchen. The kitchen was equipped with industrial appliances. Off the kitchen, a giant pantry housed the utilities and a hallway led to the greenhouse, keeping all food in close proximity.

There was also an exercise room, since living underground didn't easily afford the natural exercise of the outside world. Still, I preferred to walk the hallways around the complex instead of spending time in one room walking on a treadmill. The exercise room was two stories deep. Aside from the usual gym equipment, there was a rock-climbing wall across one side of the room that was tall enough for an added basketball net.

Another common room included a library and music area. Father was concerned that the arts would disappear in the wake of a doomsday scenario, so there were various instruments and lesson books for anyone who wanted to learn. There was also a large music collection as well as books. He bought up copies of famous art prints, since they could not afford originals.

The doctor maintained an operational clinic. Everyone still had to go to church every Sunday, with activities and fellowship on Wednesdays. There were two offices in the same section as the church, one for father and one for the pastor.

Father erected an armory at the back of the complex for emergencies, which he spent nearly a decade stocking with guns, ammo, and reloading equipment. There was even a general store. There was no currency to speak of, but the store held extra supplies, clothing, materials, and personal hygiene items. And, of course, there was a schoolroom.

Living underground for nearly half our lives didn't mean we got a free pass on education. The school was stocked with learning materials from kindergarten through high school and even some college texts prior to closing the doors.

All compounder kids attended school Monday through Friday.

Aside from the common rooms, there were pods. . . or family

living areas. Each pod had its own bathroom facilities, so there were no common restrooms.

Each family had one pod, but there were several unoccupied pods for future growth, should we remain underground for many years. Aside from the bathroom, the remaining area was one large room with modular walls that could create rooms as needed to accommodate any given family.

Of the remaining pods, two were for routine storage and one for a clothing storage unit. There were a couple of sewing machines and fabric for anyone wanting to create something new or special. There was also virtually every size of clothing for boys, girls, men, and women for every season and every reason.

The last pod housed what was left of the luxury supplies that rotated through the General Store.

Pod 7 was designed specifically for me.

We moved to the compound shortly before my tenth birthday. Prior to that, we spent many weekends and summers there.

As my father saw his beloved country falling deeper into darkness and was certain of impending doom, he readied the family to move to the mountain.

Then the stock market crashed. The nation saw a deep recession that politicians refused to admit. While they spouted praises and plans of a rebound, they continued to raise the deficit and sell out to China. Citizens saw an increase in unemployment and deterioration in resources. While America continued to fight a war in the Middle East, father felt one brewing right here at home.

Not in America! That's what many thought. He frequently recited the phrase, "United we stand, divided we fall."

After a series of elections showing an extremely divided nation, he determined the time was right to move everyone to the compound, permanently. We packed up everything of use, sold off the rest, and moved to our little mountain.

Father had created a network with others of like mind. He was very cautious with whom he shared information and had very specific jobs he wanted filled in the event of a true socio-economic collapse. He didn't follow suit with normal doomsday preppers in his selections. He was already well prepared in weapons, hunting, and defense and was handy with most maintenance issues that might arise.

Mother was an incredible cook. Between the two of them, the group could survive for a long time, but he wanted more for me and Charlie. He sought to create as normal a life as possible, even while preparing to live indefinitely underground.

The compound had a doctor, a teacher, a preacher, a supply

manager to run the general store, extra hands for hunting and gathering, security, and people who could cook for large groups. Even during doomsday, Charlie and I went to church every Sunday and school every day. That was our father's dream.

Those invited into the bunker began calling themselves the compounders. The location and the specifics were always kept secret. No one really knew everything my father had created on the compound until they moved there.

When we first arrived at the bunker, the door was locked only at night, so Charlie and I spent carefree days roaming the woods around the compound and playing in that tree house. Shortly after we settled into our new home, life in the United States began to change quickly, just as our father had always predicted.

A series of events saw a rise in racism. Still other events led to cries for drastic gun control, which caused even greater division amongst the people. Politicians, trying to regain control of the country, turned away from democracy and invoked socialistic laws that eventually led people to rebel against the government. As the people rose up, the government employed martial law to reestablish peace. By then, the last compounder purposefully chosen by my father had moved into the bunker. Four years after the last of us arrived to the bunker, we closed the doors and locked ourselves away from the world below.

Living life underground isn't always easy, but we're surviving.

What has become of the United States of America since that day? We do not know.

* * * * *

"Holly, are you about done with that paper?"

"Almost, Mom."

Holly thought, but dared not write, *I dream of the day my father opens those doors so I can run through my woods and spend the rest of my life discovering what's out there!*

* * * * *

Chapter 1

THEY STOOD in silence, not daring to move or breathe for fear they would make a sound and be discovered. It seemed like an eternity waiting for them to pass. After some time, they began to relax. It had been quiet long enough, and the excitement of impending danger was waning. The excitement changed with the realization that he would soon whisk her away from this dungeon forever.

Turning towards her, his piercing blue eyes looked straight into her soul. Her heart began to beat faster with each passing second. He reached up and tucked a stray hair behind her ear, ever so lightly brushing her cheek, and she felt her body respond and come to life at his touch. His arms wrapped around her, and he pulled her close. She could feel every rippling muscle beneath his shirt; her body felt on fire. Her breath caught as he closed his eyes and slowly lowered his head toward hers. A light shudder shook her body as she felt his breath on her lips, and her eyes closed slowly. As she leaned in closer...

WHACK

A pillow hit her in the head.

"Wake up Holly!"

With a groan, she opened her eyes to find Charlie standing over her on the bed, his bare ass shining bright white and waving in the air. "Happy" was on one cheek and "Birthday" on the other. It was her annual birthday mooning dance! She screamed and chucked a pillow at him as he scrambled to pull his pants back up while falling to the floor. Their mom and dad walked in and looked down sternly at him.

"Charlie, you will be eighteen in two weeks. When are you going to grow up?"

He grinned, looked at Holly, and winked. "Never!"

Mike sighed, showing his frustration with this large man-child sprawled across the floor surrounded by 100 balloons in honor of Holly's seventeenth birthday. While she was mostly displeased that they woke her from such a dream, she was secretly happy that despite their journey into adulthood, her big brother was the one unchanging constant in her life.

She was just seven years old when Charlie decided it would be funny to write Happy Birthday on his butt and dance around the room singing to her. In the shock of the moment, mother had screamed and chased that mischievous little boy around the room for twenty minutes, knocking over a table, stepping on the family cat, and causing a spectacle that sent Holly into hysterics.

She smiled now, remembering that moment. Much to the chagrin of their parents, that was the start of a new birthday tradition. Looking over at the scowls and sighs coming from her parents today, she couldn't help but giggle. Charlie reached up and pulled her off the bed, and the two lay on the floor amongst 100 balloons, laughing like the small kids they once were.

"Happy birthday Holly!" Mike said as he rolled his eyes and turned to walk away.

"When you two hyenas are done, come on down to the kitchen. I have a surprise waiting for the birthday girl," mother said. Just as Holly knew she'd be serenaded with her brother's ass at some point today, she also knew her 'surprise' was her favorite breakfast of banana pancakes with strawberry topping. In their simple life, some things never changed.

* * * * *

Charlie and Holly lay on the floor staring at the ceiling. He would be turning eighteen in two weeks and, while they both longed for adventure, excitement, and a break from the monotonous life they lived here underground, there was a nostalgic sadness in knowing they were growing up and things would inevitably change.

After several moments in their separate thoughts, Charlie broke the silence. "You know, Milo's been hanging around dad even more so than usual lately."

Holly pondered that for a second. "You okay with that? It should be you he's grooming to run this place someday, not Milo."

Charlie chuckled. "You know dad will never look at me like that. I will never be the son he dreams of following in his footsteps. If Milo can be, more power to him. At least it keeps the glares off me for a bit. That's not what I meant anyway. I've seen how Milo looks at you. I'd say dad's grooming him to take over more than my inheritance, Hols."

She laughed, shook her head, and punched him in the arm. "You've lost your mind, Charlie! Do you actually think that dad would condemn me to boring old Milo Weaver? You're crazy! It'll never happen."

He hesitated before proceeding. "Hols, as I understand it, he's already formally asked dad to" ahem... he cleared his throat and swallowed hard... "court you. And I don't think dad could be more excited than the possible union of his beloved daughter with the golden boy."

Holly made a noise somewhere between a laugh and a growl, and through gritted teeth said, "The mere fact he'd use the word 'courting' in this day and age is a testament to what a disaster that would be! Milo Weaver and I have absolutely nothing in common. Dad has to know that."

Charlie shrugged as he got up to leave. "Just thought I'd give you the heads up, little sister."

She huffed off to the shower thinking of Milo Weaver. He was two years older than her and the eldest son of Pastor Weaver. She had heard rumors that Mike invited the Weavers to the bunker, not just because father was in search of a preacher, but also because the Weaver's had three sons around Holly's age. Milo's brother, Chris, was her age and her very best friend. Eric, the youngest, was just a year younger. Eric was a classic baby brother, always tagging along and annoying Chris and Holly. Milo was just, well, Milo!

* * * * *

Milo Weaver was quiet as a kid. He always had his nose in a book and often spent more time with the adults than the kids in the compound. He was the eldest of all the kids and mature beyond his age. In a nutshell, he never did anything unexpected. He was the picture of perfect and, to Holly, that was the picture of boring.

Looks-wise, he wasn't so bad. He had grown taller and leaner the last few years. He worked out in the gym daily, and it showed. The other girls in the compound liked to watch him workout, and a few had big crushes on him; but there had to be more to a guy than good looks and a nice body. Milo couldn't possibly make that cut, unless he was the last man on earth. With a frown, Holly realized he almost was. That thought sat heavy as she finished getting ready and headed to the kitchen.

As she entered the community room, she saw the Sawyer twins on the lookout. One of them jumped up and ran to the kitchen screaming, "Here she comes!" The other took her hand and escorted her into the dining room. As she entered, everyone greeted her with a big "Happy Birthday Holly!"

All the residents of the compound were there to celebrate, and mom walked over with a big stack of banana pancakes covered in strawberry sauce and a lit candle on top. Chants to make a wish arose. Holly closed her eyes and thought, *I wish for adventure, excitement, and romance outside the walls of this bunker. I long to be free and run in the sun and sleep beneath the stars again. That is what I wish, not a perfectly safe, planned union with Milo Weaver, and stuck in this hole forever.* With a slight frown, she blew out the candle to the cheers of everyone present.

The remainder of the day was light and uneventful, with everyone taking the day off in celebration of Holly's birthday. It was a relatively quiet day of fellowship and games. After dinner, everyone retired to the community room, not wanting the day to end. Holly managed to avoid Milo all day but caught him watching her several times. She was conscious of it after Charlie's words of warning and hung back to help clean up. Milo lingered behind too.

Once the final dish was cleaned, the remaining group headed for the community room. As she passed by, he reached out and took her hand. His hand was cool, slightly clammy, and a little shaky. He was clearly nervous. Holly turned to face him, curious by this sudden attention. He looked down and smiled, relaxing a bit. With his other hand, he produced a small wrapped box and handed it to her. He let go of her hand so she could take it. He grinned a boyish grin that she had never seen before, leaned in, and whispered, "Happy Birthday, Holly." Then he walked away and disappeared into the community room with the others.

She unwrapped the small box, hesitantly. When she saw it was a jewelry box, her eyes widened, she gulped hard, and her pulse began to race with unwanted nerves. Shaky hands opened the gift and found a beautiful oval locket. It was simple and not very ornate, but when she opened it, her heart skipped a beat. Inside, instead of pictures of people or confessions of unfounded love as Charlie would have bet on, were two tiny pictures. The first was a tree, a real tree with sun shining brightly through the branches. On the other side was a picture of the moon and stars.

How did he know? How could he know? She could not help herself. She held the locket close to her heart and smiled, feeling warm all over. She had never received a more perfect gift. In that moment, everything she had ever thought of Milo Weaver changed.

Slightly confused, she made her way into the community room with the others. Milo was already sucked into a game of billiards with several others. She avoided eye contact and made her way to one of the couches where Chris and Cassie were waving to her.

* * * * *

Cassie Worthington was the oldest of five. Her parents managed the greenhouse and grew the most amazing fruits and veggies year round. The entire family worked in the gardens, and Cassie had already proven herself to have just as green a thumb as her parents. More importantly she was Holly's other best friend. Holly, Chris, and Cassie had become fast friends even before they all moved to the bunker, and the three of them had been inseparable since. Often called the Three Musketeers, the trio was well known by all for their adventures and often-thoughtless antics. Any one of them by themselves could have been a handful, but together they were a constant in their gift for trouble.

As the three sat talking late into the evening, she could feel Milo's eyes on her and absentmindedly twirled the locket in her fingers and fell silent. Chris and Cassie didn't seem to notice.

* * * * *

Something jolted her attention as she heard her father talking with Colton Evers who was in charge of the armory and security. "Mike, I'm telling you there must have been ten turkeys on the cameras this week. Imagine what a Christmas feast that would be!"

"I dunno Colton. Remember the last time we tried to hunt for Thanksgiving?"

"I know Mike, I know, but that was two years ago. I monitor the perimeter cameras daily. There hasn't been a soul in sight in more than a year now, and with that many turkeys, clearly no one's hunting them. We haven't had fresh meat in ages. I think now is the time."

"Okay Colton, we'll discuss with the others and if they are in agreement we will open the doors for hunting."

Holly's heart leapt. *They're considering opening the doors!* She wanted to scream it for all to hear. Her heart jumped out of her chest just at the thought. She said a quick prayer that all would go well, knowing that if it did not, her father would lock them all away forever.

* * * * *

Chapter 2

IT HAD been just over two years since the bunker doors were last opened. The men were out hunting turkey for the Thanksgiving feast and something bad happened. Holly still to this day did not know exactly what occurred on that dreadful day, but the compound lost a good man, and the elders shut the door for the last time.

Holly had long since stopped praying they would change their minds and open the doors once again. There used to be a time when people came and went all the time. They lived in a full compound, not just stuck in an underground bunker. The area surrounding the bunker provided many resources and, for Holly, it provided freedom and some privacy. Even when things got bad and the doors closed initially, groups would still go out during the day for hunting and gathering, but not since that Thanksgiving hunt two years earlier. They shut the doors and never opened them again. She resented the bunker for those very reasons but wouldn't dare admit it for fear of hurting her father.

Mike Jenkins was a good man. Everything he did, he did for the common good. Ultimately, the bunker, the compound, and the entire mountain within which they lived was his. The others looked to him as their leader, and he always had final say in decisions; but Mike didn't want to live in a dictatorship. He dreamed of a land of true equality to raise his children. Instead of running the compound his way all the time, he created a Board of Elders where the head of each household had equal say in compound matters. The entire community voted on things beyond that, but general business and decisions remained in the hands of the elders.

* * * * *

Holly had always been good at sneaking around. She knew how to be quiet and where the best hiding places were, and she knew that the elders always held their meetings in the chapel. There weren't many places to hide in a room such as that, but Holly knew from years of snooping on important grown up meetings that her father's office provided coverage and easy listening, since it was originally part of the same room. The walls constructed to create the office were built as a last thought and were thin enough for someone to hear on the other side. There were even some cracks in a few places from which to peek.

And so on this night, she found herself crammed against the wall in her father's office behind his reading chair, which at one point would have concealed her. It had been so long since anything important enough for her to snoop had happened. She was remembering a space much larger than the spot she now awkwardly tried to cram into with no hope of actually concealing herself.

Too late to turn back now, she thought.

The men and a few women that comprised the elders group were already assembling in the room just on the other side of the thin wall. She strained against it to hear what they were saying.

"How can we be sure our men will be safe out there this time?" Mrs. Lamay asked.

"Patty, we know how you feel after the attack on Jerry. It was terrible, but that was two years ago. And from the wildlife cams as well as the surveillance cameras, we haven't seen any activity in the area for a very long time, not even further down the mountain on any side."

Holly struggled to tell who was speaking.

"We'll take precautions, of course, but fresh meat from a hunt would do much for the morale of this place, not to mention the stomachs."

Everyone laughed, and Holly strained to put a face to the voice she heard through the wall. She finally gave up and moved to a small hole in the wall she had once been able to see through and hoped it, too, hadn't shrunk over the years. Since her father's office was dark, it was not too difficult to see where the cracks and weak spots were located. She moved aside a small bookcase as quietly as she could, praying that no one heard and became suspicious. Light flooded into the room. It took a second for her eyes to readjust before she dared peek through. What she saw there made her gasp and jump back. Standing on the stage just to the right of her father was Milo Weaver.

Holly could not put the voice to a face because she had never once considered that Milo was now a member of the elders group. While she tried to concentrate on what they were saying, her mind couldn't help wandering as she tried to grasp the concept that he was part of the elders. He was not just an elder; he held a place of authority on stage with her father.

She couldn't imagine why he would hold such a rank within the bunker, unless... Her eyes widened, and she choked down a groan as she remembered what her brother had said that very morning. Certainly, her father would know better than to try to arrange her love life without consulting her first.

* * * * *

She was so caught up in her thoughts, cursing her father, and growing more and more angry by the second, that she did not notice the meeting had adjourned until she was shocked back to reality when the lights suddenly came on in her father's office. She jumped and instinctively squeezed her body as tightly as possible, praying the chair that seemed so small now would actually conceal her.

Milo noticed the bookcase was slightly off almost immediately upon entering Mike Weaver's office. He just needed a piece of paper from the desk and would be in and out quickly. He saw Holly sneak out of the common room earlier, before they called the meeting to order. He was hoping he could catch her in the gym before bed.

As he rummaged the desk in search of the paper Mike had asked him to retrieve, he saw a slight movement from the corner of his eye. He jolted in that direction and at first saw nothing, and then he noticed something odd from under the chair. Was that a leg?

He moved in for a closer look and peered behind the chair. He was thrown off by the sight of Holly crouched awkwardly behind it. He laughed out loud, a full belly laugh that nearly brought tears to his eyes.

She cringed at the approaching footsteps and jumped slightly as a roar of laughter rang out from above her. She turned her head for a better look, trying hard not to be detected, but her position wouldn't allow it. The next thing she knew, he pulled the chair away, and she found herself splayed out across the floor of her father's office, with Milo Weaver laughing at her.

Not my best moment, she thought to herself. She jumped up, trying not to show the cramps in her body as she stretched back into a normal shape. She glared at him, then turned and stomped off.

He quickly put the bookcase and chair back into position, grabbed the paper from the desk, and hollered after her. "Holly, wait up."

She stopped for a second, and then decided to continue and ignore him.

"Holly, come on. Wait up."

She turned, irritated more at herself for getting caught, but also at him for laughing at her.

"What Milo?"

"Um, what was that all about? What were you doing in there?" He didn't have his normal critical scowl; he honestly looked amused, which irritated her even further.

"I was trying to listen to the meeting, if you must know. It's not as if anyone will actually tell me anything that goes on around this place. So I've realized it's my job to stay informed on my own." Her chin obstinately jutted out in self-resolution that she was in the right for snooping in on the meeting, regardless of what he thought.

Milo laughed. "You didn't need to go to all that trouble; you could have just asked. I didn't even know a human being could possibly get into that shape you were in, let alone hold it for so long."

She realized he was trying to be funny, but it made her feel even more embarrassed and angry. "Don't you dare tell my father about this, Milo Weaver!" She turned on her heels and started to stomp off, realizing it was a childish move but not caring.

He sounded almost hurt. "You really think I'd do that, Holly?"

Something in his voice made her stop and turn to face him. "I don't know Milo. I really don't know what you would do or say. We may live in the same bunker, but I don't really know you at all."

As she turned to go, she realized that she hadn't meant for her words to sound so mean, so she turned to look at him one last time. He really did look hurt. "I didn't know you were an elder now, congratulations." She tried to smile but she didn't sound completely sincere. She appeared more irritated by it and consciously made an effort to soften her voice before speaking again. "Thanks for the locket; it was perfect." She smiled at him, and he beamed.

She turned and continued down the hall thinking, maybe a little too perfect. She'd have to talk with Chris and hoped he wasn't entertaining the idea that she suspected may be running rampant. *Milo and Holly?* She almost laughed at the thought. *No,* she thought, *that will never happen!*

* * * * *

Chapter 3

WHEN HOLLY woke up the next morning, she showered, dressed, and headed for the range. At the very back of the bunker near the emergency back door, her father, along with Colton Evers, had designed an armory and range. The thought was that each person within the bunker should be proficient at shooting.

The range itself consisted of four old school buses in a line, extending out away from the primary bunker area. It allowed for two lanes of shooters. The armory housed every weapon within the bunker, with exception of a stocked small safe room at the primary entrance for emergencies. No one ever carried within the bunker. Everyone had to check guns, knives, bows, and even slingshots in and out through the armory, as needed.

Years ago, this meant a lot of people came and went through the back entrance as most would check out a weapon just to go for a walk in the fresh air. Now, the area remained largely secluded, except for those wishing to keep up their skills with weapons. At one point, it was mandatory that everyone spend time each week on these skills. As years passed without a need, however, people grew slack and rarely put much effort into marksmanship. But not Holly. She spent many hours every afternoon working on her shooting, becoming more proficient as time passed.

This morning, she wanted to get to the range and go through her routine early, fearing that news of the bunker doors possibly opening would drive more people to go and brush up on their skills for the upcoming hunt.

When she reached the range, Colton Evers was already there, talking to Milo Weaver. Holly sighed. In a world as small as theirs, it would be impossible to avoid him, and she seemed to find his presence everywhere lately.

"Morning, Holly. You're here awfully early today." Colton greeted her.

"I know. I was worried perhaps others would be coming down today, and I wanted to get my practice in before it got too crowded."

She still didn't know if the elders had actually agreed to open the doors for the hunt. She almost laughed to herself as she realized she was so distracted by Milo that she did not hear the final verdict the night before.

"Yeah, you're a smart girl. As word spreads about the doors opening for the Christmas hunt, there's bound to be plenty rushing down to dust off their shot. Not everyone is as diligent at keeping up their skills." He prattled on, but she tuned him out, as the excitement of hearing the doors would definitely open for a Christmas hunt overwhelmed her.

"Holly? Holly?" Milo was trying to get her attention.

"Um, what?"

"What weapon do you want?" Colton asked.

"Oh, just the usual, Mr. Evers."

She grinned at the older man as he handed her a pink Beretta Nano and a box of 9mm ammo, which he had already gathered the moment he saw her arrive.

"Thanks!"

Milo eyed her suspiciously.

"You have a 'usual'?"

He was a bit surprised, having never imagined the princess of the compound to be an avid shooter.

"Of course, don't you?"

She really didn't know if he did but was put off a bit by the incredulous tone that she would actually have a 'usual' at the range.

Colton handed Milo an AK47 with a box of 7.62x39 ammo, and Milo grinned back at Holly, "Of course," he replied. She looked down at the tiny gun in her hands and shrugged her shoulders. As they walked over to the range, she felt the need to comment, which irritated her.

"I know it's not the most beneficial for hunting, but it'll do the job for self protection, and it's fun to shoot."

She put on her ear and eye protection, loaded the magazine, and looked smugly at him before firing off six rounds dead center on the target.

He was impressed, but he loaded his magazine and set off a round equal to hers. He turned and smiled back at her just as smugly, knowing that she was watching him.

She was surprised to find him such a good shot. She unloaded her Nano and offered it to him. He did the same with the AK47. They both loaded the new guns and fired off a series. Both hit bull's-eyes with each round.

Holly's eyes were big with amazement to find Milo had shot so well with her small gun in his large hands. He was equally impressed at her skills with the AK. She took back her gun, replaced a few loose rounds into the box of ammo, and returned it to Colton. She asked for a 12ga shotgun instead. Milo did the same and asked for a Colt 45 Peacemaker. Colton smiled at them both and shook his head as he issued the requests.

Colton Evers knew that Milo and Holly were the two best shots and most avid shooters in the entire compound, himself excluded of course. But he but found it humorous that they obviously did not know that about each other.

They changed the targets, loaded the new guns, and shot off a round each. Both bull's-eyes. They switched weapons and did the same, with the same result. Milo was openly appreciative of Holly's skills. She was competitive, though, and upon return of her weapon, requested another and another. After the sixth round, they were equal in matches. Milo requested a bow and arrow. Holly grimaced, knowing it was her weakest weapon, so she chose the slingshot.

"A slingshot? Holly is that even a real weapon?" He scoffed.

"Why? Are you giving up and ready to admit I'm the best shot?" She was serious, but he was grinning. He had enjoyed the morning's events, but wasn't competitive enough to keep up with her temper if she lost.

He wasn't sure what came over him in that moment though, and, as he opened his mouth to concede, only one word came out, "Never!"

She huffed and took the slingshot. "You're going down this round, Weaver!" She was glad she sounded stronger than she felt. She couldn't take him with a bow and arrow. She suddenly remembered him as a young child, practicing repeatedly with the bow. She knew he was a decent shot back then and could only imagine how much better he was now. It was not in her, however, to back down from a challenge.

She replaced the target and, using a large BB, pulled back her slingshot and let it fly perfectly through the bull's-eye. She turned to him and grinned, satisfied with the look of shock on his face.

He loaded his arrow, pulled back on the bow, and, just as he was about to release it, she spoke. "By the way, I really did love the necklace and forgot to say thanks; it was really sweet."

As he released, he moved ever so slightly and landed the arrow just to the left of center mass. He stopped, put his head down and shook it, then looked over at her and grinned.

"You play pretty dirty there Jenkins," he said with a laugh, "But I'm glad you like your birthday present."

She smiled sweetly, "Don't blame me because you crack under pressure, Weaver." She offered him the slingshot.

He just shook his head and laughed. She realized he didn't seem so uptight and disgustingly perfect when he laughed like that. She thought, *He should do that more often, and maybe people won't always assume he walks around with a stick up his...*

Milo interrupted her thoughts, "Here goes nothing." He pulled back on the loaded slingshot and let it fly barely clipping the right corner of the paper. He hung his head in shame before making a bowing motion to her as he conceded.

"If Goliath ever shows up at our doorstep, I'll be glad to have you fight beside me," he said in mock appreciation.

She just laughed, realizing that she had actually enjoyed her showdown with Milo. The thought bothered her some, but she didn't want to dwell on it. It put a slight damper on her mood.

"Got to get going. Keep practicing; maybe someday you'll be good enough to take me." She tried to sound cute and playful, but when she smiled, it was forced and not the same easygoing smile she had given him all morning.

He noticed the cool look in her eyes. Everything had been going so well, and he was enjoying their time together. He wasn't quite sure what changed so suddenly but felt he had spooked her somehow. He tried to replay the events to figure out what he had said or done wrong but couldn't understand it.

He had been getting a lot of pressure from his dad, Holly's dad, and several of the elders, persuading him to pursue her. He had honestly not thought of her as anything but his little brother's pesky friend until they put the idea into his head. He had spent the last several weeks watching her from a distance. She often surprised him with her kindness toward others, especially when she thought no one was watching, which told him she was naturally good and caring and not at all the attention seeker he had assumed she was.

Despite his observations, he had been in no way prepared for the spontaneous meeting that morning at the range. He was more than a little shocked at just how good a shot she was. He was also pleasantly pleased at how well it had gone, for the most part, and more than a little surprised at how much fun he had with her. He just wished he knew what caused her to turn cold so suddenly.

* * * * *

Chapter 4

IT HAD been two days since her last encounter with Milo at the range. She had successfully avoided him since, as word of their showdown had circulated throughout the compound. Chris had even cornered her just that morning asking about it.

"So, Holly, Milo?" he asked. He didn't have to ask a full question as he and Holly had practically read each other's minds since childhood, always finishing each other sentences and asking partial questions that not even Cassie could keep up with or understand.

"Really?" was all she said. He raised an eyebrow that made her blush when she didn't mean to.

His eyes widened a bit, and he shot her a condemning look.

"What do you want me to say? We battled it out on the range to see who the better shot was; that was all." She tried to sound convincing.

"I'm cool, ya know," he told her. She knew he meant with her and Milo, IF there actually was a Holly and Milo, which she was certain, would never happen. She responded as if she didn't understand.

"Sure, you are, Chris." She said sarcastically. He knew she was just teasing him.

"Seriously, Hols. If that's what makes you happy, then I'm happy."

She groaned at him and shook her head no.

He grinned back. "Yeah, I didn't think so!" He pushed her playfully.

Cassie came over, rolling her eyes. Holly thought she saw Cassie and Chris stare at each other a fraction too long and then dismissed it. She was just having an off day all around. But the next morning the doors would be open for the big Christmas hunt and that excited her more than anything.

The remainder of the day, Holly was worse than the little kids on Christmas Eve. She was so excited about the Christmas hunt. She knew her dad would never allow her to go, but she prayed every second that everything would go smoothly and it would lead to future hunts. Maybe even one day, the opening of the bunker and the life of the compound would resume both inside and out.

She stalked and interrogated every elder or person with potential knowledge to find out all the details she could of the hunt. With that, she knew only five men were going out, and she was more than a little irritated to find that Milo Weaver was among them. She was a better shot, and it should have been her, but daddy would never allow his little princess to be out there. It irritated her, and she had to hold her anger in check as best she could when she ran into Milo that evening.

The cold look she gave him did not go unnoticed. He sighed. Maybe he had been right all along and never should have let the elders get into his head about her. He was excited about the hunt and being a part of it, but he suddenly wondered if part of the anger he saw just beneath the surface was just jealousy because he was allowed to go and she was not. He knew she was a far better shot than any of the four men assigned to the job. He felt sorry for her, but there was nothing he could do about it. Mike Jenkins would never put his daughter in harm's way.

Holly knew the hunters would be leaving the bunker at 5:00 a.m. and had strategic spots that each was to setup at before sunrise. She fell asleep knowing that she would be there when those doors opened and slept dreamless for a change.

She awoke with a start. Someone must have turned her alarm off. She had set it for 4:00 a.m., and the clock display said it was 4:45. She almost missed it. She jumped out of bed still in her PJ's and ran through the bunker to the back door where the five hunters would be assigned their weapons and the door opened for the first time.

Mike Jenkins sighed as he saw his daughter round the corner, sock footed, in her pajama bottoms and a loose tee shirt. He had sneaked in and turned off her alarm just before 4:00 a.m. that morning in hopes that she would not come to disrupt or make a big deal out of the opening of the bunker. His plan failed.

She skidded to a stop, nearly colliding with him. "Daddy I promise not to get in the way. I just want to see outside, breathe fresh air for the fraction of a moment that the door opens. I won't try to follow; you won't even know I'm here!"

She was sleepy eyed and makeup free, and her hair a mess, as she had not even stopped to brush it. Milo had never seen her like that. He had to admit that she looked good, natural, and carefree, just as he always thought of her. To him, she was a free spirit. One her father seemed to want him to tame; but he secretly admired her too much for that.

Mike begrudgingly agreed to let her stay, but only because he knew she wouldn't accept no for an answer. He knew he didn't listen to his wife enough when she warned him to choose his battles when it came to their daughter. As long as she didn't try to make a run for the open door, which he really wouldn't put past her, he knew this was a battle he wouldn't win, and he didn't want to waste time fighting. "Fine," he told her. "Just please don't get in the way."

She knew if she tried to join them or got in the way, he'd simply shut the door and never open it again, so she stayed to the side, helped Colton issue weapons, and didn't get in anyone's way.

When the moment came, they opened the door. No big ceremony; no crowning moment. As Holly saw through the door to the outside world, she saw a light dusting of snow on the ground and the bare branches in the trees beyond the door. She closed her eyes and swore she heard trumpets sounding in the distance. She inhaled the cold air as a burst of wind came through the doorway. She shuddered with the chill, and when her eyes opened, her senses were on fire. She had never felt so alive.

Milo watched in fascination, stalling until the other men passed through to the other side. He couldn't imagine what was going through her mind just then.

She saw him give one last nod and a knowing look her way, but she wasn't sure what exactly he thought he knew. He was so comfortable and confident inside the bunker that he couldn't possibly understand what it was like for her. When the door finally shut behind him, she felt deflated with the disappointment of it and headed back to bed with the hope and prayer that they would all return safely and successfully and that this would not be her last taste of the world beyond the bunker doors.

* * * * *

Holly did little that day. She tried to finish wrapping the small gifts she had made for her family and Chris and Cassie in an attempt to distract herself. She tried to read a book but couldn't focus. She tried to go to the gym, but after nearly falling off the treadmill, she gave up that idea, too. She was shooed from the kitchen twice. She tried to nap but was too anxious for even that. By late afternoon, with no word from the hunters, she headed down to the armory. Colton Evers was amongst the hunters selected, so no one was at the armory.

She sat on the floor with her back up against the wall, staring at the back door of the bunker. She remembered there were spare walkie-talkies in the armory and searched around for one. She sat back on the floor and turned on the radio, searching through stations to see if she could find the one they were using. It had been so long since she used them, she could no longer remember the frequencies. All she heard was static until the static broke out a voice she didn't recognize.

"Sarge? Come in Sarge." It was so faint, she almost couldn't make out the words, and then it was gone. She listened for what seemed a long time, but no other voices came though that channel. She thought she had imagined it and flipped through the other channels, finally hearing Milo's voice across the radio.

"It's 4:30. Rendezvous at the door at 5:00. I'll call it in."

He sounded so official and authoritative, Holly wondered just when he had grown up so much. She still thought of him as Chris's big brother. The Golden Boy, as she and Charlie had always called him. Milo could do no wrong in the eyes of the adults. He never got in trouble, never walked outside the perimeter, and never colored outside the lines. He was the perfect child and, more than once, she had been reminded of it... told that she should be more like him. However, this was not a child she was listening to; he grew up when she wasn't looking. He was a man now.

She turned the radio off, returned it to its place in the armory, and sat back down and waited. Milo must have called Charlie because he came around the corner within a few minutes.

"Chris was looking for you, Hols. Should have known you'd be here." He tousled her hair, and she smacked his hand away, "You were here all day?"

"No, I just got here a few minutes ago. It was getting late, and I didn't want to miss their return."

"Come to welcome the Golden Boy home safe and sound?" he asked teasingly.

She flashed red and punched her brother in the arm. "NO! I just wanted to see outside one last time. I'm hoping the sun isn't fully down. It wasn't up when they left this morning."

"Not gonna make a run for it this time are ya?" He wasn't entirely teasing this time. He knew Holly could do it. She was stubborn enough, and he knew how much she resented being locked up in the bunker all these years.

"No, I'm not," she said seriously. She wanted this to work, wanted them to open the doors permanently, and she wouldn't risk that chance by doing something spontaneous and stupid like darting outside.

At exactly 5:00, there was a series of three knocks at the back door. Even knowing they were coming, Holly jumped, and her stomach knotted with anticipation. Charlie laughed, then unlocked and opened the door. As all five men safely returned, they came bearing seven turkeys, three deer, and several bags full of squirrel and rabbits. It was a great day for a hunt, indeed!

Despite the excitement over the kills, Milo saw Holly staring out into the wild with a look of contentment and happiness on her face until the door completely closed and the bolt clicked into place. She suddenly seemed to deflate before his eyes with a look that reflected his own emotions at the sound of the final latch. He vowed to himself that he would continue working with the elders to encourage them to open the doors again, and again, and again, until they remained open for good. He understood how Holly felt, and he wanted the freedom and peace of the outdoors as much as he suspected she did.

* * * * *

Chapter 5

CHRISTMAS was bright and cheerful. Everyone stuffed themselves with fresh turkey and venison. It had been such a long time since any of them had fresh meat that they cooked the majority of it and held a great feast. It seemed to revitalize the entire bunker, even Holly.

With the successful Christmas hunt, the elders decided that a New Years Eve hunt would take place to stock up the freezers with fresh meats for the remainder of winter, which turned into weekly hunts for the next month.

By March, they were eating fresh meats daily, with a rotating group of men hunting in groups of three and five. Holly was getting more and more anxious with each day's hunt until finally in mid-March, Milo cornered her in the gym during an intense workout.

"Holly, what are you doing tomorrow?" he asked, which irritated her even more than him actually disrupting her workout.

"Hmmm, let's see," she said sarcastically. "First, I'm getting my hair dyed pink at that new boutique, and then I have an appointment with the dentist to file my fangs. Maybe I'll stop by my favorite restaurant in town on my way back home." She rolled her eyes at him but when he didn't comment, she just shook her head and moved to the kick boxing bag and resumed her workout. "I'm going to school, coming to the gym, having lunch with Chris and Cassie, and maybe going to the library to study. More likely, I will end up frustrated and back in here. You know... the same things I do every day!"

He cringed a bit at her resentment. Her life really didn't sound so bad to him; while he enjoyed the outdoors, he loved the peace and comfort the bunker provided. He didn't understand why she was so miserable at times. Still, he was doing this for her.

"Not tomorrow then; tomorrow is a day of change! Be ready at 6:00 a.m. I'll pick you up." He turned and walked away.

She was completely shocked and had no idea what he was talking about, so she just kept kicking until she was totally exhausted. Then she walked back to her pod, showered, and climbed into bed without dinner.

* * * * *

There was a knock on her bedroom door at 6:00 a.m. the next morning. She was just in a tee shirt and underwear when Milo walked in.

"Wake up Holly," he said. "I told you to be ready at 6:00 a.m." He sounded slightly irritated.

She looked at the clock and groaned. "You were serious?" She tried to put the pillow back over her head, but he walked in and grabbed it.

"I'm not kidding, you need to hurry."

She sat up sleepily and stretched before standing up. He turned around quickly, and she realized she was wearing only a tee shirt and underwear. She grabbed the blanket from the bed and wrapped up in it.

"Just let me take a quick shower and wake up."

"No time for that. Here." He took some clothes off the chair next to her bed and threw them in her direction. "Suit up fast or we're going to miss this opportunity; now let's go." He sounded adamant. She was tired but didn't want to fight, so she picked up the clothes. They were heavy and there were a lot of them.

"What is this?" she demanded.

"It's cold out today, you'll want them. Trust me." He sneaked a peak backwards, grinning so big it made her heart flip a little.

None of what he said fully registered until she was standing at the armory receiving her pink Beretta Nano and an M1A Scout with a suppressor. When she shot a look at Milo, he was still grinning. She looked around; only Milo and Colton were in the vicinity.

Milo grabbed a slingshot off the shelf and tossed it her way. "Just in case you need to protect yourself." He laughed, remembering how she had taken him in a shoot off with that slingshot.

She tucked the slingshot into her back jeans pocket beneath the several layers of clothing she wore. Her heart pounded hard and fast in her chest. She was sweating from the thick layers of clothing, and as Colton walked out of the armory to the back door of the bunker and gave an all clear for them to leave, her heart nearly pounded out of her chest, and she jumped up and down and squealed like a small child.

Milo laughed and gently nudged her out the door.

* * * * *

Holly stopped just outside the bunker door, looked down, and dragged her foot in the dirt, making a circle on the ground. She looked up and relished the sun shining on her face. She breathed deeply and felt the cold air burn through her lungs. She was ready to run, climb a tree, and swim in the ice cold water at the waterfall they had named Holly's Hole. She had dreamed so long of this day, and her heart soared.

Milo watched with fascination. He could feel the adrenaline kick in and thought she might just take off and run away, so he spoke up. "Rules Holly. I had to do many favors to make this happen. The deal is, you stay with me at all times, got it?"

She thought he sounded condescending and felt irritated. *He always has been a fun sucker,* she thought.

"Promise me, you won't try to run off by yourself. Your dad will never let you out again if you try. Promise me you will stay with me today." He wanted to set her free, but he couldn't chance it. He knew she resented the leash he had to keep on her but at least she was outside, and he would let her be as free as he could. He sighed.

She didn't want to spend the day with Milo and his rules, but she would give anything, even promise what he asked, just to be outside for a while. "Okay, Milo." She gently touched his arms and looked at him. "I'm grateful to you for doing this. Whatever you ask... I promise that I'll behave." She smiled at him.

He noticed the smile didn't reach her eyes. She wasn't as happy as he thought she would be. He suspected that she would rather be locked inside than spend the day with him. He had hoped this would be a change between them for the better. He wasn't so sure now but secretly vowed to make the most of the day.

"Come on. We're supposed to actually hunt today, but we can go for a walk and explore wherever you want."

She smiled back at him. She knew he was trying. She wasn't entirely sure why, but she could be thankful for that, at least. "Sure, I'd love to just walk around the compound and see how much everything has changed."

They spent the next hour just walking, largely in silence. At times, she could even forget he was there. She visited the old tree house and walked down to Holly's Hole. She wanted badly to dip her toes in the icy cold water, but refrained. She walked over to the old garden and was sad to see it overgrown and dead. It had once been beautiful and thriving.

When she got to the edge of the meadow, it was brown from the winter's cold with only hints of green splashes showing signs of the impending spring. She could no longer contain herself. She stopped at the edge of the woods and checked the perimeter as was engrained in her to do. When she was certain there was no danger, she put her guns down and took off at a full run across the meadow. The wind blew through her hair, and the cool wind stung her eyes, causing them to water. Her legs burned. Her lungs burned. She never felt so alive. The heavy layers of clothes weighed her down, so she slowly shed them as she ran back and forth across the meadow.

* * * * *

When she took off, Milo cursed under his breath. They had warned him about this. This is what couldn't happen, but something held him in place, and he just stood and watched her. He breathed a sigh of relief when she reached the far side of the meadow and turned to run back toward him. He hadn't realized he'd been holding his breath. He watched her run on and on for what felt like hours. After all, hadn't he done the same the first time they allowed him out alone? This, he could give her. He smiled, feeling happy as he watched her soar through the field.

As she began to wind down, she turned and ran straight back to him. Her hair was windblown and her cheeks bright red and tear streaked. *More likely, they were watering from the cold air,* he thought. He had never seen her cry. She looked alive and truly happy, and he was thankful that he could give her that.

When she approached him, she walked right up and, before she even realized what she was doing, stood on her tippy toes and kissed his cheek. "Thanks Milo!" she said with a laugh at the look of shock on his face. She looked back at the meadow. "Maybe just one more lap!" She grinned and took off running the perimeter of the field.

His insides knotted up. Things were going far better than he ever imagined. He froze in place as he watched her run, and his heart leapt when she turned and waved to him; then it plummeted when he saw movement in the trees just behind where she ran.

* * * * *

Holly heard a noise in the trees and whipped around just in time to see a large black bear come charging out of the woods right for her. Her heart stopped for a moment. She dropped to the ground face in the dirt, but that didn't deter the bear. He came right for her. She lay as still as she could, but he took his mighty paw and batted her back and forth with it. Pain surged through her body but she did not yell out and did not move. He stopped toying with her and began to walk around her, growling.

She felt on the ground and found three small stones. She slowly and carefully reached into her back pocket and retrieved the slingshot as the bear continued circling. She was thankful she had shed those extra layers. Just as the bear reared up on his hind legs and let out a loud roar, she rolled onto her back, loaded her slingshot, and let a stone fly, hitting the bear right on the nose.

The bear stumbled back for a second, then reared up and roared again. She let the second rock fly, then the third, all hit perfectly on the bear's nose. He stumbled backwards, and she heard a gunshot and saw the bear scramble to his feet and run back into the woods.

Blood was pumping hard in her ears, and she was shaking when she felt Milo's arms wrap around her. She hugged him back and winced in pain.

"Holly, are you okay? Where does it hurt?" He was already checking her over.

When she finally found her voice she said, "I'm okay Milo. A few bumps and bruises, but okay." It wasn't entirely true and she wasn't sure, but thought she may have a broken rib. She would secretly ask the doc to look at her later, but she couldn't let Milo suspect anything might be seriously wrong or she would never get this opportunity again.

As the adrenaline subsided, Milo couldn't stop talking. "Oh my God, Holly, did you see the size of that thing? I thought for sure you were a goner. I couldn't get a clear shot, and missing the target wouldn't do anything more than piss him off and make things worse. I've never been so scared in all my life. When he started batting you around, I thought I'd throw up." He rambled on and on until Holly just lay on the ground and started laughing. He finally shut up and lay next to her, laughing too. Neither really thought it funny. It was more like the hysterical laughter that sometimes comes with great danger. At that moment, laughter was the only thing keeping them from acknowledging what could have happened.

"I was only kidding with you about the slingshot, Holly. That wasn't the smartest thing to do with a bear, but did you see the look on that thing's face when you nailed him right in the nose? Priceless!"

She laughed harder. "Playing dead wasn't working; I didn't know what else to do. I wasn't thinking; I just reacted." Then she turned serious. "Thanks for having my back, Milo. I thought I was a goner for sure."

He hugged her close. "You're okay; everything's going to be okay."

She wasn't sure if he was trying to convince her or himself. "Maybe we shouldn't mention this to anyone. Just between you and me?"

He liked the way she said 'you and me' and smiled down at her. "Absolutely! Your father would not only lock you away forever, he'd have me shot before a firing squad for putting you in danger like that!" He laughed, but they both knew it wasn't far from the truth.

Holly trusted Chris Weaver with her life and just about every secret she'd ever had, but she had never expected to trust Milo in the same way. She wasn't entirely sure she did now; but what else could she do?

* * * * *

Chapter 6

OVER THE next few months, everything changed back into life in a compound once again. As spring came, more and more people made their way outdoors. Mike Jenkins still wasn't comfortable with it, but as people came and went without incident, he slowly lost the battle.

Milo and Holly had spent many days hunting side-by-side through the remainder of winter and well into early spring. They developed a sort of bond, almost a friendship, during that transition time. As the compound came alive again, she no longer needed him to come and go as she pleased. They seemed to drift back to the ways things had been before. He was spending more time with her father and the elders, adjusting to the changes, while she was free to roam about and do as she pleased... as long as she maintained her responsibilities.

By May, her high school graduation came and went with little notice due to the excitement of spring outside the bunker. The gardens that had been overgrown and dead just two months earlier were alive and thriving with abundant produce for harvest. Cassie's family headed up the restoration of the gardens and Holly spent endless hours throughout the spring helping cultivate the land again.

It wasn't her favorite thing to do, but it kept her outdoors for countless hours every day and was worth it to her. She'd have to think about what she wanted to do now that school was over. She knew her dad wanted her to do some independent college coursework, and that would buy her some time to figure it all out.

As spring changed into summer, she seemed to be happier than ever. She smiled more and was friendlier to everyone, especially Milo. Cassie and Chris teased her often about a budding romance, but she always brushed them off. It wasn't like that for her. She had grown to like Milo, even respected him. Besides an occasional flutter in her stomach when he looked at her in just the right way, she didn't really feel anything for him. She had always been an avid reader and had big ideas on love and romance. Milo Weaver just didn't fit that picture.

* * * * *

One day in the early days of summer, Milo sought Holly out to ask her to go for a walk. She should have been harvesting strawberries with the Worthington's, so he knew she would agree to go and use him as an excuse to get out of her assigned work. It had become clear in the preceding weeks that people in the compound had begun to link them together. He knew that she was horrified and angry at first, but something changed and she was more agreeable lately.

People wanted to see them together so badly that she could get out of just about anything as long as she was with him. Chris warned Milo that he thought this was the case, and he knew Holly better than anyone, so Milo took it for truth. He was okay with that and thought he, too, could use it to his advantage. She would use it to her advantage to get out of her assigned work and do things she wanted to do. He would use it to get to know her better and, hopefully, grow closer to her before she realized it. He felt a little guilty about that, but the elders were so certain they should be together. He liked her well enough to try, at least.

* * * * *

She rounded the corner, heading toward the kitchen, when she spotted Milo leaning up against the wall, deep in thought. Her first thought was to turn back and get away from him.

She wasn't in the mood for the smiling faces and nods of approval they seemed to get whenever they were together. It irritated her and wasn't even worth getting out of her chores.

"Hey Holly, I was just coming to find you."

Too late, she thought. "Hey Milo, what's up?" She tried to sound nonchalant.

He stared at her with his piercing blue eyes in just the way that sometimes sent butterflies through her stomach, made her cheeks pink involuntarily, and caused her heart to beat faster. He smiled warmly at her, and she couldn't help but realize just how handsome he really was. As the gap closed between them, he reached out and took her hands in his, which took her by surprise. They were cool, a little clammy, and not entirely confident. She wondered what he was up to but couldn't think past the pounding of her heart.

"I have off today and was wondering if you'd like to go for a hike up to the top of the mountain. I haven't been up there since the compound reopened and, well, it's a beautiful day. I know you're supposed to be harvesting today, but I think I can make arrangements." He grinned sheepishly.

She wasn't sure what to think. They had gone on several walks around the compound, spent hours hunting side-by-side. However, this felt different, and she wasn't sure what to do or say, so she just nodded yes.

"Yes?   Well, okay then!" he seemed relieved at her agreement. "Say we meet at the back door in about an hour?"

People had stopped coming and going through the back door now that the front of the bunker was fully open. The safe room near the front door had been set up as a checkpoint for weapons, so rarely was anyone, even Colton Evers, at the back entrance. She knew the back door was the easiest place to climb up to the top of the mountain. She was more familiar than anyone with that side of the mountain. Everyone else would have naturally gone out the front, around, and up the marked paths. It would be counterproductive to leave through the back door and swing around, down, and then back up to find the marked paths. There were no marked paths from the rear of the bunker, so she was a little surprised and curious that he would choose to go that way.

* * * * *

Exactly one hour later, Milo came down the hallway to the back door. Holly was waiting anxiously to see what he had in mind, and he was happy to see her ready and seemingly excited about their journey. He led the way up and over some of the boulders in a cut-through that she knew would lead them straight to the spring. She thought she was the only one who knew that route. It was a major shortcut that allowed her at least an hour of free time when she was younger and tasked to fetch water from the spring.

When they reached the spring, he stopped and filled the empty camel bladder from his daypack. He wasn't sure if she had thought to bring one, so he offered her a second empty one to fill and helped her fit it into her daypack. He took a long drink from the cold spring, closing his eyes and enjoying the clean, cool sensation.

He never fully understood why they did not pipe the spring water directly into the bunker, but during the construction, Mike had covered all his basis, so while they lived off spring water, it was pumped in and then distilled and treated before circulating through the bunker for fear of water contamination. The process removed all the natural minerals that gave the spring water that taste of perfection. He sighed, thinking how heavenly the cold spring water tasted.

Holly smiled at him. "I always preferred the spring water too."

They started their journey up to the top of the mountain. The day passed quickly and mostly in silence. She was amazed at how well he seemed to know his way around this side of the mountain. A part of her felt a little uncomfortable by it as she had always thought of this as her territory, but he seemed almost as familiar as she was. The closer they got to the top, the more certain she was that he was taking her to the large, flat boulder that provided a perfect overlook out to the mountains and valleys below, which wasn't exactly the top of the mountain but close enough.

As they reached the boulder and he helped her up to the top, she commented, "This has always been one of my favorite spots, especially for sunsets."

He was visibly shocked to hear that she had been up there
before. "Really? I can't believe you even knew this place was
here." He thought about it for a second. "When you were a
kid, you were always running off by yourself. Even Chris
didn't know where you went. Is there where you'd come to
hide?"

"Sometimes."

She hadn't allowed herself to think of that for a long
time. As she looked out across the valley, with the sun just
beginning to set, she closed her mind and tried not to think
about it.

The sunset was beautiful, and they stood just before the
last bit of light sunk behind a distant mountain. He took her
hand, and it was warm for once, but still a little clammy. She
didn't mind so much; she expected it. He turned to face her
and looked into her eyes. Her skin was all goose bumps, and
she sighed just as he closed the gap between them and ever
so gently pressed his lips to hers. Her eyes had barely closed
before it was over. He hugged her tightly to him, and they
watched as the last of the sun disappeared and night washed
over them.

"It's a long way back in the dark. You up for it?" she asked
him, knowing she could have found her way back blindfolded.
This was her land, and it housed all her most precious places.

"I've come prepared. We'll be okay." He reached into his
daypack and pulled out two headlamps, placing one on his
own head and one on hers, letting his thumb linger a bit and
brush down her cheek. It sent chills down her spine. *Always
prepared; always safe,* she thought. *Even when he's trying to
be adventurous, he's still in complete control.* She wasn't sure
why that irritated her.

They talked lightly on their walk back to the bunker. It
was late, and she was sure he was going to try to kiss her
again at the door to her pod, but he just lingered there, gazing
into her eyes for longer than would be considered normal.
Then he said good night, turned, and left for his own pod.

* * * * *

Holly lay in bed and replayed the day's events. Her first
kiss. It wasn't as magical as she had imagined it would be,

but it was nice. She would have liked to kiss him more, just to experience the sensation of it. Then, again, it was Milo... and at the end of the day, Milo was still Milo in her mind. She had been happy with his chosen site and still amazed that he even knew it existed. He seemed so confident and comfortable getting them there and back. Maybe there was more to him than she suspected. Maybe he had his secrets too.

Secrets.

She let herself think about and long for the place she had mourned for so long after they finally shut the doors and she was cut off to the surrounding world. The Cave.

* * * * *

Chapter 7

THE CAVE! Holly had tears in her eyes just thinking about it. She lay there crying and reminiscing. She had been just a little girl when she stumbled upon the cave. She had grown to love the place and would hide there whenever she could sneak away. She stored and hid all her most prized possessions there.

The entrance to the cave was a hole in some of the boulders not far from the entrance to the back door. It was hidden amongst a thick patch of blueberry bushes. She found it accidentally, literally falling into the hole while picking blueberries one day. At first, she was terrified, but soon she began to relate it to Alice and Wonderland. It was her very own rabbit hole, a place to escape and live out adventures as she dreamed and reenacted countless stories, casting herself as the heroine who would save the magical land below.

The Village. She hadn't thought of that place in a while. It had taken a long time to work up the courage to explore the cave beyond the bottom of the hole. What she found inside was a large cave with a section of wall that just seemed to disappear. A rock slide long ago perhaps. To her, it was the most amazing, most beautiful place on earth and provided her with her very own picture window to the world and the lovely village below their mountain.

What had become of it?

As she contemplated the flood of memories, she found herself vowing to search for the cave once again.

As bad luck would have it, much of the weeks to come had her busy around the compound, and her resolution to rediscover the entrance to the cave went unresolved. She allowed herself to think about it and daydream about it, though.

Cassie teased her, thinking she was daydreaming about Milo. Holly sighed at the thought. She hadn't spoken to him much since their journey to the boulder near the top of the mountain. She wasn't avoiding him; she'd just been too busy to spend time with him or even think of him. If she were honest with herself, she didn't want to dwell on any of it.

* * * * *

Holly had yet another full day planned, but as she came to the entrance of the common room, she overheard her father and Milo talking. She registered immediately that they were talking about her and how best to proceed with their relationship. It frustrated her and made her more than a little irritable. How dare her father interfere with her love life, or lack thereof! She decided to skip breakfast and get away from the bunker for a bit. Maybe she'd even skip her chores for the day. She'd worry about the aftermath later. She wasn't in the mood to care at the moment.

She went out the back door to avoid as many people as possible. While she stewed over her meddling father and the mess with Milo, she now knew with certainty that many, if not everyone, assumed they were a couple. She found herself wandering toward the boulders where the blueberry bushes had once stood. She didn't expect to find them. The gardens were dried up and overgrown, and she expected to find the blueberry bushes in the same condition, but they were wild and didn't need tending. She found them big and full of delicious blueberries, just ripe for picking.

Her eyes searched for the crack in the rocks before she even knew what she was looking for. Was it gone? A rockslide could have buried the entrance forever. What if she had grown too big to fit through the entrance? She didn't think that was possible, as it seemed so big to her as a child. Then she remembered the now small space behind her father's chair in his office and worried that perhaps she couldn't get through that opening.

She immediately felt the need to find that sacred place, a place so special that she never dared share it with anyone. This was her secret place. In all these years, she hadn't once muttered about its existence. The blueberry bushes had grown so large that she was having trouble getting her bearings. When she saw a familiar looking rock, her eyes grew wide. It had to be around here somewhere.

Blueberries were a great excuse for her escape. She would take a book and a couple pails, eat blueberries until her heart's content, and lay out on a rock and read. She always brought a full pail or two home. Her brother teased her endlessly upon her evening return, always dirty with purple stained lips and fingers. No one ever suspected she'd been playing in her cave, not even Charlie.

She couldn't let this moment pass. She poked around the bushes near where she thought the hole had been, and there it was! A blueberry bush almost completely concealed the entrance, but she was certain this was it.

It certainly was smaller than she remembered. Had she grown too much? Would she fit through the opening? Stubborn pride wouldn't let her just walk away without trying. After a momentary pause and wondering what would happen if an animal had actually taken up residence there during her time away, she sighed but forged on. She pushed the bush away, sat at the hole, lowered her legs into it, and slid on her back into the darkness.

As a small child, it was like going down a sliding board, but this time, her head barely cleared the top before her feet hit the cave floor. She lay there and laughed, hoping she wasn't stuck. Then she lowered herself to her knees, twisted, and turned, trying to slither the rest of her body through the short tunnel and into the cave.

She was clear at last. "It should be fun to get back up there," she said aloud to herself.

It was dark in this part of the cave. As a kid, she hid a flashlight under a rock near the entrance. Why hadn't she thought about that before? Carefully feeling for the walls, she advanced forward slowly.

Trying not to trip, she slid one foot forward slowly. When her foot settled into its new place safely and securely, she shifted her weight and proceeded forward with the next. It was a slow process, but she knew it was only about twenty yards before the cave would cut sharply around a corner, and then she would take a right and one more left. Then she should be able to see some light from the large window in the cave overlooking the valley below.

As she rounded the last corner, she saw light just ahead. She began to walk swiftly with an urge to see the mountains and beautiful valley below, home to her picture perfect village that had been the setting for so many stories and dreams inside her. The light was getting brighter, and she knew it was just up ahead. Excitement grew within her.

Then she stopped suddenly and froze in place. Had she heard something? Something was wrong. She wasn't certain what it was, but something set her entire being on edge, and she froze. All her senses heightened, telling her to run the other way, but she couldn't. She held her breath, listening for any sound out of place, still unsure of what had set her off but she dare not move.

A slight scuffle across the ground just up ahead. She was sure of it this time. Something or someone was in her cave. She began to panic. As a child, she had prepared for such things at all times. She even stocked her cave with weapons and survival gear as her father would have done. However, it had been years, and a moment of nostalgia had led her here today.

She knew if she turned back now, she would surely be heard trying to get back out of the hole in the rocks. As she cursed herself silently for coming down here, her eyes subconsciously scanned the area. Her eyes adjusted quickly to the small amount of light coming from just up ahead, and she suddenly remembered every inch of the place as her survival instincts kicked in.

A few feet away would be a hole behind a rock where she often stored stuff. If she could just get there, perhaps there would be something she could use to defend herself. As quietly as possible, she made her way to the spot she knew so well. She crouched and felt around, still unable to see her surroundings fully. Her hand stumbled across something cold and hard. A can of food? She pushed past, identifying a can opener, a pencil, a book, her binoculars, and, finally, her hand rested on her trusty old sling shot.

She wrapped her fingers around it, pulling it up while simultaneously picking up a rock off the cave floor, and getting into position. She sat like that for what seemed an eternity. Nothing! Not a single sound. Perhaps she had scared off whatever it was with her entrance into the cave. Perhaps it was waiting, as she was. She strained her ears for any sound, and all was silent. After a few moments, she sighed. "Guess my imagination can still get the best of me!" She whispered to herself.

She shoved the slingshot in her back pocket and stood, then made her way toward the light ahead. When she rounded the last bend and came into the large cave with her picture window, her heart soared and all fears and hesitations subsided.

She sat down on the large, familiar rock she had called her couch and looked out at the beautiful mountains in front of her. "Huh," she voiced her thought aloud, "I really thought everything would change somehow, that Dad was right and life outside was terrible, but look how beautiful everything still is! How can it be?"

"It's been a long time since I've heard anyone talk like that." She whipped around, crouched low behind the rock she had been sitting on, and grabbed for her slingshot, poised and ready. He slowly came out of the shadows off the tunnels to the left. He raised his hands, and his voice was smooth and calming. "Relax, I won't hurt you," he assured her.

When he fully stepped into the light, she took a quick assessment. He was tall and sturdy, with broad shoulders and visible muscles. He was tanned to a golden brown, which recalled memories of years past.

She was so pale now after years away from the sun. Everyone she knew was, but not this man. Her eyes continued making their path up. No visible guns at his sides. She relaxed just a bit and looked him square on. Golden brown hair with eyes seemingly the same color that sparkled like gems in the sunlight.

He took a step closer, and she caught a glimpse of the compound bow strapped to his shoulder. He reached for it and she yelled, "Drop your weapon!" He signaled for her to be quiet and moved swiftly toward her. She squealed and let the rock fly hitting him right between the eyes.

She tried to run, but he was at her side quickly. He wrapped his arms around her in restraint and covered her mouth with his hand. With a stern look, he shushed her. The panic subsided, and she froze. He signaled to the rocks below out her picture window. Then she heard him. "Griffon, are you okay? What's going on up there?"

He loosened his grip on her and put a finger to his mouth, motioning for her to be quiet. Then he walked to the edge and looked down. "Sorry man, it's pretty dark in here. I walked right into a stalagmite; it got me right between the eyes." He looked over and glared at her, and though she knew she should run and try to get away, she couldn't help but stand there and giggle.

"So ya see anything of value up there?"

"Nope, nothing. This is just a cave in the rock. Neat spot to look out and meditate, but all the tunnels are too small to get through, so looks like a dead end here."

"Hell. I ain't climbing any further, then. You okay to find your way home?"

"Yup"

"Okay then, I'm heading home. Lily will be waiting for me, wondering what the hell kind of trouble you got me into this time."

"Okay, think I'll hang out a bit. I'm off tomorrow, so expect me the day after."

"Okay, you be safe. That woman will kill me if anything happens to you."

"See you in two then."

He stood and waited for his old friend to get safely back down the rocks then turned back toward Holly. Her eyes were wide with amazement and curiosity. He had never seen a more beautiful creature. When he was certain it was safe to talk, he spoke. "I hate to lie to him like that, but I'd imagine you would not have been very happy with two strangers invading your space.

I really didn't mean to scare you. At first, I thought maybe a bear was holed up in here, from all the noise. Then, when it got quiet, quickly, I knew it must be a person, so I hid to wait and see. Really didn't mean to intrude on your conversation with yourself after all." She glared at him, and he grinned from ear to ear.

"I wasn't talking to myself, exactly."

His eyebrow raised in this, really? I'm not buying it, sort of expression.

"Okay, so what if I was talking to myself! No one else was supposed to be here. What are you doing here anyway? And, who are you? Where did you come from?"

He held up a hand to silence her. "Slow down a bit there. I have all the same questions for YOU!" Then he continued, "Okay, I'll start. My name's Griffon. See that small town down in the valley? That is where I'm from."

"Really? You live in the village? I have always dreamed of that place. So safe and snug in the valley. Picture perfect place to live. It must be wonderful!"

He looked genuinely stunned and stood there in awkward silence before blurting out, "Where are you from? Do you really think my town is any less affected than yours just because we're small and nestled into a mountain?"

She felt anger behind his words and, having no clue as to what he meant, just stared blankly at him. After a moment he continued.

"Where are you from? I demand to know!"

"You 'demand' to know? You don't have the right to demand anything!" She could feel her temper rising and blood pulsing through her veins. *How dare he! Just who does he think he is?*

"Are you a migrant? If so, just keep on moving lady. We have more than our fair share of problems without adding yours. If you think the AMAN haven't infiltrated our life in our quaint little 'safe village' you are dead wrong! I don't know what you're here for lady, but it would be best if you just kept moving."

She could tell he was mad, but so was she, and her temper flared at his audacity.

"Best if 'I' keep moving? I'm not the one trespassing here,

now am I?" She wanted to add, "And just what exactly is the AMAN?" but feared she'd already said too much. Looking out, she could see the sun low in the sky. It would be setting soon and she needed to get back.

"What do you mean, I'm trespassing?"

"It doesn't matter. I'll have to be going soon, it's getting late."

"You aren't setting up camp for the night here?"

"No, why would I do that?"

He glared at her with that incredulous look of his but his tone changed this time. "Seriously, who are you?"

Holly began to retreat toward the darkest tunnel of the cave. He remembered that was the direction she came from, but where and how? He knew he had frightened her or angered her or something. He hadn't meant to, but her optimism and happy countenance initially had set him on guard. From the look on her face, it was as if she'd never heard of the AMAN, but how could that be possible?

He touched her shoulder lightly and changed his tone. "Please, don't go."

"I must." She sounded almost disappointed as she said it, and she was. She had so many questions she wanted to ask, but she must always remember to protect her family first, and to ask would raise questions on why she didn't already know. She bit her lip and turned to leave.

He tried one last time.

"Will you be back tomorrow?"

"I don't know."

"Please?"

"I'll try."

"Wait, I don't even know your name."

She stepped away and turned to face him. For a moment, she just stared into his golden eyes. "My name is Holly," she said sweetly and shyly. Then she lowered her gaze and turned to walk away.

* * * * *

Chapter 8

WHAT A strange ending to the day. Griffon was certain
that Holly was some wild migrant, strong, independent,
and stubborn and one hell of a good shot with that slingshot
of hers. He rubbed his forehead at the impact point. Ouch!
In those last moments, his opinion of her changed. She was
sweet and innocent. He half expected her to curtsey upon
leaving, like something you'd read in a book from long ago.
If books were legal of course.

His mother had been the town's librarian, and while it
took a little longer for the AMAN to reach Wythel, VA, reach
it they did. He could still remember how helpless he felt
watching the library burn to the ground. His mother was
a mess, falling to the ground and crying hysterically. She
had never again been quite the same. No one knew how he
and Lily had gathered all her most beloved books and hid
them in the rafters of their home. They could still be hung
for possession, if caught, but he dreamed that one day they
would be able to present them to her and see the light return
in her eyes.

Perhaps Wythel hadn't faced the wrath and destruction of
the AMAN as other areas had, but it was bad enough.

The AMAN, the Armed Militia of the Allied Nations. It
had been sheer luck that he was not drafted, himself. Their
power over the Allied Nation was strong. It was impossible
to avoid them, so how was it that Holly seemed so unaffected
at the mention of their name?

Women and young girls didn't venture out alone. Ever! It wasn't safe; yet, here she was. What if I had been an AMAN scouting this cave instead of a nobody rebel in search of food, illegally hunting high in the mountains and just praying not to get caught?

His mind wandered to that thought, and he didn't like it one bit. The thought of the AMAN crossing paths with her invoked anger in him that he didn't fully understand. Within moments, he convinced himself that the pure sweet debonair Holly must be protected, and then he scratched his head and felt the wound she had left. He laughed aloud to himself. She was, perhaps, not so sweet and innocent after all. With his final memory of her still so fresh, it was hard to remember the slingshot firecracker he originally encountered.

He hadn't planned to spend the night here, but he knew he couldn't leave. What if she returned tomorrow? He had to wait and see.

* * * * *

Griffon? What just happened? She climbed out of the cave and stumbled over the rocks, mindlessly heading back to the compound. With a million things running through her head, she ran right into Milo without even seeing him. She was thinking only of Griffon and the millions of questions she wanted to ask but hadn't dared.

Looking up at Milo with his dark, almost black hair and bright blue eyes set in a pale ivory face, she found herself subconsciously comparing the two men.

"Holly, are you okay?"

"Uh, yeah, I'm fine."

She shook her head yes to show she meant it and attempted to clear her head. *No one must know about my encounter with Griffon. It wouldn't be safe for him, and I know father would lock me away forever if he thought I was in the slightest danger. No, I must keep him to myself. Perhaps not asking questions like who are these AMAN people? and why are you on my mountain? was a good thing. The less I know, the less chance I'll slip and say something to endanger my family.*

Milo helped her up after their collision. As she stood, she found herself face-to-face with him. She smiled, and he leaned down and brushed his lips against hers. He lingered there this time, and her head spun from the shock of it. Her hand was in his, although she didn't remember taking it. She made no move to remove it as he escorted her back to the compound. He was becoming bolder with his intentions. Mostly, she didn't mind and was becoming used to him being around. Tonight, all her thoughts were on Griffon, and that irritated her.

* * * * *

Before Charlie could ask too many questions as to her whereabouts, she announced the discovery of her blueberry bushes. He shook his head and laughed... same old Holly. She told her mother that she wanted to take some buckets to pick some in the morning, and then she adjourned for the night without raising too much suspicion.

She tossed and turned all night, thinking about the stranger in her cave. Tomorrow, she would question him. She just had to know. Why was he there? Who is the AMAN? What had happened to the United States?

There was something about him that made her want to trust him. She wouldn't say anything. He could form his own opinions of her but there were things she just had to know.

Griffon had an old thermal emergency blanket he found in the first aid kit of an old Chevy scavenged out by the old Buckman farm. Not much in way of comfort, but he hoped it would be warm enough to keep him until morning. He knew it was stupid to sleep up here. He had next to no supplies, only a few pieces of jerky, and a small canteen of water to sustain him. He had certainly lived through worse over the years, and he just had to see her again. Trying to ignore the grumbles of his belly, he fell asleep dreaming of the sweet wildcat he had met that day.

* * * * *

The next morning, Holly awoke before dawn and found four buckets and two books along with a note from her mom. "Have a great day of peace, Holly. I love you, mom." She giggled to herself. Her mother always thought she understood her daughter's need for solitude, despite father's objections. This note was her get out of jail free card for the day.

She jumped out of bed, showered, and changed, smiling all the while. For a moment, she thought of Griffon and how awful sleeping in the cave could be. He'd only had his bow and backpack. Did he even have food? She felt bad for not having thought to ask yesterday, so she made her way to the kitchen and, upon finding it empty, whipped up a feast for the two of them before heading off on a true adventure. Thankfully, no one interrupted her time there.

Making her way quickly to the blueberry bushes, she filled two buckets and a partial third. She hid them near the hole in the rocks and climbed down, taking the third bucket and a picnic basket with her. She remembered a flashlight this time, making her journey through the tunnels much easier. As she rounded the last curve, she saw him sprawled out on the cave floor with a rock for a pillow and an emergency blanket partially draped over him but not big enough to cover him fully. She stopped short and listened just before entering the cave, making sure there were no other sounds.

He heard her coming, but lay there, unsure if he was dreaming again or not. It had been a terrible night for sleep. Not because of his temporary living conditions but because he couldn't stop thinking of her. When her footsteps stopped a few feet away, he called out in a deep, sleepy, husky voice, "I'm alone and unarmed."

"But are you hungry?" came the sweet voice that had played through his mind all night long. He rolled over and looked up at her, grinning. To his amazement, she was perfectly groomed in clean clothes with damp hair, and she smelled lightly of vanilla. He couldn't remember seeing anyone so well cared for in years. How had she managed it in the middle of nowhere, and what was that tantalizing smell coming from her basket? It was like a vague memory he couldn't quite place.

She sat down and set a picnic blanket on the floor beside her. She motioned him over as she withdrew a container with hot eggs, bacon, hash browns, toast, and gravy followed by a stack of pancakes and syrup. She had picked fresh blueberries in the bucket. He honestly thought he was dreaming. He hadn't seen such a feast in over five years.

"I wasn't sure if you had any food with you. I don't know what you like, so I whipped up a bit of everything. I hope it's not too much. I don't exactly meet too many new people, so I'm afraid my hospitality is a little rusty." She motioned him to eat, and he dug in as if he hadn't eaten in days.

Halfway through the stack of pancakes, he stopped and asked if she was eating and apologized, admitting he was hungry and hadn't seen food so plentiful in years.

Holly hadn't thought of that. All these years, food had never really been an issue for her, and she still didn't know what had become of the world outside the compound. She told him she had already eaten, that it was all for him. She knew he needed it more than she did. She sat quietly as he polished off the eggs, bacon, and hash browns, asking if it was okay to save the rest for later. She told him that was fine and showed him a cool place in the cave to store the food so it wouldn't spoil.

They settled down on the rocks and stared out into the mountains without a word. The silence wasn't awkward today, though.

Griffon wondered where she had come from and how she had managed so well up here seemingly sheltered from the world below. Holly wondered how to go about getting answers to her questions without sounding naïve and stupid.

* * * * *

He broke the silence first.

"Thank you! That was the best food I've had in years. I know how scarce food is and what a burden that must have been. So, thanks. Really, I appreciate it... I'm rambling, aren't I?"

He grinned a sheepish grin and shook his head. "Sorry... and thanks again."

She laughed and punched him playfully.

"I'm not hanging out here, if that is all you're going to say all day. I guess I got a little carried away in the food department. I just wanted to butter you up to answer some questions, no pun intended, ha ha ha!"

She made a mental note... food no longer plentiful.

"So I guess your family doesn't have a lot of food? You know, times are tight right now?" She was trying to ask politely if that was just his family without sounding like it.

"No one has access to food like that anymore Holly, no one." He looked at her seriously, and she knew that he knew she was different. She sighed and shook her head in acceptance.

He continued on, answering questions she hadn't yet asked.

"It's bad out there Holly. Now I don't know how you have managed over the years, and I don't guess I need to know; but the rest of us don't live like this anymore. Hospitality?" Griffon snorted, "If it weren't for my stubborn mother, I wouldn't know what that word was.

"People don't talk like that anymore. People don't give food crumbs, let alone a complete feast to strangers. People don't shower and put on clean clothes every day. I smelled a hint of vanilla on you yesterday but this morning it's strong and fresh and your hair's wet."

He reached over and smelled her hair. "It smells of shampoo. Holly I can't even remember the last time I saw a bottle of shampoo! I'm lucky to get a bar of soap a year."

She dropped her gaze and nodded. He knew. She didn't have to tell him. He knew, or suspected, or something. Her just being here gave them all away. Yet she wasn't in fear. She instinctively trusted this man.

With a sigh she said, "Start from the beginning Griffon. I need to hear what happened. I need to know."

* * * * *

For the next several hours, he told her a tale of how happy he and his family were growing up in the quaint little picture-perfect village below. How the nation began to divide, and how the militia rule began, leading to the next civil war. A war divided not by states or localities, but by town versus town, neighbor versus neighbor and, in some cases, brother against brother.

"The world went crazy. The military turned on the people to restore order by the President's decree, but instead, the people turned on the President. He was hung on the White House lawn, and law and order were gone.

"Small towns like Wythel held together. The cities were like war zones. For a long time, they thought it couldn't come to them, not here; but it eventually did.

"Over a year of chaos and groups formed. One of those was the Armed Militia of Allied Nations. It was a good play on names that made people believe we banded together for a common cause and were working toward peace.

"At first, it was great. They'd bring food and supplies and help provide protection too. Under the direction of General Steinfeld, their territories grew, which required more resources. They began taxing the towns. Those who refused were destroyed.

"We were told by others without the protection of the AMAN. We now know it was BY the AMAN. They needed more recruits, so they began demanding one child from every family."

* * * * *

"When they came to our house, I was prepared to go, to do what I needed to protect my family, but they took pity on my father and left me, his only son. Instead, they raped my eldest sister in the middle of our family room and burned the emblem of AMAN into her skin, marking her as an AMAN wife.

"AMAN are not allowed emotional ties to any one person, so the wives are a general pool of women for any soldier to have at will for the purpose of pleasure and procreation.

"I was barely seventeen at the time," he said, with a faraway look in his eyes as he recalled the moment.

Holly had tears running down her cheeks, and he was shaking from his memories. She wrapped her arms around him and cradled him as a mother would a small child. Through tears, she told him how sorry she was for everything he had gone through.

She wouldn't ask him anything more. She wasn't sure she wanted to hear any more and she couldn't put him through the pain of reliving his story again. This was worse than her father's biggest fears, and she silently thanked him for his protection.

At that moment, her stomach growled, which lightened the mood some. "Must be time for lunch," she laughed.

"I'm not sure I'll eat again for a month after that breakfast," he teased.

She produced a loaf of fresh bread from the picnic basket, along with two fat slices of ham, two chunks of cheese, and fresh cucumber slices with homemade ranch dip.

"Oh shoot! I guess we'll just have to share because I ran off and forgot cups. Do you like sweet tea?"

His mouth watered as he nodded. She bowed her head and thanked the Lord for their meal before eating. He watched with fascination. He couldn't help think how proud his mother would be if he were to bring Holly home to meet the family. Perhaps in another time or another world. He chuckled to himself at the thought and ate the lunch she provided, aware that she was watching him the whole time.

* * * * *

"You know, if you were to meet my father, the first thing he would ask is, "Son, are you a God-fearing man?" She had lowered her voice to give her best interpretation.

Griffon chuckled, and, for a moment, wondered if she was thinking much the same as he. "Well, yes, I am. However, Holly, I should warn you that under AMAN law, which governs this territory, you would be hung in the center of town just for asking. Organized religion of any kind is strictly forbidden. The AMAN says there is no God."

"No God?" She gasped in disbelief. "How can they stop people from believing in God?"

"Well they can't, but they can stop people from openly practicing religion. It started about two years ago. They went from town to town, gathered all the priests and ministers of any religion, and killed them. Think Salem Witch trials. Anyone vocalizing such blasphemy was to be killed."

He hesitated for a moment, knowing he shouldn't go on, but he did anyway.

"Our minister died a week before our town was attacked. They killed three other ministers in the area. Pastor Campbell was already grooming his youngest son to take over in his place. The younger Mr. Campbell is not a true ordained minister, but he's the closest we have. There is a small group of us that still practice in secret.

"I don't know why I am telling you this. You could have my entire family killed with this knowledge alone. There's just something about you. You're different from any woman I have ever met."

She took a moment to let his words sink in. She took a deep breath and proceeded into dangerous territory.

"First, I am not an AMAN. Let me put your mind at ease if the idea ever crossed it. Until yesterday, I had never even heard the term, as I know you already suspected. How is that possible?" She took another long breath, "My father was once what people called a Doomsday Prepper. He built a bunker up here on the mountain or rather in the mountain, and we've been living there all this time. I haven't been off this mountain in over seven years. And now I have just handed you my family's secret and safety, too."

She bit her bottom lip and watched as he processed her words.

He laughed a deep full belly laugh.

"You're Crazy Old Man Jenkins daughter?"

"He's not crazy, and he's not old either."

She crossed her arms in a defensive way and that stubborn fire he saw on their first meeting blazed through.

"I didn't mean anything by it, really. It's just that some folks around town remember your dad. As time passed, the story grew more and more. People don't want their kids wandering up on this mountain, so the story grew to discourage it. Crazy Old Man Jenkins cried Doomsday all the time, so he built a cabin at the top of this mountain and moved his family here.

"No one could survive such winters, and the first winter took his daughter and son. His wife was so distraught, she took her own life, and old man Jenkins lost his mind.

"They say he still wanders this mountain in search of his family, capturing young boys and girls and holding them captive in replacement of his own kids until he realizes they aren't them and kills them and feeds them to the bears.

"That's why the bears are so much bigger on this mountain and why no one comes up here. There have even been sightings of the ghosts of Old Man Jenkins' wife and children for years, still roaming the mountain. Even the AMAN won't come near this mountain."

Holly laughed out loud. It was the most ridiculous thing she had ever heard. People actually believed it? She couldn't resist the moment.

In her creepiest voice, she chanted, "Griffon... I am the ghost of Crazy Old Man Jenkins here to lure you to my father!"

She got up and walked around with her arms out in front of her, making ghost sounds.

"Holly," he groaned. "Are you a ghost or Frankenstein?"

They both laughed.

They talked late into the afternoon. Both knew they needed to leave but neither wanting to. They had fallen into an easy friendship that neither wanted to see come to an end. Griffon explained his work schedule as four days on and three days off. He was due back in the morning. They agreed to meet in the cave again in five days time, said their goodbyes, and parted ways.

* * * * *

Chapter 9

I**T WOULD** be five days until Holly saw Griffon again, and that made her feel sad. She had only just met him but knew she would miss him over the next several days. He had shared a lot with her. She knew that things outside her compound were worse than she had imagined. Worse than anyone could have imagined. Her father had been right to build this sanctuary and hide them away from such evil.

It would be hard knowing and not saying anything to those she loved. She must carry this burden on her own for now. She would have to take certain precautions now. She couldn't just stand by and let something bad happen to her family by withholding such knowledge; but how could she go about it without alarming everyone? As she reached the compound door with buckets of berries in hand, she thought of Charlie.

Charlie had been at odds with their father over the need for information. He was rallying a group together to go down to the town and find out what was happening in the world. Holly had been encouraging him, but now she knew she had to stop him. He could not go down to the town or anywhere. It was too dangerous.

Deep in thought over this dilemma, she rounded the corner to her family's pod and ran right smack into her father. He had been prepared to scold her for her disappearing act over the last two days but melted when his little girl looked up at him with worry in her eyes. She hugged him tight as she had done so often as a little girl.

"I love you daddy!" She wanted to say so much more. *You were right all along. Thank you for keeping us safe from the AMAN.* She knew she mustn't speak those words.

This was a rare treat for Mike, and his frustrations with her melted away in that moment.

"Are you okay sweetie?"

"Yes Daddy, I'm fine. I did a lot of meditation and prayer today, and I don't think Charlie should go down the mountain in search of news. We don't know what's happened in the last five years. What if the world isn't as we remember? Maybe some reconnaissance from afar to watch the people and see how they are now living before strolling into town? It's a small town; people will know he's not from around there. They will ask questions. He could put us all in danger."

Mike's heart soared at his daughter's words. "That's exactly my thought too. I like the recon idea. Perhaps that will keep him occupied long enough for us to figure out the next step. He won't be happy, but it should be a good compromise."

Her father continued to talk as they walked to their pod, but Holly was already lost in her own thoughts. Charlie would be furious with her. That was certain. She'd have to accept those consequences for his safety. Maybe someday, she could tell him the entire story.

"Seriously Hols, have you lost your mind? You're siding with him?" Charlie was in a rage over her defecting to team Dad and he yelled at her for more than ten minutes. Her father did not attempt to hide his happiness over this turn of events, which only infuriated Charlie more. She let him vent until he stopped yelling and sat down defeated. "Why Holly?"

"Charlie, you know I am always on your side. I just have a bad feeling about this. You've always trusted my instincts, and I need you to do that now."

She took his hand and looked him straight in the eyes. "Please Charlie. It's not safe down there."

He could see she knew much more than she was letting on, but he was also smart enough to know that now wasn't the time to push her. If it was that important to her, he had to listen.

"Okay, I'll stop pushing the issue. I promise."

She hugged him and squealed, "Thank you, thank you, thank you!"

He grinned. "I'll focus on recon from a distance... for now. But someday, you're gonna tell me the real reason why."

He kissed her on the forehead, gave her an all-knowing look to let her know he'd be watching her more closely now, and left to find their father and discuss the details.

Exhausted from the encounter with Charlie, Holly decided to call it an early night. As she drifted off to sleep, she thought of Griffon. Had it really been just that morning that she met him with a picnic basket in hand, determined to find out what was happening in the world? His stories changed her life forever. She had grown up today, and she drifted off to sleep with the weight of all she now knew.

* * * * *

Day One. Holly decided to sit in on Charlie's recon planning meeting. His first plan of action was to set up three lookout points where they could discreetly and safely observe the town below. Wythel, according to the map, was the only town on the western side of the mountain and the smallest and most easily accessible to begin their recon. Three other towns on the eastern and southern sides of the mountains could serve as future targets, but that would take more time and planning.

Holly felt a twinge of guilt as they discussed possible lookout points. She knew the cave was the best and safest point on that side of the mountain, but she wasn't ready to give that up, especially now that it wasn't just her spot. She thought of Griffon and began to worry. What if they caught him coming up the mountain? She'd have to warn him to be extra careful now.

As they brainstormed possible areas, Holly strategically routed them away from the cave. It was no secret that she was most familiar with that side of the mountain with her beloved blueberry bushes. She used the rocky terrain as obstacles in that area, steering them more toward the woods northeast and southeast of the town. Only one point was of concern, but it was the closest to the town, too. A person would have to look back just in her direction and with binoculars to notice anything. That was the best she could do and she'd let Griffon know the locations so he could make it up the mountain without being seen. It was a risk, but excitement pulsed through her at the thought, and she knew it as a risk worth taking.

* * * * *

Day Two. Holly spent time outdoors with Chris and Cassie. The three of them had been friends for so long, inseparable really, but lately she pulled apart from them both. She was preoccupied with her own life. She knew it would be hard not to tell them everything, but she was also excited to spend a carefree day catching up with them both.

A part of her longed for school and seeing her friends every day. It amazed her how quickly her time filled up with other things since she graduated three months earlier. Summer vacation was nearly over, and Chris and Cassie would be back in school soon for their senior year. She had never really thought about what that would mean for her, and she regretted not spending more time with them. Since the doors of the compound were open, Holly had done everything possible to stay outside and away from everyone. Sitting here now, watching her two best friends, she felt like a third wheel. She could see a change in them. They were closer, more playful with each other. She didn't fully understand and would have to think it through later. For now, her stomach was growling loudly, and they all laughed.

"Lunch should be here shortly," Chris announced.

"You've already made arrangements?" Holly felt completely confused.

"Not me! You should know me better than that."

They all laughed and nodded in agreement. As if on cue, Milo came out of the woods and into the clearing. Cassie jumped up and assisted him. Holly smacked Chris on the arm, "What's he doing here?" Chris grinned. "Holly, it's okay. I know."

"You know what, exactly?"

"I man the perimeter videos two nights a week now, ya know. I've seen what's been going on between you two. Hey, it's okay. I'm cool with it. I can't imagine a better sister."

He was partly teasing, she could tell, but mostly she thought he was being serious.

"There's nothing going on with me and your brother."

"Oh really?"

She couldn't help but blush from the knowing look on his face.

"It's 'nothing' to steal kisses at the back door or walk hand in hand while watching the sunset? Come on, Holly, I wasn't born yesterday. Like I said, it's cool."

Cassie and Milo finished setting up the picnic, and Chris ran over to join them. Holly suspected all day that something more was going on between her friends, but if there was any doubt, it was quickly laid to rest as Cassie fed Chris a grape and he sneaked in for a quick kiss as she giggled in protest.

How had she missed all of this? Milo was waiting for her. She gasped as she realized this was a double date, and they were waiting for her to join them. A part of her wanted to turn and run, but these were her friends, her family. She decided to make the most of it and joined them, trying hard not to think and just live in the moment.

To Holly's surprise, she had a fantastic time with Chris, Cassie, and even Milo. It was comfortable and safe. Everything she had once thought she didn't want. Milo walked her home that evening, and they sat up talking for some time. She was surprised at how easy it was to talk to him. For the most part, conversation was kept to the basics... weather, gossip, hunting, Cassie and Chris, and compound politics like Charlie's recon mission. He opened up and told her some stuff personal to him, like how he had always wanted to fly planes for the Air Force. It was a nice evening alone with him, and when he went to kiss her good night, she didn't hesitate this time.

* * * * *

Day Three. Holly woke up on the wrong side of the bed. She spent the morning silently berating herself. She had spent a perfectly good evening with Milo. He was kind, considerate, handsome, and smart... everything that would make any girl happy. So why had she spent all night dreaming of Griffon? Griffon. She had all but convinced herself that he was just part of her imagination. Griffon. He was gorgeous, adventurous, and exciting, the complete opposite of Milo Weaver. She knew they could never be together. They were from two different worlds that must never collide, but the romantic in her couldn't stop from dreaming and longing. He hadn't shown any interest at all in her like that, but there was something irresistible about him that she just couldn't turn off, and it left her in a terrible mood.

She was what her mother called an open book, so when she walked into the kitchen, everyone knew to steer clear. She ate, and Milo came in as she was washing her dishes.

"Ouch. I rather expected to find you in better spirits. At least I hoped."

He let the word trail off, and she knew he was fishing. She smiled in spite of herself and assured him he wasn't the cause.

"Well then, I'll have to try to leave a happier impression after our next date. Speaking of which, are you free on Thursday?"

Thursday? Griffon would be here then. For a second, the voice in the back of her mind said, *If he actually shows.* She pushed the thought away.

"I have an eval for next school term on Thursday. I'll be tied up all day."

It wasn't a total lie. She had been putting that off and knew she had to make a decision soon.

"Oh." Milo sounded disappointed. "How about Saturday evening then?"

She calculated in her head and knew Griffon would have to be heading back home early Saturday, so she agreed.

Milo was thrilled. He stole a quick kiss and disappeared before she could change her mind.

She chastised herself for basing it on Griffon. *He won't even show,* she thought.

She ran into Charlie later in the day.

"What's wrong with you?"

"Nothing, what's wrong with you?" She countered.

"Absolutely nothing. Life is good. We got the lookout stations completed today. Tomorrow we'll have all three stocked, and we begin manning bright and early Thursday morning."

"Thursday?"

"I know, right! The boys and I are moving in record time. Pretty exciting, huh, Hols? Right?" He looked up from the clipboard he was using to go over the plans and saw his sister walking away. He shrugged and got back to work.

Thursday is too soon! How can I warn Griffon in time? Her day went from bad to worse, and she spent the day grumbling and obsessing over what to do.

* * * * *

Day Four. Holly had tossed and turned all night but knew she had to try to warn Griffon. He hadn't told her anything about what he did or exactly where he lived, but she was determined to warn him. She knew it was ridiculous and crazy, but she felt she had to try.

She packed a lunch in a backpack, checked out her pistol so everyone would think she was hunting small game, and headed down the mountain. She knew this was the craziest thing she'd ever done. As she approached the edge of the woods, she crouched low behind a thick bush and pulled her binoculars out for a look around. It was still early, and everything looked calm and peaceful. The buildings were a bit more run down then she'd imagined, but otherwise she still thought it a lovely little village.

Just after 7:00 a.m., the place seemed to come alive. She could smell fresh baking bread and saw men and women heading off to their jobs. What did they do? She couldn't help but wonder. She watched for an hour or so, but saw no sign of Griffon.

She decided to change positions and moved along the tree line about a mile, just watching people go on about their daily lives. She came to a small farmhouse on the edge of town and noticed a little boy and girl playing ball in the yard. How familiar the scene was, like something out of her personal memories. She found a safe spot and crouched low to watch them. A woman came out and shooed them both inside. Something was wrong. Holly could sense it. A man was yelling from inside for them to hurry. Holly recognized the man's voice. Griffon's friend had come up the mountain with him. Holly knew his name was Amos and his wife Lily.

A few moments later, the woman, who must be Lily, came outside with the children and told them to run and hide. They each had a little backpack on now and ran straight for the woods. Holly didn't know what was happening but sensed it was bad. She could see the children through the trees a few yards away. The little girl had something bright pink hanging off her backpack. Surely, whomever they were hiding from would see it too.

Holly knew she had to move quickly. As quietly as possible, she made her way to the children. She put on a smile and held her finger to her mouth as she approached them. She reached into her bag, grabbed a camo blanket, put it around the kids, and motioned for them to get down behind a thick patch of blackberry bushes. They were wide-eyed and frightened but obeyed.

There was a scream from the house and the sound of someone kicking in a door. She could hear Amos talking, but his words were too muffled to make sense. There were sounds of breaking and destruction as their house was ransacked. Holly remembered she had packed some cookies in her lunch and retrieved two for the kids. Their eyes were wide, and they giggled with delight. She reminded them to be quiet.

A loud crack and more yelling from the house and Holly had two pair of big golden brown eyes staring at her. Griffon. These were Griffon's eyes. Holly wondered for a moment if they could possibly be his children. She pushed the thought aside and grabbed for her iPod. Not knowing if the children had ever seen or heard anything like it, she put an earbud in each child's ear and played some music. Their big eyes stared back in astonishment. She smiled and placed her finger on her mouth to signal them to keep quiet. A few moments later, the back door flew open and three men walked out with Amos and Lily following closely behind.

"We've told you before, there are no children here."

Holly took a moment to look over the intruders. They were all dressed in camo pants with black tee shirts cut off at the sleeves. They each had a tattoo on their forearm but Holly couldn't make it out. Their hair was long and pulled back into a ponytail. Combat boots. Each was outfitted with what appeared to be an M4 strapped to their back, and she could make out at least two side arms on each man.

A fourth clone stuck his head out, "All clear Sarge. There ain't no sign of kids in this house."

"So it would seem," the man replied.

The man called Sarge stepped up to Lily and ran a hand down the side of her face, "My apologies Ma'am."

Holly could see Amos using every ounce of restraint not to fight back. Sarge spit a wad of tobacco at Amos's feet and paused for a response. When he got none, he yelled, "Roll out boys."

Six men, all identical in appearance, piled into a jeep and drove off. Holly looked down and saw the kids smiling and bobbing their heads to the music. She was thankful they hadn't seen the full encounter though suspected this wasn't the first time they'd been through this drill. Another few moments passed and Lily called out for the children. Holly removed the headphones and signaled for them to go. The little girl stopped and turned around.

"Are you an angel?"

Holly smiled, "No sweetie I'm not an angel, just a person like you."

The girl shook her head, "Mama says God sends angels to help us when we need them. You must be an angel."

Then she turned and ran off screaming, "Mama an angel saved us!"

The boy must have been telling them, too, because next thing she knew, Amos was grabbing a stick and heading her way, ready to take all his anger from the encounter with the AMAN out on her. She couldn't get away fast enough. As he got near, she jumped up.

"Amos, stop."

That threw him off guard. He hadn't expected her to know his name.

"Who are you?

"It doesn't matter."

"How do you know my name? I ain't never seen you before."

"I know. Look, I don't have a lot of time. I need you to get this note to Griffon. It's important. He could get hurt without this info."

Lily stepped forward. "Griffon? You know my brother?"

Holly could see the same golden brown eyes on her. At least that explained the kids.

"Yes. I have to go, please see that he gets that note."

She turned and disappeared into the woods.

* * * * *

Word travels fast in a small town, and news of the AMAN attack at Amos and Lily's came moments after it occurred, but no news of the outcome. *Did they find his niece and nephew? Was Lily okay? Did Amos hold his temper?* These questions burned through Griffon all day. When the whistle blew to signal the end of his shift at the lumberyard, he took off running and didn't stop until he was at Lily's front door. She teared up when she saw him and gave way to the fears of the day, crying in her brother's arms. He and Lily were three years apart and though she was the elder sibling, he had always been her rock. They had an undeniably close relationship that few understood. Amos was mostly thankful that Griffon could handle all the emotional girlie sides of his wife. Lily was strong with everyone but Griffon. He quickly learned everyone was okay.

When Angeline tried to tell him about the angel that saved them, her parents cut her off and scolded her. That was not to be mentioned in the presence of others and, right now, many neighbors and friends were stopping by to check on them.

After all were gone, the five of them settled down for dinner. Little Trevor said the blessing and they began to eat. Angeline jumped up, "Now Mama, now?"

Lily laughed at her single-minded daughter, thankful for once that a new nightmare was not in the making. Griffon noticed a strange look on Lily's face as she watched him...

with curiosity, perhaps? He couldn't quite read her tonight, so he tried to concentrate on Angeline's tale of the angel.

Trevor piped up, "She gave us cookies!"

"Shh, I'm telling the story Trevor! She put a blanket on us so no one could see us, and she put magic buttons in our ears that played music. Real music, Uncle Griff!"

Griffon raised an eye toward his sister. They had all finished eating, so Lily shooed the kids upstairs to wash up and prepare for bed.

"What?" he asked.

"So do you want to tell us about this angel of yours?"

"MY angel? I assure you I don't know any angels. You should be interrogating your kids. Maybe they just made it up to get through today."

Amos spoke up, "Sorry, my friend, but the angel asked us to give you this." He handed him the note.

Griffon looked at it, "What's this?"

Amos said, "I dunno; you tell us."

Lily piped in, "It's a piece of paper you morons; hasn't been that long since you last saw one."

Griffon shook his head and mumbled, "I know what a piece of paper is… " while he opened it.

What he found was a hand drawn map with three X's marked and a note from Holly explaining they were monitoring the town to gain intelligence. She only told him to be careful if he decided to come back up the mountain and avoid the three spotters in the locations marked on the map. Griffon threw the note down and headed for the door.

"Relax. She's long gone, my friend. This was hours ago, and she was heading up the mountain," Amos said.

Griffon spent the next five minutes pacing the floor and yelling at himself or someone. They weren't sure whom he was mad at but let him have his moment.

"What was she thinking?"

"The AMAN was right here! What if they'd seen her?"

"All to protect me? ME?"

"I'll wring her neck when I see her!"

After a while, he settled down and looked like a deflated balloon.

"All done there, lover boy?" Lily teased. "Wanna share with the class what's going on exactly and who this mystery girl of yours is?"

Griffon reluctantly told them about the cave and meeting Holly. He tried not to go into too many details, and they didn't ask.

"Wow, after all this time, the Jenkins really are still up on that mountain?" Lily was surprised and impressed. Holly was an angel who saved her babies, so that was already a plus in her book. From the looks of it, she had her brother wound tighter than a drum. It was about time as far as Lily was concerned. He needed a good woman in his life, besides her of course.

Griffon made up his mind. He would head up the mountain that night. This time, he packed appropriately with blanket, pillow, flashlight, food, water, change of clothes, and, of course, his climbing gear and bow. He showered, grabbed his gear, and said goodbye. He let them know where he was going and that he would be back on Saturday. Amos tried to talk him into waiting until morning, but his mind was set.

It was an uneventful climb up the mountain to the cave. He was there within two hours and settled in for the night.

* * * * *

Chapter 10

HOLLY PRAYED that Lily and Amos got the note to Griffon in time. She was nervous and anxious all evening, and she couldn't get the sight of the AMAN out of her mind and shuddered just thinking of it. She wrapped a warm blanket around her shoulders.

"You've been shivering all night. Feeling okay?"

It was Milo.

"I'm fine, thanks."

"You looked a million miles away during dad's sermon tonight."

She knew he was right, but had hoped no one noticed. Wednesday nights were fellowship nights. Pastor Weaver always said a few words and everyone at the compound was expected to be there. Holly wasn't in the mood for fellowship but didn't know how to get out of it.

"Milo, come on over. I want to run something by you before we adjourn."

"Sorry, Holly, I have a meeting tonight. Talk to you later?"

"Sure. Later." She was thankful to get out of the spotlight. As Milo made his way over to her father, she sneaked out of the room and headed to bed early, wondering what Griffon was doing just then.

At that moment, Griffon was also laying down for the night. The sun set, and the cave grew dark. He was exhausted after a long day's work, the emotional roller coaster of the AMAN attack, Holly's role in it, and then the long climb up the mountain. He had taken a risk and come up by way of the lowest lookout on Holly's map. It was a good lookout, but there were much better spots on the mountain, with the cave being the best. He couldn't help but wonder why they hadn't chosen that point. He'd have to ask her about it tomorrow.

* * * * *

Since Holly went to bed so early, she was up before dawn. She tried to go back to sleep but it was a losing battle. She just wanted to get to the cave and wait for Griffon. A part of her wondered if he'd really come. She headed to the kitchen to fix breakfast and pack lunch. She was surprised to find her mother already there, sipping on a cup of coffee. She asked Holly to sit down and join her. How could she say no?

"I knew you'd be up bright and early this morning. A lot is changing quickly around here. How are you holding up?" Her mom reached over and tucked a stray hair behind her daughter's ear.

"I'm okay, I guess. Lots to think about, right now. I'm going to take the next few days and figure out this college stuff. The school year's coming fast, and I know dad will stop stressing when I have a plan in place."

Her mom considered that. She always seemed to know exactly what Holly needed and when she needed it.

"Fall will be here soon you know. Not too many warm nights left. I've noticed you've been needing your alone time more than usual lately. Why don't you grab a tent and sleeping bag and head up to that special place of yours for a few days? If life were still normal, we'd have given you a week away to the beach or something with your friends for graduation. You are welcome to ask Cassie to go with you, but I think a little alone adventure would do you some good. Figure out what you want, and I don't just mean with school."

"Thanks mom. I would love that! Do you think two nights would be okay? I'll be back on Saturday."

"Take all the time you need, sweetie."

"Well, I have a date with Milo Saturday night." She blushed.

Her mother smiled her all-knowing smile and gave her a quick hug as she left the room.

"Get on out of here, and I'll break the news to your father this afternoon. Enjoy it honey. And don't forget a flare gun just in case."

She knew her father would not be happy. For a moment, she sat there. What just happened? Was she dreaming? Before the shock of her mother's plan wore off, she packed enough food for three days, with extra for Griffon. She gathered the gear she'd need and swung by the schoolroom to pick up the books and syllabi she needed to make her school plans for her college years. Then she left the compound and headed to the cave.

She froze at the cave entrance. What was she doing? What would happen if Griffon actually did show up? The voice in her head was sure he wouldn't. Well, she wasn't giving up this opportunity either way. Three days all to herself.

She was almost giddy as she dropped her things down the hole. The sun was just starting to rise, causing the sky to turn pink around the mountains to the west.

She was much earlier than he expected... and dragging something heavy from the sound of it. He saw her enter the cave with her back toward him, definitely dragging something big.

* * * * *

"Good morning sunshine, you're up awful early."

She screamed, her heart pounding. "What are you doing here? You scared me half to death!"

"Sorry," he laughed at her as he said it.

"It's 6:30 a.m. How did you get up here so fast?"

Looking around, she knew the answer.

"Did you sleep here last night?"

His voice was deep and sexy, husky from still waking up. "Heard a crazy story about this angel who flew down from the mountain." He gave her an accusatory look. "What were you thinking, Holly?"

She just stood there, stunned. A part of her really didn't believe he'd come back, and she didn't know what to do or say now.

"Holly? Holly?"

She shook her head, still fighting a fog of confusion. "Uh good morning."

"You okay?"

"Yeah, I'm just surprised to see you, that's all."

It was Griffon's turn to look confused. "Didn't we make plans for today? And didn't you risk your life to come warn me to be careful on my way up?"

"Yes, but I wasn't sure you'd actually come. Really, I did not risk my life. Don't be silly."

He was at her side, holding her by the shoulders. "You were a couple hundred yards from the AMAN. You saw them... that's way too close. You can't come down there, it's not safe."

Then he hugged her close, but only for a brief second. It dawned on her that he had been worried about her.

"What is all this?" He asked.

She was suddenly embarrassed and not one hundred percent sure how this happened or how to tell him. Oh well, she might as well be honest.

"It's been a strange morning. I have a three-day camping pass. Not my plan. It was actually my mother's idea. I don't get a ton of alone time, so I jumped on it and grabbed everything I thought I might need."

He raised an eyebrow and asked the obvious question. "You're staying here?" A grin spread across his face that made her blush.

"It's not like that," she protested. "This all happened this morning. I didn't have time to think it through. I have a tent, so I can go up the mountain to camp."

"No need. This place is plenty big enough for the both of us." He put his hands in the air trying to look innocent, "I'll be a perfect gentleman. Promise."

She shook her head. "Have you eaten yet? I'm starving." She started unpacking food, more food, and more food. He wasn't sure he had ever seen so much food in one place.

"Didn't seem smart to start a fire in here, so I grabbed a camp grill. Set it up over there, and I'll fry us up some eggs."

He looked at the pile she had dragged in. Six bags in all. One was a tent, one a sleeping bag, and the one she took had the food. That left three more. He found clothes and personal care items in the first. The second was filled with books. The last bag contained a small camp stove and kitchen stuff with some miscellaneous items. He set it up and went back to the bag of books. He fingered them mindlessly, with memories rushing through his mind.

"Where did you get these?"

She looked up. "Oh, the books? Yeah, sorry, I have to look them over this week and come up with my plan for college next term to get my dad off my back."

"College? How is that possible?"

"Well, before we moved up here, dad prepared for everything, including school." She rolled her eyes. "I graduated high school last May. So far, school's been largely in a classroom setting. This year, it's all independent study. I'm not looking forward to it, and let's face it, after all you've told me, what is the benefit of a college degree?"

Griffon was truly amazed by all she said. "Don't ever second guess an education, even in this world." He hesitated a moment, then told her again about the AMAN law against books and about his mother.

"I guess it would be more helpful if I asked what's not illegal!"

He laughed.

Breakfast was ready, and they ate and fell into easy conversation. After breakfast, she announced it was clean up time. He looked around and asked if she had water. He had some but it would barely sustain him for three days, let alone her and cleanup. He cursed himself for not thinking it through better.

"Silly boy. Grab your flashlight and that bucket and let me teach you the secrets of the cave."

* * * * *

She led him down a series of tunnels. She knew every inch of the cave. He couldn't help but be impressed. He had no idea where they were or even how long they'd been gone; all he could do was trust her.

She stopped, "Shh, do you hear it?"

He heard something but couldn't quite place it. The sound grew louder with each step. He could see a faint light ahead just around a corner. The light grew stronger as they approached, so did the noise. At last, they came to another cave. The light wasn't bright like the main cave, but there was some, and he could see a magnificent waterfall and pool. It looked like something from a fairy tale with water reflections bouncing off the walls.

"Spring water," Holly said. "We can fill the bucket up here. Best water on the mountain."

Griffon got down and scooped up a handful. It was ice cold, and he couldn't remember water ever tasting so good. He filled the bucket, and they made their way back.

"How do you know so much about this place?"

"This was my secret place. I used to hide up here in the summer, even before we moved here permanently. You're the only other person who knows about it. I've never told anyone. Not Chris or Cassie, or even Charlie."

Griffon hadn't considered there were others up here. He knew she said "they" were watching the town in her note, but he had never stopped to consider who "they" were.

"So who are these people? Are they your siblings?"

"Charlie's my brother. Chris and Cassie are my two best friends. They're dating right now, so that's a bit awkward. I found out a few days ago on a surprise double date. Surprise being on me not realizing I was on a date." Holly rambled on without really thinking.

He tried to keep up. There were definitely more people than just her family up here. "A date? You have a boyfriend?"

That thought certainly hadn't crossed his mind, and he didn't like the idea, which really surprised him. It was like a punch in the gut.

"Oh, I dunno!" Holly said, exasperated.

He stopped.

"You don't know if you have a boyfriend or not?"

"It's complicated. I won't bore you with the details." She knew she had rambled on without thinking and certainly had never meant to bring up Milo. She hoped he'd drop the subject, and for a while, he did and switched topics to the others.

"So there are three families living up here?"

"No, there are far more than that."

"How is that even possible? Your cabin must be enormous."

"Um, something like that." She tried to side-step the question. She was good at reading people, and she trusted him, maybe too much. She didn't want to put her family or anything from the compound in danger.

"I don't mean to pry. I'm just fascinated. You've lived untouched by all the ugliness in life. I don't fully understand how. I didn't believe anyone like you existed anymore."

* * * * *

They arrived back at the main cave, and he started cleaning the breakfast dishes. "Hey, last night I swung by your lookout, the one closest to town. Good work. I was impressed but have to ask why there? If you wanted to spy on the town, there are much better, more direct points."

"They were starting up a group to go down to the towns and find out what's going on. I was supportive until I met you and learned of the AMAN. It took a lot of convincing to stop him. We compromised on recon from a distance. Wythel is the closest town, so the logical place to start.

"Since Charlie knows I have always roamed this side of the mountain, he asked for my advice, and I may have steered him away from a direct point of view for my own selfish reasons. I had no idea he would get things rolling so quickly, and I'll admit, I freaked a bit, envisioning you getting shot or caught and interrogated trying to get back up here. It was total luck that I stumbled across your sister's place. I recognized Amos's voice from the other day. I hadn't planned to get so close.

"I was hoping to find you. Stupid, I know. I just couldn't sit there and do nothing. The little girl had her pack open, and I could see bright pink poking out from fifty yards away. I didn't know what was happening but knew it must be serious. I couldn't just not do anything. Sorry if it caused you any grief but when I realized it was Amos, I took the opportunity."

"Caused ME grief?" He laughed. "We owe you everything for that. They were strangers to you. That was a pretty stupid risk to take."

He saw her cringe at the words.

"Angeline thinks you're an angel sent from God. I think Lily might too." He chuckled.

She really was an amazing woman. The thought of a boyfriend popped into his head again and hit him like a ton of bricks. Holly Jenkins wasn't just any girl! Jealousy rose in him over the thought of another man in her life. He knew he needed to keep his guard up.

She invoked strong feelings in him, and he knew he could fall hard for her. He almost accepted the inevitable doom that was to come from it. They were truly from different worlds. No one outside his family would have risked what she did to protect his niece and nephew, much less two complete strangers. She was a remarkable woman.

She spoke, breaking into his thoughts. "No one who really knows me would ever call me an angel!"

* * * * *

The day passed quickly. They had no shortage of conversation and felt very comfortable with each other. They didn't do much else but talk, and she promised to show him more of the cave the next day.

As evening set in, she knew she would need to set up camp, but the thought made her feel awkward and clumsy. She had sleepovers before, so this shouldn't be a big deal. She knew her parents wouldn't agree, and that made her nervous as if she was doing something wrong.

She pushed the thoughts from her mind and started laying her stuff out. She grabbed her toothbrush, soap, and pajamas and headed to the spring to wash up for bed. Griffon stayed behind to get his stuff ready.

When she returned, she found him laid out on his blanket in nothing but a pair of shorts, and right next to her own sleeping bag. She stopped and gawked at the sight. She couldn't seem to pull her eyes away from his bare chest, so golden brown and rippling with muscles.

She knew she was staring but she couldn't stop herself. He was acutely aware that she was staring. He didn't mind. He rather enjoyed it but couldn't help but comment. She looked irresistibly cute in that moment.

"Nice! Hello Kitties." He said with a grin.

She broke her stare. Something flashed across her face that he didn't recognize. What had he said? She straightened, almost obstinate, and walked over and climbed into her sleeping bag. They watched the sun go down in silence. Then she rolled onto her side with her back toward him.

She was deep in her own thoughts. *He thinks I'm a child. Why would he even stay up here? He's a grown man with responsibilities. What is he doing here? I'm just a little girl with a crush. A crush? I just met him. I barely know him. Nothing would ever happen between us. I was stupid to think such a thing.* It felt like something, at least to her. She was flooded with emotions she didn't yet know how to process. Then she felt a hand on her back, gentle, but strong enough to send a ripple through her body.

"Holly, are you okay? You're awfully quiet tonight."

She rolled toward him, not realizing just how close he was. Finding herself face to face in his arms, she couldn't look him in the eyes. He reached out and tipped her chin up to face him. He couldn't tell what was going through that pretty little head, and when he brushed her cheek to tuck a stray piece of hair behind her ear, her body warmed and she shivered involuntarily.

"You're cold," he said and pulled her closer to him.

Cold? It was ninety degrees outside, and her entire body was on fire. She had to get some space between them. Her heart was pounding in her ears. Her senses acutely aware of his presence. His scent flooded her. She never fully understood what the smell of masculinity was until now. She met his stare and, for a brief moment, thought he was going to kiss her.

Don't be silly, Holly. You're just a kid he feels responsible for after saving his niece and nephew. He doesn't think of you like that. Space. You just need some space.

"I'm fine, really." She smiled at him reassuringly, trying to roll away but unsure how to do so without making her escape attempt obvious. "Just tired, and it's a bit warm in here actually, don't you think?"

* * * * *

She felt trapped... in his arms and in the sleeping bag. She was an over-thinker. She needed time to process this. She wiggled out from under her sleeping bag, but he was still right there. She moved to adjust the bag back under her and as she went to sit up, her head smacked into his chin.

"Ouch!"

"I am so sorry!" She cradled his face in her hands, checking to make sure he was okay. Instinct took over, and she was not entirely aware that she was practically lying on top of him.

"I'm fine," he said in a husky voice. Then he wrapped his arms around her and pulled her in for a kiss. Her body took over and responded in kind before the reality of the situation made it to her brain. They were both breathless when they came up for air. She rolled onto her back while he repositioned to his side in order to face her.

"I've wanted to do that all week," he confessed.

"You have?" Her voice couldn't hide her surprise. "Why?" She asked the question before her brain told her not to.

He chuckled. "Really? You're kind and caring. You're fearless and smart, not to mention extremely sexy. You're the most beautiful woman I've ever met."

He leaned in and kissed her again.

Sexy? A woman? No one had ever said such things about her before. At seventeen, she was just beginning to understand the truth in his words. "Even in my Hello Kitties?"

"Especially in your Hello Kitties," he whispered with a grin as he stole one last sweet kiss.

He rolled back to his back and held her hand, his thumb slowly caressing it almost absentmindedly. She wondered how that small motion seemed to send shock waves to every part of her body. They talked of lighter things and soon drifted off to sleep hand in hand.

* * * * *

The next morning, Holly woke with a smile on her face.
The cave floor wasn't the most comfortable nights' sleep, but
it was worth it. Her hand flew to her mouth, and she sighed
contentedly with the memories of his kisses. The sun was up.
She wasn't sure for how long. The cave was already warming
more than usual. It was going to be a hot summer day.

She reached for Griffon and sat up, realizing he wasn't
there. His stuff was there but he was nowhere in sight. She
looked around with the momentary panic that he had left.
Then she realized that the water bucket was missing. He
must be at the spring. She set about preparing breakfast,
certain he hadn't eaten without her. When breakfast was
done and there was still no sign of him, she decided to go
look for him.

* * * * *

Chapter 11

HE WOKE up early. For a while, he just watched her sleep next to him. She was so peaceful that he didn't dare wake her. He felt a bit like a sap for nearly professing his love for her last night. He hadn't meant to but she seemed genuinely shocked by his kiss, and he felt the need to reassure her with words. He worried a bit over just how much she really meant to him. They had just met. It seemed crazy when his brain stopped to think, but there was no denying his heart. He didn't know what to do about it and decided it best to just take things one step at a time.

He wanted to do something nice for her and decided to try his hand at cooking. First though, coffee. They were low on water so he decided to try to find his way back to the spring.

He tried to remember the path, but after a while, he knew he must have missed a turn. A voice in his head kept telling him to stop and wait... that she'd find him. He felt so stupid; he just kept going. Around another bend, he saw faint natural light ahead and headed in that direction. It opened into the spring room but from a different tunnel. He set to work collecting the water, still not sure how long he'd been lost in the tunnels. He got up, looked around, and tried to get his bearings straight. Then he saw her.

"Let me guess, you took a left instead of a right at the second fork."

He gave her a sheepish grin and headed toward her. "What gave it away?"

"I'm impressed that you made it here at all. There are so many twists and turns on that side, you could have been lost for days in there."

He hugged her, gave her a quick kiss to test the morning water, and then lingered for a longer one. He pulled away smiling and feeling that she wanted much more, too. "To be honest, I wasn't sure I hadn't been in there for days!"

They both laughed and headed back to the main cave.

They ate breakfast and straightened up. He noticed that she was very agitated and wouldn't sit still.

"Holly, am I making you nervous or something today?"

She laughed but he didn't know why.

"No, not at all."

When he raised an accusatory eyebrow, she continued.

"Really, it's not you this time. Maybe it should be, but it's not." She was rambling now, a side of her he hadn't fully seen before, and she paced absentmindedly while she talked.

"You would think that a girl who spent nearly half her life living under ground could handle a few days of rest in a cave, but not me."

She was talking faster and more animatedly, and he had a hard time not laughing out loud at the scene before him.

"Who am I kidding? I can't sit here day-after-day just lounging around talking. What happens when we've run out of things to say? Awkward! No, it's best to do something. I need to do something."

He couldn't help it. He laughed out loud, which stopped her ramblings.

"I'm sorry, really. You are ridiculously cute right now, but let me see if I'm following you. You're stir crazy already and want to do something today?"

"Yes! That's exactly what I was trying to say." She sat down, exasperated.

"Well why didn't you just say so?" He was giving her an irresistible grin, and she knew he was mocking her, but she didn't care.

"We can't exactly go out wandering the woods. Someone might see us and it's crazy hot today," she said. "Tell you what; I have to get this college plan done, so you can help me with that. First though, we work out."

"We what?"

"Work out. It's a well-known fact that I cannot work the brain before the body. So we will work out; then I can concentrate on the books."

He was old enough to remember his mother working out to fitness videos on TV when the stuff hit the fan. He knew what a gym was, *but those didn't exist anymore, did they? Certainly not in Wythel.* He shrugged and decided to let her lead. *It could be fun, right?*

* * * * *

"Come on champ, you can do this. No gym in here, but we can make the most of it." It sounded almost like a dare. He snorted. He was easily twice her size and all muscle. With his job, he worked out for a living. How hard could it be?

She began with a series of yoga stretches. He thought they were silly at first and mocked her but they gradually grew harder. A few were so sexy that he had a hard time concentrating on her instructions and found himself gawking at her instead.

"I didn't even know that position was even possible," he said out loud, which broke her concentration.

"Down boy," she said with a laugh. "Enough stretches, let's get started."

I thought that was the workout, he thought to himself.

Two hours later, he was sprawled out on the cave floor gasping for breath while she laughed as she finished her cool-down stretches. Every muscle in his body ached.

"You're a machine. You can't be human." He complained. "I'm a lumberjack. Did you know that?"

She shook her head no. She knew he worked, but he hadn't mentioned what he did.

"I climb trees and cut wood fifteen hours a day, four days a week. On my days off, I help Amos with construction. I'm in great shape." He was still breathing heavy as he said it.

She laughed, "Who are you trying to convince there, Champ? Yourself or me?

He groaned.

She laughed again.

She grabbed her books and sat down on the rock couch. He crawled over beside her, still sprawled across the floor, but now with his head in her lap to see what she was doing.

She knew she took education for granted. She also knew from Griffon that they burned books and the written word was dead. *Did he even know how to read?* She was looking over a list of classes as she thought it.

"Calculus? Physics? Economics? Latin? You are a machine!" He half joked.

He can definitely read, she decided.

He was enormously impressed as he looked through the course list from which she had to pick.

"In another lifetime, I had plans to go to Virginia Tech after high school. Preferably on a football scholarship, of course." He smiled at the memory, and she made a mental note to bring a football next time.

She stroked his hair and allowed him to continue. "Now it's the biggest AMAN fort in this area. The football field is used for combat training and arena games for the entertainment of the soldiers.

"It's often hard to remember how the world used to be, but you bring back so many good memories, not to mention many great new ones in the making." He gave her a knowing smile, and she bent down for a quick kiss.

After they hashed over the list and she was confident in her schedule for first term, he sat up next to her. "Now what boss?"

She grinned and acted bolder than she felt, as she pressed close for a kiss. He groaned softly in response and pulled her close, parting her lips to explore every inch of her mouth. Her heart leapt into her throat, her pulse throbbing. She was thankful they weren't standing because her legs wouldn't have supported her.

His hand was massaging the nape of her neck. Her hands seemed to have a mind of their own, exploring the hard muscles across his back. She had been kissed before, but never like this. She was amazed at the feel of his body beneath her hands, which roamed up and down his chest and across his shoulders. As they moved lower and discovered the hard ripples of his abs, he broke the kiss and pulled away with another moan. She wanted more, much more, and she could tell by the fog in his eyes that he did too.

He put some distance between them. Wringing his hands through his hair he said, "Holly, we can't. I mean, I want to, but we can't."

He threw his head back and groaned, wondering why he had to be so damn honorable. He knew she wanted him as much as he wanted her, but he cared too much to rush things in that direction. He forced himself to breathe deeply and regain some control before he did something they could both come to regret.

She watched him from where she sat. She was mesmerized. How did she manage that kind of effect on a man? She didn't know she had it in her, and the awareness of what she'd just done to him made her heady with a strength she had never known before this moment. She knew she could not have broken that connection from him, though she was glad he had. She knew neither was ready for that. She could tell he was still trying to gain control of himself and decided to lighten the mood.

"Hey champ, you bring a bathing suit, or at least an extra set of clothes?"

He straightened up and looked at her with one brow raised.

"Maybe... what exactly is going through that evil little head of yours?"

"Relax; I'm not going to attack you. Thought maybe we could both use some cooling off. So if you don't mind getting those shorts wet, then follow me, otherwise change quickly and let's go."

He wasn't sure what she had in mind exactly, but was thankful for the change in atmosphere between them. He could tell she wasn't upset that he had halted things so abruptly, and he was relieved she had redirected them both, for now.

She led him deep into the bowels of the cave again. After several twists and turns, he again heard the sound of water. It was different this time, louder and stronger than the spring. As he saw light begin to stream in, he stopped and asked her, "What is that? It's not the spring, is it?"

"Nope, it's the waterfall. It spills down into Holly's Hole, named after me since I was the one who discovered it. On a hot day, like today, there are probably plenty of people cooling off there, but we should be unseen as long as we stay on this side of the falls."

He wasn't sure what to expect, but as they arrived at their destination, he was astonished at the beautiful site before him. She motioned for him to keep following and walked around a rock that opened up to a brightly lit area just behind the main waterfall.

She pulled him to one side where he could see out around the water into the world beyond. Then she pointed down, and he saw people swimming and sunbathing in the pool beneath the falls. She pointed to something on the cave wall... 'Holly's Hole'... and smiled and gave him two thumbs up.

Talking was pointless here, as they could not hear each other over the falls. It was like something from a picture book or movie from long ago. He had never seen such incredible beauty, never dreamt it could truly exist, and for that moment, it was as if every worry, every fear, past and present, were gone. In that moment, life was simply perfect.

As if slapped back into reality, Holly began taking her clothes off, and every inch of him was ready to spring with desire. She saw it on his face, and was already coming to recognize that dark look in his eyes. She laughed and waved him back as she discarded her clothes to reveal a bathing suit. It may have been a one piece, but left little for one to wonder what lay beneath. He groaned to himself and shook his head to clear a fog already setting in just from the sight of her.

She ran her hand across the water and splashed him. It was cold and shocking. He retaliated and imagined she was squealing in fun. They splashed, played, and teased much of the afternoon.

She was surprised when she noticed the sun laying low in the sky. She looked back down into the hole and everyone was gone. *Off to supper*, she imagined.

She took Griffon's hand and led him carefully to another set of rocks in the sidewall. As they got closer, he noticed she was heading for an opening that led to a path that twisted and wound down, eventually spilling out into the pool below. About halfway down, the noise lightened significantly and they could once again talk.

"That was absolutely incredible!"

She smiled. "It's one of my favorite places in the world. I'm glad you enjoyed it."

"Where does this lead to?"

"Down to the water hole."

"Is that safe? Weren't your friends down there?"

"Everyone should be in for dinner by now. It's getting late, so how about an evening swim before heading back up?"

"Lead the way, boss!"

* * * * *

As they came to the last turn, something caught her attention. She froze in place and put her hand up to signal Griffon to do the same. They inched a little closer. Voices, she could hear it more clearly now, but couldn't quite make it out.

"Mr. Jenkins wants you to do what? You can't propose to her right now, Milo; she isn't ready. You know that. If you push her, she'll run the other way. Trust me; I know how stubborn Holly can be."

Oh no! Panic set in. It was Chris. She closed her eyes and fought not to throw up. This could not be happening! She glanced back at Griffon and signaled him to go back the other way in hopes that he hadn't heard any of that conversation, but from the look on his face, she knew it was too late.

"I don't know what to do Chris. Mom's already pulled Grandma's ring out of the safe and polished it to a shine. All the elders are just waiting for the big announcement. I just don't know. What do I do? I mean, I like Holly, don't get me wrong. She's gorgeous; who wouldn't like her? We get along well enough. She's no longer jumping out of her skin when I kiss her, so that's improvement; but I'm not sure she's the one."

She was watching Griffon with his big eyes in shock. She could see him visibly tense, and when Milo mentioned kissing her, she saw his hands ball into fists and his muscles tighten.

She moved close and put a hand on his chest, hoping to calm him down. When he jolted and looked at her, she just shook her head no, as if to say, don't do anything stupid.

"You know I love Holly. I was relieved at how cool she was about Cassie and me. She's always been like a sister to me and so you know I'd welcome her to the family with open arms. But you seem a little leery here, and I know she likes you a lot, but I don't know that she's actually in love with you either, yet."

"Yes, I'd agree with that assessment. We have a real date, just the two of us on Saturday. Got any ideas on how to spice things up?"

Their voices faded in the distance, signaling that they were moving away from where Holly and Griffon stood. She closed her eyes and prayed it was just a big nightmare, then opened them and looked straight into his eyes. She knew it had really just happened. She wanted to crawl under a rock and hide forever.

He turned and made his way back up to the waterfall. He needed that cold shock from the water to calm him. She had mentioned a boyfriend; she hadn't kept that from him, but an engagement? 'It's complicated' he remembered her saying. Anger filled him. *Complicated... yeah, I'll say.*

What is she doing here, with me? How can she be in my arms one day and run back to this other guy the next? That picture didn't fit with anything he knew of her. One thing for sure, she was already taken. She would never be his, and that thought cut through his heart like a knife.

He knew he had no right to her, that she wasn't really his, but he was unable to convince his heart of that. He was aware that she was respectfully keeping a distance and letting him cool off.

He knew from the look of terror on her face that she hadn't purposefully led him to hear that, but for now, he just couldn't talk to her or look at her. He was angry, upset, brokenhearted, everything all at once. In that moment, it went from the best day of his life to the worst.

They walked back in complete silence. He wouldn't even look at her. The sun was setting when they arrived back to the cave. She got busy cooking dinner while he sulked on the stone couch. When dinner was ready, she handed him a plate, which he at least took. She sat down to a painfully quiet meal. When she finished and he was still largely picking at his plate, she had brewed to a boiling point and couldn't keep quiet any longer.

"This is ridiculous, Griffon! I'm sorry you heard all that, but so what? Why are you mad at me? I told you it was complicated!" She was angry and frustrated too. Not at him but at the entire situation and at herself. "I'm sorry! I don't even know what else to say."

She stood up at some point, and he jumped up too. He felt so many strong emotions. In three strides, he crossed the space between them and grabbed her with arms stronger than he intended. He kissed her with all the anger and frustrations he was feeling. He wouldn't give up so easily. Dammit, she was his girl! His!

His kisses were hard and hot. Nothing like before. These were demanding and possessive and awoke in her feelings she had only read about in books she sneaked from the library, knowing her mother would disapprove. She met him with equal passion.

They were both breathless when he finally pulled away and stepped back to stare at her. He was horrified by how hard and aggressive he had been with her, but she didn't look scared or horrified by the event. Why had she kissed him back with seemingly equal passion? What did it mean?

She gave him a few moments while she caught her breath and tried to regain control of herself. Then she softened and sat down, almost deflated.

"I'm sorry," he said quietly. There was agony in his voice; she could hear it. "I didn't mean to be so rough. Didn't mean to scare you."

"I'm not scared of you Griffon, and you don't need to apologize for kissing me. I wanted you too." She had never been so direct with a man before, but she needed to make her intentions clear to him. "I apologize for the pain or confusion or whatever you felt when you overheard Chris and Milo today. I apologize that I put you in a position to be hurt. I do not apologize for my actions and do not accept apology for yours.

"That was Chris and Milo Weaver. Chris is one of my best friends. I told you about him. Milo is Chris's older brother and, well, the complication. I didn't hide him from you or disguise the situation. It is a situation. I don't love him. I never will, not like that at least. Our families... "

Wait. Did she just say she doesn't love him? Did she mean it? What else did she say? Something about her family?

"Griffon?"

"Uh, what? What were you saying?"

ARGH! "I was trying to explain the, uh, complication. Seriously, did you just tune me out? I'm trying to be honest with you, here."

He grimaced a bit. His mind had wandered, and he didn't hear much after 'I don't love him'. He grinned an irresistible, boyish grin and said, "Okay, I'm listening. Start again from the 'I don't love him' part."

She couldn't help but laugh at him and threw her pillow at his head. "Really? That's all you heard?"

He snatched her up into his arms and kissed her sweetly this time.

"Hmmm, that was all I needed to hear!"

Morning came quickly and Holly woke first this time, with a heavy heart. She couldn't just go back to life as normal. It was Saturday, which had come much too quickly. They had talked some more late into the night with no promises of tomorrow, only what if's and wishes that they both knew would never come true. She would just be thankful for this week and any other time she may get to spend with him.

Griffon woke and watched Holly in deep thought as she prepared their meal. This sight was becoming much too familiar. He knew in his heart they could live in this cave forever, and his life would be filled with nothing but happiness. It was a great dream, but too much to ask of her.

"Good morning, Sunshine!" He smiled, remembering his first morning here and how he had scared her half to death. It felt like a lifetime ago.

She looked up and smiled back at him. She knew they'd have to say their goodbyes soon, and she was restless with the sadness that thought brought her.

"Good morning. Sleep well?"

"No, kept having these crazy wild dreams about some red head."

She didn't have to look over to know he was grinning. She was too.

The day passed much too quickly, and by midday, they knew they couldn't keep stalling. It was time to say their goodbyes.

He asked what they both were thinking. "So, any chance I'll see you in five days?"

She didn't hesitate. "YES!" She threw her arms around him. Before they broke the embrace, she told him, "I don't know how to make this happen, but I will definitely try, and I will be here five days from now and will understand if you don't make it."

It was a vague statement, she knew, but he understood. They were from two different worlds wanting to promise each other everything while knowing they could not.

* * * * *

Chapter 12

WHEN HOLLY arrived back at her family's pod, her father was waiting for her. She had left much of her gear at the cave and was only carrying the bare minimum. He eyed her suspiciously but didn't say a word, just sat there watching her.

She smiled, gave him a quick kiss on the cheek and, without a word, handed him the completed portfolio of the first semester college plans that she and Griffon had worked so hard on. Mike looked at the folder, then back at his daughter. He was surprised to find it complete and thorough. Pride welled up inside him.

"I see you've been busy these last few days. I'm glad you're home where you belong. You're mother's been terribly worried."

She laughed. "It was all her idea Dad, so stop worrying. I'm fine."

He could see that she was better than fine even. His baby girl had changed somehow. She had grown up over those three days away. He couldn't quite put his finger on it, but there was something different about her, more mature, more aware somehow.

He was shocked by this sudden development. As she walked away, heading for her room, he noticed a new confidence in her that he had never seen before. He didn't want to admit his wife was right to let her go. He wasn't ready to let go of his baby girl.

She showered, changed, and headed for the kitchen. Her mother was there, discussing something with Mrs. Worthington. Her mother looked up, smiled, and motioned for her to come over.

"I'm just going to grab a quick bite to eat first."

When her mother was done talking with Mrs. Worthington, she turned her attention to her daughter. Holly felt her mother watching her. When their eyes met, Holly found a knowing glare, and her mother had a smile on her face.

"That's better," her mother said. "Some fresh air has done you well."

Holly hugged her. "Thanks mom."

She knew she couldn't tell her mom about her little trip, but she always suspected her mom wouldn't ask. "Dad didn't look so happy when I got in."

"Oh, you already saw him?"

"Yeah, I think he relaxed some when I gave him my completed portfolio."

"You finished it?"

Holly nodded.

"That's pretty impressive, Holly. I'm proud of you. I know that will set your father's mind at ease some. He might not complain quite so much next time."

She gave her girl a squeeze. "It's really good to have you home, though."

Next time? She said next time? Holly's heart soared! She was certain that her father would have forbidden her to leave like that again, but her mother's words gave her hope.

She decided to hunt out Cassie for a little girl time and found her in the gym with Chris. She knew this was just something she'd have to accept and get used to, and while it was making her feel like a third wheel, she really couldn't be happier for them.

"Holly! You're back! We've missed you," Cassie squealed. Holly noted her use of the word 'we'. That was definitely something she was going to have to get used to hearing.

"Everyone's been worried about you," Chris chimed him.

"I'm fine, great even. Mom was right; it was just what I needed." She smiled, and Chris and Cass both caught the knowing look in her eyes. "So, what do you guys have planned today? I'm completely free this afternoon."

"What about your portfolio? Shouldn't you be working on that? You're dad's climbing the walls with frustration over it," Chris said.

"Not anymore. All complete and submitted to him for review this morning. He looks pleased so far."

Both her friends' jaws hit the floor.

"You're done? All of it? How?" Cassie choked out, clearly in shock.

Holly grinned. "What do you think I've been doing for three days?" She laughed to herself, knowing all that really happened.

"Wow! Congratulations Hols. We're all in shock here." Chris laughed. "So what do you have in mind to do today?"

"I have absolutely nothing in mind. Just haven't seen you guys much lately and thought it would be nice to catch up and just hang out."

That's exactly what they did. Holly learned that they had been dating for three months. She was more than a little surprised to hear that but accepted that they didn't need to tell her everything and knew that she certainly was keeping plenty from them as well.

They filled her in on all the summer gossip she had been ignoring, such as the chaos the little Sawyer twins were causing these days, or how Cassie's little sister trapped a field mouse and tried to keep it as a pet only to have it escape in the compound. It sent everyone into hysterics chasing the poor thing. She noted that they added mentions of Milo here and there and knew from overhearing Chris and Milo that they would be happy to see the two of them together. The thought weighed on her.

Milo left messages at her pod that he would pick her up at 6:00 p.m. She couldn't help but wonder what he had planned, and she felt somewhat guilty about the three amazing days with Griffon. She was also stressing about his comment to spice things up. She just couldn't imagine what that meant to Milo Weaver. He was such a precise planner. She had no doubt that every second of the date was scheduled.

He would show up in a suit or polo and dress pants, because that would be appropriate for a date. He would have something planned for dinner. They would stroll around the compound hand in hand, outside, weather permitting. Otherwise, they would sit in the fellowship room and talk. Boring!

It irritated her, and she rolled her eyes. She knew she had to play along, though. If anyone suspected she was seeing Griffon, her father would do everything in his power to stop it. *How can I kiss Milo when I'm certain that he will know I've kissed another man?*

Maybe I'm worrying unnecessarily. She tried to relax and not think too much about it. She couldn't get out of it, so she was determined to do her best to get through the night as quickly as possible.

* * * * *

Milo was late, and he was never late. At 6:15, she was beginning to worry; then she heard the knock at the door. She opened it about to chide him for being late and rush to get moving, when she was stopped in mid step. Milo wasn't wearing a suit or khakis; he was in shorts and a tee shirt, and he was holding a dozen balloons.

"Hey, you in a hurry to get moving?" When she didn't answer, he just smiled and handed her the balloons. "These are for you. I was going for flowers and then thought... 'Holly is a free spirit who needs room to soar like a bird,' and these seemed more appropriate. I hope you like them." He gave her a quick kiss on the cheek. "I missed you."

Who was this man? She was truly stunned and immediately softened.

"They're perfect!" She kissed him softly on the lips and felt relieved that that first kiss was over. She had done it, and it wasn't so bad. She didn't think he suspected anything, so maybe she could relax, and, who knows, maybe he would surprise her.

He looked her over. She had a quiet assurance about her that he had not seen before. He liked it. He noticed she was wearing a dress.

"You look beautiful." He said "But, you may want to change into shorts for tonight."

"Shorts? Um, okay; just give me a few minutes to change."

Shorts? What is he up to? In no scenario of a date with Milo could she fathom him not wanting her dressed up nicely and on display. Not since they were kids could she remember him ever wearing shorts, and, she recalled, he was actually tan, legs and all, and not the usual pasty white complexion typical for everyone in the compound. Tonight could be more interesting than she suspected. *Is this what he meant by spicing things up a little?*

When she returned wearing a pair of khaki shorts and a navy, v-neck tee, he thought she had never looked prettier and told her so. He liked how she blushed at his compliment. He would have to remember to do that more often.

"Are you ready for an adventure, Ms. Holly Jenkins?" He offered his hand.

She smiled. "Okay, let's do this."

He wasn't in any hurry. They strolled hand-in-hand through the compound and out the front door, stopping to say hello and address those they passed in the process. For once, he didn't seem to be on a timed schedule. *This is a refreshing change,* she thought.

He stopped just outside the door and gave her an almost wicked grin, then pulled a piece of paper out of his pocket and handed it to her. Before he removed his hand from it, he told her, "Okay, this should only take about 20 minutes. So get a move on."

She looked at the paper in their hands and back at him. "What's going on?"

"Just follow the clues, and you'll find out soon enough." Then he gave her a quick kiss. "Now hurry. I'll see you on the other side." He ran back into the compound and left her just standing there.

Okay, let's see what he's up to, she thought and opened the paper he had handed her.

What feeds our body and nourishes our soul? Find your next clue there.

That was what Mrs. Worthington always said about her garden, that it feeds the body and working the garden feeds her soul. Mrs. Worthington had a garden in the greenhouse that had sustained them for years, and she had this year's planted already. Since he led her outside, she decided to try the outdoor garden first and headed down the path in that direction. When she arrived at the garden, she found a basket of fresh bread, cheese, and berries with a note attached.

What heals all that ails you? Find it and you'll find your next clue.

She thought for a minute. *What heals all that ails you?* She picked up the basket and thought for a second? *Heals? Doc? TEA,* she thought. *Doc always said tea would fix anything from tummy aches to broken hearts.*

She smiled thinking of him. Not everyone knew, but she did, that Doc had planted various herbs years ago near the old tree house. She wondered if Milo knew that too and headed in that direction to find out.

Sure enough, there was a backpack. It wasn't just any backpack. It was the picnic backpack from the compound that contained a blanket, plates, silverware, two wine glasses, and a chilled bottle of sparkling cider. There was no alcohol in the compound but her father enjoyed the sentiments of toasting for New Years and celebrations and had a stock of sparkling cider and grape juice for such occasions.

They often joked that, after so many years, his stash probably was wine by now. She retrieved the next note, anxious to see what would follow. She put on the backpack, picked up the basket, and read the next clue.

Flowers are necessary for any special date. You are one of a kind that stands out above the wildflowers.

She read that one several times because she didn't understand. Where's the "go here" and "get this?" This was more like a statement than a clue. *Wait! Wildflowers?* There was a patch of wildflowers not too far away in the open meadow.

Maybe he was talking about those. She headed in that direction but when she arrived, there wasn't a basket, backpack, or anything obvious. She read the clue again, carefully. *Flowers are necessary for any special date. Okay, so am I supposed to pick a flower and bring it? Which one?*

She read the rest of the clue. *You are one of a kind that stands out above the wildflowers. Above?* She looked up and out into the patch of wildflowers. They were so beautiful.

She scanned the area above and something caught her eye. The wildflowers there were largely yellow, purple, and blue, with some dark red and light pink thrown in the mix. Just beyond, up on the hill, was a striking bright red rose bush. She couldn't ever remember seeing it before. She headed up to it and noticed there was freshly dug dirt around it. She grabbed the note and read it quickly.

Cut flowers in a vase would never work for you. Your roots run deep, and your soul longs for wide-open spaces. Red for my redheaded firecracker who stands out amongst all the others. I hope you'll return and think of me often. On to the next clue: What adventure could be complete without a buried treasure? Find the next clue in your hidden treasure chest.

Her heart fluttered reading the first part, and she broke into laughter at the clue. Chris! She couldn't believe he even remembered. Would she? A lifetime had passed since that beautiful sunny day that she and Chris pledged their friendship with spit and blood and buried their most prized possessions. She had forgotten all about it.

Could she even find it after all this time? She assumed they had since he said the clue would be with the buried treasure. She made her way back to the tree house and walked around it slowly. She couldn't find the mark on the tree to signal the point from which they counted off their steps, and how much smaller those steps must have been. So much brush had grown up in the area since then.

She was excited and amazed that he remembered and found it. Then she noticed a couple of broken twigs in the brush and pushed them to the side. There on the ground, she saw it, freshly dug dirt with an X marking the spot. She grabbed a rock and began to dig in the dirt.

She uncovered the note first, but threw it aside and kept digging. When she hit something hard, she filled with excitement. She pulled out the little metal Strawberry Shortcake lunch box that had belonged to her mother before her. She had once used it as a pencil box, determined to be a writer.

When she opened it, she still found a couple of pens and her old journal inside, along with Chris's favorite matchbox car and three pieces of paper. The first was dry and seemingly nothing. She knew it was the napkin they both used to wipe their hands on after shaking hands in their own spit to seal the pact of friendship. Another napkin covered in droplets of blood smeared together and a hand written note signifying their union as best friends forever. She sat there laughing and smiling as the memories flooded back to her. She opened the journal and read the last entry.

Today Christopher Michael Weaver and Holly Ann Jenkins became best friends forever. Not just friends. Chris is now my brother in all ways that matter, and someday I hope to make that official when I marry his brother, Milo.

Her jaw nearly hit the ground. She had forgotten all about that. She had such a huge crush on Milo Weaver that summer. Of course, she was nothing but his brother's pesky little friend back then. Chris had to have shared that with him. She wanted to crawl down into the hole and die. Chris was a walking dead man. He would pay for this! She was embarrassed but she knew she'd have to move on... Milo must be waiting for her. She picked up the clue and read it out loud.

There's another treasure hidden in the hole at the base of the tree, retrieve it, and go to the point where the water falls from the sky every day, all day long. I will be waiting.

Holly decided to bury the lunchbox back in its place. Then she searched the tree to find the hole and retrieved a messenger bag. Curiosity couldn't stop her from peaking. Inside was a new notebook and pens. She hadn't had new in so long that it brought tears to her eyes seeing them. She assumed they were for her, but she would wait and see. She wiped the tears, read the clue one last time, and knew he must be at Holly's Hole.

When she arrived, Milo was waiting with his back toward her, looking out into the valley below. She just stopped and watched him for a moment. He stirred so many memories and emotions in her with his little treasure hunt that her heart and mind filled with confusion. Confusion over this man standing in front of her and the one she had said goodbye to just that morning.

He turned toward her and smiled, seeing that she had all the things he needed.

"Did you have a nice adventure?"

"It was incredible, thank you!"

He could tell by the look on her face that she truly meant it, and it warmed his heart. He was anxious to get started on the next part, though. She had taken longer than he thought, and his stomach was grumbling.

He took her hand, and, with a wicked grin, said, "The adventure's not over!"

He led her away from the swimming hole toward the steep part of the mountain. She, of course, new the area well; *where was he going?* This direction was a dead end, and they stopped at the edge. He wrapped his arms around her waist and held her close.

"Isn't it amazing Holly? You can see for miles. It just goes on forever. What has happened to this world, no matter how bad it may be, this hasn't changed. It's God's perfection." His voice was like a soft lullaby, and she was swooning in it.

"Sorry," he said shaking his head and looking embarrassed from having lost himself in the moment.

He is a romantic, she thought.

It embarrassed him, but it was there. For the first time, she wondered what it would be like to kiss him. Really kiss him, as she had with Griffon, and, in this moment with Milo's guard still down, she did just that.

It wasn't the burning desire she felt when Griffon kissed her, but it was intoxicating. Her body warmed and enveloped her. She felt comfort and security, but not in the same way she once had. This was like floating on a soft cloud. She could envision them right here eighty years old and feeling just as much love. It was a beautiful moment that shattered everything she had once thought of him, and it shook her to her very core. There was promise in this kiss.

She took him by surprise. He had kissed her hundreds of times by now, but never anything like this. His entire body turned to mush. He wasn't sure how they were still standing. This was better than anything he had ever read about, anything that he had ever dreamed or imagined. He went along with his father's wishes to court Holly but, until this moment, he never dreamed it could possibly work between them.

As they parted, he had a dreamy look in his eyes and a soft almost husky voice that gave her chills. "Hmmm, I don't even remember what we were talking about." He was still living the moment.

She smiled. "Sorry, I guess we got caught up in the moment."

"Oh I'm not complaining!" The way he said it made her laugh. It was so unlike him. Or was it? She could get used to this Milo, which worried her some.

"Okay, let me think... oh yes, are you scared of heights?"

"What? Me? No, why?"

He gave her a sheepish grin. "Ever been rappelling?" She shook her head no. "Well, just follow me."

First, he attached a rope to the basket and two bags she had brought with her and slowly lowered them by rope to a ledge about twenty-five yards below them.

"Wait, we're going there? Down there?"

"Yeah. I'm gonna show you my little secret spot and favorite place on earth. Now, wrap this around you, and pull this rope through here; now clamp this down, and follow me."

Once she was hooked up, he started down and encouraged her to follow.

"That's it. Just step off, the rope will hold you. There you go. Keep your feet on the rocks so you don't get turned around."

"Where did you learn to do this?"

"Emma Grace taught me."

Emma Grace was their teacher's daughter. She was a couple years older than Milo and nearly fully-grown when they closed the door to the compound. She was never considered "one of the kids," and Milo was always thought of as "the eldest of the kids." Emma Grace was quiet and kept to herself and, despite living together for more than half a decade, Holly really didn't know her and was surprised to hear that he did.

"A few more feet and you're there," he told her after having already reached the ledge. The ride down was thrilling, and the views were magnificent. How could he have known she would love something like this? She and Chris had never done anything like this before or ever talked about doing something like, so she knew this was all him this time. A completely new side of him that she never knew existed.

He grabbed her waist just as her feet touched down on the ledge.

"Steady now, you're here. Just unbuckle here, and I'll help you out of this gear."

He helped her wiggle out of the gear, then opened the backpack and spread the picnic blanket on the ledge. They sat down, and he served her the bread, cheese, berries, and sparkling cider. He rose and moved carefully around the side of the ledge and disappeared. She got up, peaked around, and saw the ledge continued on around. He reappeared a few minutes later with a large basket containing a meal of hot fried chicken, potato salad, green beans, and biscuits, which were still warm. She eyed him suspiciously.

"How are these still warm? You had to have brought them down hours ago."

He grinned, "I have my way."

"You're just full of surprises today."

"Good surprises, I hope."

"Very good," she admitted and blushed in spite of herself.

They toasted and enjoyed the meal in comfortable silence, each lost in their own thoughts, looking out across the beautiful valley.

They talked; they cuddled; and they kissed. *This is a surprisingly very romantic evening,* she thought. As the sun set in the sky, she sat up suddenly.

"Milo, how exactly do we get off this ledge? Are we climbing back up?"

He laughed. "Not this time, but maybe some other time. I guess it is getting late, so we best make our way back. I told you I was going to show you my favorite place on earth, remember?"

"Wasn't this it?"

"Not quite! Help me clean up, and I'll show you."

They hadn't left much to clean up, so they finished quickly, and he led her around the ledge in the direction he had disappeared to get the food. She followed, a little nervously, as the ledge narrowed quickly. She was so busy looking down to watch her footing that she didn't notice the cave in the side of the cliff. He pulled her inside, and when she realized where they were, her heart jumped into her throat.

He has a cave, too, was all she could think. Then panic set in. Could this be part of her cave? How much had he explored? Would he find her special cave?

"Where are we Milo?"

He was grinning with happiness and contentedness. "This is my cave. My get away place. I know it's silly. I mean we live underground. Why would I pick something dark, dreary, and underground for comfort? I dunno. I just really like it here, and I love the ledge with its views, it's like my own personal little condo."

This time he blushed. He knew she'd think it was silly. "I know you prefer your big wide open spaces at the top of the mountain, but this. This is me."

Oh God! They were more alike than she ever imagined. How is this happening? Why is this happening now?

He brought some headlamps with him to show her around, and she felt right at home. He was thrilled that she was so comfortable there and genuinely seemed to like it. She asked many questions, especially regarding the tunnels. They looked around a few of them, but all dead ends. Milo explained that he believed one of them might have connected to a bigger cave in the mountain, but that it had caved in at some point. She knew exactly where that point on the other side would lead and had often wondered exactly what was on this side. She was smiling uncontrollably, and he was thrilled to see her so happy.

They seemed to stay there for hours, although she had no real idea, as time just seemed to stand still. Eventually, they both began to yawn and knew it was time to call it a day.

"So, how exactly are we getting home?"

"Follow me." He led her down one of the tunnels they had yet to explore. It twisted, wound, and spilled out into the other side of the mountain. The entrance was covered with brush, and when he helped her through to the other side, she was astounded to find them at the above ground spring. How had she never found this place? Cassie and Chris were there waiting.

"We didn't think you two were ever coming out of there," Chris said. "It's nearly midnight."

"Yeah, we were making bets on whether you had thrown each other off the ledge or moved in permanently," Cassie laughed.

"You two knew about this place all along and never told me?"

"Nah, we're not that good with secrets Hols. Milo needed a little assistance so he 'caved' and showed us his secret lair." Chris laughed at himself. He always thought he was funnier than he actually was.

"So that's how you got fresh, hot food out there! You are so busted!" Holly teased him, and he swept her up in his arms and kissed her as Chris and Cassie hooted and cheered.

Then he lunged at Chris, and they skirmished to the ground laughing.

"You're not supposed to give away my secrets little brother."

Holly had never seen this playful side of Milo. Not ever. He was like an entirely different man, and though she wasn't quite ready to admit it, she liked it.

* * * * *

Chapter 13

Holly's life was falling into a pattern with which she wasn't entirely comfortable. From Saturday to Wednesday, she largely spent her free time with Milo. Everyone at the compound was thrilled and wedding rumors were growing louder. Thursday through Saturday, she sneaked off to the cave to be with Griffon.

Her father disapproved of her regular disappearances, but her mother intervened and forbid him to discuss it. It was Holly's life to do with as she pleased.

Milo was beginning to question and persuade her to stop with the lone wolf act. She knew what they expected of her. She knew she was to marry him, settle down, and start a family, but part of her continued to rebel against those expectations. She had grown to care deeply for him, but was it enough? How could it be when she still constantly thought of Griffon and spent crazy nights making out with him in their cave?

She didn't have to lie to Griffon. He knew her, the real her. He had no expectations; they just lived in the moment and were thankful for every second they were together.

It was late October, and the nights were often cold now. Thanks to a milder than usual fall, they were able to continue their meetings longer into the year than they had expected but they were on borrowed time. They both knew they wouldn't be able to continue meeting in the cave much longer. The thought weighed heavily on Griffon. He noticed she seemed more agitated than usual and wondered if it was weighing on her too.

"What's on your mind, Holly?"

She sat in silence for a while, contemplating so many things and wondering if he was truly ready to hear what she was thinking. Milo was prepared to propose any day. Her time with Griffon was ending, at least until spring, and that seemed like a lifetime away.

It felt like nature was forcing the direction of her life. She would lose Griffon just as everyone pushed for her to marry Milo. She wanted to rebel against it. Part of her was defeated and just ready to walk through the life that they carved out for her, with little regard to her wishes or feelings.

"Milo is ready to get married," she said, staring out into the valley below, unable to look at him as the words rolled off her tongue.

"And you? Are you ready to marry him?"

He was angry at the thought, and she could feel the resentment in his tone.

"I mean what are we doing here anyway, Holly? I can't offer you the life he can. You don't know how much I wish I could."

"I dunno," was all she could muster. She didn't know if she could marry Milo. She didn't know if she could be happy with him. She didn't know if she could be happy without him. She knew she wasn't ready to give up Griffon but she didn't know how to keep him either. At this moment, life just seemed unfair.

"There's a lot and absolutely nothing in that response, ya know." He had never seen her look so sad. His heart ached to hold her, but he didn't dare. He hadn't meant to snap at her like that. He had no right to make it harder on her, but it was hard on him too. This was something she had to work out for herself, and he had no right to interfere with that decision. He had nothing to offer her but perhaps a few more nights in secret before the snow set in and it would be too cold and dangerous to try to continue camping in the cave. He felt hollow and empty.

"I'm not ready to lose you," she said and turned to look at him. Her eyes pierced his heart, and he knew he would spend the entirety of his life pining for this woman. She was like a bird that he knew he had to set free, but didn't know how or even if he could.

"You'll never lose me, Holly. I'll always be here for you in whatever capacity you need."

She knew in those words that he would continue to love and support her, no matter what she decided about Milo. She also knew in her heart that they could never be just friends. She would have to choose one man over the other.

"I am not ready to make any decisions. My family will push for a decision over the holidays; I am certain of that. I am not ready to make a commitment. They won't understand, and it won't be easy, but I'm too young and not ready to be anyone's wife. That is the only thing I am certain of anymore."

His heart soared with new hope. It would be a long hard winter, but could he dare hope she would still be there waiting for him when winter broke? He knew without her saying as much that she had come to care a great deal for Milo, too. He tried not to let jealousy consume him.

"Come on," he said as he got up and pulled her to her feet. He needed to move; he needed a change of scenery and a change of topic. He knew they didn't have much longer together like this and, should the snow set in early this year, he might not be able make it back up the mountain. This was not the last encounter he wanted to remember with her.

"Where are we going?"

"To the spring."

He led the way as they walked in silence, hand in hand. He now knew every twist and turn in this part of the cave and no longer got lost. He had grabbed a blanket as they were leaving, and when they entered the spring cave, he led her away from the spring and laid the blanket on the floor, pulling her down with him. They lay side-by-side, holding hands, and staring up at the ceiling as the reflections from the water danced across it.

After some time, he rolled to his side and dropped his head low so that he could talk in her ear. The constant running of the waterfall into the spring made it noisy and difficult to talk.

"The first time you brought me here, I was in awe of this place. It seemed magical with its dancing lights and beautiful waterfall. It reminded me of a book my mother once read to me as a child. This place is untouched from the world outside. Here, anything is possible, even us, Holly." He leaned down and kissed her, offering her everything without saying it in words.

She couldn't take it anymore. The stress of being torn between two worlds, two lives, two men, was breaking her down. She knew in her heart that everything she wanted was right here, but she didn't have it to offer him or the strength to take it. The emotions of that moment took over, and she cried softly.

He had never seen her cry before, not from injury, illness, anger, or anything. He was used to women crying; after all, he only had sisters. But this was different, and he didn't know what to do, so he just held her close and watched the shapes change across the ceiling, occasionally pointing out something he saw in them to her, which made her laugh out loud or merely put a smile back on her face.

Neither knew how long they had been there, but when they returned to the big cave, they were surprised to see it was dark. They said little that night, but Holly slept peacefully for the first time in weeks in the arms of this man she was ready to accept she truly loved but would have to say goodbye to.

As Griffon packed up to leave the next day, he took more stuff with him than usual. He knew instinctively that snow was on the way. While it had been a milder than usual fall so far, it was common for the area to see snowfall before Thanksgiving, and the weather was shifting, and the nights growing colder with each day. He was not certain he'd be up again before spring, but he wasn't ready to say goodbye either.

"Well, I guess we take it one week at a time from here on. I know I can't be back up next week. I'm sorry. I've been putting off a lot back home, coming up here on my days off. I have to prepare us for winter if we're to survive it. I have some guys helping chop wood next week, but if the weather continues to hold, I'll try to get back up the week after."

"No promises," she said. "I know."

She was determined not to cry. "You take care of your family Griffon, and be careful down there." She wanted to tell him she loved him and would wait for him, but she knew she couldn't.

He hugged her close and kissed her one last time.

"See you," he said before disappearing down the side of the cliff.

She sat in the cave watching him until he completely disappeared down the mountain. She felt empty inside, and her stomach was growling. She didn't pack up her stuff and clear the cave as he had; she was not ready for that finality.

* * * * *

On her way out, Holly headed to the outdoor spring for a cold drink of water, hoping it would clear the fog settling into her head. She suddenly saw Milo as he exited his own secret cave. He stopped when he saw her. He hadn't seen her in days, and she looked so sad, he wasn't sure if he wanted to retreat to the comfort of his cave or wrap his arms around her and kiss away her sorrow.

Before he could decide, she looked up and stared right through him. She moved toward him, and he knew he couldn't retreat. He opened his arms and she flew inside for the safety and comfort she knew she'd find there. She couldn't keep the tears back any longer. He just stood there, holding her for what seemed like an eternity.

He realized he had never seen her cry before, not even when she was six and fell out of a tree, breaking her leg. He had carried her back to the bunker to find Doc.

She was acting strange in the days before she escaped this time, off to wherever it was she went to hide religiously three days a week for the last several months. He hadn't wanted her to go this time. They had fought about it, and, in the end, she went anyway. He was prepared to sit her down and discuss the matter when she returned, but he wasn't prepared for her to return like this.

He stood there holding her until her tears ran dry. She looked so vulnerable. Vulnerable? Holly? That was not something he would ever have expected, but he rather liked it. He liked feeling needed, and she wasn't the type that ever seemed to need anything except space and alone time, which didn't work too well in a relationship.

"Want to talk about it?"

"No! Just hold me, please."

She knew she was being selfish, but for once, she didn't care.

"Come on, let's get you home."

She started to protest. She wasn't ready to go home and face normal life but she let him lead her anyway. When they arrived back at the bunker, he steered her down the family hallway and stopped at Pod 9. It was right next to Pod 7, which had been hers since they built the bunker. She knew that someday she would move into it and raise her own family. Pod 9 was supposed to be empty, but Milo led her in, and she was surprised to find it furnished and livable.

"What's going on? Is this your Pod now?" she questioned.

"Yeah, I moved in this week. Thought you could use a little more time to pull it together before facing the masses." He rolled his eyes as he said it.

Did he feel the pressure of their inevitable union, too? She hadn't considered maybe it wasn't what he wanted, either. She was grateful for some more time away from the spotlight in the warmth and safety of the bunker. She didn't want to live in a fishbowl today.

When he returned, he brought food, including some coveted Oreos her dad kept hidden for himself. Even slightly stale after all these years, they were still a heavenly treat. She wished she'd known so she could have told him to bring a jar of peanut butter with him. No sooner had she thought it than he produced a jar.

"Chris always thought it disgusting, but I always loved dipping Oreos in peanut butter." He grinned, looking like a kid again.

"I know; me too." She smiled at a long forgotten memory. "You taught me that!"

She was surprised as she remembered. "I was six or seven, and Chris and I were following you around trying to torment you the entire summer. You ate Oreos and peanut butter every day for your afternoon treat while Chris hooted and gagged and teased you on how disgusting it was.

"You dared us both to try it. Chris chickened out, but I tried it and feigned disgust. I loved it but I couldn't let Chris know, so I'd sneak them in the kitchen when he wasn't around." She smiled genuinely. "I had forgotten all about that."

Milo hadn't known that about her. No one did. She looked through the box he was carrying to see what else he had brought and found fresh fruit, veggies, chicken salad sandwiches, a couple bottles of water, and a portable DVD player with several movies he had checked out of the library.

She gave him a questioning look. "Are we settling in for the day?"

He grinned and sat down beside her on his couch. He set up the DVD player and motioned for her to pick a movie.

"It is my day off, and you look like a quiet day in would do you some good. I did tell your mom that you were back and I'm holding you captive for the day. I didn't want her to worry."

He is always kind and considerate, she thought.

It was easy to like him. She could almost envision herself loving him. Marrying him would be easy, comfortable, and safe. She wouldn't have to worry about the pain her heart felt saying goodbye to Griffon.

Griffon. If he hadn't come into her life and opened her eyes to a completely new world, would this have been enough? Could she have been happy with Milo? Just for today, she wasn't going to think about any of it; she was just going to be here.

* * * * *

Milo put on the movie Holly chose and settled in beside her. He was somewhat surprised when she took his arm and moved it around her shoulder so she could snuggle into him. She had been a bit moody and distant the last few weeks, so he was relieved to find her relaxed and comfortable with him today. He never realized that he had an impact on her growing up, but he couldn't help but smile remembering her account of the Oreos dare.

Chris had teased him and told him that she had a huge crush on him as a kid. Even knowing that, he was shocked and pleased when he read it in her own childish handwriting in the diary buried by the tree house. He knew her as a wild, outgoing rule-breaker, constantly testing the limits and an occasional loner who chose to walk her own path. He knew she was a complicated woman, but he really wasn't prepared for the full capacity of that.

For today, they largely sat in silence, watching a movie and cuddling. At some point, she turned to look at him and noticed he was watching her and not the TV. She smiled at him, which softened the serious look on his face, and he leaned down and kissed her softly, just testing the water.

Griffon's face popped into Holly's mind and in her determination to push it away, she kissed Milo back more aggressively then she would have if she were thinking clearly. His throaty moan jolted her back to reality. One look and she knew she had managed to arouse him in ways she had never intended.

He seemed to awaken and come alive, and she found herself lying on the couch with him on top, kissing her madly. His blues eyes were a dark gray she had never seen before. She didn't know how long they had lain there kissing, but she was jolted back to reality when she felt his warm hands on her stomach climbing higher under her shirt.

Breathless, she tried to tell him no. It wasn't right. He was a man of integrity, and, although it took her a couple tries, he, too, was jolted back to reality. He was shocked by his own actions and her response. He sat up quickly and apologized for getting lost in the moment.

She laughed and reminded him that she wasn't exactly pushing him away. She had wanted that distraction. She needed to feel without thinking, but was glad she had come to her senses before it had gone any further. The haunting reality that she was using him as an escape for the loss she felt over Griffon wasn't fair to either of them. It was too easy an escape, but when her head was clear, she knew that was all it meant to her.

To Milo, it was so much more. He knew she was passionate but never realized how that could affect their personal relationship. In his conscious mind, he would never have acted so aggressively toward a woman. In reality, he felt empowered and strong, and he loved it.

The day went much quieter for them, watching movies and talking, but Holly noticed a new strength in him. An assurance she had never seen before, and it worried her.

* * * * *

Chapter 14

THEY LEFT his Pod only to attend dinner, and Chris and Cassie came back to the Pod with them afterward. They played card games, teased, and chatted throughout the evening. They put on another movie and Chris and Cassie were soon making out on one end of the couch. Normally, this would embarrass Milo, but not today. Today he took the opportunity to join them in his own make out session with Holly. By the end of the night, Chris was teasing them both but looking very pleased with this turn of events.

Cassie decided to call it a night and pulled Holly out with her for a few moments of girl talk before leaving.

"Spill it... what was that all about? I thought you didn't really like him, you know, like that."

"I don't, or I think I don't. I don't know. I'm so confused. How could I have let this happen, Cassie?"

"From the looks of things, you better get it straight quickly. Your dad was on cloud nine watching the two of you at dinner tonight. While I am always first and foremost your friend, he is Chris's brother. I don't want to see Milo hurt, either. We'd be thrilled to see the two of you together, but only if that's what you really want." Cassie hugged her and left before Holly could say a word.

That night, Holly tossed and turned. Nightmares set in. She was tied to a board in some sort of medieval setting. Her feet and hands were bound with rope, and she was being pulled in two different directions. She was strapped to the table and unable to make it stop. She felt helpless and scared as she awoke screaming.

Charlie ran to her when the screams began and woke her from the nightmare. She was white as a ghost and covered in sweat.

"Hols, it's okay. It was just a dream."

She sat up and hugged him tightly. "What am I going to do, Charlie? Please just tell me what to do. I can't live like this anymore!"

He wasn't sure what she was talking about so he just held her close and soothed her until she fell back to sleep. He stayed up watching to ensure she was okay.

When she awoke again and saw him sleeping in the chair next to her. She didn't remember why he was there. It was early, but she needed to move, so she grabbed her iPod and headed to the gym. She had been working out for a good hour when she noticed Milo watching her.

"Morning," he said. "You were pretty zoned in there, and I really didn't want to disturb you. Do you mind if I join you now?"

She had no idea how long he'd been there watching her. She wasn't ready to talk to him, so she just nodded and continued working out side-by-side with him. This became a normal morning routine over the next few days. She'd wake up to find Charlie sleeping in a chair next to her or laying on the floor, and Milo waiting in the gym for their morning workout.

On Thursday, she woke to the same thing but with a heavy feeling. She should be packing up to head to the cave, but she knew Griffon would not be there. She stepped over Charlie so as not to wake him. He looked tired these days, and she wasn't sure why he continued to sleep in her room.

Had she started sleep walking again? She hadn't done that in ages. She shrugged and headed down to the gym, surprised to find it empty. She felt just as empty on the inside. Where was Milo? She wondered. No Griffon; no Milo. She was in a sullen mood and set about to take it out on the kick boxing station.

About an hour passed when Milo walked in laughing and talking with Emma Grace. It was clear that they were there to work out together. He stopped short and his eyes were wide with guilt when he saw her.

"Holly? What are you doing here?"

She hadn't seen him look quite so uncomfortable in a long time and wondered if it had anything to do with Emma Grace standing next to him. She glared at Holly, and it was hard not to see the hatred in her eyes. She started to walk away but Milo stopped her. She was curious at this interaction.

"I'm just working out, same as any other morning."

"Oh, sorry, I thought you'd be gone by now. You know it's Thursday, right?"

She nodded, realizing that he expected her to be away for the next few days. She had never once wondered what he did on those days but now wondered how much of that time he spent with Emma Grace who was still shooting daggers at her.

"Supposed to be a cold couple days, and I didn't think I should be out in it."

"Oh, sorry, I didn't realize or I would have been here earlier. Emma Grace and I usually work out together on Thursdays and Fridays. Are you okay if she joins us?"

She took a long look at Emma Grace, and her heart went out to the girl. She wondered if Milo had any clue the woman was in love with him. She suspected he didn't. She knew too well that terrible feeling of loving someone you couldn't have. She couldn't have Griffon on this day but she wasn't heartless enough to take Milo from Emma Grace and decided to retreat.

"I'm about done here, just cooling down. No worries." She smiled at Emma Grace. "I'll get out of your way and let you have it. Have fun." She giggled to herself at the look of shock on Emma Grace's face.

Milo shrugged. "See you later then."

She waved without turning around to look at him as she left the room.

* * * * *

Holly went back to her Pod, showered, and changed before waking Charlie. It was time to talk.

"Hey there roomie, wake up."

Charlie groaned and rolled over.

Holly kicked him, "Get up! We need to talk."

"I don't want to talk; I need sleep." He groaned but got up and moved to lay on her bed.

"So, what's with the night guard duty?" she asked accusingly. "Got word I spent a day alone with Milo in his Pod and trying to make sure I'm not sneaking off for hot make out sessions in the middle of the night?" She was teasing him and rolled her eyes.

Charlie rolled over and frowned at her. "Nightmares, Holly."

"Oh, I'm sorry, why didn't you tell me? Want to talk about them? Used to help me a lot when I was a kid."

"Seriously?" he asked and groaned at her. "I'm not having nightmares; you are!"

"What? What are you talking about?"

"Hols, you wake up screaming almost every night. Even woke mom and dad with them one night. I've been sleeping in here to calm you down when they hit. Last night was particularly bad. You were up four times before I got you settled."

"Oh."

She vaguely remembered nightmares. She often woke up in a cold sweat in the mornings feeling restless.

"Have we talked about them yet?" she asked a little hesitantly.

Did he know about Griffon? Would she blurt something like that out in a restless moment?

"No. You haven't woken enough to discuss them but you call out in your sleep often. It's bad, little sister. What's up with you these days?"

"I dunno. I'm sorry. I didn't even realize." She shook at the thought. Were her dreams so bad that she blocked them out even from herself?

"You talk a lot about being torn in two in your sleep. It's Milo, isn't it? I keep telling dad to back off and stop pushing him on you. You don't have to marry him, you know. I don't care what dad says, I'll intervene for you."

She smiled, always grateful for her big brother. He always looked out for her, but she knew this was her battle to fight alone, and she couldn't explain to him that it wasn't just dad and Milo, but Griffon, too, who had her so torn.

"Thanks big brother! But this battle is mine alone to fight."

"What are you doing here anyway? Isn't it Thursday?"

She groaned. "I'm going to hear that a lot today aren't I?"

She pouted, knowing that she should be with Griffon but she knew that she couldn't let him consume her thoughts. "It's getting cold. I'm not sure how many more outings I'll get in before spring."

Charlie could see the sadness in that statement even if he didn't fully understand it, and he felt bad for her. "It'll be okay, Hols. I'm sure Milo is thrilled!" He was raising his eyebrows up and down and giving her a wicked grin.

She hit him with a pillow, which turned into a battle. They laughed and squealed so loudly that their mother and father burst through the door to see if everything was okay.

Mom gave them both a stern look of reprimand while Dad just grinned and puffed his chest in delight.

"Isn't it Thursday? My baby girl's home to stay?!" He phrased it simultaneously as a question and a statement.

Holly and Charlie looked at each other knowingly as she groaned and rolled her eyes. He smacked her with one last shot of the pillow.

Once the chaos of the morning subsided, she had already run into Cassie, Chris, and most of the bunker and heard, "Welcome back Holly" and "Isn't it Thursday? And Good to have you home Holly!" more times than she could stomach. She retreated to the library. Cassie and Chris were both in school, and she had several assignments for school coming due. Mostly, she just needed the quiet.

* * * * *

She was deep in concentration on the writings of Shakespeare when Milo and Emma Grace came in giggling. They clearly hadn't expected anyone to be there at that time of the day, and both looked shocked and guilty upon seeing her. If it wasn't for the fact that Holly was all but engaged to this man, she would have found the situation amusing. Instead, given her sullen state to begin with, she just looked at Milo quizzically.

"Hey Holly, sorry. I completely forgot you were home today."

He ran over to give her a quick kiss, and she noticed another death stare from Emma Grace.

"Emma Grace is tutoring me in Molecular Biology. She's been doing an apprenticeship under Doc, so she knows a ton about this stuff."

He was gushing in his praise of Emma Grace, although Holly suspected he didn't mean to nor did he realize he was doing it. She noted the pleased look that flashed across the girl's face at his praise, which soon disappeared.

"Sorry. I've tried to plan as much of this sort of stuff on the days you're gone so it frees up more time when you're here. Guess I'm a creature of habit."

He looked so guilty, she had to smile.

"It's okay. I understand. I'm not going to interfere with your routine. I can take this back to my room if I'll be too much of a distraction."

Holly liked pushing people's buttons, and she was suddenly curious about Milo and Emma Grace. She grinned wickedly and stood up to gather her stuff, but not before giving him a kiss that neither he nor Emma Grace would soon forget. As suspected, Emma Grace could not contain the look of hatred as she glared at Holly while trying to put on a smile as if everything was okay.

On the way back to her room, she thought about the Emma Grace encounters of the day. She honestly didn't remember ever seeing the girl that much in any given day. She clearly had feelings for Milo, and her hatred of Holly probably stemmed from that. She decided she wanted to know more about Milo and Emma Grace and would need to do a little recon.

It made her feel like a kid again. She had spent more than one summer spying on Milo Weaver. This time, it was for a good cause. Holly had no illusions that Milo was in love with her, and it was obvious that Emma Grace was in love with him. She needed to know just how Milo felt about Emma Grace.

She knew they were in the library and, with the door open and them in a back corner, it was easy to sneak in and sit in the stacks within earshot. She sat quietly and listened.

"Em I know you don't like Holly, but please, you're my best friend, and she's going to be my wife someday. Please try to get along with her... for me."

Holly noted the use of a nickname. *Em?* She had never heard anyone call her anything but Emma Grace. Interesting, and *"best friend"*? She hadn't thought about Milo having a best friend. She knew from their first real date that he had obviously spent a great deal of time with Emma Grace but hadn't really thought much about a possible friendship. He never really mentioned her.

Emma Grace interrupted Holly's train of thought, "But she's not right for you Milo, you've said so yourself. Why do you go along with this nonsense? She'll just make you miserable, and you know it. The elders are wrong to force this."

Holly couldn't totally disagree with her on that one! She didn't completely understand her reference to the elders, but knew her dad was certainly doing more than his fair share of encouragement.

"I know, Em. I thought they were wrong, too, but I went along to keep the peace. Now I'm not so sure. She's not like we thought."

Holly assumed she was the "she" to which they were referring.

"Have you fallen in love with her?" Emma Grace's voice was demanding, with a touch of hurt. Holly felt sorry for her.

She couldn't help but think about Griffon. It was bad enough they had to be apart, but how would she feel if he didn't love her back. He had never said the words to her, but she knew he did. She was certain of it. Some days, it was all that kept her going. Since their last encounter when she realized she was truly in love with him, she had been more open and honest with herself.

If she married Milo, it would be for the family and what was best for their community. It had nothing to do with love. She admired him and enjoyed spending time with him. When the guilt of Griffon wasn't at the forefront of her mind, she could even enjoy kissing him, but she wasn't in love with him. Maybe someday she could love him in a safe and comforting way, but not in the all-consuming passionate way that she loved Griffon.

She had to shake her head to clear her own thoughts so she could pay attention to Milo and Emma Grace. Judging from the awkward silence, he hadn't said anything.

"Well?" Emma Grace asked.

"I care about her Em. I don't want to hurt her. Sometimes I wonder if pressuring her is the same thing though."

He was being openly honest with her, and Holly couldn't help but think that he could never be so open with her.

"That's not the same thing as love, Milo"

"I know, and I don't know if I'm falling in love with her. I just don't know. What is love? What does it feel like? Do I even know? I have strong feelings for her, but I don't know what that means, Em."

Emma Grace was stunned silent. She didn't like what she was hearing.

Holly had heard enough. She backed out of the room to think things through. Perhaps she would discuss this with Chris and Cassie later... but could she? They were her best friends, but could she confide in them about this? They were rooting for her and Milo as much as the elders were.

* * * * *

Holly kept it to herself until Charlie came in at bedtime. She was still awake but didn't realize she was waiting for him.

"Hey, you," she said.

"Hey, yourself. Didn't think you'd still be up this late. What's up?"

"I have a lot on my mind, Charlie."

"Oh, have you discussed with the terrible trio yet?"

"No, I don't think I should."

"Uh-oh this sounds serious, and I'm guessing it's about Milo?"

He raised a questioning eyebrow her way.

"Want to talk about it?"

He was already settling into the bed next to her as he had so many times when they were kids talking late into the night. Holly only confided in him for the most serious stuff in her life.

"Yes! No! I dunno!"

She blurted out everything she had done and overheard that day.

"And I honestly think Milo might be in love with Emma Grace, too, even though he will never admit it as long as I'm in the picture."

"That's pretty serious, Hols. What are you going to do about it? I mean on the one hand, that could be an easy out for you, although dad and the elders would be devastatingly disappointed!" He said it with mock exaggeration.

"On the other hand, you know what's expected, and so does he. It seems you're both willing to accept that. I think you deserve more! I'm not your conscience, and I'm not your father. I am your brother, and I just want you to be happy. Can you be happy with Milo? That's what you need to figure out, but for now, just go to sleep! I'm exhausted. Try to have sweet dreams tonight. I'm too tired for nightmares." He rolled over and drifted off to sleep immediately.

She lay there, thanking God for her brother and thinking over what he said until she drifted off to sleep. That night, she had good dreams but awoke the next morning uneasy in her realization. Her thoughts were all about Griffon. Charlie was still sound asleep.

* * * * *

Chapter 15

N<small>O SIGNIFICANT</small> change occurred in Holly's life over the last month. Milo was still Milo. He continually bounced back and forth between her and Emma Grace. She encouraged him to spend more time with his friend, but after one of the elders took notice, he backed off. The few times she saw Emma Grace, she recognized the open hostility and hatred. Why did men have to be so stupid?

Rumors were still running rampant about a possible Christmas wedding, although Milo had not officially proposed... and she was thankful for that.

She hadn't seen Griffon since that last time in the cave. She sneaked down a pumpkin filled with candy for Angeline and Trevor on Halloween. It should have been Griffon's day off, but he wasn't there. Lily told her that he was working and had been working too much on his days off since the cold set in. She seemed worried about him.

* * * * *

With Thanksgiving less than a week away, everyone was encouraged to hunt. The entire bunker looked forward to fresh game for the holidays, and Holly was more than happy to assist. Normally, they hunted in pairs, but on this day, she found herself in the woods alone. She had already killed two turkeys and one deer this fall.

She crouched low, watching a flock of turkeys just a few yards away. She found the biggest and sighted it in. One clean shot to the head, and the turkey dropped to the ground and the rest set off in every direction. She could have taken out more than one, despite the craziness, but she was satisfied with her prize. Realizing how far down the mountain she already was, she made an impulsive decision to clean her game on the spot, bag it quickly, and take it down to the farmhouse at the base of the mountain where Griffon and his family lived. The turkey was heavier than she thought. He'd make a fine Thanksgiving feast.

* * * * *

As the woods thinned out and the house came into view, Holly squatted, watched, and listened. When she was certain nothing out of the ordinary was going on there, she ran swiftly to the back door and tapped gently. She heard Angeline scream inside and her mother scold her for it. Lily was hesitant opening the door, but when she saw Holly, she relaxed, threw open the door, and hugged her tightly. There was no sign of the kids as Lily pulled her inside.

"You are a sight for sore eyes. It is so good to see you!" Holly knew she genuinely meant it.

"Sorry for spooking you. I was hunting further down the mountain than I expected and thought it would be easier to carry this guy down than up."

Lily's eyes grew wide and teared up when she saw the big turkey in the bag, already cleaned and ready for Thanksgiving dinner. It had been a long time since they had fresh meat. Griffon wasn't hunting anymore. He never went near the woods and worked himself to death all the time. Lily suspected it was to keep Holly off his mind but he never admitted it.

Holly broke the silence, "so where are the kids hiding? Can I at least say hello to them before heading back?" She was rubbing her hands from the cold.

"Oh, you must be freezing. Go and sit by the fire. Knock twice on the bookcase to the left of it." She knocked slowly twice on the counter to demonstrate, then turned to address the gift Holly had given them.

There was a fire roaring in the fireplace, and Holly quickly rubbed her hands together to warm them. Then she knocked twice on the bookcase as instructed. It swung out toward her to reveal a secret room with bunk beds and a few toys. The room was painted bright and friendly.

This was Angeline and Trevor's room where they often hid from the AMAN. When they saw Holly, they both squealed with delight and ran to her, knocking her over in the process. There was such commotion that Holly didn't initially hear the gruff husky voice from the next room.

"Hey, you guys, knock it off in there, I'm trying to sleep!" Her heart lurched into her throat. What was he doing here? Much to her disappointment, she knew it should have been a workday for him.

"Uncle Griff's sick," Angeline reported.

"And very, very grumpy!" Trevor informed her.

"You should go cheer him up." Angeline giggled.

"Yeah, make him feel better so he's not so grumpy." Trevor added.

She smiled at the pair of them and walked to the room she assumed was his. The kids were giggling so loudly that Griffon jumped up and swung the door open, already barking, "I told you two..." the sight of her standing there cut his anger short.

"Sorry Uncle Griff." Angeline said. "Come on Trevor let's go see what mama's doing."

She took her little brother by the hand and led him back upstairs, but not before Trevor turned to Holly and tried to whisper a little too loudly, "Pleeeease make him in a better mood!"

Griffon ran his hands through his hair, unable to believe she was standing there. "I must be running an awful high fever, cause I do believe I'm seeing things." He shook his head to clear the image before him, not believing she was actually there.

She smiled at him. "You look terrible!"

He grinned. "Thanks! Thanks a lot." He pulled her close, still uncertain if she was real, but not really caring. He missed her so much it hurt, no matter how much he tried to work and busy himself so as not to think of her. He usually ended up exhausting himself enough to crash at night with dreamless sleep.

She was worried but allowed him to pull her into his arms for a minute. "Oh, my gosh, you stink!"

He laughed and kissed her anyway. "You're burning up. What happened, Griffon; what's wrong?" She was immediately in nurse mode, ready to tend to him when Lily came downstairs.

"Well a smile on that grouch is improvement!"

"How long has he been sick?"

"Three days. I can't get him to eat, and we can't seem to get his fever down. He's been downright nasty to everyone. I'm hoping that you can at least help in that department."

Griffon frowned. "You brought her here?"

"No, you idiot; she came down on her own. But I'm gonna use her to my advantage where you're concerned, that's for sure." Lily winked at Holly before exiting, and then turned. "He's refusing to bathe or be bathed; perhaps you can help with that, too." She gave Holly a wicked grin and retreated upstairs.

Holly ran upstairs to talk to her. "Have you given him anything? Tylenol? Motrin? Anything to help break the fever? How about hot tea and a thick blanket in front of the fire?"

Lily frowned. "No medicines left around here to give. Doc recommended tea but didn't say anything about a blanket and fire. I'm willing to try just about anything."

"Okay, if you can make some hot tea, I think there's some Tylenol in my field kit. It's expired, but better than nothing. How about a bucket and wash cloth to de-funk him?"

She blushed at the last part, and Lily laughed and gathered what Nurse Holly asked for. Holly looked through her field bag, found not only Tylenol but also a bar of soap and hand sanitizer. "Woo Hoo! Forgot that was in here. He won't stink for long!"

Lily saw the bar of soap, new and still in the package. She was in awe. It had been forever since she had last seen anything like it. It was better than gold!

Holly handed her the hand sanitizer. "I know water is hit or miss down here at times, so I'll leave this for you and the kids. It's hand sanitizer. It'll keep the germs at bay and, hopefully, keep you guys from catching whatever he has." She took the bucket of warm water and the rag and headed back downstairs.

Griffon was nearly asleep, smiling, and talking of Holly. He honestly thought it had all been a dream until his lights came on. He groaned and protested as she pulled the blankets back, and there she was, looking not so pleased to see him.

"Holly?" he asked confused. "What are you doing here?"

She put a hand to his head. *Too hot,* she thought.

"Sit up; I need you to take these." She shoved two pills in his hand and held out a glass of water, waiting.

"What is it?"

"Tylenol."

"They still make that stuff?"

"I dunno, and it doesn't matter. You are going to do exactly as I say. No grouching, and no objections. Got it?"

He smiled; he had never seen her like this before. "Got it, doc." He swallowed the pills. "Now what?"

"Get up and go to the bathroom. I was going to give you a sponge bath, but you really need a full-blown shower. So let's go."

He obliged.

He was wobbly and weak, so she knew she'd have to help him. "Okay, strip."

"What?"

"Come on, you don't need me to do everything, do you?" He gave her a quizzical look. "Fine, if that's how you want it." She proceeded to strip him down to nothing but his boxers. She knew they had to go too, but hesitated. She knew the differences between men and women. She had a brother; it wouldn't be the first time she'd seen those parts but not on a fully-grown man and certainly not on Griffon.

She started to remove his boxers when he stopped her.

He was laughing now. "Relax! I can shower myself, though I'd much prefer the sponge bath." He paused with a wicked grin. "Turn around; some thing's need to be saved for our wedding night."

Holly's mouth dropped open. What did he just say? She tried to remind herself that he was half-delirious with fever and not read too much into it. Nevertheless, excitement bubbled in her at the mere thought.

When he was done, he yelled over the curtain, "Towel." She threw it over the top, and he emerged covered in nothing but the towel at his waist.

She leaned in and hugged him. "Better! Now, brush your teeth, get yourself dressed, and come sit by the fire."

"Yes ma'am," he said with a grin.

She retrieved a blanket and set it by the fire, and Lily came down with the hot tea. "Full shower?"

"Yup."

"You are my hero! Would you mind stripping his bed while he's up?"

"Sure, do you have clean sheets to put on?"

"In the closet."

"Thanks." She set about stripping and making his bed.

When he emerged, he looked a hundred times better. "Much better!" She praised him, and then motioned him over to sit on the floor with her. He obliged. She kissed his forehead and noticed it was still very hot but perhaps not as hot as it had been. She wrapped him in the heavy blanket with only slight protest and forced him to drink the hot tea. He insisted that she snuggle close to him.

"I feel terrible," he admitted

"I know. Hopefully, this will help that fever break; you'll be feeling better soon."

"I don't mean the sick. I mean about you. I hate living life without you. Stay with me. Run away with me. Live in the cave with me forever and ever. Whatever. Wherever. I just don't want to lose you again."

He drifted off to sleep as he said it and, again, she had to remind herself not to get caught up in his words. He wasn't thinking clearly from the fever and didn't mean it. He fell asleep in her arms, and within an hour, he became restless and clammy. She could tell by the beads of sweat on his forehead that his fever was trying to break and she was glad.

Lily came back to check on him and was visibly relieved at the difference.

"You will always be our personal angel sent from God! Thanks for taking care of him."

When Amos came home, he helped Holly get Griffon up and back into bed. He woke only briefly during the transition and fell back to sleep quickly. His fever was down, and he was sleeping peacefully. Holly wanted to wake him to say goodbye but didn't dare.

"Feel better, Griffon," she whispered and kissed him lightly on the lips. "I love you." She left him. It was late, and she had to get back up to the bunker. Amos and Lily thanked her for the turkey and for caring for Griffon, and she hugged the kids goodbye, wished them a happy Thanksgiving, and disappeared up the mountain.

* * * * *

Chapter 16

THANKSGIVING Day was loud and festive in the bunker. Everyone was in good spirits. Hunting was prime this fall, and the outside garden had produced an abundance of food over the summer. They would feast!

The dining room wasn't quite large enough for everyone at once, so they added tables and chairs around the great room to accommodate the children and young people, while the adults were seated in the main dining room. They ate turkey, ham, mashed potatoes, gravy, corn, green beans, fresh rolls, collard greens, spiced apples, and pies of every variety.

Holly couldn't help but wonder what Griffon and his family managed to add to the turkey she had brought to them. What would they have eaten if she hadn't brought it? Did they even celebrate Thanksgiving anymore? She hadn't even thought to ask. She felt guilty for the feast before her, knowing how they struggled for food in the town below.

She made her plate, feeling a little less festive and was about to retreat to the great room to find her friends when Milo motioned her over to the dining room table.

"We've been invited to sit with the adults this year," he informed her, looking pleased.

"Why?"

"Please sit."

She noticed Charlie was there, too, as well as Emma Grace and all the elders. She didn't want to sit with them; she wanted to sit with her friends, but did as she was told, looking to Charlie for answers. She didn't like the look of warning on his face.

Dinner was peaceful, quiet, and more than a little boring. It turned out to be a disappointing Thanksgiving. As they moved on to dessert, she ate a fat piece of pumpkin pie and sighed with thanks over the treat. At least she had that.

Halfway through her pie, she became acutely aware that all eyes were suddenly on her. She tried to think of what she was doing wrong and looked over at Milo, who looked very nervous.

"Um, Holly," he cleared his throat. "There's something I've been wanting to ask you." He pushed back his chair and got down on one knee.

She nearly jumped out of the chair and ran from the room but with all eyes on her, she froze. A look at her brother's face nearly reduced her to tears. This was really happening.

"Holly Jenkins. . . will you marry me?" Milo looked up at her. The expression on his face wasn't of love and devotion, it was almost apologetic. She glanced over his head at the horrified look on Emma Grace, who was clearly trying to hold back tears. She felt trapped and terrified.

She looked at the ring and smiled as best as she could. "It's beautiful," was all she could muster. That must have been close enough to yes because cheers went up all around, and Milo noticeably relaxed and slipped it on her hand.

Her father said, "Kiss her, son!" and Milo obliged. It was forced and awkward, and everything happened so quickly that she didn't have time to think. They filled glasses with sparkling cider and made toasts all around. She couldn't manage to eat the last of her pumpkin pie. Only Charlie seemed to notice.

That was it. She was engaged! Her life as she wished would never be the same. Word spread quickly to the great room, and celebration was in full swing long into the night as everyone congratulated the happy couple. Holly noticed Emma Grace was nowhere in sight.

Charlie was waiting in her room when she finally retired for the night. "Well, you didn't actually say YES! You can still back out, you know." He felt bad for her, knowing this was not what she wanted for her life.

"I don't even know how, Charlie!" She began to cry. He cradled her in his arms and let her cry herself to sleep.

* * * * *

Holly was arguing with her father, as they often did these days.

"I don't want a Christmas wedding!"

"It'll be beautiful Holly. Everyone's expecting it," her father said, choosing the wrong words for this argument.

"I don't care what everyone expects. I'm engaged, you should be happy enough with that."

She was trying not to lose her temper.

"I won't be eighteen for a few more weeks. Why are you so determined to rush this?"

He sighed. "In another world, sweetie, I'd never consider eighteen as marriage age, but in the world we live in now, it's smart, practical, and necessary."

"What if I don't want smart and practical, dad?"

"Will you do something with her?" He looked pleadingly at his wife.

"Holly, what time of year do you want to get married?" Her mother was trying to remain diplomatic.

Holly frowned. *Never,* was the first answer that came to mind. She, instead, smiled sweetly and said, "I've always dreamed of a fall wedding mom, you know with the beautiful colors of the changing leaves."

"Fall? That's nearly a year away!" Her father was astounded at her answer.

"Why is that such a bad thing, Michael?"

His wife appeared to be on their daughter's side, so he knew he wasn't going to win this argument. He finally agreed. The wedding wouldn't take place until next fall.

Holly sighed in great relief. At least that bought her some time to get out of this mess!

* * * * *

Milo was surprised to hear of the delay in the wedding. Mike had informed him and not Holly. He was glad of that because Mike didn't notice the moment of relief he felt with the news, and he knew Holly was relieved as well.

He did what he had to do, but he still wasn't sure he even wanted to marry her. He knew he would have to stop thinking like that. She said yes, sort of. He didn't miss the absence of an actual acceptance but that didn't seem to concern anyone else.

He was acutely aware of Emma Grace's disappearance. She was avoiding him like the plague now, and he mourned for his friend.

Holly hadn't been around much either. He didn't think she was actually avoiding him, but he wasn't certain.

He felt trapped and was determined to climb out of this funk, do the admirable thing, and be the best fiancé possible. He owed Holly that much. He got them into this mess, and he had to make the most of it. He could learn to love Holly or at least have a comfortable life with her... maybe.

* * * * *

Holly was relieved with her father's acceptance of a fall wedding. That would give her time to catch up with Griffon in the spring and really talk to him. She knew he wouldn't offer her marriage. He would never want her to be a part of his world below, not really. He worried too much for her safety as it was.

She was okay without marriage, though. She was okay with a part-time relationship with Griffon as long as it meant he would be in her life. The track she found herself on had no room for Griffon, and that scared her. She didn't want a life without him.

She couldn't alert the others to him, either. They would never understand. For now, playing the happy, dutiful fiancé would bide her the time she needed to figure this all out, so she was determined to be the best bride-to-be that she could be.

She hadn't spoken to Milo much since the proposal, and she knew that would alert suspicion, so she headed to dinner early, knowing he preferred it and was surprised to find he wasn't there. She hung out in the great room visiting with everyone. She endured people gawking at her ring on the all-important finger and tried to smile and appear happy. It was nearly 8:00 p.m. before he came strolling in.

She jumped up to talk to him.

"Hey," they said in unison.

"Are you okay? I thought you preferred to eat in the early round."

"I do," he said. "But you usually stroll through right around eight, so I thought I'd wait for you."

"Yeah, I've been hanging out since five waiting for you."

"We need to talk." They both said it at the same time and laughed.

"Let's grab some dinner and take it back to my Pod, okay?"

She liked that he asked and didn't assume or demand. She smiled and nodded.

They filled their plates quickly and headed to his Pod. Both were aware of the nods and smiles of approval as they exited.

Before she settled in the room, Milo was pacing and talking.

"I'm really sorry, Holly! I wanted to warn you and give you a heads up. I didn't want to ambush you like that, but I kinda got ambushed and guilted into it at the last moment. Mom brought the ring to dinner with her, and they shoved it in my hand and said, 'Now's the time; get on with it boy; what are you waiting for?' and I didn't have the guts to say no. I'm sorry."

She got up and stopped him from pacing.

"Hey, it's done; it's over; it's okay. We both knew it was coming. Neither of us are brave enough to tell them no or to butt out of our lives."

She hugged him, feeling they were now allies. He still didn't want to get married, either, and the realization was surprisingly freeing. "We'll get through this, Milo. It's going to be okay."

He grinned sheepishly at her, "They may not have cared, but don't think I didn't notice there was no actual yes to my proposal!"

She laughed. "My momentary act of defiance. What can I say?"

They both relaxed. Friends they could be. A pretend engagement they could handle. They'd figure the rest out as they went along.

* * * * *

To the rest of the bunker they were a happy couple excited about building a life together in the bunker. The first of the second generation in the making. It was almost poetic, if any of it was true. Milo and Holly had an understanding and an alliance that brought them closer each day. As days passed, she could sometimes forget that it was all a hoax.

The elders eased their schedules to give the 'happy couple' more time together during the engagement period, which meant more free time for the both of them. The downside was that they had to spend much of it together and, thus, found common ground and a comfortable routine.

She couldn't talk to Chris and Cassie about it. She and Milo had agreed that no one must know. She was thankful to have them as friends and confidants, even if she couldn't tell them everything. She cost Milo his best friend in the process, and that bothered her more than anything. She knew Emma Grace was doing an apprenticeship with Doc, so she headed down to the clinic and decided to fake an ailment so she could see her, knowing it was doc's day off.

Emma Grace didn't hide her disgust when Holly walked in. She knew this wasn't going to be easy, but she had to do it for Milo's sake.

"Hi, Emma Grace; how have you been?"

"You can stop with the polite informalities, Holly."

She turned to wash her hands, "so what's wrong with you?"

"I'm not sure,"

Holly hesitated. She wasn't sure what to say, so she looked around and saw a book open that Emma Grace had been reading. "I think I may have," she hesitated and scanned the book for the first medical looking term she could find, "syphilis. Yeah, syphilis."

Emma Grace whipped around with eyes wide. "WHAT?!" she practically yelled. "Syphilis? Holly that's a sexually transmitted disease!"

Holly's face turned bright red. "Crap!" she glanced over at the book again. "Would herpes have been a better choice?" She smiled, knowing Emma Grace had busted her.

Emma Grace noticed the book open next to the bed, shook her head with disgust, and tried not to laugh but snorted in the process.

"What are you really doing here?"

Holly jumped down from the table. "Milo really misses you. I know you're mad at him for the engagement, and I understand why." She gave her a knowing glance. "But he doesn't understand why... he's a man, and he doesn't get it! He's lost his best friend over this at a time he needs you most. It's hard enough to walk through this place feeling like we're in a fish bowl with everyone staring and smiling. People keep trying to help us along, and it's pretty miserable. I have Chris and Cassie, and Milo needs you."

Emma Grace shook her head. "You don't understand anything Holly!"

"You and I aren't so very different, you know. We both care about Milo. Go to him. He needs you more now than ever."

"Why? Why would you want me be anywhere near him, Holly? I don't just care about him, I love him!"

She hadn't meant to say that, and the look of shock in her eyes was almost too much for Holly to bear. She had to get away from here.

"I know you do, and I'm sorry I screwed everything up for you." She looked sad, and Emma Grace almost believed her.

"None of that matters right now. He needs you, his best friend. He needs to talk to someone, and that someone is you. Please think about it, Emma Grace." Holly squeezed her arm and headed out the door.

Well, there's not much I can do about that now, Holly thought. *I just hope it was enough.*

* * * * *

Chapter 17

B Y HOLLY'S birthday, Emma Grace had come around and was speaking to Milo again. He was happy and content, with fewer regrets. Holly ensured they had plenty of alone time throughout the week, secretly hoping that Milo would come to his senses about the girl. Emma Grace and Holly had an amicable understanding now, and life in the bunker, overall, was tolerable.

Holly had not been out of the bunker since the week before Thanksgiving when she helped nurse Griffon back to good health, or at least she prayed daily that she had. She left all the Tylenol she had with Lily and prayed he had recovered fast and not spread the sickness to the others in the house. She was beginning to go stir crazy fretting over them and worrying about what was happening.

On the day of her birthday, she awoke alone in peace and quiet. No balloons or signs of Charlie. She couldn't help but feel disappointed. Next to her bed was a card. She opened it and saw eighteen hand-drawn balloons that said 'Happy Birthday Hols!' on the outside.

When she opened it, a picture of Charlie's butt shot out attached to a spring for effect. 'Happy' on one cheek, 'Birthday' on the other. It read on the inside, "Worked the night shift; too tired to wake up. You were sleeping peacefully for once. Know it's not the same, but didn't want to disappoint and had to be the first to say it. Happy Birthday little sister! Love, Charlie"

She agreed, it was not the same, but it was something, and she loved her brother for being so thoughtful. She realized she had slept late, so she made her way down to the kitchen, expecting to see her mother and all her friends for her traditional banana pancakes with strawberry syrup; but no one was around.

She went to the library to see if Milo and Emma Grace were studying, but only Mrs. Lamay was there, letting her know that they had a surprise warm spell and it was 65 degrees out today, so they canceled school, and everyone was outside enjoying the spring-like weather. Milo had checked out some books, and she believed he too had retreated outdoors with Emma Grace to study.

Holly was sad and disappointed, but there was a thrill in knowing it was warm enough to leave the bunker. She packed herself a lunch and decided if everyone else would rather be out enjoying the weather than spending her birthday with her, then she could do what she most wanted, and she headed straight for the cave.

The second she stepped outside, it felt like heaven. It was warm, and the sun was shining bright. She had brought her coat, knowing the cave would be cooler. She almost decided against going because it was so nice out, but in the end, she retreated to her safe haven and favorite place on earth.

When she arrived, the first thing she did was grab her binoculars from her bag and look down into the village below. She knew it was silly but she couldn't help herself. She knew she was an engaged woman now and had no right to covet another man... but here in this place, there was no Milo, only Griffon... and it felt empty without him. She again felt disappointed.

What a terrible birthday!

She was about to leave and go hunt down Chris and Cassie or pretty much anyone. She'd rather hang out with Milo and Emma Grace than spend her birthday alone and depressed. Then she heard some movement on the rocks outside the cave. She felt a moment of panic. What if it was Milo and Emma Grace exploring this part of the cave? What if it was the AMAN? She retreated into the shadows to observe the intruders.

When Griffon's head appeared over the edge, and he pulled himself up into the cave, she breathed a sigh of relief. He stopped and looked around, sighed heavily with disappointment, and slumped down on the rock they called their couch. He fumbled with something in his hand and set it down next him.

She wasn't sure why she hesitated and just sat there and watched him but she couldn't bring herself to move. She wasn't prepared to face him. She was ashamed of how weak she was in agreeing to the engagement, and she knew instinctively that he would not be happy, even with a fake engagement. However, today was her day, her selfish day, her birthday, and the man she loved was here to see her when everyone else forgot.

Griffon rose and strapped on his gear to leave, ready to leave. There were clearly no signs of Holly having been there anytime recently. He had hoped with the nice weather that just maybe she would show up, but he would have made the trek up today no matter the weather. It was his girl's birthday, after all, and even if she wasn't here, she would find her gift the next time she returned and know he was there and thought of her on her special day.

"You used to be more observant than this, Champ. What's your hurry?"

He turned and saw her standing in the shadows. "What the. . ." he couldn't believe it. "Have you been there this whole time? Why didn't you speak up?"

She was nervous. She had never been nervous with him before but so much had happened since she last saw him. "You're feeling better, I see." She smiled, still holding back, unsure if she should run into his arms or retreat in the other direction. "How's Lily, Amos, and the kids? No one else catch that flu you had?"

"No; thanks to you, everyone is just fine. I was back to my same old grumpy self within a couple days. Thanksgiving was amazing. Best we've had in longer than anyone could really remember, also thanks to you."

He could tell she was holding back but didn't know why. "Happy Birthday, Holly," he said, almost in a whisper. He was getting nervous with how she was acting but then she smiled, ran to him, and jumped into his arms. Her mouth was on his, hot and sweet. This is what he dreamed of for some time now. This is what kept him going day in and day out.

"I can't believe you remembered. It's such a nice day out, and I thought no one remembered in all the excitement... but you're here! I don't remember telling you my birth date," she said in amazement.

"Six days before Christmas. I can count, you know!" He leaned down and picked up the small box he had set on the rock and handed it to her.

She squealed with excitement. She loved presents! It was a small jewelry box, and her heart lurched, remembering the last box like it she had opened. She held her breath as she lifted the lid. Inside was a small wooden cross on a chain.

"It's not much, but I wanted to make you something I thought you'd like."

"You made this for me?" She was astonished. It was beautiful. "Will you put it on for me?"

He grinned and nodded "With honor, my lady." He trailed kisses from her ear and down her neck to her shoulder when he was done. "Beautiful."

She blushed at the compliment. "I love it, Griffon. It's the most perfect, beautiful gift anyone has ever given me. Thank you."

She hugged him tightly, never wanting to let go.

"You're very welcome. Now what's all this about a lame birthday?"

"Well, it's not anymore. This makes it the best birthday ever." She leaned in and kissed him.

They sat around chatting. He caught her up on all the drama below and was sure to deliver lots of Happy Birthdays from his family. When he asked how things were going with her and what was the latest drama on the Milo Weaver saga, she froze.

She didn't want to tell him, didn't want to say the words. Tears welled up in her eyes just thinking about it.

He watched the change in her and knew it wasn't good. "Is everything okay, Holly? What is it? You know you can tell me anything."

He had never seen her lock up on him like this before and panic set in. He reached for her hand to reassure her, and that's when he felt it. His eyes grew large, and a flash of anger crossed his face. She just sat there with big tears in her eyes. He lifted her hand and examined the large diamond ring on her left ring finger.

"So that's it, huh?"

He just sat there in silence, staring at her hand and unable to believe his eyes. That should be his ring on her hand. She was his. He loved her. He knew their time had come to an end. It was over. There was nothing he could do now.

She watched him in shock, and anger flooded her. "That's it? That's it? You'd give up that easily?" She fought back the hysterics she was feeling. She had no right, she knew, but in that moment, she knew she'd leave it all behind and fight for him. She wanted him and only him.

He was furious and wanted to hit something but reined it in, knowing he didn't want to scare her. *How could she? She said she wasn't ready for marriage. She said she would wait.*

"I know you're upset."

He cut her off. "Upset? Holly, I'm furious! I knew Milo was in the picture, but I thought... I hoped..." He looked so deflated.

She hugged him, kissed his cheek, and tried working her way to his mouth but he put a hand between them. "Don't. You've made your choice, Holly. It's not right. I can't do this. It hurts too much."

"I don't love him, Griffon."

"It doesn't matter. You're going to marry him; you're going to be his wife. His. Not mine. I can't come up here again."

He couldn't even look at her. He had to get away.

"Look at me. Griffon! It's a terrible situation, but I'm trying to make the best of it for now. We're trying to find a way out of this. We just need some time."

"We're trying?" Don't fool yourself Holly. He'd be an idiot to let you go."

Without another word, he gathered his gear and headed back down the cliff, leaving her sitting there crying. He wanted so badly to stay and soothe her and tell her everything was going to be okay, but he knew it would never be again.

She sat there until well after dark, completely numb. She wasn't sure she'd ever see him again, and her heart was breaking at the thought.

It was late when she climbed out and headed back to the bunker. She went straight to bed, thankful for not passing anyone.

Charlie was sleeping in his own room again. It had been weeks since Holly's last nightmare, but tonight, the screams met with uncontrollable sobs, and Charlie had a hard time consoling her. He didn't know what was wrong but something happened; he was certain of it. Even in her half conscious state, she wouldn't discuss it with him, and that really scared him. He'd have to keep a closer eye on his baby sister from now on.

* * * * *

Chapter 18

MILO FOUND her the next day to apologize for not having seen her on her birthday, as did her parents, her friends, and numerous others throughout the bunker. She always just smiled and said, "No big deal, it was just another day."

She tried to blow it off, but it wasn't just another day. It was her eighteenth birthday. It should have been the greatest day of her life and quite possibly might have been if wasn't for that stupid ring on her finger.

In the days that followed, she kept mostly to herself. She went about her duties, smiled when necessary, and spent quiet evenings with Milo to show everyone that everything was just fine.

Those closest to her knew everything wasn't fine, but they didn't know what was wrong, and she wouldn't talk to them about it. She couldn't. Griffon was her most sacred secret, and she wasn't sharing him with anyone. This was her problem, her life, and her hell to live.

With each new day, she became angrier and more determined. She loved Griffon and was certain that he loved her, even though he had never said the words.

On Christmas Eve, she had a gift for each of those she loved... Griffon, Lily, and Amos, with a new doll for Angeline and a toy truck for Trevor. She included a few luxury items for the family in the way of bath soap, shampoo, laundry soap, toothpaste, and new toothbrushes for each of them, as well as a big basket of baked goods and holiday treats that she baked over the last few days.

When she was certain most everyone was sound asleep, she sneaked out, careful to avoid the cameras as well as the guard stations. She walked in the brisk night air, thankful for no snow to give her footsteps away, and she made the trek down to the farmhouse at the edge of the woods. Everything was dark. She was certain they were all fast asleep and tested the doorknob, finding it unlocked. That surprised her a bit, but she let herself in carefully and made her way quietly down the stairs. She saw a small tree in the corner behind where the bookcase was open to the kids' room. She listened and was certain no one was stirring, and then set about putting the gifts under the tree, along with the basket of goodies. She had sneaked an angel ornament off the big tree in the great room andshe placed it on their tree where they were certain to see it.

She had one last basket tied with a bow for Lily, which had everything to guarantee them all a special day. There were fresh eggs, ham, and hash brown potatoes for breakfast... carved turkey, fresh bread, and a large bag of chips for lunch... a frozen roast, potatoes, carrots, and onions for dinner... enough food to feed a family three times their size.

She took the roast out to allow it to thaw on the stove and left the remainder in the basket with a note that simply said. "Merry Christmas."

She smiled to herself, feeling warm and happy just being here near them all but she knew she couldn't stay. Griffon was certain to still be angry with her, and she would never spoil their Christmas with her presence. She sneaked out as quietly as she had entered and made her way back up the mountain, but this time she decided to walk along the edge of the town to the old riverbed the way Griffon always came up.

She was only a few yards away when a flashlight shined around her. "Who goes there?"

She froze. She was fully exposed. What had she been thinking? "Please, I'm only passing through!" She sounded scared, frantic, and young.

"You know the AMAN patrol this area young lady. It's not safe. Do you have a safe place to stay?"

"Yes, yes sir," she managed to stutter.

"Get on then, but go back the way you came. AMAN are patrolling about half a mile up that way," he said as he shined his light in the direction she was heading.

She couldn't tell him she was about to head up the old riverbed, so she turned and headed back toward Griffon.

"Hey," the man said. "I'm Don Maynor. You have a name?"

She turned. "I'm Holly, as in Santa's elf." She giggled and ran off. The sun was rising when she arrived back at the bunker. She changed quickly and jumped in bed, knowing her parents would most likely wake her early to celebrate Christmas.

* * * * *

Holly awoke with a jolt Christmas afternoon. Charlie and Milo were carrying in gifts and a plate full of goodies for her. "Merry Christmas, sleepyhead," they said in unison.

"You missed Christmas, Hols. We tried to wake you but you wouldn't budge."

She yawned and tried to wipe the sleep from her eyes. "Sorry, didn't sleep well last night. Guess I was more tired than I thought."

Milo sat next to her and kissed her forehead. "I hope you're not getting sick or anything. You look a little pale."

She noticed that he looked genuinely concerned. "I'm fine, really."

Her mom and dad came in as well and brought dinner. Everyone assumed that she was sick and insisted she stay in bed. She felt loved. Overall, it turned out to be a pretty good Christmas, although, as she lay in bed, she couldn't help but wonder how Griffon and his family liked their Christmas surprise.

* * * * *

As the sun rose that morning, so did the kids. They didn't officially celebrate Christmas anymore but it was something they could not let go of and the one holiday they celebrated in secret, even knowing the consequences. When Angeline and Trevor walked out of their room and saw the presents under the tree, they squealed with delight.

"Mama, Daddy, Uncle Griff, come quick, come see!" Angeline was jumping up and down.

"Santa came, just like in the story you told us last night, Daddy. He was here! He was here!" Trevor exclaimed.

Still feeling groggy in the early morning, the three adults stumbled out to see what all the commotion was. Lily froze at the sight of the tree.   There were wrapped presents underneath and a large basket full of sweet treats that Trevor was already attacking. She couldn't believe her eyes, crying, hugging, and thanking her husband.

"Hold on just a second there!" You think this was me? I didn't do this!"

"Griffon, did you do this?" Lily demanded.

"Do what? What are you all carrying on about this early in the morning?" Griffon grumbled. He had been more sour than usual the last week.

"The presents, Uncle Griff! Look!"

He rubbed the sleep from eyes, and his jaw dropped when he saw all the presents and the basket full of goodies under the tree. "It wasn't me! I swear; I know nothing about this!"

"See, it WAS Santa!" Trevor insisted.

"Look, this one has my name on it, Mama!" Angeline said excitedly. "Can I open it, can I?"

Lily looked from Amos to Griffon and back at her little girl beaming brightly. She shrugged. "I guess so. It must be for you if your name's on it."

Angeline ripped open the paper squealing with excitement then just stopped and stared. Her eyes were huge. "A doll." She whispered. "Mama it's a doll of my very own!" and the little girl cried, hugging the doll closely.

Lily cried too.

Amos didn't do well with tears and gruffed, "Well come on now, you should be happy. Not every little girl gets a new doll for Christmas. You must've been very good this year."

"Oh, I was daddy. I really, really was!" She ran and hugged him. "Isn't she the most beautiful doll in the world?"

Amos had to clear his throat to keep from crying himself. He had never seen his little girl so happy and thanked God for whatever angel managed to pull this off. Angel, he thought and looked at the tree. Sure enough, there was an Angel adorning their tree. He elbowed his brother-in-law and grinned.

Griffon didn't know why Amos was so excited. He looked and saw a bunch of presents. Amos nudged him again and pointed to the tree. He saw it this time. He stopped and shook his head. It was an angel all right, and he only knew one angel capable of pulling something like this off.

He was still angry with her, but seeing his beloved niece light up, he couldn't help but thank God for her. She did this for him, for all of them. His heart fluttered with hope, and then he frowned, knowing there was none left but he wouldn't take this moment away from them.

"Mama, is there one with my name on it?" Trevor asked.

"Let's see!" She began pulling out presents. "Amos, this one's for you," as she handed him a package.

"Griffon, it looks like both of these have your name on it." She handed him two gifts.

"This one is for me, and this last one says Trevor." He jumped up and down and danced around with excitement.

"Well, open it silly," Angeline scolded.

When he did, he screamed in delight. "Daddy, it's a dump truck! Look, my very own dump truck!"

"You must have been pretty good there Trev," cheered Griffon, as Trevor ran his truck around the room, making engine noises.

Lily kept looking at her gift and the pretty wrapping paper. "Okay, I can't wait; I'm opening mine next!"

Griffon noticed how young and beautiful his sister looked. She opened her gift and started to cry. "It's beautiful!" She held up a new dark purple sweater. It was so soft; she couldn't help but rub it against her cheek.

Amos, nervous around tears, broke the moment with an, "Okay, don't go getting all sappy now. It's my turn." He opened his to find a brand new pair of gloves. He worked construction and his were nearly bare to the thread with several holes in them. Nothing could have been more perfect.

He put them on and found they fit just right. For a moment, he almost cried.

"Settle down big guy," Griffon teased. "I think daddy may cry next kids."

"Your turn Uncle Griff."

"Yeah, why did you get two?"

"I dunno. Maybe cause I was super extra special good this year?"

"No you weren't, either!"

"Yeah, you were just a big old grump!"

The two of them fell to the floor giggling.

"Sure, poke fun you two, but who here has TWO gifts?" He was laughing when he opened the first one, and found a new football inside. He smiled and shook his head. She remembered. It meant more to him than he could voice, and he was afraid that he might tear up, too. He opened the second and found a beautiful gold pocket watch.

"Wow!" exclaimed Angeline

"You're rich!" shouted Trevor.

"Wait, there's more! Look, the stockings you set out are filled, too."

Each one had a new toothbrush and two other items. In total, they found five toothbrushes, a tube of toothpaste, three sticks of deodorant, a bar of soap, a bottle of shampoo, a bar of laundry soap, a bottle of dish soap, a small bottle of perfume for Lily, and two new razors for Griffon and Amos.

Lily wasn't sure what was more surprising, the gifts or the luxury items. There was also the big basket filled with sweets, muffins, breads, candy, cookies, and more things than they could count.

"Someone went to an awful lot of trouble here. Who do you think it was?" Lily asked after the kids had taken their new toys to their room to play.

Griffon was cleaning up the mess and tossing the paper and boxes into the fire. Amos tapped on the ornament on the tree.

"Didn't you know, baby? We had an angel visit us last night."

"Holly?" she whispered, and he nodded.

"That would be my guess."

"Griffon, did you know she was going to do this?"

"Uh, no. Holly and I... haven't talked in a while. Weather and all."

He decided it best not to tell them that they wouldn't see her again, that she decided to marry another man and was no longer his.

The pain of it stabbed him in the chest, and he wondered why would she do this for them? It was supposed to be over. He knew the Holly praises were sure to come throughout the day and wasn't sure his heart could handle it so he added, "Of course, we can't be certain it was her."

Lily just shook her head, "No, it makes sense. It had to be her."

Griffon disagreed. It didn't make any sense at all.

When Lily went upstairs, she stopped and screamed much the same as Angeline had when she first saw the tree. "Come here, look!" She called for them.

They found a feast in the kitchen. More food than they would eat in a week. Griffon was certain this was Holly's doing. He even recognized her handwriting on the attached note simply saying 'Merry Christmas'. He frowned in spite of himself.

Later that evening, the rest of the family arrived to say Merry Christmas. Instead, they found a feast big enough to feed them all. When Don Maynor walked in, he greeted Griffon first.

"What's going on around here, Griffon?"

"It's a long story, Gramps."

"Santa came to visit us and brought us food, treats, and gifts." Angeline filled us in.

"And soap!" Trevor concluded. "You were on duty last night, weren't you Gramps? Did you see Santa? Did he fly in on his sleigh with his reindeer? Did he Gramps?"

"Nope. All I saw was a pretty little elf." The kids giggled at the thought, then ran off to show off their toys.

"A pretty little elf, eh?" Griffon questioned.

"Yeah, never seen her before. She was over near the old riverbed. I don't know where she was headed but because the AMAN were patrolling out that way, I turned her around the way she came. Seems she headed back this way. I know I spooked her, so I tried to keep my distance but she just sorta disappeared on me."

"And did this elf have a name Gramps? Maybe something like Jack Daniels?" Amos laughed at his own joke.

"Laugh all you want son, but I know what I saw. I even got her name. Holly. Yeah, it was Holly. She said was one of Santa's elves."

Griffon asked, "What the hell was she doing by the old river bed? She could have come up and down right here by the house. She doesn't need the riverbed."

Don looked at his grandson but didn't say a word.

* * * * *

After dinner, Don cornered Griffon for some answers. "Okay grandson, spill it."

"Spill what?"

"Well you didn't seem too keen on my elf being near the river bed, something about going up and coming back down. Don't tell me she's one of those Jenkins." He paused and recognized the shock on Griffon's face."

"I don't know what you're talking about Gramps." He started to walk away.

"Don't you walk away from me boy! You tell me everything you know about this Holly girl. I'd given up hope they'd survived up there after all these years. Now, you tell me the truth. Was that or wasn't that Ms. Holly Ann Jenkins?"

Griffon realized he didn't even know her full name, yet he was certain his Gramps did.

"How do you know the Jenkins, Gramps?" He was fishing and the old man knew it, but Griffon was holding his ground and not prepared to reveal anything just yet.

"Okay, I see how this is gonna go, so I'll tell you but only because I suspect you already know. Back in 1999, Mike Jenkins bought that whole mountain up there for a couple grand. He set about putting in some sort of safe house for him and his family. I never met him, but your Grandmother, God rest her soul, befriended his missus.

She'd come down for groceries when the family was in town and bring her two young'uns. Charlie and Holly Ann. Cute kids. Used to sneak them peppermints.

Anyway, rumor was the Jenkins moved up there for good just before all hell broke loose. Of course, you know the stories about Crazy Old Man Jenkins and all that nonsense. Never believed a word of it. Now was that really the same little red haired gal with pigtails that your Grandma was so fond of?"

"Yeah, Gramps, that was Holly Jenkins. I don't know why she was over near the old riverbed. Usually, that's my path up there, but she never uses it. She knows the woods better than I do and goes up and down that way. I'm glad you were the one to find her. If I see her again, I'll wring her pretty little neck."

"IF?" Lily asked laughing. "As if Holly could stay away. She has quite the thing for this handsome grandson of yours, Gramps. She never stays away for long."

"Not safe for that girl to be running up and down that mountain like that. Her father is either dead or she's sneaking around behind his back. Her parents would never allow her to traipse all over the mountain like that." He saw Griffon grimace at his comment.

"She's the one who brought all these goodies down?" Gramps asked Lily.

"Yeah Gramps, we think so." Lily confirmed. "She's something special to us. You've heard the stories of the Angel who saved my babies?"

Gramps nodded.

"That was Holly. Nursed Griffon back to health last month too." Lily was very proud and protective of her friend but knew their family could be trusted with her safety. Soon the entire extended family was listening in and learning all about Griffon's mystery woman.

Griffon didn't have the heart to set them straight.

* * * * *

Chapter 19

HOLLY TRULY thought, with the mild winter they were having in January, that Griffon would come up to the cave at some point to see her. Every nice afternoon, she rushed over to check if there was any word from him. She hoped that with her Christmas surprise, he would have softened some and at least want to thank her. January went by, and there was no sign of him. February came and went, and, still, no Griffon.

In the bunker, people were beginning to evade her. She was short-tempered with everyone. She didn't mean to be, but couldn't seem to stop herself. Milo made excuses for her, but even he wanted to avoid her.

They seemed to be arguing all the time now, and he wasn't even sure why or where they had gone wrong. Everything was going so well, he even hoped that they could actually make a marriage work. Now, he wasn't sure he could handle another day with her, let alone a lifetime. But, he was faithful. He made a commitment, and he intended to see it through for better or for worse... and this was definitely worse.

Chris finally got through to her. She was in the gym yelling at the Sawyer twins for jumping rope wrong. They were on the verge of tears when Chris intervened. "Holly what are you doing? Leave them alone."

She started to snap at him, then stopped. He was right. She had no right to take her frustrations out on others.

"You have to stop this. You're pushing everyone away. We care about you and we're worried. What can I do to help you?"

They were all worried about her, and she was worried about Griffon, Lily, Amos, and the kids. It had been so long since she heard any news of them and, with the guards making daily notes of increased military patrols in the area, she worried even more.

Of course, they didn't know what that meant or who they were but Holly knew that it meant an increased presence of the AMAN. Why?

There have been so many nice days throughout the winter. Why hasn't Griffon come to visit? Maybe he couldn't. She shook the thought from her head. She tried to focus on what Chris was saying. They were worried about her. They loved her, just as she loved Griffon and his family, but they could see her. They knew she was okay, only she really wasn't.

"Holly, please!" Chris was pleading.

Holly sighed. She was hurting people that she cared about and who cared about her. She had to keep that in mind.

"I'm okay Chris, really. I'm sorry I've been such a brat. I'll try to do better... I promise."

"Good." He smiled. "You can start by fixing things with my brother. He's been trying to make excuses and cover for you, but he's really worried. We all are."

"Okay, I'll fix this once and for all."

She hugged Chris, and it was nice to feel his warmth and strength. For him, she'd do almost anything, including facing his brother. She went straight to Milo's Pod and found he was not there, so she sat on the couch and waited.

* * * * *

When Milo got back to his Pod, he was surprised to see Holly there. She had been avoiding him for more than a week, and their last encounter had ended in an argument.

"Hello, Holly," he said. "What are you doing here?"

"Well, I am still your fiancé, aren't I?"

He smiled, glad to find her in a more amicable mood. "Of course you are. I'm just surprised, that's all."

"I know. I'm sorry I haven't been myself lately. I've had a lot on my mind, and I'm not coping well with the stress."

"I've noticed. I think we all have. I'm worried about you. Everyone is. You can't just run around snapping at people for no reason." He hugged her close.

She knew he had done everything to smooth over the chaos she had created, and she knew that he covered for her when she disappeared for hours or even days, and in that moment, she knew that he really cared about her, maybe even convinced himself he was in love. That didn't make this talk any easier.

"Look, I appreciate everything you've done for me. I really do. But we really need to talk. Milo, you can't marry me." She considered her words carefully so as not to lead him on. "I'm not good enough for you, and we both know it. You deserve better than this."

"You've been under a lot of stress, what with school and the wedding. I understand, and it's okay. You can take some time off from your courses. We can even push the wedding back again, if you want. But we're going to make it through this, Holly."

She stared at him. Could he really believe that? She took off his ring and held it in the air. "When you gave me this ring, I didn't give you an answer. I'm ready to now." She paused and licked her lips. "I'm sorry, but I can't marry you."

She handed him back the ring.

"I'm so sorry." She got up and ran from the room, unable to look him in the face.

She ran all the way to her room, only to find her mother there. Her mother took one look at her, held her arms out, and Holly ran into them.

"You've had a rough couple of months Holly. Tell me what's bothering you."

"I can't, mom, I just can't. I broke off the engagement. Dad will never understand, but I don't love Milo. I can't!"

She cried in her mother's arms. There was so much she wanted to tell her about Griffon and his family, which she loved as her own.

She couldn't form the words, but her heart ached for them all. Every time she closed her eyes, she saw the look of disgust and resentment in Griffon's eyes. The hurt and pain she knew she caused him by agreeing to marry Milo.

She had to make it right. She had to fix it, no matter the cost. This was step one, and it was freeing and right.

For two months, she had pined for him. She was constantly stressed and worried about what may or may not have happened to them. She had been living a lie with Milo. It was all too much. She knew she had a lot of apologizing to do still but she could hold her head up high again and feel strength in taking back control of her life.

It was March, and the promise of spring was in the air.

* * * * *

Chapter 20

L ILY WAITED until Amos left for work, then packed up the
kids and told them they would be going on an adventure.
She had never done anything like this before, but Griffon's
birthday was coming up, and she was determined to make
it special. If she could just get Holly there for his birthday
dinner, she knew that would make it extra special.

They headed up the mountain with only a few stories as
guides and no real directions from which to draw. She knew
about the lookouts but thought she could find her way around
them. They began walking this way, then that, until she had
to confess they were completely lost, and she couldn't even
see any bearings up or down the mountain. She didn't want
to frighten the children, so she stayed optimistic on their
hike, pointing out various plants and trees and animal tracks
that she remembered from outings with her dad many years
before.

From his perch, Chris saw activity in the woods. At first,
it headed north of his lookout station, then south. He couldn't
tell what it was, but whatever it was, he watched it walk in
a complete circle before heading southeast and come straight
for him.

He manned his station to the ready, waiting for whatever
or whoever it was to come into a clearing. He could hear
sticks breaking and mumblings. It was definitely people.
Whoever it was, they were not trying to hide. After what
seemed an eternity, he saw two small kids crest over the hill

just to his west, and he relaxed his weapon. What are kids doing lost this far up the mountain, he wondered. Then he saw him. Camo baseball cap about 5'10" tall. He readied his gun once more.

"Stop" he yelled from his perch. "Hands in the air where I can see them. Kids on your knees."

"Is that really necessary? You're scaring them half to death!"

He wasn't at all prepared for that sweet female voice. He jolted and put the gun down.

"Who are you, and what are doing here?"

"What? It's hard to hear you way up there. We mean you no harm. We got rather turned around on our little adventure hike in the woods and are just trying to get home."

It wasn't entirely true, but Lily thought it best with a gun pointed at her and her children to ease this man's fears. He looked barely more than a boy himself. *Could this be Holly's brother?*

Chris knew better than to disarm and come out of his lookout without so much as a warning to the others but she sounded sincere, and he couldn't help but see only the good in people, so he harnessed his weapon and climbed down to where they stood.

"Where are you from? I'll help you get back, as long as you forget ever having this meeting."

"Do you live up here?"

"No questions ma'am, please. I'm not at liberty to answer anything. This mountain is off limits but I can at least point you back in the right direction. Are you from Wythel?" His curiosity was peaking. If she was truly from Wythel, he had so many questions to ask but he knew his duty was to protect the compound and all its residents, so he kept quiet.

The little girl was maybe six, the boy about four. *Cute kids,* he thought. He reached in his pack, assuring them he was okay, and produced two cookies each for the two children as he grinned and fluffed Trevor's hair. Upon first bite, Angeline couldn't contain herself.

"Yum, these taste just like Holly's cookies, mama!"

Chris jolted at the name of his friend. It had to be a coincidence. He looked at the mother.

Lily noticed the reaction upon Holly's name, and she was certain this must be one her kin or a friend at least. She wasn't quite sure how much to say and studied the boy's face.

"Holly? How do you know Holly?"

Before Lily could hush her daughter, Angeline blurted out, "Holly's friends with my Uncle Griff. We call her an angel. She saved Trevor and me once from the AMAN. Uncle Griff's birthday is coming up next week, and he's been a real grump since winter set in. We want Holly to come to surprise him and cheer him up, so we went on an adventure this morning to try to find her to give her an invitation... on REAL paper! At least I think that's why my mom has us lost in the woods." The little girl shrugged and began to devour her second cookie.

Chris's eyes flew to the mom. "Is that true? What she said, is that true?"

"Yes" Lily said quietly. "Look, I know Holly has done everything to keep you safe as well as us but we've barely heard from her since winter set in. We want her to come to no harm. I see now it was a mistake coming up here. What are the chances you could just forget what you heard and forget about us?"

Lily was berating herself. What had she done? How could she be so stupid?

Little Trevor was always keenly aware of his mother's feelings and began to cry.

"Hey now, come on big guy, no need for tears." Chris had a sweet spot for little kids. Always had. He got down on his knees at Trevor's level. "Don't worry little man; your mama's secret is safe with me. As it happens, Holly is one of my very best friends. I've known her since I was about your age." *And I'm going home to wring her little neck,* he thought, but didn't add.

Angeline squealed! "So you'll give her our invitation?"

"Of course I will." He said it with no hesitation for the children's sakes, but Lily could see in his eyes the distress this news brought.

They thanked him again. He pointed them back down the mountain. Then he climbed back up to lookout point and watched closely to make certain they stayed in the right direction and didn't loop around and head back up. He didn't want anyone else to see them.

Once he was certain they were gone, he radioed the compound, and Holly answered.

"Hey Holly, any chance you can bring me up some coffee? Got a surprise for you."

"Sure I'll be right up."

* * * * *

She grabbed a large thermos and fixed a fresh pot for Chris, then headed for the lookout point. Life had been awkward around the compound lately, and Chris was thrown in the middle of things between her and Milo, making it even worse. She was nervous, but grateful for a little alone time with her friend. She bundled up warmly, determined to talk things through while he was cornered.

Chris waved her up on her approach. He thanked her for the coffee and asked her to hang out for a while.

She was thrilled.

"So, you wanna tell me where you really were off to on all those mysterious outings last year?"

"What?" He caught her off guard. We've been through that a thousand times, so why bring it up again? I told you I just needed some time alone to work on my studies and get my life in order."

"Alone?"

She shook her head yes but couldn't stop the heat rising in her cheeks. What was he up to?

Chris was getting angry. She was lying to his face! This wasn't his Holly, his best friend, so he asked her again. "Holly, I want you to be clear, crystal clear with me. Are you saying you absolutely were alone on all those summer and fall little trips away?"

There was a look of knowing in his eyes, with an edge of anger. He knew. She didn't know how he knew, but he knew. She hung her head and shook it no. "How do you know?"

He felt a great release with her acknowledgment and let out a sigh. She wasn't off the hook, but she wasn't lying to him any longer, either.

"So you were with, Griffon, is that right?" his tone was somewhat cold. "I assume that's why you've been cooling things off with my brother, calling off the engagement and all. I mean you two seemed pretty close last summer and fall and well into the start of this year. So even then, you were seeing another guy behind his back?"

She shook her head in the affirmative. She thought she just might throw up.

"Relax; I'm not telling anyone anything, but that was stupid and dangerous. You don't know anything about this guy."

"I know everything about him. I'll answer whatever questions you want; just tell me, how do you know about him?"

He couldn't help himself; he grinned an evil grin. "Wouldn't you like to know?"

"Come on; you have to tell me."

He pulled out the invitation Lily gave him and handed it to her. She stared at it questioningly.

"What's this?"

"Invite to lover boy's birthday party. The sister and kids dropped it off. They were trying to find you and got lost in the woods."

Holly sat there in shock. "Lily and the kids were here? You talked to them? They're okay? Angeline and Trevor, they're okay?"

Chris didn't understand why she was so concerned but could tell she truly was. "Yeah Hols, they're fine. Cute kids. Fed them a couple cookies. It was all good."

She started crying. He didn't know why or what to do, so he just held her and let her cry.

"Thank you. I've been worried sick about them for months. I hate winter. I've had no word since Christmas."

Chris just shook his head. "They mean a lot to you, I can tell. I was prepared to wring your neck at first, but, well, I didn't know."

"It's okay. I'm sorry you got dragged into this. Their world is very different from ours. I worry a lot for their safety."

It was like a light going off in his head. "Holly, is that why I'm sitting up here freezing my butt off on recon and why you keep siding with your father about me and Charlie not going into the town?"

"Yeah. Charlie has no idea what he could be walking into. The AMAN are dangerous, Chris. I don't want you guys anywhere near them."

"The AMAN? The little girl, she mentioned you had saved them from the AMAN. Something about being an angel. I kept thinking, no way she is talking about my Holly!"

They both laughed.

She turned serious again. "You know. Maybe there's a way this could work. Maybe you don't have to forget about running into Lily, just the part on why she was up here." She blushed. "If I tell you everything I know, maybe you could take it back and tell them you had questioned Lily and found everything out. Then Charlie could be prepared and not run down all hot headed and end up killed just to prove a point to our dad."

He thought about that for a bit. "Okay, yeah. I like it. Only I get to interrogate you, as I should have her, if she hadn't been a woman with two kids looking for my best friend. That kind of news tends to throw a guy off!"

They both laughed again and got started. Every now and then, he tried to throw in a question about Griffon but Holly would simply groan and tell him to stay on topic. She did tell him a little about Griffon, but just the basics. He was certain this was why she was pushing Milo away these last few months. It wasn't about Milo and what she did or didn't feel for him. It was about this Griffon guy and the pain she was in from being separated from him. Chris felt genuinely sorry for her.

Milo came to relieve Chris from his shift. He had passed Holly on the way down, and it was as tense as ever. He truly did not know where he had gone wrong. Where they had gone wrong. She wouldn't discuss it or talk to him. He had hoped that maybe she had been talking with Chris, and he proceeded to quiz his brother the second he arrived, and felt cornered.

This was his brother, but she was his best friend. He didn't like being put in the middle and told Milo as much before excusing himself, briefly explaining the day's events and how he needed to get up to the compound and call a meeting with Charlie.

Chris tried to keep everything sorted in his head. What he could tell, what he couldn't, who supposedly told him what, and so on. It was giving him a headache, and the sooner he got it all out, the better.

Charlie gathered all the elders and anyone from the recon team not on active duty the moment he heard Chris had met a local and had news to share. This was what he had been waiting for. He envied the boy this opportunity and prayed he didn't screw it up. They needed this information. He needed to know.

"Okay, Chris. We're all here, so start from the beginning."

Chris said a quick prayer that he wouldn't completely blow it, took a deep breath, and began the story Holly had relayed to him. "The United States of America no longer exists. It is much worse than we feared."

Several of the ladies in the room gasped.

"Please. Just let me tell all the gruesome details and then we can have a discussion."

All heads nodded, and he began again.

"Like I said, there is no more United States of America. The country is divided into many parts under the leadership of many different people. Our particular area is part of what they now call the Allied Nations. It was unclear how much of the U.S. makes up the Allied Nations but for our immediate area, that is all that matters. A ruthless general by the name of General Steinfeld runs it. He seized the former Virginia Tech campus for his main fort. His soldiers are the AMAN, the Armed Militia for the Allied Nations, and if her intelligence is correct, we have every right to be worried.

"Let me back up because I'm sure you all have many of the same questions I did. Number one being, what happened? According to Ms. Lily, the nation went into disarray after the last of us moved up here. The economy continued in a downward spiral, and life in the cities got bad, really bad.

"There was rioting. Neighbors fighting neighbors. Food couldn't be transported from one town to the next without being looted, and, eventually, they just stopped the trucks altogether. It became a race war. Another damn Civil War.

Blacks against Whites, Asians against Hispanics. Each group out for themselves and their kind.

"The President tried to send in the National Guard and declare martial law but they didn't have enough to cover the entire country. The smaller towns banded together and held up longer but before too long, people in the cities were starving and disease began to spread like wildfire.

"It's rumored that a few cities were nuked by our own government in attempts to regain control. Our President's life ended in a lynching on the White House lawn, and what was left of Congress dispersed quickly after that.

"The cities began to drain out into the smaller towns in search of food and safety. Wythel is pretty remote and hidden away from the beaten path, so it managed to withstand the worst of it better than some of the surrounding towns. A couple of towns to the east, off Interstate 81, were burned to the ground during riots as the city folk attacked the towns people, trying to take everything they had. In the end, no one had anything.

"General Steinfeld was said to be a good man. He recruited young men up and down the east coast and formed a fine militia. At first, they came in and brought food and supplies to the small towns. They taught them basic defense and assisted in securing the areas.

"After some time, things changed. A few towns to the north got fed up with the restrictions that were put on their people and the tax levies to support the militia... because the AMAN didn't help for free... and they opted not to pay the taxes.

"Within two months, one town was burned to the ground and brutes came in and took everything. General Steinfeld used the incident as an opportunity to launch a survival campaign that doubled the taxes on the remaining towns, and he took one child from every family in his territories to build his army.

"Now, it's common knowledge that the AMAN staged it to look like brutes in order to gain more support from the other towns in fear the same would happen to them. My informant's sister was taken as an AMAN wife and dragged from her family's home, kicking and screaming.

"They are ruthless and brutal, and they control absolutely everything... the roads, the food, the weapons, and the people. They are strategically killing off all remnants of the past. First, they confiscated and burned the U.S. flag and replaced it with the AMAN flag, and then they burned the written word. They ended religion with the slaughter of all religious leaders.

"They take what they want, who they want, when they want, and they're rewriting history as things go in their favor. It's only been five years, but many have forgotten the ways of the past. They still have power and electricity, running water, and what not, but you wouldn't know it as the AMAN strategically manage it all. Many are basically living like the dark ages down there."

Several of the women gasped and cried as he relayed the stories Holly had told him. The men remained stoic, trying to tame anger and frustrations for the benefit of the women present. Things were worse than they suspected.

Many of them, even at the point of which each of them decided to join the others in the compound, still did not believe the world, as they knew it, would end. Things were bad and getting worse, but they honestly expected to ride out the wave in the compound and return to their homes and their lives at the end of it all.

Now their homes may no longer exist.

It was a surreal moment that took them all by surprise. Yes, they were prepared for the end of the world. It's what they had worked for, and they swore an allegiance to each other to ensure the survival of their loved ones and themselves.

People never let themselves believe that things would get so bad. That the United States of America would cease to exist. The air was thick and stifling in the room as Chris's words sunk in, and they all realized they would never go back to the life they once lived.

Mike stood up, and all eyes turned to him.

In that moment, he was their savior. This was his plan from the start, his vision of the future unfolding before them. Without Mike Jenkins, where would any of them be today? Their hearts were open to him in a way they never were before. He was their leader, and no AMAN could take that from them.

Mike cleared his throat. "In light of what Chris has told us, I would like to hold all questions for now. I don't know about y'all, but I could use a little time to let this news sink in before we discuss a plan of action and decide what we need to do to ensure our safety in this new world that we don't yet understand.

"We're overdue for dinner and fellowship anyway. After all, it is Wednesday night, and I think everyone will agree that we have a lot to be thankful for and a need to be prayerful right now. Pastor Weaver will hold his usual Wednesday evening service after dinner. I think we can agree that it's more important than ever to maintain now. So I'd like to adjourn this meeting for the moment and reconvene in two days."

There were mumbles and whispers as everyone dispersed. Discussions of what they just heard continued in smaller groups into dinner, throughout the Wednesday service, and well into the night. Life in the compound was now changed.

* * * * *

Chapter 21

MIKE JENKINS banged his gavel on the desk. "Order," he said. "This meeting will come to order." He banged it again to no avail.

Charlie gave a shrill whistle that caught everyone's attention, and the room fell silent.

"Thanks Charlie. Now, I know everyone's wound up, and we have a lot to discuss, with many differing views, but nothing is going to get resolved if we keep yelling over top of each other. We need order and respect, and I promise, everyone will be heard. Now, Charlie, as head of the recon team, why don't you give us a brief review and update to get us started."

"Thanks, Dad," Charlie said. "By now, I think even those who were not in attendance the other night know what information Chris Weaver was able to abstract from his informant in the village, so I'm not going to re-hash everything that was said. Bottom line is that if anyone has questions, we will try our best to answer, but all we know right now is third party intelligence. We can combine that with what our own recon team has observed over the last six months and conclude that Chris' information is very likely true."

There were whispers and talk amongst the people at this confirmation.

"Please!" Charlie held up a hand to silence them and began again. "We've been watching Wythel for quite some time, and some of what we've seen is fitting into the puzzle as described."

He put up a slightly blurred image on the projector screen that depicted a man with dark hair pulled back into a long ponytail wearing all black and obviously carrying weapons. Charlie pointed to the picture. "We believe these are the Armed Militia of the Allied Nations."

Noise rose once again in the crowd, and Charlie, again, waved them quiet.

"If they are AMAN, it appears that only one or two actually reside in the town, and they are the only ones noticeably armed. Large trucks full of AMAN arrive every Monday, Wednesday, and Saturday like clockwork around noon to pick up or drop off supplies.

"The townspeople will often gather for their arrival and, even after the crowds have dispersed, they often roam the town for several hours before leaving in the late afternoon.

"The people in town at first appear normal. They get up, go to work, and go home. But they don't normally gather together, except on the days the AMAN arrive.

"There are shops down Main Street, yet no one goes from store to store except to start the day and end it. The church has been completely empty in the six months we've observed them, with exception only to the cemetery as they occasionally bury the dead. There are no signs of an actual funeral, though.

"We've caught movement late through the night, but it's too dark to see what's going on. In some cases, it looks like a small gathering of sorts, from what we know. We suspect there are groups meeting in secret late in the night. That gives us hope that perhaps the people of Wythel are still proud Americans who want a change. If that's the case, we stand ready to fight beside them and bring the United States of America back from the dead."

The noise in the room grew louder, with several in thunderous applause shouting "Hoo Rah" back to Charlie. Others yelled "Noooooooo" in unison. Others continued to talk above it all.

For a brief moment, Mike felt proud watching his son and seeing a man where a boy once stood. Charlie took control of the situation, but fighting wasn't the answer as far as he was concerned. His final words, met with mixed emotions, frightened and angered Mike.

"Hold on," he said, holding up a hand to silence the room yet again. "Hold on. No one is talking about fighting here. This isn't our fight. We have to protect ourselves. My son is admirable in his desire to help those people, but we must take care of ourselves first. We have to secure our grounds further and consider once again closing the doors to the compound where we can live in peace and prosperity."

"Prosperity?" Holly asked before her brain had engaged. "How is being shut off from the rest of the world being prosperous? What about our neighbors in Wythel? If they need help, supplies, or sanctuary, it is our obligation as humans to help them."

Mike couldn't believe his ears. His own daughter disrespecting him in public with her verbal outburst. He had never been more disappointed in his children. He tried to contain his emotions. "That's very admirable Holly, but we don't have the supplies or space to support an entire town."

His words were sharp and meant to signal there would be no further discussion on the subject. Holly knew that tone in her father's voice well. It had stopped her in her tracks as a child. As a young woman ready to fight for her family and friends both here and in Wythel, it only ignited a rebellious spark in her.

Doc stood up then, and everyone quieted to hear what he had to say. "I hear what the young people are saying, and I hear what Mike's saying. I agree with Holly in that we have a human rights obligation to assist anyone seeking help and asylum. It doesn't mean we move them in here, but accommodations in the old tree house perhaps or one of the caves in the area would be the right thing to do."

Holly smirked at her father and before Mike could object, Doc continued. "Mike, I know you're number one concern will be and always has been the safety and security of this family, and we all thank you for that. Without you, where would any of us be right now? We need to stay diligent and true first and foremost to the people in this room, but in the name of what's right, there are other factors to consider."

Mike glared back at Holly with the face of victory, but Doc went on. "Charlie made some valid points, too. We cannot just live under a rock. We have to prepare ourselves to fight. Maybe we don't rush down to aid our neighbors, but at some point, some day, the AMAN are going to find their way up this mountain, and we have to be prepared for that."

* * * * *

Chapter 22

HOLLY TURNED the invitation over in her hand. Tensions in the compound were at an all-time high. Nothing was decided yet, just a lot of debating. She knew her dad was keeping a closer eye on her now.

Everyone was cautiously watching out for everyone else. She desperately wanted to surprise Griffon at his party, though. It had been too long since she last saw him. She made herself believe that he was gone for good, never coming back to her... but Chris had mentioned how Lily said he was equally miserable, and that gave her hope. She knew she would do almost anything to get to him now. She just needed a plan.

Chris had not revealed all of her secrets to the group. She thought there was a chance she could go in through the cave and climb down the rocks, taking the path Griffon had always favored. She had never done that before, but thought that, just maybe, she could borrow some rock climbing gear from Milo and make it down. Would that work or would he insist on going with her? She was deep in thought when Cassie sneaked up behind her.

"You're not going down there alone, Holly."

Her friend knew her better than anyone, and, of course, Chris would have told her everything. She made a mental note to punch him next time she saw him.

"It's dangerous; you said so yourself. I can't just stand by and let you wander off down there by yourself. If this guy means half as much to you as Chris suspects, then I also know you won't give up the idea without a fight."

Holly turned to look at her friend, "So you came to fight?"

"Nope. Chris and I are going with you. I know you will try to make it down there, and Chris and I can't just rat you out. You know we're not like that. At least there's safety in numbers, and we'll watch your back and see you safely down and back up the mountain."

Holly grinned. It was a good plan but still... *how would they avoid the spotters? They had doubled in numbers, which meant they were covering more area than ever before. How could they possibly get around them without being seen?*

Cassie watched her friend closely and saw the thoughts flashing through her head. They had been friends for so long, she could practically read her like a book. She wondered just how Holly had managed to keep this mystery man from her all this time. It was so visible now. She shrugged and decided to let her friend off the hook.

"It's already been decided, so relax. Chris and Charlie worked it out this afternoon."

"WHAT?!" Holly practically yelled. "You told Charlie?"

"Do I look that stupid? Of course we didn't. Charlie has a list of questions he wants answers to. Chris is the 'contact,' right? It took a lot of convincing on the stance that the three of us have wandered these woods looking out for each other since we were kids, and he knew that you and I were capable of watching his back.

"Besides, his contact is a woman, right? He convinced him that with us, she wouldn't be so nervous and would be more likely to open up. Of course, he didn't run this by your father or the council. This is strictly off the books, but he's handling the lookouts to get us down and back without issue. You just have to lead the way."

Holly just stared, stunned! Tears welled up in her eyes as the reality of what her friends were doing for her hit home.

"Don't you dare, Holly Jenkins! You do not cry, ever, and you aren't starting now. That's my job." Holly could see Cassie's eyes glistening, too, and she threw her arms around her. For a moment, they just held on to each other.

"Thank you," Holly whispered to her friend.

* * * * *

Charlie was not happy with Chris's decision to take Holly and Cassie down to the village but he couldn't argue with his reasoning, either. He vowed to himself that he would keep a close eye on them from a distance so as not to spook the contact. He just couldn't, in all good conscience, send his baby sister down there unprotected like that.

He trusted Chris, but not with his sister's life.

Charlie had always been too protective of her; she was his baby sister, always had been, and always would be. He had struggled watching Milo step in over the last year and was about the only one in the compound to be relieved when that fizzled out. He knew his parents and many others were still holding out hope for a Milo and Holly wedding, but Charlie was sleeping better at night knowing the likelihood of that was very low now.

* * * * *

Chris, Cassie, and Holly woke up early the next day. They were all nervous, excited, and a bit fearful. They ate breakfast together in the kitchen and chatted casually, trying to appear as normal as possible.

"Look at this," said Holly's mother. "The three of you back here together. It's been too long since all three of you spent any real time together. I do hope you have a full day planned with one another."

Cassie looked around nervously, and Holly rolled her eyes behind her mother's head thinking, so much for acting normal. Chris just grinned and spoke up for the three of them.

"Yes ma'am. We're going to do some hunting and have a picnic up on bluff's ridge, then see what other kind of trouble we can get into."

Her mom was a bit preoccupied, as she often was. "Mmm, yes, sounds good dear. Be careful. Watch out for each other, and stay out of trouble."

She gave Holly a quick peck on the cheek as she passed, heading out of the kitchen while mumbling something about them always being up to no good.

Cassie let out of big breath of relief when she was gone. She had never been good at lying. As kids, Chris and Holly never told her where they were going or what they were doing until they were there and doing it. They feared that she would blow the entire day's adventure. Holly knew they had to get out of there before she did just that, today.

They packed a picnic basket before splitting up to retrieve their backpacks and meet at the armory to pick up rifles with suppressors. They hunted with suppressors now, with the threat of the AMAN. Since that was their cover story for being gone all day, they needed the props to go along with it. Chris also felt better armed while going down to the village.

Scouts reported two days earlier that the AMAN had moved out of the area. From past accounts, they knew that meant they were not due back for another two weeks, and aside from the few who stayed year round, it was relatively an AMAN free zone right now. Of course, Lily would have known this and planned accordingly.

Holly suspected she also planned the party mid day, knowing that most of the people in town would be working. It gave Holly plenty of time to come down, spend time with them, and get back up before the threat of spying eyes could be an issue.

* * * * *

As they exited the compound and began the descent along the path Chris and Charlie had agreed upon, Holly's spirits lifted. The further down the mountain they went, the lighter she seemed to become. Chris and Cassie watched in awe as their friend transformed before their eyes. Even from a safe distance behind, Charlie noticed it too.

The trip was uneventful. Holly was amazed at how smoothly everything was going. Her heart jerked as the farmhouse came into view, and she stopped in her tracks. She was nervous. It had been months since she had seen Griffon.

What if he doesn't want to see me? she thought.

Lily thought he would, though. Right? Why else would she have risked everything coming up here to deliver that invitation?

Chris and Cassie left her to her own internal argument. They smiled at each other over her head. After a few minutes, Cassie broke the silence. "Holly, she risked a lot to invite you to this party. He'll want to see you. She wouldn't have done that if he didn't."

Her friend knew her so well; it was scary, at times.

Chris chimed in, "Besides, she's probably been living with the same grumpy, short-fused monster we've been dealing with these past several months. Probably as tired of walking around on eggshells with him as we are with you."

Cassie punched him in the arm. "Idiot!"

Holly laughed and cleared her head. She knew they were probably both right, and she knew she wasn't going back up that mountain until she saw him, so she might as well get it over with. She told them to flank to the right and wait by the blackberry bushes for her signal to come on down. She took a deep breath and slowly walked toward the farmhouse below.

Charlie was following a bit too close and had to take cover quickly when they stopped unexpectedly. He could see them talking, but he wasn't close enough to hear them. Holly seemed to be the focal here. *Maybe she was having second thoughts,* he thought to himself.

Something in their movements made it appear that Holly was in charge. It didn't make sense to him.

After some discussion, she squatted down and pointed to something below. He saw her signal Chris and Cassie to the right as she proceeded down by herself. Charlie was furious. How could Chris put her in danger like that? Lily was his contact, so why would he send her down alone? When he was sure they were all out of sight, he crawled slowly down to the spot where they had stopped. He squatted down low in some underbrush, and, from there, he could see a farmhouse below. Holly was walking right toward it while Chris and Cassie were cowering behind some bushes, watching.

Charlie tried to wrap his head around what he was seeing. Holly taking the lead while Chris hid undercover in the safety of the bushes at the edge of the forest. It didn't make any sense. Holly was almost to the edge of the yard. A few more steps and she'd be out in the open.

He was about to yell to her to stop when the back door of the farmhouse swung open. A little girl came running out of the back of the house. It appeared she was giving some sort of signal and, at the same time, he saw his sister run out of the woods and right toward the little girl. She grabbed her in her arms and hugged her, swinging her around until they fell to the ground giggling.

Charlie stumbled back and slumped against a tree. He was in shock at what he was seeing, and anger boiled in him. This wasn't Chris's contact; this was Holly's. She seemed to know this young girl very well.

He thought of all the time she had spent out on her own last summer and well into early winter. Could this have been where she was hiding all this time? Would she lie to him? Him?

He wracked his brain trying to remember what she had said about those times away. She had always needed her space, and he was too preoccupied to have taken much notice.

If this is where she'd been, then she knew all along about the AMAN, about everything. Why would she tell them now? Why now? He began to panic as she entered the house and disappeared from view. He wanted to run after her, to protect her, but instead he just sat there paralyzed with disbelief.

* * * * *

Holly was happy to see Angeline. The two of them giggled, lying on the ground as the child tried to fill her in on all that had happened, talking a million words a minute. Holly laughed, enjoying the moment.

When the little girl calmed down, she said more coherently, "I sure hope seeing you puts Uncle Griff in a better mood. He's been terrible to live with all winter. Praise God for spring!" Holly hugged her close, and they got up and walked, hand-in-hand, into the house.

It was dark inside. The front windows had the blackout curtains down. Lily ran over and told Angeline to get in place. "It's a surprise and you made it just in time," she informed Holly. "He's about to walk in any second." She pulled Holly down with her behind a couch.

When Griffon walked in, everything was dark, and he felt comforted. He had been in such a low place for so long that to come home to a dark, empty house somehow felt right. Now that spring had sprung, he was having an even worse time not running up the mountain in search of Holly at every opportunity.

She was surely married by now; he was certain of it. He let it happen. He should have fought for her, for them. He sighed wearily. The memory of her consumed him constantly. It felt like a part of him was missing, and he knew he wasn't coping well.

He felt bad that he often took his frustrations out on those he cared about most. They said they understood, but he felt guilty about it all the same.

Today was his twenty-second birthday, and he knew the house wouldn't be quiet long.   Lily had been scheming something up for weeks, and the fact that he wasn't able to crack the details from Angeline and Trevor told him it must be big. Might as well enjoy the quiet and try to focus on something for a change. He could put up that pretense for them today.

He plopped down on the couch without turning on the lights. Holly and Lily were hiding behind him. He rubbed his temples and tried to think happy thoughts. Angeline would be so disappointed if he couldn't break out of this funk in time for their surprise festivities.

Everyone in the room was silent for what seemed like an eternity to Holly. Angeline couldn't hold it in anymore and began to giggle.

"What the..." Griffon shot up off the couch. The lights came on, and everyone jumped out yelling, "Surprise!"

Angeline flew into his arms yelling, "Happy Birthday, Uncle Griff!" She hugged him tightly. He couldn't keep from smiling at that kind of reception, no matter how much of a funk he had been in just moments before. Angeline craned her neck around the room looking for something. Griffon wasn't sure what.

Lily kicked Holly lightly and offered a hand to help pull her up. In all the excitement, Holly had just frozen in place. Her heart was pounding in her chest. Surely, everyone in the room heard it. Everything in the room was suddenly quiet as Lily pulled her up.

Holly knew all eyes were on her. Several of these people, she had never even met. Griffon took a step back, almost dropping Angeline in the process. Then he froze, like a statue.

Holly couldn't tell what he was thinking, and everyone was watching. She did the only thing that came to mind. "Surprise! Happy Birthday." She tried to smile but had never felt so awkward in her life. Amos broke the silence, slapping Griffon on the back and striking up conversation. The room came back to life slowly but Griffon was still staring at her.

She's here. That's my Holly. The words ran over and over in his head. He was in shock. *How? Why? Lily!* As his bewilderment waned, his eyes instantly shot to her left hand. He had to know.

Seeming to read his thoughts, Holly lifted her left hand, and it was void of a ring. She shook her head no. Relief, happiness, and joy flooded him. His chest hurt as the release of the wall he tried to build around it broke free, and he jumped over the back of the couch to get to her.

His arms were around her, tight and safe. She held back tears as emotions consumed her. He kissed her face sporadically until his lips found hers. Hoots and hollers rose up around them, and he was laughing when they finally broke apart. In that moment, the world was set right again.

No one seemed shocked or surprised to see her there. They were, after all, his immediately family. He introduced her first to his Grandfather, Mr. Don Maynor.

"Hey, I know you," Holly said with a smile as she remembered their encounter at Christmas.

The old man grinned and handed her a peppermint that brought back a memory or a familiar feeling she couldn't quite place. He gave her a wink as Griffon steered her away.

She met his mom and dad and, then, his sister Laurel and her family. She heard as much about them as they had apparently heard of her, and she was welcomed with open arms.

Angeline came over to talk and blabbed all the secrets she had worked so hard to keep in the last few weeks.

"It's too bad Mr. Chris couldn't make it too, Holly."

"Mr. Chris?" Griffon asked, looking down at her.

"Oh crap!" Holly said. "Chris and Cass... I forgot all about them. I'm a terrible friend! How long have I been here?"

"Nearly an hour," Lily chimed in.

"They're gonna kill me!"

She looked so guilty that Griffon couldn't help but smile.

"Lily, do you mind if I invite two more people?"

A couple of people in the room seemed on edge with her request. Lily looked at Amos, who nodded his head yes. Holly ran over, gave him a kiss on the cheek, and thanked him profusely.

"Much has happened in the last few weeks, mainly thanks to Lily."

Holly gave her a knowing look. "I needed some assistance getting down here undetected."

She ran out and signaled to her friends. Several people strained their necks out the back door and windows to see who was out there. Chris and Cassie caught the signal, stood up, and walked over.

"Bout time," Chris said.

"Geez, Holly, we thought you had forgotten all about us." Cassie chimed in. Holly could tell by the tousled hair on Chris's head that they had found plenty to occupy their time.

"Come on, I want you to meet everyone."

As they approached, Cassie hesitated. "Holly, you're sure about this, right?"

Before she could answer, Griffon walked outside to meet them.

"Cassie, Chris, this is my... uh... Griffon; this is Griffon." She caught herself off guard, not even sure how she planned to finish that sentence. *My... what?* she thought.

"Griffon, these are my two best friends in the entire world, Chris and Cassie. They helped me get down here today."

"Then I am forever indebted to you both," he said as he hugged Cassie and shook hands with Chris.

Charlie, still watching from above, fumed with the scene he witnessed below. That was certainly not Lily. He noted that none of them had their weapons. For the first time, he remembered Holly didn't have hers when she first went down, and Chris and Cassie had obviously stashed theirs away somewhere, too. Defenseless in the enemy's house. It was too much.

He started to get up and head down to stop this madness unfolding before him but, once again, remained silent. This time, it was like a fist to his chest as he saw this big brooding stranger put an arm around his baby sister and guide her back inside. He stumbled backwards and just sat there in shock.

* * * * *

Chapter 23

INSIDE, GRIFFON introduced the newcomers around. It only took a few moments for the anxiety to pass and the party to energize again. Of course, they hadn't been able to bake a cake, as Lily was not able to get hold of enough of the ingredients. Instead, she made Griffon's favorite meal of meatloaf and mashed potatoes, and she turned that into a cake.

It was delicious and a fun treat. Cassie, however, had come prepared. Remembering stories of food shortages in Wythel, she had baked and prepared a cake the night before and brought the icing and decorations with her. After dinner, she gathered Griffon's nieces and nephews together in the kitchen and shooed the adults out. They set to work decorating the cake with icing and candies. From the other room, all anyone could hear were giggles and shhhh's.

When the cake was complete, Trevor led the way with all the kids surrounding the cake and still giggling. As they sang Happy Birthday, they moved aside to reveal their masterpiece. It had been so long since any of them had seen anything like it.

The adults just sat and stared. Griffon's mother cried happy tears. Most of the kids had never seen or tasted cake, and they treasured and enjoyed every bite.

Holly said a thank you to her friend over the heads of the sugar-crazed kids who had obviously been sampling their creation in the kitchen.

While the others fought over the last precious pieces of cake, Griffon grabbed Holly by the waist and pulled her into a tight embrace.

"Did you make your wish?" she asked.

"What could I possibly wish for? Everything I ever want is right here in my arms." He kissed her breathless.

The afternoon passed too quickly. Holly was not ready to leave when Chris announced it was time to go. She knew she had to go but, for a moment, she thought of just staying down here with Griffon and his family. Then she looked back at Chris and Cassie and knew with a heavy heart that she could not. This felt like the hardest goodbye they had ever faced. Griffon must have felt it, too, as he rose. With a head nod toward the back door, he gave her a minute to say goodbye to his family, and they both headed outside.

Chris and Cassie held back, giving the couple a few more minutes to say their goodbyes. Cassie was battling back tears. Her soft heart ached for her friend and the tragedy of the situation. She knew Holly was truly in love with this man she had wanted so badly to hate. She knew that Griffon loved Holly, too. It was obvious, but it was a love that could never be. There was a solemn feeling throughout the room.

Outside, Holly and Griffon walked to the edge of the forest hand-in-hand in complete silence. He pulled her in close and held her tight. He wanted to promise her things that he had no right to promise. The promise of hope, of love, of a lifetime together. Right now, all he had to offer was goodbye.

Seeming to read his thoughts, she shook her head no. "This isn't goodbye. We'll find a way to make it work."

He hugged her tightly as she said, "I can't lose you again; I love you."

Her final words weren't much more than a whisper, but his heart soared! Never had she verbalized those words before. He had felt it, and he was certain of his own feelings. Hearing her say it out loud empowered him like never before, and he knew in that moment that he would do anything to be with her. Holly was his. Forever.

Just then, they heard a rustling in the woods and froze, eyes darting around to find the source. Reality slamming back into them both.

Charlie had watched the two of them kissing and cuddling near the edge of the woods. He sat up on that hill for hours watching the house for any sign of risk for her safety, and this was too much for him to handle. He could no longer restrain himself and marched down the hill with guns at the ready. Griffon and Holly saw him at the same time. Holly tried to jump in front of him, but Griffon pushed her behind him. The look he shot her froze her into place, and she didn't dare move.

Charlie stopped a few feet away with his gun aimed directly at the guy's chest. He wanted to protect his sister. He was confused and angered by the situation. "Holly, get over here, now!"

She wanted to speak, but one look cut her short. "Let her go!" Charlie demanded.

"Drop your weapon!" Griffon countered with equal demand.

"Holly, are you okay?"

She placed her hand on Griffon's shoulder and stood on her tippy toes to whisper assurance, "It's okay; he'll never hurt me." Griffon did not relax, but when she moved, his eyes were pleading, not demanding this time.

She walked around and stood directly in front of Griffon. Body-to-body, shielding him from Charlie. She reached for his arms, wrapped them securely around her waist, and patted his hand for reassurance.

"There, now put the gun down. You will have to get through me to get to him. And we both know you aren't going to shoot that gun at me."

Charlie was furious! "Hols, what the hell do you think you're doing!"

As he advanced closer, even while putting the gun away, Griffon's grip tightened and he swiveled his body in a protective, possessive manner to shelter her. Even through his anger, Charlie noticed the move. He laughed. "Really? You think you can protect her from ME? Just who do you think you are?"

Griffon immediately noted the possession in the man's voice and thought it must be Milo. He looked from the stranger to Holly and back again. She was obviously furious, which gave Griffon the okay to shut this situation down. She had said she loved him. As far as he was concerned, she was his and only his. He would no longer settle for sharing her.

"You need to back off and head on back up that mountain. I don't know who you think you are, but Holly is my girl. Mine. She is not your problem to worry about anymore."

Holly's heart swelled with love and pride. She was his girl; he said it! Then, she came back to reality with a thud. She knew instinctively that he thought this was Milo. She saw her brother about to strike from the corner of her eye and quickly jumped in the middle of the two.

"That's not Milo, Griffon!"

"Charlie, STOP!"

Both men stopped and took a step back.

"Charlie? Your brother?"

"Milo? How the hell does he know about Milo, Hols? Who the hell is he?"

"It's okay, both of you. Really. This is a good thing."

"What's good about this Holly? There is nothing okay with this," Charlie said. "I can't believe you'd put our lives in danger like this. Not you. You know that we have to protect each other. Family first."

She cringed at his words. "How much have you told him? You've put the entire compound at risk. I can't believe you could be so stupid! Naïve is never a word I would have used to describe you before today. I can't even believe this is happening. Not you, Holly."

Charlie was pacing absentmindedly now. *Never a good thing,* she thought.

Griffon watched her as her brother spoke, and he spoke up on her behalf. "Enough," he said, which stopped Charlie's pacing. "Can't you see you're hurting her? She hasn't put anyone's life in danger. Not from the likes of me and my family. Holly's part of us too. We'd protect her with our lives and that goes for all of you up there just because you're important to her. She's all I care about in this God-forsaken place."

Charlie took a good look at Griffon and knew without question that this guy meant every word. He sighed, the anger and frustrations of the day easing off. His sister was in love. He was as certain of it as the stars in the sky. He didn't understand it, and he couldn't begin to figure out how it had happened, but he knew it as absolute fact, just as he knew that this man standing by her side meant every word he spoke.

Resolutely he shook his head. "Did Chris at least get my questions answered?"

She smiled, threw her arms around her big brother's neck, and kissed his cheek. "You're gonna love him too, you'll see," she whispered so Griffon couldn't hear. Louder, she said, "In all the festivities, he forgot about it. He's working on it now, giving us a few minutes alone to say bye... which you kinda blew there, big brother." She was teasing now and both men began to relax some. They even managed to shake hands, and Griffon invited Charlie in to meet his family.

* * * * *

As the threesome entered the kitchen at the back of the house, no one paid attention. Then Trevor spoke up loudly. "Who's that?" The entire room went on edge.

Holly was quick to reassure them, and Chris let out an "Oh crap!"

She laughed. "It's okay, Chris. They've already duked it out and are well on their way to being friends." They rolled their eyes at her, but she hugged them both equally close to her. "Everyone, this is my brother, Charlie."

Commotion in the room ensued. Griffon's mother fretted over him, needing to reassure herself that he wasn't hurt in any way. Cassie, feeling guilty as ever, was blabbing everything to Charlie and filling him in on several missing details. Holly just stood in the middle of all the madness, grinning from ear-to-ear.

"For a woman torn between two worlds, you sure are happy there, little sister," Lily said.

"Who wouldn't be? I have the two greatest men on the planet by my side. My family is together at last!" The two women looked at each other knowingly. Lily felt the same way about Holly. They accepted her as family. Griffon had made his choice, and, today, he solidified it.

Chris had to break up the happy fest, noting the time, and the others reluctantly agreed. Charlie, surprisingly, fit right in and was busy talking security with Amos and Liam, Griffon's other brother-in-law. Cassie and the ladies were swapping recipes and sharing gardening secrets. She made mention that the area hidden just behind the blackberry bushes in which she and Chris had been feverishly making out at just hours ago, would make a splendid garden that could remain hidden from the AMAN.

They agreed to meet and discuss it again soon, and everyone moved outside to say their final goodbyes. Griffon grabbed Holly's hand, led her back to his bedroom, and closed the door.

Before the door was fully shut, his mouth was hot and wet and everywhere. Her head was swimming, and the need in her grew quickly. As far as she was concerned, she was his, and she wanted him more than she could fathom. As her hands slid under his shirt and up his chest, she heard him moan deep in his throat but he pulled back, knowing they didn't have time. He wasn't sure he'd be able to stop himself if they headed down that path.

He was still breathing heavily, but his eyes were no longer clouded. He cupped her chin in his hands and caressed her cheek.

"I love you Holly," he said sweetly and confidently, and her entire body warmed. "I've loved you since the first moment I saw you. If you hadn't shot a rock at my head, I would have kissed you right then and there."

She smiled at the memory of their first meeting and traced the spot on his forehead that now held a tiny scar preserving that moment forever.

"I know," she said and kissed him again. This time was not the feverish all consuming kiss of the moments before. This was a strong, confidant, possessive kiss of a woman, and it took his breath away.

There was a knock on the door, and Lily walked in. "Sorry guys; it really is time to go, Holly."

"I know."

Lily noted a new, quiet confidence in the girl.

Holly took Griffon's hand unashamedly and led him out to

see the others. For a moment, Lily thought Holly might just try to stay, but after a moment's hesitation, she said goodbye to each of them, gave Griffon one last kiss, and walked away without looking back. They hadn't discussed tomorrow but they both knew tomorrow would come.

The foursome walked back up the mountain in silence. After quite some time, Charlie dared to glance back and was not at all prepared to see the strength, determination, and love so raw on his sister's tear streaked face. He stopped and hugged her close.

Although he had always considered her someone to treasure and protect, he admired her strength and power. He could only remember seeing her truly cry three or four times in her life, and his heart was breaking for her now.

"It's gonna be okay," he tried to assure her. He wasn't sure how or when, but he knew they'd find a way to make it work. They had to. All those miserable days of winter, he knew with certainty that she was dealing with the loss of Griffon, and without being told, he suspected their bond only grew stronger today. He knew it wouldn't be easy, but somehow, they'd have to make it work.

* * * * *

Chapter 24

TENSION continued to run high in the compound. Mike stood firm that they must lock themselves away from this cruel and evil world before it infiltrated their sanctuary. Many of the elders sided with him, as did Milo Weaver. Others, like Charlie Jenkins and many of the younger men and women, felt compelled to reach out and help the town below.

Charlie formed a task force with the begrudging approval of the elders to go down and meet Chris's contact in the town below. What Charlie was really doing was strengthening the alliance his sister had already established for them.

He chose carefully who would be on this new team. Of course, Holly, Chris, and Cassie were members. In the end, he chose four others, including Big Jim and Milo, at Mike's insistence. Having Milo on the team could cause some issues for Holly. She'd have to be extra careful now.

To keep Holly and Griffon's secret and keep Griffon's family safe, the team would wait for the AMAN's weekly town check, then move down onto Main Street and meet some of the local townsfolk. Each person was armed with a list of questions and a basket of food in hopes to win the people over and convince them to keep their mouths shut when the AMAN were around.

With their plan in place, the eight new members of the community relations task force team found themselves up late with anticipated excitement. Talking late into the night, each knew they had a long day ahead of them... but the thrill of this new adventure had pure adrenaline pumping through them all. Holly most of all.

This could be her chance to make a difference and bridge the gap between her family and the safe, secure life in the bunker and the town below and, someday, a real life with Griffon. As the others broke off to finally head to bed, she found herself tossing and turning until restless sleep finally won.

She dreamed of sunshine, happiness, and fields of flowers. She was dressed in white, and her friends and family were there smiling at her. Her dad was leading her down a path toward something, no someone. She could see him in the distance looking back at her but no matter how long they walked, they never seemed to get any closer. Dark clouds rolled in and thunder boomed around them. Dark figures ran over the hill behind the man waiting for her. She could see a fight ensue as lightning streaked across the sky and rain poured down. The storm blurred the image further, and she ran as fast as she could, but she never got any closer.

She awoke with a jolt and quickly discovered it was her alarm clock going off. She had a heavy feeling in her heart. She couldn't exactly remember the dream but the helplessness and unease weighed on her. It was not the way she envisioned this day.

"What's wrong with you?" Charlie asked her over breakfast.

"Nothing. I'm fine," she snapped as she grabbed a muffin and headed for the door. "What's taking so long? Let's get this over with, already," she said over her shoulder.

Chris, Cassie, and Charlie looked at each other in confusion. She should have been as happy and excited this morning as she was last night.

Cassie followed her friend. "Holly, what's wrong?"

"Nothing! I said I'm fine." Even so, she knew her friend wouldn't let it go. "Sorry; bad dream; rough night. I'm just tired and ready to get moving."

"We'll just be a few more minutes. We're waiting on Milo," Cassie said, and Holly rolled her eyes.

"I can't believe he's actually coming. It feels so wrong!"

She was thinking back to her dream. The field of flowers. She could clearly see one red flower standing out above all the other flowers, and her heart sank. Was she dreaming of Milo or Griffon? Even after everything, she still wasn't certain, and the thought of the two of them meeting face-to-face did not sit well with her.

* * * * *

Another hour and they were finally ready to head down the mountain to the tiny town of Wythel. Stopping at the last checkpoint, the one closest to town, they confirmed no AMAN were in the area. With anxious relief, they made the final trek down, stopping again just at the edge of town. They decided to break into groups of two, and each group headed in a different direction.

Milo grabbed Holly's hand and held it high as each began pairing off. Charlie felt really bad for his sister, who looked as if she was in shock and trying not to throw up. But, what could they do?

Holly jerked her hand away a little harder than she intended, and Milo eyeballed her suspiciously.

"Okay, which direction do you want to go?" she asked, trying to sound more cheerful than she felt and praying they didn't run into anyone who would recognize her and respond without thinking.

Milo led her straight to Main Street, and she decided it would be best if she just follow along and keep her head low and mouth shut. As they turned the corner onto Main Street, she walked right into someone and found herself in Milo's familiar arms keeping her from falling. In the chaos, she closed her eyes, desperately trying to disappear. Milo righted her as the man apologized. She heard his voice and froze.

This could not be happening! She panicked and wanted to bolt. Milo was already introducing himself and shaking hands. "It's nice to meet you, I'm Griffon Maynor. You're not from around here are you?"

"No, no, we're just passing through."

With that, Holly took a step back and turned, praying Milo's back was to her. It was, and as she saw awareness creep into Griffon's eyes. She shook her head no and knew that he saw the panic she was feeling.

Griffon couldn't help but stare. He saw quickly that Holly didn't want to be here. As he tried to fight his desire to check on her, wrap his arms around her, and kiss her a thousand times over, he instinctively knew they weren't supposed to know each other. *Who was this guy, and what were they doing down here?*

"I'm sorry... what did you say your name was again?" Griffon asked.

"Milo. Milo Weaver," he said with confidence. "We're really sorry for running into you like that. This is Holly."

She politely shook his hand and when she did, she felt her body warm as he brushed his thumb lightly across the top of her hand. Her eyes widened and warned him to behave. She knew from his look that he was well aware of who Milo Weaver was.

"So, what brings you two to Wythel? If there's anything you need, please just ask."

"Thank you." Milo again shook his hand, this time quite enthusiastically. "We really weren't sure what to expect down here, and it's a relief to find you so hospitable."

Griffon glanced at Holly just in time to see her roll her eyes, drop her head, and shake it from side to side. It took everything in his power not to laugh at her discomfort with the situation.

"Well, do you need a place to stay? Food? Work?" Griffon asked, knowing full well that they had it all nearby.

"No, no. Thank you, but no. We live not too far from here, and it has been so long since we have had any news of the outside world. We thought perhaps a visit into town would be nice."

Milo was trying too hard to sound nonchalant about the situation. It was almost comical.

"Well, we certainly don't get many newcomers strolling through town, what with the AMAN patrols controlling the roads and all. I must ask; where did you come from?"

"Oh, just over the mountain," Milo said, pointing to the wrong mountain to throw him off. There was something about this Griffon fellow that set him a bit on edge. "We are hoping to meet others and establish trade and communications with the people of Wythel."

With that, Milo set his concerns aside and began talking and asking questions as they strolled down Main Street. Milo and Griffon walked side-by-side, and Holly just followed behind the both of them.

Chris and Cassie came down Main Street and saw the entire scene unfold. They both couldn't help but laugh and caught the attention of some ladies in a local shop knitting and mending clothes with what few supplies they had. One of those ladies just happened to be Lily.

"This really is a small town!" Cassie exclaimed.

Lily did not hesitate and walked over to her new friends, embraced each of them, pulled them inside, and introduced them to the other ladies in the shop, none of whom were surprised to meet them. They were clearly part of the Maynor's inner circle.

Lily gave them a quick tour of the shop and explained that their jobs were to mend and sew clothes for the people in the town. It was a good job. They all got along well and, although gossip often ran dry, they always managed to find something or someone to talk about. They were especially excited to have newcomers with whom to talk.

Chris continued to watch the scene on the street. Even from behind, he could tell Holly was about to die and wanted nothing more than to melt into the sidewalk and disappear forever. He couldn't help but laugh at the situation, which drew the attention of the ladies.

"What's so funny?" Cassie asked.

"Poor Holly looks like she's going to bolt at any second! If we were truly good friends, we'd go rescue her."

"Holly's here too?" Lily asked. "Griffon's unexpectedly off work today and should be coming by for lunch anytime now. I do hope he doesn't miss her."

"Oh, he didn't!" They both said at the same time and burst into laughter.

They explained what had unfolded on the street and how poor Holly was stuck walking Main Street with both Griffon and Milo, both of whom had their chests puffed out and shoulders back, both clearly marking territory over Holly.

"We have to do something! You two should be ashamed of yourselves," Lily scolded. "What is Milo most interested in?"

"Church, but that won't help much down here," Cassie said.

"Planes!" said Chris. "But unlikely there's an airfield around here."

"Actually there is!" exclaimed one of the ladies who had been introduced as Mrs. Little. "Jeb has a few crop planes in a little airstrip not even a mile from here."

Lily clapped her hands together. "Well that's it then but Chris, you're going to have to sacrifice and go with him while we pull Holly out of the fire for a bit."

"He'll never go without her," Cassie said.

"I dunno about that. She'll still be with you and my local contact, which may help soften him some. And he'll be hard pressed to turn down a chance to see the planes," Chris said, then pulled her close and gave her a quick kiss. He smiled down at her. "For luck... I'm gonna need it!"

With that, Chris headed across the street, very animated. He told Milo about the crop planes and asked if he wanted to see them. He told him about the ladies in their knitting circle, said how Cassie had already settled in to help them, and asked if Holly could stay with her while they went. Just then, Lily came out and walked over to them.

"You must be Milo," she said and hugged him, signaling Griffon to get out of there. "Chris has told me a lot about you. I'm Lily. Chris and I met and spoke a couple times in the woods. I see you've met my baby brother, Griffon."

Milo was a little overwhelmed but managed to nod his head yes.

"Griff, Pops is looking for you over at the old barn. I know today is your day off, but he has some odds and ends he needs help with." She smiled sweetly with a stern look that said GO!

With Griffon gone, Milo relaxed. "Chris says there's some crop planes nearby that we could take a look at?"

"Absolutely! Mrs. Little was just about to head home to get some lunch for her and Jeb. You're welcome to join them, and he'll be glad to show you around." Lily continued being most hospitable.

"Holly, do you want to go look at planes?" Milo asked hopefully.

She tried not to sound too excited, but reminded him that we were supposed to stay in pairs for safety, and if Chris really wanted to go that badly, then she should really stay with Cassie and would see the planes next time. Milo grudgingly agreed.

With Milo out of the picture, Holly calmed.

"What a nightmare!" she said as they entered the little shop.

"I honestly thought that you were gonna die right there on the street." Cassie laughed and hugged her friend. "Just breathe, Holly. It's okay now."

"Why didn't y'all send word you were coming down? We would have been ready." Lily introduced her to the rest of the ladies.

"I couldn't believe Milo was stubborn enough to insist that we pair up, and when I realized it was Griffon we just literally ran into, I almost died! I can't believe that he kept his cool through it all."

"You looked so pathetic. I knew I had to play along. Besides, I wanted to get a feel for this Milo of yours," Griffon said standing in the doorway.

"He's not MY Milo."

"I certainly didn't get the feeling that HE knows that," he said accusingly before snatching her up in his arms and giving her a quick kiss.

She blushed as the ladies in the room all gushed before switching the conversation to memories past and settling back into work.

Cassie picked up a shirt, needle, and thread and set to work, too. Noticing how dull the needles were and how worn the clothing being repaired already was, she said, "We mostly brought food with us this time but if there are ever any other supplies that you need, please just ask. We're hoping to come down at least once a week, and I can bring whatever you need... newer fabrics, stronger thread, sharper needles. It's not a problem, just let me know."

* * * * *

Griffon led Holly to the back room. Lily stopped her midway. "Here," she said, handing her a shirt in desperate need of mending. "When the boys return I'll say, 'Holly, do you need any help? It's the green one.' And you'll know they're here."

"Thanks Lily. I love you. You're the best!"

"Right back at ya girl."

Lily gave her a quick squeeze before getting back to work.

Griffon grabbed her hand and pulled her into the back room, which held baskets of clothes. The back door was open to allow plenty of light. He checked the area and found it empty, then pulled her into his arms and kissed her senseless.

"I'm really sorry for today," she started.

He silenced her with another kiss. "Don't be. I happen to run into my favorite girl, quite literally and completely unexpectedly. You made my day!"

"I meant about Milo."

"I know what you meant. Unfortunately, he really does seem like a nice guy. I wish I could hate him, actually, but I don't. I see why you like him."

"I never said I..."

He silenced her with another kiss.

"It's okay, Holly. This is me. We always tell each other the truth. I know you had feelings for him, maybe even still do. I envy him. He gets you every day. But I know your heart, and you told me that you love me, ME."

He held her hands up to his chest. "I don't even understand why sometimes, but I do know that you wouldn't have said it if you weren't sure."

He kissed her sweetly and then changed his tone. "So, he can puff his chest and act like he owns you, but I know the truth!"

His cocky, mischievous grin made her heart lurch. She wasn't always sure why, either. It was just meant to be.

They spent the afternoon sitting quietly on the back steps, holding hands and talking. When they heard Lily's voice raised in question over a green shirt, they hesitated, gave each other one final kiss, and parted ways. Holly walked back into the room with the shirt in hand.

"This one?" she asked, handing the shirt to Lily.

"Thanks; that's the one." Lily squeezed her hand affectionately, hating the pain she knew goodbyes caused them both.

Milo glanced around, obviously looking for Griffon and smiled with relief when he was nowhere around.

Griffon stood and stared at the empty space where Holly had just been standing and thanked God for the few precious hours they had together. Then he turned and walked away, knowing it would only raise questions if he were still hanging around.

She told him they would try to come to town one day a week and explained how they wanted to build strong relations with the people in the town. He smiled to himself, remembering how she had blushed over his eagerness to help build those relations. She agreed to meet him for one night at the cave in just two days time. He would not let his happiness darken with even a thought of Milo Weaver.

Once back at the compound, all were abuzz with the information they had found and the friendships they were beginning to forge. It had been a positive and uplifting day for all, and even the elders rejoiced in celebration. Perhaps the world hadn't changed as much as they feared.

Holly hugged her brother and thanked him with a quick kiss on the cheek. He raised an eyebrow and, without a word spoken, she knew he was asking if she had seen Griffon. She shook her head yes, and her smile lit up the room. Charlie had never seen her quite so at peace in the bunker, and he knew what they had done today was right and would lead to good things in their future.

* * * * *

Chapter 25

THE COMMUNITY relations task force team continued to go down to Wythel one day a week, every week throughout spring and well into summer. They watched carefully for signs of AMAN discourse that would signal someone was talking to them about those in the bunker, but there were none to be found.

The team eventually befriended the former mayor and police chief, who continued to be the dominant figures of authority for the people. Charlie put Milo in charge of those relations, which negated the previous buddy system.

This meant that Holly was free to see Griffon while in town and without so many watchful eyes, and they continued to meet at the cave from time to time as well. In town, they tried to hide their relationship as much as possible, but word gets around in a small town, and Griffon's interest in the outsider, Holly, was soon the talk of the town.

Milo was uncomfortable with the chatter but brushed it off as mere gossip. *So what if Griffon was interested in Holly? There was no way she could be interested in a guy like that. After all, everyone in the bunker knew that he and Holly were going to marry.*

Mike Jenkins had all but guaranteed Milo a fall wedding, despite the engagement break up. Holly was friendly with him again, and, while he was not pressuring her right now, he felt they were slowly growing close again. Everything seemed right on track.

He was busy establishing himself both in the bunker and in the town of Wythel. People respected him, and knew he would soon be able to give Holly the life she deserved. He told Emma Grace his plan, knowing this goal was consuming him. He was hurt that she had been distant and refused to talk to him since. He missed his friend greatly.

Emma Grace was more remote than ever, spending time alone in nature or stuck in a book in her room in the bunker. Rarely did anyone see her anymore. She was heartbroken. She had always held out hope that Milo would eventually see that she was the right woman for him. His confessions of love for Holly had been her final straw, and so she locked herself away from everyone, even him, and mourned the loss of what could have been.

Holly was always in the spotlight, whether in the bunker or in the town. She had befriended practically everyone and often spent more time in town than at the compound. When the rumors of her and Griffon finally hit Mike, he was furious. Milo tried to assure him that it was nothing more than rumor, but he would not have his little girl's name slandered like that.

When Holly came home late one night after one of her little getaways, Mike was up waiting.

"Holly, can I talk to you for a minute?"

"Sure dad. What's up? I didn't think you'd still be up this late."

"And I didn't think you'd be out so late," he scolded

She shrunk a bit. It angered her at how her dad's words could make her instantly feel like a small child again, no matter that she was a fully-grown woman.

"So what's up?" She felt tension in the air but was unsure why.

"Griffon Maynor" was all he said as he pursed his lips and stood, glaring over her.

"Griffon? What about him?" She tried to hide the defiance and need to protect him that she so strongly felt.

"Rumor has it that he's been courting you."

"So I've heard," she said, with complete conviction. She would not deny or agree with the statement and dared him to go on.

He saw it there in her face. An open book just as her mother always proclaimed. He lost before the battle began. However, he was a man of stubborn pride and pressed on just the same.

"I don't like it. I don't like hearing rumors of some heathen from town courting an engaged woman, especially my daughter. I won't stand for it!"

He was so loud; he woke her mother, who now stood at the door, sleepy-eyed, watching it all unfold. To her, and to Holly's own amazement, Holly did not fly off the handle with her own stubborn pride. She simply bit her lip, gathered her thoughts, and had her father second-guessing himself before she even opened her mouth.

"Number one... I am NOT an engaged woman, nor am I a practically engaged woman or even close to marriage in anyway, and most certainly not with Milo Weaver, despite your best efforts at meddling around in MY life."

"Number two... I am a fully grown woman, and I'm more than capable of making my own choices in life." She paused just a bit to let that one sink in.

"Number three... I do not appreciate you or anyone else spreading rumors regarding my relationships, or lack thereof, regarding any man, most particularly Griffon Maynor and Milo Weaver."

"So you admit that you know this Griffon fellow, and he's been courting you without my approval?!" Mike erupted.

She bit the inside of her cheek, closed her eyes, and said a quick prayer for patience.

"If Griffon Maynor wishes to court me, he does not need your approval. I am not a child, Dad. I am free to date whomever I want, when I want. You best remember that." With that said, she turned and walked away, shutting her door behind her.

Mike looked at his wife who was already scowling at him. He shook his head, "Well, now, I'm more confused than ever. Is she seeing the boy or not?" She rolled her eyes, closed the door, and went back to sleep, listening to him ramble on, "and she is still my child. Eighteen or not, she will always be my child. A woman? Ha! When did that happen? Why I never..."

* * * * *

Holly slept in late the next day. It was the day they all went to town, but after last night's argument with her dad, she wasn't in any hurry to get moving. She also knew that Griffon would be working all day, and she wouldn't have time to see him until late this evening. What she didn't know was that her father's meddling was just getting started.

Mike Jenkins awoke early, dressed in his best clothes, and headed down the mountain with his son to the town of Wythel. Charlie wasn't sure why his father was going today, but was happy to see him coming around. Mike was on a mission to find out as much as he could about one Griffon Maynor.

When they got into town, Charlie took him to the old courthouse where they would find the mayor, the sheriff, and other elders of the community. He introduced him to everyone, and Mike was cordial and polite, fitting in immediately, until Don Maynor walked in.

"Dad, this is Don Maynor, his family's been around these parts for some seven generations now. They are still upstanding pillars of this community."

"Maynor?" he asked accusingly while shaking the man's hand. "Is your boy Griffon Maynor?"

"My grandson actually," Don said proudly.

"I'm very concerned with the rumors going around regarding that boy and my daughter," Mike said frankly.

"Well," Don looked uncomfortably at Charlie, who just hung his head in embarrassment. "I'm not up on many rumors, sir. I find it best to leave that to the ladies."

"I'd like to meet this grandson of yours for myself," Mike said, completely unoffended.

"I'm not sure that's the smartest idea, but I don't fight Griffon's battles for him. He's working today. We'll take my truck."

"Much obliged, Don. I have a hell of a time keeping after my Holly. She's too stubborn for her own good and doesn't have a clue what's best for her. She doesn't understand how rumors such as this can cause problems for a young lady, especially one already spoken for."

"Spoken for?"

"Oh yes. Holly is to be married to Milo Weaver. I'm sure you've met Milo. Now THAT is an upstanding young man."

"I have met Milo, and I agree that he is an upstanding young man but I've also met Holly. She's a smart, brave girl. She saved my great grandbabies once. My family's quite fond of that girl and quite protective of her, too. The Holly I know has a good strong head on her shoulders and knows her heart and mind better than most twice her age. Now I don't normally meddle in the affairs of our young people, but if my Griffon's wronged her is some way, I will gladly step in and talk to him."

Mike was stunned. He didn't know all that about Holly. *She saved some kids? From what? How? This man seems awfully close to her. How was that possible after only a few weeks?* He had a thousand questions going through his mind, but snapped back to reality when the truck stopped and Don jumped out. Mike followed suit.

They promoted Griffon after the previous foreman caught ill during the winter and passed away. He oversaw logging. Today, one of the new young guys, whose name Griffon didn't know, yet, was climbing and got stuck. Fortunately, he remembered to anchor himself and was currently dangling some one hundred and fifty feet in the air off that anchor alone. Griffon didn't trust anyone else to go up and get him. He knew that he had to do it himself.

When Don and Mike arrived on site, Griffon had just a few feet left to climb to reach the kid. He was able to right him quickly but it took another hour to talk to him down. Griffon just sat up there with him with all the patience of a saint until they finally began a slow descent back down.

For nearly two hours, Don and Mike watched him from below. People came and went, stopping occasionally to talk to Don.

"He ain't trust no one of us to get that kid down safe and sound."

"I'd have cut him down before sitting up there like that for all this time. Man's got the patience of a saint!"

"Best thing they did was promote him to foreman. We all know he has our back. Heck, he probably don't even yet know that noob's name, but he's one of Griff's boys and that's all that matters."

"He'd do the same for any of us, and God knows, we'd do it for him!"

Mike couldn't help but find himself conflicted while watching this brave man rescue a boy he didn't even know but felt responsible for saving. Hearing the words of his crew painted a very different picture than the one he had conjured up of Griffon Maynor.

Don sensed the change in Mike's attitude. "I understand you're a father worried about your little girl, and I don't know much about Milo Weaver, aside from he seems like a good young man in the few times we've met, but that grandson of mine, well it just don't get much better than my Griff. What I do know is that Griff is fiercely in love with that daughter of yours and, from what I've seen, I'd say it's not one-sided. Maybe you should talk to Holly."

His words were like a punch in the gut. *Holly's in love?* "I've tried. She's determined to shut me out." Hearing his own words caused him unbearable pain.

"Holly's a good girl. You've done raised her right. She has a good head on her shoulders, but I see the stubbornness in you, and I clearly recognize it in that child who has cloned temper. So maybe you should try really talking to her."

He nodded and was about to turn to leave, knowing he was wrong to come here, when Don said, "Hold up a second. Griff, come on over here. I want you to meet someone."

Griff was shaking hands and receiving claps on the back as he made his way over.

"Hey Gramps, what brings you out here today?"

"Griffon, I want you to meet someone. This is Mike Jenkins, Holly's dad."

Griffon paused in shock for a second. He dusted off his clothes nervously and ran a hand through his hair as best as he could before shaking the man's hand.

"Mr. Jenkins. It's nice to meet you." He said glancing over at his grandfather with questioning eyes.

"Griffon. It's nice to put a face to the name. My children have spoken a great deal about you." He eyed up the young man in front of him. *Can Holly really be in love with this man?* His heart told him it was possible, and he surprised himself by offering an invitation he hadn't meant to offer. "You know, we are harvesting strawberries tomorrow. If you aren't busy, why don't you come on up and give us a hand. We'll have a celebration afterward. Bring your family."

"Thanks Mr. Jenkins. I'm off tomorrow and would love that." He hesitated slightly. "You're sure?"

Smart boy, Mike thought, and laughed in spite of himself. "Yes, I'm sure."

"Alright then, just tell me where and when, and I'll be there."

Mike purposefully did not give a time or location. Something told him he already knew their whereabouts and was pleased to be wrong. "Can you read a map if I give you some coordinates?"

"Yes sir."

"Okay then." Mike reached in his pocket, pulled out a piece of paper and a pen, and jotted down the coordinates, which were just slightly off.

"Thank you sir, I'll see you tomorrow." Griffon shook hands with Mike, then hugged his grandfather and scurried off to work.

"Thanks Mike. I know that must have been hard for you, but I don't think you'll regret it."

"We'll see," he replied. "We'll see."

* * * * *

Charlie met his father back at the courthouse, and Mike was busy discussing some security issues with the sheriff. Don Maynor pulled Charlie to the side for a little talk.

"Not sure what's going on. Your father was steaming upset with Griffon when he got here. Against my better judgment, I took him on out to meet him. There was an incident up at the trees, and I think watching Griff in action softened him some. In the end, your dad invited him strawberry picking and to a harvest celebration tomorrow. Give Holly a heads up, will ya? I'm not real sure what your old man has up his sleeves. One minute he's spouting off about how Holly's engaged to that Milo kid. Next, he's offering invites to Griff up to your compound. I dunno, but I don't have a good feeling about it."

"Yea, doesn't sound real good, whatever he's up to. Thanks for the heads up, Don."

They shook hands, and Charlie went to break up Mike and the sheriff so they could head back up before dark.

On the way up the mountain Charlie asked, "So, did you really invite Griffon up to the compound tomorrow?"

"Yeah. Is that okay with you?"

"Yes sir."

Charlie was quiet on the way back; so was Mike. Both men were deep in thought over Holly.

As soon as they got back to the bunker, Charlie ran off to wash up and find his sister before dinner. She was hanging in the gym, playing basketball with Milo. Mike was already at the doorway watching them, too.

"Tell me Charlie, what do you think of Milo and Holly?"

"I dunno dad. I like Milo just fine, but I don't' think Holly loves him. I don't think pushing marriage on her is going to help her fall in love, if that's what you're after." The words were out before Charlie could bite his tongue. He immediately regretted it, but his father didn't look angry, just deep in thought.

"And what do you make of this Griffon Maynor?"

"He's a stand up guy. Reliable. Solid. I really like him, dad."

"And your sister? Does she really like him, too?"

"That's not my place to say. You want to know how Holly feels about either of them, you're going to have to ask her yourself."

He shook his head in agreement. "I know that son, but as her big brother, your job is to look after her. I've been hearing rumors coming back that she's seeing this Griffon guy. Milo says not to worry, that it's nothing. Do I need to be worried?"

"I suppose that depends on what you're worried about." He clapped his dad on the shoulder and left him to think about that.

"Got room for one more?" Charlie asked Milo and Holly.

"Sure big guy. What ya got for me today?" She taunted him.

Milo laughed. "I'm out. She's kicking my butt! Maybe you'll have better luck. See ya later Holly."

"Bye Milo."

Charlie looked back at the doorway and noticed their father was no longer standing there. He walked to the doorway and looked around, and no one was in sight.

"Paranoid much? What's going on?"

"Dad got wind of you and Griffon somehow. Don told me he invited him up tomorrow for our strawberry festival."

"Griffon's coming here, to the bunker? Tomorrow? Did he meet dad?"

"Yeah, I think so, Hols."

"Well if he invited him up here, it must have gone okay, right?"

"I dunno what he's up to, but he's going to be watching you like a hawk, that's for sure. He's still spreading those wedding rumors, too."

"I know, and I think Milo is starting to take them seriously. He mentioned something about things being different after this fall. Ugh! What am I going to do? I've already told him no. Why won't he listen?"

"I dunno but I feel like tomorrow is some sort of test, so watch your back. I'll warn Griff when he gets here. I've already changed the schedule to make sure I'm on watch around the time he should be arriving."

"What am I supposed to do Charlie? Do I just tell him? I feel like he'll lock me away forever if he knows. Do I pretend to be uninterested? Just tell me what to do?"

"I can't tell you that Hols, you know that. I'm on your side, whatever you decide to do. I like Griff, you know that, right?"

"Yeah, I know you're okay with us. I'm just not sure dad ever will be."

He hugged his sister. "Who knows what tomorrow will bring!"

* * * * *

She didn't sleep well again. She tossed and turned much of the night worrying about the next day. By 4:00 a.m., she gave up on sleep altogether. She found her dad sitting in the main living room.

"What's wrong dad? Can't sleep?"

He jumped. He hadn't heard her come in.

"Yeah, can't sleep. You, too?"

"Yup."

"I've been doing a lot of thinking the last few hours. You know that I love you with all my heart, right? And I only want the best for you."

She nodded.

"I also want you to be happy, baby girl. That's all I ever want, especially in the crazy screwed up world we live in."

Her heart soared. He was really going to be okay with it after all!

"I know that Milo will make you a good husband. He will give you babies, take care of you, and make you very happy. I know that he has already asked for your hand. Why do you continue to turn him down?"

Her heart sunk. He didn't understand her at all, and he was never going to change.

"Dad, I don't love Milo. I've tried; God knows I have. I've tried to make you and everyone else happy. I like him a lot. He's a sweet guy, but I don't love him."

"Sweetie, you're too young to know what love is. Love is solid, stable, and safe. It's warm and comforting. Is that not Milo for you?"

"Daddy, love is also thrilling and exciting... it's knowing that you can face the world with anything it throws your way. It's acceptance and understanding and knowing exactly who you are and who they are and accepting it unconditionally."

"Sweetheart, you read too many of your mother's books! That's not the real world."

She sighed, knowing it could be.

* * * * *

Chapter 26

M ORNING CAME and went; Holly was tired and grumpy
with everyone. Charlie went off to stand watch before
she could tell him anything. She did not know what today
would bring but knew she wasn't looking forward to it.

When it came time to go out to the garden for strawberry
picking, she hung behind. She showered and dressed in a
cute flowered sundress. This was going to be one awkward
afternoon. She might as well look pretty in the spotlight.
Feeling angry and rebellious, she walked out to join the
others. Not to anyone's surprise, she was paired up in a
group with Milo. Fortunately, Chris and Cassie were also
there, and Charlie would be joining them soon.

Just great, she thought.

When Charlie arrived, he had Griffon with him. Her
father's face dropped. Holly could overhear part of the conversation, something about finding him wandering through
the woods as the coordinates he gave were to the water hole
and not to the strawberry patch.

Her father feigned embarrassment but she was on to him
and knew it was the first test. He wanted to know if Griffon
already knew their area. *Well, at least that backfired on him,*
she thought.

Charlie invited Griffon over to their group. Perfect. Once
again stuck in the middle of Griffon and Milo.

Griffon said hello to everyone and even shook hands with
Milo. You could cut the tension with a knife. Most people

seemed not to notice but it was hard to ignore the tension in the air.

He politely said hello to Holly, too. He wanted her to run into his arms and shout her love for him before them all, but he knew today would not be that day.

They worked side-by-side with little conversation. Milo on her left, Griffon on her right. Both jumped to assist when she tripped over a rock and stumbled. Both grabbed a sandwich for her when they broke for lunch. They seemed to one up each other all day.

When they had picked all the strawberries, and it was time to head in, they both reached for her bucket at the same time and knocked it over. Strawberries went everywhere, and as they scrambled to pick them up, they began arguing over who was picking up more.

Holly sat down on the ground, picked up a handful of strawberries in each hand, and chucked them at both men.

"Hey!" they said in unison.

"What's that for?" Milo asked.

"Yeah, what's with you today, Holly?" Griffon asked.

"I am sick and tired of all of this. I am tired of my father playing with my life. I am tired of you," pointing to Milo, "not taking no for an answer and not seeing what you have right in front of you. You're an idiot, Milo Weaver, for listening to my father. I am not marrying you. I have told you no once already and that isn't changing. I infuriate you. I know I do. I can see it all over your face. How many years do you think you can just bite your tongue with me just to please my father, before you explode? Emma Grace looked lovely and completely miserable today, while you fumbled around like a bumbling idiot trying to one up this guy."

"She loves you Milo. Why are you too pigheaded to admit that you love her, too?"

He froze. "Who told you that?"

"No one told me. I have eyes and can see plain and clear."

"I've never told anyone that, not even her."

"Ya think! Why are you so quick to make her life so miserable? She loves you, too, you know. Although why, after the way you've treated her, is beyond me. But she does."

He sat down. "Do you really think so?"

She rolled her eyes. "You're incorrigible and pigheaded! Go to her!"

"But your father. He already has a fall wedding planned for us. It's a done deal." He looked miserable.

"Yes, I have heard the rumors." She laughed. "I don't care what my father thinks he's doing. I do not love you as a wife should love a husband."

"I know that. If it wasn't for this idiot," pointing to Griffon, "maybe you could." He sounded hopeful.

"No Milo, I couldn't. You're a good friend and I've enjoyed our time together, but it's not the same. I don't want the love of peace and comfort that my father envisions. I want passion and excitement, understanding and acceptance. It wouldn't matter if Griffon was here or not, it still wouldn't be enough for me."

"And you do love him, don't you Holly. Really love him?"

"Yes I do."

Griffon's face lit up, and his grin spread from ear to ear. Holly chunked another strawberry at him. "We'll talk next. You aren't going to be any happier with me when we're done," she said seriously. He didn't like the sound of that at all.

"It's okay Holly, and you're right. I don't love you. I am in love with Emma Grace, I've just never let my dad, or yours, down on anything, and I feel like I am giving up on you."

"You can't live for them, Milo. You have to be the man you were meant to be, not the man they dream you'll be."

"Thanks, Holly." With that, he leaned in, hugged her, gave a quick wink to Griffon, and kissed her hard on the mouth.

She shook her head. "Incorrigible! And you," pointing to Griffon, "calm down. He's just trying to goad you. Now it's your turn." She motioned him over. "Look, my family means the world to me, and while I agree with every word I just told him about living life for yourself, I'm not brave enough to follow through with it. Just the thought of us being together is tearing my dad up. He's not sleeping, he's barely eating because he's stressed about what we may or may not be doing. If I choose you, it would be over him, and I can't Griffon, I just can't. I love you; you know that. That hasn't changed. But I can't do this to him. I don't have the strength."

She shook visibly, holding back the tears.

"Honey, don't please, don't cry." He held her close to him, and she couldn't keep the tears from flowing.

"I have to say goodbye to you. I won't be back down in the village. I just can't see you every week and feel this pain repeatedly. It's time you went home, Griffon."

She stood up and tried to walk away.

"Like hell!" He said and grabbed her arm, turning her toward him. He kissed her with every ounce of his being. "I won't lose you Holly, I can't! You're dad will come around. We'll make this work, I promise."

He was begging now. She took a step back. Her eyes were distant, as if she were already gone. She shook her head. "I'm sorry, Griffon. Goodbye!" She turned and ran off straight for the cave. She needed to be alone.

* * * * *

Charlie came back to the strawberry patch looking for Holly and Griffon. He was all smiles and laughing until he saw Griffon's face.

"Griff, what's wrong? Where's Holly?"

"She's gone Charlie. I've lost her."

"What are you talking about? Don't be ridiculous. Milo is out of the picture now. He just walked in and, out of nowhere, got down on one knee and proposed to Emma Grace. Emma Grace! Can you even believe it? She actually said yes! Everyone's inside celebrating. You and Holly should be, most of all."

"You aren't listening, Charlie," he said in a stone cold voice. "She's gone. She won't see me again. She made that clear."

His voice was cracking, and he was about to lose it. He had to get away.

"Wait!" Charlie said. "Tell me what happened."

"After she lectured Milo and told him that she's never going to marry him and he's an idiot for not telling Emma Grace how he feels about her, she broke up with me. Said she couldn't choose me over her father and family and it was over. Then she just ran off."

"She didn't come back inside."

"She's probably at the cave."

"What cave?"

"It's her special spot. It's our special spot." He looked in pain as he said it. "Look, I have to go." He turned and headed back down the mountain.

Charlie stood in disbelief. *Where is the cave?* he wondered. He needed to find his sister. For over an hour, he searched the area that he thought she headed when she needed her alone time. If Griffon knew where she went, why didn't he go after her? Charlie was angry with them both.

Just then, there was a strange noise echoing off the mountains. Birds filled the sky, and Charlie's stomach hit his throat. He was certain it was a gunshot. Another sounded, then another. He was certain there was gunfire in the area.

He headed for the closest lookout to get a report. Shots fired on the outskirts of town near or at the Maynor farmhouse. Charlie was in shock but immediately headed down the mountain to check on his friends.

The lookout signaled him to get down. There was movement in the woods not one hundred yards away, and it was too dark to tell if they were friendly or hostile. Whoever it was, they were moving fast and not concerned with being discreet. Charlie hid behind the tree, held his breath, and waited for an all clear. He had to see what happened.

He heard a gun click from the stand above him.

"That's far enough. State your business," said the sentry above.

"Fred Maynor and family. It's Griffon. He's been shot."

There was a flurry of activity, and Charlie came out of cover to meet them.

"How could he be so stupid?" Charlie asked aloud before he could stop himself. He knew Griffon was upset but didn't think he'd do anything this stupid.

"AMAN," said Lily. "We didn't know what to do or where to go. They have our doctor under guard, just waiting for him to show up for help. I don't know what they want, but it was clear they came for him. They had us under house arrest for hours before he arrived. He just went nuts and fought back as if he had a death wish or something. I've never seen him like that before."

She was talking fast and without conscious thought. She was in shock. They all were. Charlie had to stop and think. They had to be smart about this. Even a half-decent hunter could track the mess they made coming up here so far. Charlie was numb and acted on survival instinct. He quickly formulated a plan in his head that just might work.

"You, up top... throw down your field kit and poncho."

"Yes sir," returned the sentry, who immediately produced both.

"Okay, we need to keep moving back in the direction you came. You've trampled a lot of underbrush already so unfortunately we're going to have to do more of the same to throw them off."

As he talked, Charlie was already digging into the field kit and tending to Griffon's wound. Griffon moaned at his touch but was unresponsive overall. There was a lot of blood.

"We need to move him away from here. There's a clearing not too far. We can lay him down there, and we'll be far enough away to keep our lookout safe."

They worked together to move him. Once at the clearing, Charlie opened Griffon's shirt to examine the wound. Lily held a flashlight in her shaking hands, so he could see.

"It's worse than I thought," Charlie said. "He's losing a lot of blood. We need to move fast."

He cleaned the area, noting that the bullet did not exit his body. He dressed the wound as best he could but he was bleeding through faster than Charlie could apply clean gauze. He ripped a large piece of Griffon's shirt and managed to tighten it around his shoulder, across where the bullet entered.

"That should keep some pressure on it, but it's not going to hold long."

He listened carefully but didn't hear any gurgling or struggling to breathe.

"I don't think it punctured his lung. That's good news, but we need to try to keep him as still as possible while we move. The bullet is lodged in there and could shift to cause further damage. Help me wrap him in this poncho. Hopefully, it'll keep any more blood from dripping and giving away our location."

Once they secured the poncho around him, Charlie gave instructions for most of the group to trample back toward the farmhouse, get out of the woods, follow the tree line down to the old riverbed, and come up that way. He kept Fred and Don with him to help move Griffon.

"We have to be very careful now. We cannot leave a trail for the AMAN to follow. Help me lift him and follow exactly."

* * * * *

They made their way back to the lookout and had the sentry call for someone to meet the others at the old riverbed and escort them up. Charlie then led Fred and Don, with Griffon, up the mountain, using a virtually undetectable path frequented between the bunker and lookout point.

Once in the bunker, Charlie left them to run ahead for Doc. Although it was late, everyone was still up celebrating in the common room. He ran in and grabbed Doc. There was much commotion as everyone searched for answers.

They moved Griffon into the infirmary and laid him on the table. He was still and looked lifeless and pale.

Doc quickly set to work to find the extent of damage. He removed the poncho, now pooled with blood, saw the makeshift dressing, and cut it away to get to the injury. Even while he worked with great concentration and thought, he commended Charlie for an excellent field dressing.

"If this boy survives the night, it'll be thanks to you, lad."

Once he cleaned Griffon's wounds and a put a compression in place to stall the blood flow, Doc checked his vitals.

"His blood pressure is dangerously low. He's lost a lot of blood. Go see if anyone knows his blood type."

Charlie ran out to ask and was relieved to hear it was O+. Most in the bunker were O+, and they all donated regularly to prepare for a need such as this.

"Wonderful!" Doc exclaimed and set to work, starting a line for transfusion, an IV for fluids, and a morphine drip.

"That bullet's gonna have to be removed but we need to stabilize him some or I'll for sure kill him trying."

Charlie left the room to check on the others. As he rounded the corner, he met his dad face-to-face.

"Are you crazy? Have you lost your mind? What the hell were you thinking, bringing these people here?"

"Dad, it's Griffon! What did you want me to do, just let him die? What about Holly?"

"This has nothing to do with your sister! Nothing! You've put us all in grave danger."

"These people are our friends, and they're in danger. We will give them asylum here, and you'll have to kill me to stop it!"

For the first time, Charlie noticed they were not alone in the hallway. Everyone was silent but clearly listening.

Mike had never heard Charlie speak with such authority. Normally, the stubborn side of him would have backhanded the boy for having the audacity to challenge him in front of everyone like this but he just stood there in stunned silence.

Charlie was the class clown that no one took seriously, but this man before him commanded respect. For the first time in his life, Mike seriously looked at his son and saw a true leader stepping up and controlling a bad situation.

"Okay son. Okay. If this is what you feel is best." He clapped his hand on his son's shoulder and gave a squeeze before walking away, nodding his approval.

Those around stared with shocked curiosity. Charlie hesitated only a minute in disbelief of what had just transpired. Then he shouted orders to whoever was around. Within an hour, they had the entire Maynor family comfortably set up across two pods. After updating the family on Griffon's status, Charlie gave them a quick tour, introduced them to those they hadn't met before, and left them to settle in for the night.

It's been one hell of day, Charlie thought, wondering, again, *where could Holly possibly be through all of this?*

* * * * *

Chapter 27

WHEN HOLLY left the strawberry patch and walked out on Griffon, she felt numb and lost. Her instincts took her to the cave, which had always been a safe haven for her. She sat emotionless, staring out into the beautiful valley below with no thoughts or feelings. She slept restlessly in the cave that night.

When she awoke, the excruciating pain of the events from the day before flooded her. She felt pained from the absence of Griffon in their special place. It was no longer hers, it was theirs, and she knew immediately that she had been wrong to come here.

For three days, she clung to that pain and emptiness. She knew she had done the right thing with her sacrifice, but was not ready to move on with life, so she sat and embraced the loneliness that she would have to learn to live with.

Her stomach growled. She couldn't remember with certainty when she had last eaten, but the stabs of hunger in her stomach told her it had been too long. She got up and was surprised to find her body stiff. How long had she been sitting there wallowing in her own self-sacrificing self-hatred?

She stretched her legs and looked around in search of food. All she could find was a can of Spaghetti O's, which she opened and ate cold before heading to the spring for water.

* * * * *

Griffon was shot three days earlier, yet he remained still and lifeless, although his vitals were improving a little more each day. Doc was optimistic that surgery would be possible by the end of the week. In the meantime, he kept Griffon heavily sedated on morphine.

Charlie was getting more frantic by the day. Where was Holly? He went out daily and searched for her, without a single sign of her existence anywhere. The bunker was on lock down. No one was to be out of the compound without just cause, though Charlie refused to follow those orders, disguising them under the pretense of patrolling the area. They started a rotation to staff the doors and monitor the video 24/7. The fear of the AMAN was great now.

Most of the Maynor's were settling in nicely. They found things they enjoyed and helped around the compound but Amos was used to working outdoors, and three days stuck inside was enough to drive a man like him mad. He begged Charlie to let him go on patrol with him, and Charlie finally consented.

Once out of the bunker, Charlie headed back toward the rocky side of the mountain. He called out to Holly as he had every day, and just like every other day, he received no response. Amos watched, realizing what he was doing.

"You don't think anything happened to her, do you?"

"I dunno, Amos. Judging by Griffon, I'd say she was probably pretty messed up when she took off. She's gone off on her own for days at a time before. I'm sure she's fine and will come back eventually, but, man, I just need to find her. She'll want to know about Griffon, ya know?"

"Any idea where she would run off to?"

"I honestly do not know! It's driving me crazy. Griffon mentioned something about a cave, but I'll be damned if I can find it."

"A cave?" Amos lit up. "You mean where she used to meet Griffon up here?"

"Yeah, that's the one. You don't know where it is, do you?"

"Well sorta. I ain't never been up there, but I can show you the entrance Griff uses. If you have some climbing gear, we can get up there. I'm not sure where he keeps his."

Amos led him down the mountain instead of up and over toward the rocky terrain that was nearly impossible to maneuver. He stopped and pointed up.

"See that opening way up there?"

Charlie nodded.

"That's it. That's their cave."

"How the hell did they ever find that? There must be another way in, Holly would never be able to make it up there with all the stuff she's drug out over the years."

"I dunno. But that's how Griff gets in."

"Holly! Holly!" Charlie began to yell and Amos joined in.

There was not a sound.

"Here, help me find a rock. We'll tie a note to it and throw it up there. If she is up there, maybe she'll see it. Thanks man, at least it's something. I feel so damn helpless."

It took several tries but eventually, the rock sailed perfectly into the big hole in the side of the rocks. Content with that, they headed back to the bunker.

When Holly arrived back at the main cave, from the cool mountain spring where she had showered and refreshed, she stumbled over a rock. It took her by surprise, as she generally knew every rock, stalagmite, and uneven spacing in the cave. She picked it up to toss it out and saw a note tied to it.

"Holly, come home. RED."

Holly's heart skipped a beat. *Red??* That was her dad's code for extreme danger. She began to panic, and fear set in. *What the heck happened? What's going on?* She could never live with herself if something had happened to her family while she sat and wallowed in self-pity, hiding away from everyone. She got to her feet quickly and headed for the bunker.

* * * * *

When she arrived at the bunker, they had shut the door. She moved to open it and found it locked. She began to panic again and took two big breaths.

Think, Holly, she told herself.

She remembered the video camera that guarded the door, which she had so carefully bypassed for years. She moved to it now and waved. A moment later, she heard a click and finally breathed, not realizing that she had been holding her breath. Colton Evers was manning the doors.

"Sweetheart, where have you been? The whole place has been frantic worrying about you!"

"I'm fine. What's going on? I got a RED alert. Why is the door locked?"

She was asking a thousand questions at once, knowing she wasn't giving him time to answer.

"Calm down, girlie. That was probably Charlie sending you that RED. We've had an incident. I'm going to let him tell you about it. It's not my place."

Colton got on his radio and dialed in for Charlie.

She headed for her pod to wait for him. She didn't pass anyone, and Charlie wasn't in the pod when she got there. It was several long moments before he appeared in the doorway. He ran to her and swept her up in his arms.

"Don't EVER do that to me again! Where have you been? We've all been worried sick."

She apologized and told him about the talk she had with Milo and Griffon before disappearing.

"I just needed some time alone, Charlie. I'm sorry. Now, what's all this RED business? Was that you leaving me that note? How did you find me? It better not be to get me to come home!"

He paused and hugged her again. "I don't even know how to tell you this." He ran his hands through his hair trying to formulate the words when their father walked in.

"Holly!" He ran to her side and hugged her close. "I'm so sorry about Griffon, baby."

Her entire body went stiff, and her eyes darted to her brother's. She saw immediately that something was terribly wrong.

"Wh... what happened to Griffon?"

Her father looked at Charlie and an exchange occurred that only frightened her more.

"Charlie, tell me! What's happened to Griffon?!"

Mike looked at his baby girl and saw a young woman in her place. He knew with certainty, now, that she loved Griffon, and it pained him deeply to tell her the news.

He glanced at Charlie, who stood frozen and unable to help.

Mike took her by the arm and led her out the door and down the hallway, patting her with reassurance. She trembled and shook her head, fearing the worst. They stopped outside the infirmary door.

"Baby girl, it's bad. I'm so sorry. Griffon's been shot."

Her world crumbled in that moment. It couldn't be. What kind of game were they playing? Her father didn't even like Griffon. Why were they doing this to her? She turned, opened the door, and forced her feet to move forward. She felt dazed, as if she were watching someone else run to Griffon's bedside and collapse in tears over his still, pale body. She must be watching someone else scream while two men held her tight.

They tried to get her to leave, but she would not. She sat there holding his hand and consoling herself as much as him. He was cold and unresponsive, much the same as she felt on the inside. Days and nights blurred together. It was never easy to keep time in the bunker but, in this instance, there was no concept of time at all. Time just stood still.

The day came when Doc was ready to attempt the removal of the bullet but Holly refused to leave his side.

Lily came in to talk to her.

"Holly? Honey, you can't just sit in here day in and day out. It's not healthy."

As she had been since she arrived at his side, she remained unresponsive with a distant look in her eyes.

Lily had enough.

"Holly!" she yelled. "Get up! You stink. You are not helping him like this. You need a shower, food, and a swift kick in the rear!"

Holly looked up, and the fog lifted slightly from her eyes. Lily took her by the arm, yanked her up, and forced her out the door. She only mildly resisted. Lily took her back to her pod, started a shower, and shoved the girl in, clothes and all.

The cold water jolted her back to reality.

"What the... ? It's COLD!"

"Good! Maybe it'll knock some sense into you."

Holly warmed the water, undressed, and stood under the faucet, letting the warmth spread over her. She started to cry for the first time and sank to the floor of the shower. The sobs came harder, the tears flowed faster, and she was consumed with guilt and grief she had held in for too long.

Lily stayed nearby. It broke her heart to see her friend in this condition.

"It's my fault. It's all my fault! I wasn't strong enough to stay with him. I couldn't choose him over my family. I hurt him. If I hadn't, Lily, he'd still be here with us. It's all my fault! He should have been here at the bunker, celebrating, with me by his side. I devastated him, then sent him to his death. I can never face him again. It's all my fault!"

The guilt was all-consuming. Lily's heart ached. No one knew exactly what happened between Holly and Griffon before the accident but Lily knew, in her heart, that she was right. He had a death wish. He wouldn't have wanted to live without this woman in his life but what happened was not Holly's fault.

"Just let it all out, Holly. I'm here, I'm listening, and it's not your fault. It's not. This is the AMAN's fault, and whether he had stayed and celebrated with you or left and come home an hour earlier, it wouldn't have mattered.

They were there for him, Holly. They came for him. We don't even know why. They kept us captive for hours just waiting for him, and they would have waited for hours more, so this is not your fault. It's terrible, and we're all upset, angry, and feeling guilty. But this is not your fault, and you can't keep blaming yourself."

* * * * *

Holly finally composed herself enough to stand up. She finished bathing, letting the soap and water cleanse her body and her soul. When she was done, dry, and dressed, she hugged Lily.

"Thanks!" was all she could muster. They hugged each other for a long time.

"I should probably get back to Griffon now."

"Not so fast!" I'm happy to have you somewhat back. That catatonic Holly was scaring us all. Next, you eat."

"I can eat in the infirmary."

Lily hesitated. "No Holly, you can't. I didn't just get you out of there for your own good. Doc's doing surgery to remove the bullet today. You can't go back in until he's done."

"What?? Why didn't you tell me? I should be there."

"No, you shouldn't. You're in no condition to be of any help. Come on, let's get you some food. You've lost too much weight already. You look like crap!"

She laughed. "Thanks a lot!"

Just walking to the kitchen, Holly was surprised at how weak she felt and knew Lily was right. She ate as much as she could physically get down. Her mother, Cassie, and Mrs. Worthington came in and fussed over her, thanking Lily for bringing her back to life. They spent the afternoon in the family room as others came and went, stopped to talk, and checked on her. Everyone was waiting for word of Griffon's surgery.

* * * * *

Doc did not have access to an x-ray machine to see the details and extent of damage the bullet had caused. He would have to cut and open him up blindly to see what he was dealing with. Emma Grace had been studying under him for months now but had never assisted in a surgery before today. They were both in uncharted territory, making the best of a bad situation.

It took six hours and two blood transfusions to get through the surgery. In the end, Doc removed the bullet and stitched several internal tears to control the blood loss he was still experiencing. Overall, it was a successful operation, and Doc was pleased with the damage assessment.

They hadn't hit any vital organs, and his heart and lungs were untouched. His clavicle was partially shattered from the impact of the bullet, and they cleaned up that mess as best they could. It would take weeks still for him to heal but Doc was now optimistic that he would survive. With the surgery over, he lessened the morphine dose in hopes that Griffon would soon be conscious.

Doc and Emma Grace looked exhausted when they entered the common room. Many were there waiting for news and keeping Holly company. Doc was pleased to see her up and around, and she had some color back in her cheeks. He smiled and nodded his head.

"He's not out of the woods entirely, but thanks to the help of my wonderful assistant," he smiled at Emma Grace, "I am optimistic that Griffon will make a full recovery."

Cheers went up in the room. Someone broke into the sparkling cider and passed glasses all around. Doc accepted one with thanks. It had been a long day.

Somewhere in the midst of the celebration, Holly disappeared. She wandered down the hall and made her way back to the infirmary. She entered the dimly lit room without turning on the lights, went to his side, leaned over, and kissed his forehead lightly. He stirred and moaned softly.

"Shhhh," she said, knowing he really couldn't hear her. "I'm sorry for what I said last week. I'm sorry for the way I behaved. I'm going to be stronger for you. We're going to make it through this. I love you!"

She was holding his hand and her head was down. Somewhere in the middle of her talk to herself, Griffon opened his eyes. The world around him was fuzzy, and he couldn't make out his surroundings.

There was a soft glowing light above his head, and his right shoulder felt on fire but he was too surprised to acknowledge it. He had images of lights flashing and of Holly watching over him. He was certain that he was dead. *Could this be heaven?*

As his eyes began to focus, his ears began to waken. He hadn't realized how quiet everything was. He heard Holly's sweet voice and knew he was either dreaming or dead. *Did she just say she loved me? If only it was enough.* His entire body cringed as memories of their last night together hit him like a ton of bricks.

She felt his body jolt and looked up.

"Griffon?" she spoke softly. "Griffon, can you hear me?"

He looked dazed and confused.

"Holly?" he tried to say. His voice sounded hoarse, and his throat burned. He tried to sit up, and pain seared through him like fire.

"Don't move. Let me get Doc."

She started to get up but he held her hand tightly. His strength surprised her.

"Holly? Is it really you?"

"Yes, shhh. Try not to move. I need to get Doc."

"Where am I?" he continued, as if he hadn't heard her.

"You're in the infirmary. Do you remember anything?"

He shook his head, and the room blurred again as pain shot through his head.

"Ouch; that hurts."

"What hurts?"

"My head, my... everything."

"I'll be right back." Before he could stop her again, she ran from the room.

* * * * *

Griffon tried to move his head to look around, but his neck was too stiff and sore. Everything hurt, and the fire in his shoulder intensified. He closed his eyes again and just lay there wondering where Holly had gone.

When Doc and Holly returned, Griffon's eyes were closed, and he looked once again unresponsive. Holly went to his side.

"Griffon?"

He didn't answer.

"Griffon?" she said, again.

This time he stirred and moaned.

"Griffon, I have Doc here. He's needs to talk to you."

He moaned again but this time, he opened his eyes.

"Remarkable!" exclaimed Doc. "My bet was on another day or even two, before you'd surface. You are one tough lad. Now, how do you feel?"

"Hurt. Everywhere. Burning." He tried to move his left arm to point to his right shoulder and found it tangled with the various IV lines running them it.

"Now, now, don't try to move just yet. You've been through a lot this week."

"Week? What do you mean, this week?"

"Well, tell me what you remember, lad." Doc said sweetly.

Griffon shut his eyes and tried to think.

"Holly and I got into a fight, and she ran off. I was mad and headed home early." He scrunched up his brow and tried to recall. Holly felt a sharp stab of guilt over his last memories. "My family!"

He tried to sit up, but Doc held him back down. "My family! The AMAN were holding them prisoner. We fought. We fought and... I can't remember anything after that.

"Let me up. I have to go. I have to make sure they're okay. A week? Have I been out that long? What's happened to them?"

He looked so scared, it made Holly's eyes burn with fresh tears.

"Shhh," she said. "It's okay. They are fine. Everyone's here, safe and sound. You're in the bunker, remember?"

Her fingers trailed down the side of his face and she ran a hand through his matted hair. "It's okay now. They are fine, and you are going to be fine, too."

Her touch and soothing voice calmed him, and his eyes drifted shut again.

Doc noted the calming affect Holly had on the boy and decided it best if he go and alert the family himself.

"Stay with him, lass, in case he wakes again. He'll be in and out like this for a while yet. I'll go fetch the family."

Griffon moaned. "I'm still here." It was all he could say before the darkness took over once again.

When he awoke next, Holly was the first thing he saw. He smiled and tried to reach a hand to her. Pain stabbed him again but she instinctively knew what he wanted, and her hand was in his almost immediately. He tried to look around. This time, his head didn't hurt as much.

"Doc upped your pain meds some to help with that," she said, as if reading his thoughts.

* * * * *

"Griff?" Lily said. "Hey, it's Lily. How are you feeling?"

"Not sure yet," he replied noting again how dry his throat felt. "Water?" he asked.

Holly picked up her water bottle. It had a straw on top, so she placed it in his mouth, and he sipped happily. The cool refreshing sensation in his throat was heavenly.

"Thanks," he smiled. "Better."

"Is everyone okay? The AMAN. What happened? No one told me about the AMAN."

"They were waiting for you. We don't know why. There was a fight, and they shot you."

His eyes flew open. He tried to sit up as pain burned through his right arm.

"Settle down," Holly soothed once more. "It's all okay now. Everyone's fine. Charlie moved them all up here to be with you and keep them safe. Angeline, Trevor, your mom, and dad, everyone's here. They are all fine but you've been through a lot and need to rest so you can heal."

"She's right, Griff. That pain in your right arm is from the bullet. Doc was able to remove it, and you're going to be fine. It will be a slow recovery, so don't push it," Lily scolded.

"What's the bunker like Lil?"

"It's amazing! You won't believe it when you see it. They have everything here. It is the most incredible place in the world. I can't wait to show it to you, but you need to rest first. Everyone is getting impatient. They want to see you for themselves, so I'm sure you'll have an exhausting stream of visitors tomorrow. For tonight, though, try to get some sleep."

He nodded and closed his eyes, trying to take it all in.

"Holly, come on. Let him rest. You need a good night's sleep, too."

"Does she have to go?" Griffon asked, his eyes still closed.

"She's been worried sick and has barely left your side for days. She'll be back tomorrow."

He squeezed Holly's hand tightly and opened his eyes. "Don't disappear on me again, okay?"

Tears sprang to her eyes. She leaned down, hugged him, and kissed him sweetly on the lips. "I'm sorry," was all she could say before Lily pulled her away.

Mike walked into the room, as Holly was saying goodbye. His heart hurt watching his baby girl and knowing the part he played in her pain. Charlie saw to it that he knew everything that happened.

"Get some sleep sweetheart," Mike told her. "Doc's going to try to do the same, so I volunteered to keep him company throughout the night."

Holly froze, and her eyes grew wide. "Dad, are you sure?" She wasn't comfortable leaving them alone like that, especially when Griffon was too weak to fight right now.

"Relax," he assured her. "He's going to be fine. We're going to be fine." He hugged her, which did little to reassure her but Lily shoved her out of the room.

* * * * *

Chapter 28

MIKE JENKINS stared at this pale, lethargic man sleeping soundly, and he was flooded with a thousand thoughts. Who was Griffon, really? Where did he come from? How did he meet Holly? How long had they been seeing each other behind his back? How was it that Holly couldn't tell her own father about this man, whom she obviously cared for greatly?

He got down on his knees and prayed for understanding and acceptance. He asked God to heal this man that he only knew through the words of others. He prayed for peace for his daughter. He prayed for forgiveness in his part of it all. While he prayed, he felt Griffon's hand on his shoulder, embracing him.

They had spoken little more than a casual greeting of introduction, but Griffon knew this man. He understood Mike's need to protect his baby girl from everything, even him. He understood that kind of love, and he knew that he had to make amends with him if Holly was ever going to find peace.

"This is not your fault, Mr. Jenkins," he started. "None of this is your fault. Holly loves you, dearly. She could never do anything against your wishes. When you told her not to see me again, she ended things completely."

He paused as the pain of that moment filled him again.

"I'm not sure how I came to be here with you all, but I want to thank you for protecting my family. It means the world to me. I love your daughter, sir, and I would never do anything to jeopardize her relationship with you. I will respect your wishes as best as I can. She's a stubborn woman, your Holly, but I will ask her to keep her distance while we are here, and we will move on as soon as I am up and around."

Griffon said what he needed to say and then shut his eyes in stoic determination to follow through with his promise.

Mike listened to the young man who he feared had already stolen his Holly from him. He was an admirable guy, trying to do what was right, and he liked him immensely, no matter how much he didn't want to. He sighed.

"I'm sorry, son. I only wanted what was best for my baby girl and didn't trust her to know for herself what or who that was. I have watched her struggle with the guilt of everything that has happened, and I realize now the part that I played in it. I can never make that up to either of you. It'll take me some time to get used to it, but you have my full blessings. Holly loves you, and you obviously love her. Anyone would have to be an idiot not to see that, and I'm tired of being the idiot." He was waving his white flag, surrendering to the inevitable.

Griffon did not say a word but drifted off to sleep and slept peacefully that night. When he awoke, Mike was gone, and he was certain that he had dreamed it. He felt disappointed.

Mike walked in with a food tray and coffee in hand. The smells made Griffon's mouth water, and his stomach grumbled in protest.

"Good morning, son. Your stomach was growling most of the morning. Doc said you could try a liquid diet this morning, if you feel up to trying to sit up a little."

Griffon eyeballed him suspiciously. Had he just called him son? Could it be that he was not been dreaming last night after all? He was too surprised to think it through clearly.

Mike elevated the bed carefully to allow Griffon to eat without choking.

He bit the inside of his jaw so as not to scream in pain. He couldn't let this man see him as weak, but Mike did see through it.

"It's okay, ya know. I'd be bawling like a baby, if I were you." He smiled knowingly. "It's okay to hurt. We know you're still in a lot of pain. Recovery will come but it's going to require patience."

"I don't like feeling weak and helpless." Griffon surprised himself by admitting.

Mike smiled. "I'd be more concerned if you didn't feel that way, son. Now, I know you have a lot of wires and tubes coming out of that left arm but I would not recommend attempting to eat with your right. The gunshot wound is in your right shoulder. You probably know that by now, or suspected as much." Mike undid some tape and loosened wires that helped free Griffon's left arm a little.

"Thanks, Mr. Jenkins." He felt less out of control now that his left arm was somewhat free.

"It's okay to call me Mike. We're all like family around here, son," he said with an affectionate tone. Griffon still was unsure how to take it, but he was gracious and thankful for everything.

Mike assisted with his breakfast of chicken broth, Jell-O, and coffee, and he laughed at the disappointed face Griffon made over the meal.

"I know; it sucks. Hey, hold this down, and I'll smuggle you in a ham and cheese sandwich for lunch."

"That's a deal!"

Holly walked in as Griffon was finishing his breakfast, and her heart lurched seeing him and her father laughing and joking together. He was sitting up, and his color was coming back slowly. She was grateful that her father was doing this but refused to get her hopes up that he would ever accept Griffon into their lives. She tried to discreetly back out of the room so as not to antagonize her father.

"Told ya I wouldn't kill him in the middle of the night, baby girl," her dad joked affectionately.

Holly rolled her eyes as he motioned her to the bed.

"I've got work to do this morning, so he's all yours," he said with a smile and winked at her on his way out.

"What just happened?" she demanded

"Heck if I know!"

He wanted badly to get up and walk across the room to kiss her good morning. He tried to shift on his own and grunted in pain. She was by his side immediately, scolding him while he grinned his sheepish, boyish grin at her.

"What?" She demanded, laughing.

He lifted his left arm, thankful for the freedom, and pulled her close enough to kiss. There was a spark of surprise in her eyes that stabbed at his heart. "Good morning," he said with a wicked smile.

Doc walked in at that time.

"Your patient's feeling much better today, I think," she informed him.

"You ready to run a marathon, then, lad?"

"If you'd cut me loose from all these wires, I just might do that, Doc."

"Splendid! Let me check you over. It's good to see your spirits so high." Then, almost to himself, "With Mike here, we were all making bets on whether you'd both even survive the night." He laughed at his own words.

"It was enlightening. . . or I dreamed it all. Either way, it feels good this morning!"

Holly raised an eyebrow and gave him a questioning look. He knew there would be an interrogation later. He also knew that he had definitely not lost her, at least not yet. That realization made him feel stronger. He tried to shift positions again and put a little too much pressure on his right side. Maybe not that strong, he reminded himself.

* * * * *

The next few days fell into an easy routine. Holly spent every morning from breakfast through lunch with Griffon in the infirmary. She left to do her chores when someone else came in to keep him company. She returned in time for dinner and stayed until bedtime. He was sleeping alone overnight, now.

By day four of post surgery, Griffon was going stir crazy. He wanted to shower, and he wanted to get up and walk around. Doc had only let him try a few steps the day before but he was never going to get stronger lying in that bed. When Holly arrived with breakfast, he was in a bear of a mood.

"What's up with you today?"

"Nothing. Absolutely nothing! Just like yesterday and the day before. Just like today and most likely tomorrow. I'm going crazy in here Holly! And I stink!" He hadn't meant to announce that last part but it was true, and it was annoying him.

She laughed. "Well, I can at least help with the last part." He eyeballed her suspiciously, as she grabbed a pan from a cabinet nearby and filled it with warm water. She retrieved a washcloth and a bar of soap that had been stored in there all these years and never needed. She carefully removed his gown, trying not to bump his IV's.

Doc had removed a significant number of them, now that Griffon was eating and drinking on his own. He still needed pain meds and some extra fluids through the tubes. She grabbed a plastic sheet from under the bed and warned him that this part could be awkward. Somehow, with not too much pain to him, they managed to get the plastic sheet under him to keep the bed from getting wet.

He was greatly amused with the entire situation until she made a move for his pants. "Uh, I'm not sure your dad will be okay with THAT!" he said, exasperated.

She laughed, "Relax, you can keep your boxers on, and we both know I've seen you in less!"

His face turned bright red. "Holly, is this even appropriate?" He surprised himself at how embarrassed he was being at her mercy.

She laughed at him, again, and, without a word, removed his pants and set to work. Once she had him washed as best as she could, she stood back and looked him over.

He looked so uncomfortable. A part of him felt aroused as he lay there with her hands roaming every part of his body. The other part of him was downright humiliated from the whole situation. Worse, yet, she seemed pleased with the obvious discomfort she was causing on both counts.

"Well, you definitely smell better, now, but you really need to wash that hair. I'm not sure how we can do it without soaking the bed. Any chance you could try sitting in a chair by the sink?"

He shrugged, secretly thrilled that someone finally wanted him out of this bed. She moved the chair into place, and then unhooked his IV lines. She left to rummage through the cabinets again until she found a sling. Very carefully, so as not to hurt him, she maneuvered the sling into place on his right arm.

He bit back the urge to scream as she set the sling. Once she finished, it actually felt better. He felt more comfortable and confident in that position. With the freedom from the IV's, he swung his legs around and readily accepted her offer to help. He knew he was still weak and had lost some muscle tone in his legs from nearly two weeks in bed, but they made it to the chair with minimal issues. She washed his hair, and he felt completely rejuvenated when she finished.

He knew that he was pressing his luck, but he really wanted out of this room for a while. He grinned at her, and she instinctively knew that he was up to no good.

"Any chance I could get dressed and attempt a short walk today?"

"I'll have to check with Doc but I don't see why not. If you're comfortable enough sitting, maybe we can make it to the common room."

She poked her head out of the room and was fortunate to find Angeline skipping in the hallway. The little girl hoped that her uncle would be up for a visit, but the adults told her not to disturb him, so she skipped back and forth, waiting for Holly to come out or someone to go in, so she could ask.

"Angeline, can you keep Uncle Griff company for a few minutes, please?"

The little girl lit up like Christmas. "Yes, yes, yes, yes, yes!" She squealed as she hugged Holly.

"Okay, I'll be back in just a few minutes. Keep him company, and don't let him get up from the chair. If he tries or if he has any problems, run and find me, okay?" The little girl nodded. "Do you know where my family's pod is?" The little girl nodded again. "Okay, that's where I'll be. I'll only be gone a few minutes."

With that, Holly ran down to her family pod and into Charlie's area in search of clothes. Normally, Charlie and Griffon would be similar in size, but even Holly noticed Griffon had lost quite a bit of weight over the last two weeks. She grabbed a pair of gym shorts with a drawstring, should they need to be smaller, and a tee-shirt big enough to go over the sling.

She raced back and, with Angeline's help, got him dressed. Getting him to his feet from the chair was a bit of a task but once up, he did okay walking. Still, Holly insisted he keep one arm around her just in case he got dizzy or lost his balance as they walked. They moved slowly and steadily out of the infirmary and down the hall to the common room, with Angeline cheering him on the whole way.

* * * * *

There were only a few people sitting in the common area when they arrived, and they assisted Holly in getting Griffon situated comfortably on the coach. She sat next to him and, even though he didn't need her anymore, he kept his arm around her and held her tightly by his side. Word traveled quickly through the compound, and, soon, family, friends, and even strangers he had yet to meet, filled the room to see him.

Emma Grace stopped by to fuss over him, and Doc came to scold Holly and praise Griffon. Lily and his mother spent much of the day fussing over him and making sure he was okay and comfortable, fetching food and drinks at his whim.

"A man could get used to this!" he teased.

Holly's mother had not officially met him yet, but she cried and hugged him when she saw him up and around.

Griffon remained in the common room much of the day and was disappointed when it was time to return to the infirmary for the night. Once Holly got him settled back into bed, he pulled her playfully onto the bed with him. He was careful to guard his right arm, which was still in the sling.

They had not spoken about the night the AMAN shot him since that first time he awoke. She had kissed him several times, but mostly when she thought he was asleep. Snuggled next to her, he needed to talk about it.

"Thank you for today Holly. Thank you for everything."

He hesitated. "I love you, and no matter what you think is best for us, for you, for your family, whatever... it's not going to change that fact."

Before she could respond, he pulled her close and kissed her passionately. All the fears and emotions of the last two weeks closed in on her. She kissed him back and deepened the kiss until she could no longer tell which parts were her and which were him. Tears fell from her eyes, leaving a salty taste in both their mouths. She only pulled back when he groaned, thinking she hurt him.

"I'm sorry, I'm so sorry. I didn't mean to hurt you."

It was all she could say as sobs took over. She was sorry for the pain that she felt her carelessness caused him. He held her close, and she cried in his arms until there were no more tears. They both drifted off to sleep like that.

Mike rose early and noticed Holly was not in her bed. He immediately went to the infirmary and peaked in, not wanting to wake Griffon if she wasn't there. They lay there, two bodies as one in that tiny bed, sleeping peacefully. Mike sighed and knew he'd have to have a talk with her soon... but for now he left in peace.

When Doc came in the next morning, he woke the sleeping pair. Even though she was groggy, she heard Doc scolding her. She hadn't reconnected his drip line for pain meds the night before.

Griffon assured them both that he was fine. Truth was, he was sore and in some pain, but it really was manageable. Doc called his bluff, removed the IV line, and gave him a pill to take... another step toward getting him out of the infirmary permanently.

* * * * *

Chapter 29

DESPITE THE lockdown, they needed to harvest the valuable crops outside the bunker. Holly was called upon to assist a group of five to carry out the task as quickly as possible. Once outside, she reveled in the sunshine. She always hated being locked inside the bunker. She set to work quickly, and within a few hours time, they had the acre garden harvested of its summer bounty. As they were gathering the last of it, a call came over the radio.

There was some activity in the woods near the low tower. Holly's heart lurched in her chest from fear as the others scurried inside with their bounty, but she stood frozen, holding her breath while awaiting an all clear.

"Friendlies. It's friendlies; stand down. It's Ben and Rhoda Hayes looking for news on the Maynor's." Holly ran down the mountain to the lookout to speak with them.

"Holly!" Rhoda squealed and hugged her with great relief. "We've been worried sick. The AMAN hung around attempting to wait them out for over a week. The last of them just moved on, but we fear they'll be back soon with reinforcements. What word do you have of them? They did make it up to you, yes?"

"Yes, Rhoda. Griffon was shot, but he's recovering nicely."

"Shot! Sweet Lord! What is this world coming to? I can't believe it!"

"Lily says they were waiting for Griffon. Do you have any news? Do you know why?"

"No, but she is right. Sarge was furious when he heard Griffon got away. Orders were clear that they were not to harm him. Sarge could have killed whoever shot him. We don't know why they are singling him out, but there's definitely something they want from him."

"Stop your gossiping, Rhoda," Ben scolded as he glared at this wife. "We didn't come up here to spread gossip. Now Holly, things are getting bad down here, and people are getting nervous. The AMAN are everywhere and threatening to bring in more, to boot. We have a group ready to stand up and take arms, but we need help. Is there some way you could convince Charlie to come down and speak with us? We need leadership, and I believe he's just the man to provide it."

"I'll have to speak with the elders, Ben. We are on lockdown up there. I was only out for harvest and wasn't supposed to come down when the call that you were here came through. Tell me what you want, and I will relay it to the elders and see what they say. We'll leave word with whoever is on sentry duty down here for you to check tomorrow."

"Fair enough! We need resources, coordination, and a plan. Right now, I have a group of loose cannons wanting to attack the AMAN when they show up again. We can't just have a few vigilantes running around after them; they'll get us all killed. It's time Wythel fights back, I agree, but we need to be smart about it. It would help to have you all on our side when this fight goes down, and, mark my word, the day is approaching quickly."

Holly nodded in agreement. "I have to get back now, but I will have a response to your request by tomorrow at noon."

They exchanged goodbyes, and Holly headed back up to the compound.

She spoke with Pastor Weaver first to let him know of Ben Hayes' request and asked him to call a meeting of the elders.

"I don't know if that would be such a good idea. Your father isn't going to like it, and, quite frankly, I'm not sure our involvement with the town is in our best interest."

"Why wouldn't it be in our best interest, father?" Milo asked.

They hadn't heard him enter the room. She hadn't spoken to Milo since he ran off to propose to Emma Grace, the day Griffon got shot. She turned to watch him. He appeared taller and more confident than ever.

"Now Milo, settle down, I just meant, well, look at what's happened. That place has turned our home upside down. Nothing is as it should be, and even if you won't admit it, you both know it's true."

Holly's eyes widened. *It was back to this? Back to them?*

"With all due respect, Pastor Weaver, if you are referring to what I think you are, you are seriously out of line. Our going down to Wythel had nothing to do with any of that. I would not be marrying your son, regardless. And for you to condemn those people down there because of any ill feelings on how this," she motioned between herself and Milo, "turned out, is truly disgusting."

She was ready to bolt, but the Pastor stopped her. His voice was cold and uncaring, so very unlike anything she had seen of him before, and it stopped her in her tracks.

"You listen here, little girl. That town screwed up everything we had planned. You were to marry Milo. We decided that when you were both still in diapers. Everything was going fine until you decided to assert some newfound independence. Then came Wythel and that heathen you're hiding here. If it weren't for you going down to that town, if it weren't for him, life would be as it should."

She bit her tongue, took a deep breath, and spoke purposefully. "You have a lot of hatred stored up in you for a man of God, Pastor Weaver. You know not of what you speak. I met Griffon long before we went down to Wythel. Despite that, I tried to do what you and the others wanted. I tried to make things work with Milo, even while loving another man. I tried to put my feelings aside for the good of this compound; it just wasn't meant to be. Two people who love others could never make a marriage work. Would you truly convict your own son to a loveless marriage?"

Pastor Weaver was red in the face and furious. Holly could feel the anger wrap around her, and it was almost paralyzing.

"How dare you!" he boomed. "I am a man of faith and an elder of this community, and you'd do best to show me the respect I'm due. My children know to obey me and don't question my intentions for what is best for us all. Something your own father should have instilled better in you."

"It must really infuriate you to know Milo fell in love with Emma Grace and asked her to marry him without your great and all powerful permission. God forbid, he should actually seek happiness for himself!"

She spoke the words without thinking. Everyone knew she had an uncanny ability to provoke people. 'Stop poking the bear' her mother had frequently told her as a child, but even Holly knew better than most not to provoke the wrath of Pastor Weaver.

She had shivered as a child when Chris confessed to her the spanking and lecture he received when he disobeyed his father's orders and sneaked off to play, instead. While he paraded around helping others and preaching the Lord's message, his own children walked on eggshells, scared of anything that might set him off.

Overall, he was a good man, but he had a terrible temper, and he took everything out on his wife and children. Holly knew that her father had intervened in a few instances and never understood why he allowed the pastor to stay. The thought hit her that, perhaps, his security within the compound was tied to her marriage to Milo. If it were not for his boys as prospective suitors for her, her father would have had him thrown out years ago. That would certainly explain the hatred toward her that he was not even trying to conceal.

In the silence of the moment, as the thoughts flooded her, she was not aware of the anger continuing to build inside him until Milo stood in front of her, grabbing the arm that was ready to strike her.

"You will not lay a hand on her, father, now or ever." Milo's voice was extremely controlled and cold as he spat the words out and threw the old man's arm away, which caused the Pastor to stumble.

Pastor Weaver's eyes flashed with anger before he carefully reigned in his anger and transitioned to the cool, calm, and collected loving minister most knew him to be.

She shuddered, watching the transition and knowing what lay just below that cool exterior.

"If a meeting with the elders' council is what you want, fine. I will call it this evening at 8:00 p.m., here in my office." With that, he turned and walked out.

Holly was shaking from the encounter. Milo was furious! He wrapped his arms around her to steady them both and to stop himself from going after his father.

"I'm so sorry Holly. You weren't supposed to see him like that."

She looked at him, filled with sympathy, and he knew in that moment that she had known about the monster within his father. She probably knew that all along.

"I shouldn't have provoked him like that," she hesitated. "I knew better, Milo."

He nodded, confirming what he thought.   Chris had confided in her all those years ago. He held her tightly. It felt good to have her in his arms again, and he chastised himself for even thinking it. Then something she said hit him.

"Hey, what did you mean about not having met Griffon in Wythel? I thought you two met that first day we went down there and you ran into him." He paused, trying to remember that day. "What a minute... you already knew him, didn't you, Holly?"

Her eyes were wide and nervous, and he knew that he was right. "How? Where? When?"

She just stood there in silence, and he laughed. "Relax, Hols, it's okay. I'm happy with Emma Grace and don't really give a rip what my father thinks about it. I won't say I didn't care for you. Heck, I still do, just not in the same way that I do Emma Grace. I was just curious, and that's all. You said that you had tried to make things work with me even while loving him. I was just curious. If you don't want to tell me, it's okay."

"No, it's fine."

She wondered if perhaps she and Milo could actually be friends after all that had happened and decided to confide in him.

"There's a place in the rocks. A cave very similar to your cave; in fact do you remember that rock slide that blocks those paths you've always wondered about?"

She paused, and he nodded.

"They would have connected to my cave," she grinned sheepishly. "After the bunker was opened last year, I searched for the hidden entrance. It took me a while, but I finally found it, and when I got into the main cave, well, Griffon was there. He and Amos had been out hunting and were hoping for a bear or something hiding in the cave. He came up by way of the old rock slide, and I met him there."

Milo's eyes grew wide, "Holly that was over a year ago. That was before we even started dating."

She shrugged sheepishly. "It was right around the same time, actually. I knew about the AMAN but couldn't tell anyone."

"That's why you switched sides and started agreeing with your brother about us going down there."

She answered with a soft, "Yes."

"So, I gotta know... which of us did you kiss first?" He was grinning at her.

"Really?"

"I'm just teasing you, Hols. Griffon's a good guy. There have been days that I have prayed to see some kind of fault in him just to appease my own selfish ego, but really, I like him. He's good for you. Anyone can see how happy he makes you. That's all I care about."

She hugged him and gave him a quick kiss on the cheek. "Thanks Milo!"

Emma Grace walked in at that moment, and the look on her face made them both feel guilty. He quickly let go of her, and Holly spoke up first.

"It's okay Emma Grace. I'm not here to steal your fiancé. We were just clearing the air." Milo and Holly both laughed. Emma Grace still looked less than thrilled with the situation.

Holly hugged her on the way out.

"I hope we can be friends some day."

Then she left. Milo could sort the rest out, himself.

* * * * *

Chapter 30

A S PROMISED, Pastor Weaver had the elders gather in the chapel. Holly stood in front of the crowded room and relayed the information Ben and Rhoda had provided. By that point, most had already heard the news through gossip from the guards. Holly persuaded them to consider the situation and decide whether they would ally with their new friends below or leave them to their potential doom.

Mike asked her to round up Fred, Don Maynor, and Griffon, if he was up to hearing their concerns, before they made a final judgment.

Holly's eyes brightened and her heart swelled as she left the room to find them. Her father was granting them equal rights in the bunker. She had to refrain from running over and hugging him. She heard several low whispers about it as she left the room. The impact of his request was settling in with the others.

* * * * *

Holly went straight to the Maynor Pods and found Fred and Don. She explained the situation to them and asked that they join the elders meeting while she talked to Griffon.

She was on her way to the infirmary when she passed by Pod 7. It had always been hers. As a child, she kept her favorite toys in there and sneaked off to play in there for hours. As she grew, she used it as a refuge during the years of lockdown. As she looked lovingly at the door that would someday welcome her own family, she noticed that someone had opened the door, slightly. She touched it, and it flew open. She frowned. Why would her door be ajar?

She kept the key tucked away in her room, and Pod 7 remained locked so others would stay out. Poking her head in, she saw that someone had remodeled it. She had always kept it open and spacious, without limits of walls, and, now, she saw a section marked off and furnished as a living room. She heard some rustling around in the other room, and her temper flared. Everyone knew this was her Pod and that it was off limits. She threw open the door to the next room ready to rip someone's head off and stopped short.

Griffon was standing there trying to rearrange panels to relocate the bed somewhere. He was working one-handed, and it was almost comical to watch. She just stood there watching him, with her heart pounding in her chest.

Irritated, he turned around and saw her watching him with a strange look on her face.

"Well, are you gonna just stand there or are you going to help me?"

She was jolted back to the present.

"I was just on my way to see you in the infirmary. What are you doing here?"

"I'm trying to set up this Pod so I have somewhere to sleep tonight. They kicked me out of the infirmary. Doc said I was cramping his space and needed to get out."

"Who told you it was okay to move into Pod 7?"

"What? What difference does it make? I'm just trying to get settled, so are you going to help me or not?"

He was clearly getting irritated, not at her, probably with himself and the limitations of his injury while his arm was still in a sling.

She crossed the room, stood in front of him, took his hands, and looked right into his eyes.

"It matters to me, Griffon. I heard they were moving you into your parents Pod. Who told you it was okay to set up camp in Pod 7?"

His frustration subsided. He wasn't sure what she was getting at, but it clearly meant a lot to her.

"Your dad. He came by to see me as I was trying to settle into the other pod and said it wouldn't do, that I needed my space and Pod 7 would be the right one for me. I figured maybe it was a smaller one or something geared for one person, but this place is huge, Holly! Just look at it. I had to clear out a few things and add a few things, but it's coming along."

She just stood there in shock, trying to take it all in.

"Wait... you cleared stuff out? Where did you put it?"

Trying to get back to work and thoroughly confused, he told her that he packed up some of the toys that were in there and gave them to Angeline, while most of the rest were in a few boxes in the corner of the living room. She ran to the boxes to look through them and make sure all her precious belongings were there.

He followed her.

"Holly, what's this all about?"

"This isn't just a bunch of crap thrown in here. Griffon, this is MY crap!"

"Oh, sorry, I didn't know. I can get the dolls and toys and stuff back, if you want."

"No, no, that's fine. Angeline will enjoy them and take good care of everything. You just don't understand."

She sighed and dropped down on the couch, not knowing how to explain it to him.

"You're sure it was my dad that told you to move in here?"

He nodded yes.

"And Pod 7? He specifically said Pod 7?"

"Of course. I wouldn't just cop a squat in any pod. I was fine with bunking with my folks. Besides this place was locked; he gave me the key."

She smiled so big it lit up the entire room. She threw herself into his arms and kissed him.

"Do you know what this means?"

"I have no idea what you're talking about but as long as you keep kissing me like that, I am perfectly content to remain clueless forever."

She punched him. "I'm being serious here! My dad told you to move into Pod 7!"

Griffon could tell she was excited but he didn't really understand why.

"Please tell me, Holly. The suspense is killing me," he said with dry sarcasm. He just wanted to finish setting up his living area and lay down for a rest but knew it wasn't going to happen until this conversation was over. "Please, please, what is so important about Pod 7?"

She knew that he was being sarcastic and making fun of her but she didn't care. She stood on her tippy toes for another quick kiss, and then looked deep into his eyes to make sure he understood the impact of this situation. "Pod 7 is MY Pod, Griffon!"

She let it sink a little bit but knew he still didn't get it.

"It's mine. My dad assigned Pod 7 to me when he built this place. It has always been intended that when I grew I up, married, and had kids... and all that stuff... that MY family would live here. It is the biggest of all the Pods in the bunker, built special for his princess."

His eyes grew big as the impact of her words settled in, and she grinned. "We don't have to sneak around anymore. He's trying to make amends and tell me he's okay with us. I think in some crazy way, he's giving us his blessing."

Griffon grinned and pulled her close. "I've had his blessing for days. I just like sneaking around with you."

She smacked him playfully on the arm, and he pulled her in for a kiss. She tried to grasp the impact of what he just told her.

He knew he was going to have to have a serious talk with Mr. Mike Jenkins.

* * * * *

"Holly, you said you were on your way to find me for something. What was it?"

"Oh crap! The meeting! Come on."

She dragged him down the hall, trying to fill him in along the way and hushing his interruptions.

Finally, he stopped and turned to walk back. "Griffon, come on, what is wrong with you?"

"What's wrong with me? You want me to go into an official meeting with your father and all the elders without wearing a shirt? Really, Holly?"

She hadn't even noticed and laughed as he stalked back to the Pod to retrieve some clothes. She waited until he returned a few moments later.

"Sorry about that. Guess I wasn't thinking. Kinda threw me off with you moving into my Pod and all."

He stopped just outside the door.

"Listen, if you're not comfortable with me moving in there, just say so. You're not going to hurt my feelings. This wasn't something we decided. I didn't know the situation when I agreed to take it. I would never have done that without discussing it with you first, if I had known. I'm fine with moving back in with my parents."

Before she could answer, the door flew open, and they went inside. Everyone grew quiet when they entered the room. Holly noticed Pastor Weaver glaring at her, trying to control his hatred. She pressed closer to Griffon for support and comfort.

He instinctively put his arm around her waist and drew her close without knowing why. Mike motioned them to the front, so he guided Holly toward her father. All eyes were on them, and everyone in the room noticed how protective he was of her, and it confirmed all the rumors traveling throughout the compound.

She noticed that Charlie was standing next to their father, with Milo on his other side, marking him as center stage in the spot usually held by their father. Mike welcomed Griffon, shook his hand, and directed him to stand beside him. Charlie grinned at his sister and nodded his approval. There was a noticeable change in the room, both in atmosphere and physically.

Pastor Weaver would normally have stood in the spot that her father now occupied. Charlie now stood in their father's old place. Milo assumed his usual spot; the only spot unchanged in the assertive leadership lineup. In recent months, the elders promoted Charlie amongst the ranks of the compound, and he would have stood beside Pastor Weaver in the place they now offered to Griffon.

Griffon stared at Holly. He could see the importance of this meeting on her face. She looked happy but her nose was nipped red, and her eyes were glistening. He knew she was holding back tears but was not sure why. He could tell by the manner in which Mike had greeted him that this was an important moment, so he stood tall and proud and waited for them to fill him in on the rest.

Charlie broke the murmured response to Griffon's place up front.

"Okay, everyone. Welcome, and may the meeting of the elders council come to order. Please welcome Griffon, Fred, and Don Maynor to the group. I believe you have all met at this point but if not, please introduce yourselves after the meeting adjourns. We have a lot to discuss tonight."

Holly realized that she was right up front in the middle of an elders' council meeting and tried to discreetly back out of the room.

"Don't run off just yet, Hols. We need you to sit in for this one."

She looked at her brother, and he grinned and winked. She knew all eyes were on her but no one made a sound of disagreement. They rarely invited women to closed-door meetings of the council, who decided the fate of every aspect of the compound. The only exception was Patty Lamay. She was head of the Lamay family after her husband died several years back.

Mike spoke next.

"You all will notice a decisive change upfront here. Pastor Weaver has asked to step down. In his place, I've invited Griffon Maynor to join us in the interim. Of course, the elders' council will vote on this at a later date. In the meantime, I hope you will all open your hearts and minds to what he has to say."

Mike put his arm around Griffon in a protective manner, and a hush came over the room. Holly knew the others would come to accept him as their equal, too, and silently thanked her father."

"We welcome back Milo Weaver, who will continue running the day-to-day needs of the compound." With that, a cheer of approval went up. "As you know, I myself am also taking a step back. I have full confidence in the leadership and guidance of my son, Charlie, to lead us into this unknown crazy world around us, and I am proud and honored to say this was made official by a unanimous vote a few moments ago. Charlie..." everyone clapped and cheered.

"Thanks Pops." Charlie took a moment to hug his father. "Okay, the formalities are out of the way, so let's talk about why we're here today. Holly, have you filled Griffon in on what Ben and Rhoda said?"

All eyes turned to her, which made her face redden. "No, not yet."

"Okay," Charlie continued, "for Griffon and anyone else that came in late, as you all know there was an altercation down in Wythel a few weeks back, which ended with our man Griff getting shot." Griffon winced in pain at the memory. "We know from the accounts of the rest of the Maynor family that the AMAN were specifically targeting him."

Holly saw the empty look on Griffon's face and wondered what he was thinking. "That suspicion was confirmed this morning by Rhoda Hayes. Holly, can you please give account of the conversation with Mrs. Hayes?"

She cleared her throat and looked out at the people before her, trying hard not to feel like a small child about to blow a word in a spelling bee as she had done many times in front of these same men over the years.

"Well, when I arrived at the first lookout and met with Ben and Rhoda, they said that the AMAN had stuck around for more than a week and had increased patrols. Rhoda overheard them discussing Griffon on numerous occasions. The order was that he not be harmed. One of the soldiers was killed for shooting him. They are gathering more patrols and were expected to return to hunt him down."

She glanced at Griffon and saw the hard line on his forehead and his sharp, locked jaw as he was hearing this for the first time. She was sorry that she hadn't told him in person back in the Pod.

"So what happens when they come up here to get him, huh? Do we all sacrifice ourselves and our families for this outsider?" Commotion ran rapid in the room as everyone argued the point amongst themselves.

"Now hold up a minute," Mike interrupted. "I'm going to make this very, very clear. The Maynor's are NOT outsiders. Not anymore. I decided a long time ago who would be invited into this bunker and who would not, and I will continue to do so at my discretion. Anyone who has a problem with that is free to leave at anytime.

"I have already spoken at length with Fred and Don. They are here today as official elders now, not as some outsiders. They will have as much say in this as the rest of you. Holly has made it very clear that they are as much her family as any of us, me included, and the whole damn reason I built this thing was to protect her and Charlie and what they love most. Nothing's changed on that. We have the room and resources, and they have already provided a great deal to us. So make no mistake, if the AMAN come up here to get Griffon, they are gonna get the fight of their lives. We will protect him as our own."

Holly nearly stumbled back with his words. She had never in a million years even dared to hope for something like this. It was almost too much to handle. She saw the stubborn pride in Griffon's face, and her heart dropped as he spoke.

"Thanks for that, Mike. I appreciate it more than you know. All I ask is that you all protect and defend Holly and my family. If the AMAN comes looking for a fight, we'll see how that goes, but I will not choose my life over any one of yours."

Her heart sank like a brick in water, and she knew that he meant every word.

"If it comes down to a threat on the people here, I will turn myself over to the AMAN and accept whatever fate awaits me, if it means protecting all of you."

The room was quiet for a moment. Holly did not miss Pastor Weaver's snide smirk. She didn't care, though. She wanted to scream, NO, but knew she could not and knew in her heart that he meant it. She also knew that Griffon was watching her, but she couldn't bring herself to look at him.

The murmurs throughout the room changed. Griffon was suddenly one of them, and Holly felt like an outsider. Charlie regained control of the meeting, and, in the end, they all decided that the compound should send a small group down to Wythel to hear what they had to say and what they were planning before they made any final decisions. Griffon would stay behind, as a precaution, should the invitation be a setup to flush him out of the bunker. Milo, Mike, Colton Evers, Fred Maynor, and Holly made up the response team. Only Milo, Colton, and Holly would go into the town. Mike and Fred would stand guard at the tree line.

* * * * *

Chapter 31

GRIFFON WAS furious over the outcome of the meeting. He went straight to Pod 7 where Holly found him pacing back and forth.

"You're not going down there, Holly. I don't care what they say!" He continued to pace back and forth. "If I can't be there to protect you, I don't want you anywhere near that place."

She let him vent without interruption. She understood he was concerned for her safety. She was just thankful it was her going down and not him.

"I can do this, Griffon," she said softly. "The people there know me, and they trust me. They are your friends and family. I'm going to be okay. My dad and your dad will be nearby, if anything goes wrong. Colton and Milo will be there to protect me, too."

He stopped pacing. "Milo," he spat out the name. "Yeah, I'm quite certain he'll be more than happy to watch after you."

"Griffon, stop. You know it's not like that! I know that Milo would do anything to protect me. I'm safe with him."

"You're safe with ME!"

"I know that, but you aren't safe down there. What if they're just lying low and waiting? What if this is just a setup, like they said in the meeting? We don't even know why the AMAN are after you. Do you?"

"No. You know I don't. I've given them no reason. It doesn't even make sense."

"Right, and we need to find out. You're not safe until we know what we're up against. And I intend to find out."

He sighed. He saw the stubbornness in her before and knew it was pointless to argue. She had her mind made up; she was going, whether he agreed or not. He felt helpless.

That night, she slept in his arms. She knew she would have to face her mother eventually but, for tonight, she didn't care. She was where she needed to be. They talked softly late into the night, both unsure of what the sunrise would bring.

* * * * *

Feeling groggy and with little sleep the night before, Holly awoke and immediately reached for Griffon. He was there smiling down on her, just as she knew he would be. She could easily imagine waking every morning in his arms and to his smiling face. It felt good, but the daunting task ahead made it hard to be truly happy right now.

They didn't speak. They just lay in bed, holding each other tight. There was a feeling of dread looming in the air. After some time, she smiled at him, gave him a quick kiss, and darted for the bathroom. She showered and dressed for the long day ahead.

When it was time to say goodbye, Griffon's eyes locked on hers. She knew he was begging her not to go, but she had to do this. She smiled apologetically and left the room quickly. If she stayed much longer, she would not be able to tell him no.

When she entered the kitchen, Charlie and those tasked with the job ahead were already gathered. He gave her a knowing look, and she just smiled back at him, trying to brush off the questions and concerns of her sleeping arrangements the night before. Her dad gave her a look as well but never said a word.

Fred broke the silence. He gave her a quick hug and asked her once more if she were truly up for this. "You don't have to do this Holly. Milo and Colton can get the information we need." He tried to reassure her.

She knew he didn't want her down there anymore than his son did, but she tried to be optimistic, "You know they like me better than those two." She smiled, trying to be light about the situation. "Everyone will be at ease with me there, and we're more likely to find out what is really going on here."

"And that is why we want Holly to go," her father interrupted. "I understand your reservations, Fred. I truly appreciate your concern but Colton and Milo will be there to keep her safe. If I had any doubts, I would lock her up in here and throw away the key." He placed his arms on her shoulders and smiled at his beloved daughter.

She knew he meant it, but she still couldn't shake the uneasy feeling in her gut.

* * * * *

The trip down the mountain was quiet as they remained deep in their own thoughts. At the edge of the woods, they said goodbye to Mike and Fred and made their way cautiously to the old tavern just on the outskirts of Main Street as Ben Hayes had directed. The tavern was one of the oldest buildings in town. Holly knew there was a secret door in the floor behind the bar that led down to a hidden basement, which also led to several tunnels joining key parts of the town underground. She knew that this network was used long ago as part of the Underground Railroad and, later in history, to smuggle alcohol during Prohibition. Most recently, it was the safe house they used for church services after the AMAN disbanded the churches and killed all the pastors.

They would not go in through the front door. Instead, they went around back and entered through the kitchen. They stopped and listened for any sign of danger. When they were certain the tavern was empty, they crouched low and made their way from the kitchen to the bar, knowing they would be exposed for a few seconds.

Holly watched the street out front through the big picture window, looking for anything suspicious. When she was certain that all was clear, she knocked three times on the old knotted floor before lifting the secret panel and walked down the stairs it exposed. She went first, and, halfway down the stairs, in near pitch-black darkness, she heard the clicks of guns and knew they had their weapons pointed at her.

Milo's instincts were to pull her back up and get out of there, but she cut him off. "Holly Jenkins requesting entry. I have Milo Weaver and Colton Evers with me."

There was a soft murmur somewhere in the darkness, and a hand reached out and pulled her down. Milo and Colton jumped into action.

"Stop!" she shouted. "I'm okay. They're granting us entry, you buffoons."

Milo had already punched a guy in the jaw, and, as they entered into the light, she could see the red mark on Jared Hastings' face as he massaged the spot.

"Jared, are you okay?"

"I'm fine, just fine. Keep your muscles under control or we're gonna have a problem."

She scolded Milo. "What were you thinking?" She shoved him. "You'll get us all killed, acting like that."

Milo had never been in such a situation. He felt a strong need to protect her, yet she seemed in perfect control in this unknown world.

"What's going on here, Holly?" Colton asked.

"It's just a precaution, Mr. Evers. They need to protect themselves as much as we do. That's Jared Hastings over there. He's one of Griffon's boys. He's okay. Just keep calm. Ben and Rhoda warned us that everyone is on edge. That's why Charlie was so adamant that I come along. I know these people, and they trust me."

With that, Ben walked over. "Holly. I'm a little surprised to see you." He looked over Colton and Milo and then past them. "Where's Charlie?"

"Charlie's not coming. Colton and Milo have full authority to make decisions on behalf of the compound. Charlie's taken over in my father's place as head of the compound. We couldn't risk his safety by sending him down. I'm sorry, but you have my word that it's not a negative sign toward our intentions here. You know they would never have sacrificed me if we weren't here on amicable terms." She took turns making direct eye contact with each of them.

Ben nodded. "Yeah, that I do. Come on, let's get this thing started." He ushered the three of them to a small stage at the back of the room.

"Settle down everyone, settle down," Ben said to the crowd. There were close to fifty people in the room. Holly knew most of them by name.

"Where's Charlie?" a couple yelled from the crowd.

"Charlie's not going to make it but we have Holly, Colton Evers, and Milo Weaver here on his behalf," Ben informed them.

There was much talking, and a few people threatened to leave at that news. Tension was high in the room, and Holly knew she had to intervene.

"Calm down and listen. LISTEN UP!" she shouted above the noise, and everyone grew silent.

"I understand that you all see Charlie as the authority of our compound and are disappointed that he didn't come down and speak with you himself. I get that. Some of you are probably even less than thrilled that they sent a woman in his spot, but you know me. You can trust me when I say that we have made the best decision we could with the information that we had.

"Colton, here, is our head of security. You want to talk strategy... he's the best man we have. Milo and Charlie are equally ranked amongst our people, and Milo happens to be better at negotiations and more levelheaded than my brother is.

"We sent you the best of the best. We want to know what's going on and what we can do to help. I'm sure Ben has an agenda set for this meeting, but if it's alright with him, I'd like to open the floor for questions first."

She looked at Ben, who nodded with open admiration, as did Milo and Colton. Even Holly was surprised with herself and the strength and authority coming across in her words.

Jared raised his hand first. Holly looked at Ben, who motioned her to take the lead on the path she had already started. "Yes Jared."

"Is Griff alive? Cause in any world I know, there is no way in hell he'd let you come down here without him after everything that's happened." The crowd grew silent as all eyes were on her.

"Griffon is fine. All the Maynor's are fine. We didn't think it was safe for him to come down without knowing why the

AMAN is after him. He's not happy about it, but he knows it's best." They all looked at her suspiciously.

Colton piped in, "Look, I know how you feel. Griffon was not about to let Holly come down here without him, and he's one stubborn man. He doesn't trust anyone else to protect her. You all know it's true."

He let the crowd settle some before continuing. "Griffon was shot. I'm sure that rumor has already circulated down here. Now our Doc was able to operate and remove the bullet, but he's still weak, and, more than that, he's still on pain meds. So Doc may or may not have slipped him a harder pain killer this morning to knock him out, and I may or may not have locked him in his Pod to ensure that he stayed put and didn't get us all killed trying to come down."

"Colton Evers, you didn't!" Holly scolded him, and the whole group roared with laughter. That was a scene they could understand and appreciate.

Ben motioned for them all to settle down. "Okay, as we're clearing the air here, anyone have anything else on their mind?"

Jack Nelson raised his hand. Holly recognized him as one of the bakers in town. She had personally slipped him extra flour many times on her trips to town. "Holly, do the Maynor's know why the AMAN are after Griffon?"

"No, we have no idea why they would single him out like that," she admitted.

"I don't have all the answers but thought you should know that the orders came directly from General Steinfeld. He's madder than a hornet that one of his men shot Griff and now cannot find him. A couple of the local AMAN come into my bakery, and they like to gossip. Something about how the General is piping mad over it and put a substantial price on his safe return. I've overheard rumors of a wedding, too. I'm not sure what Griffon has to do with it, but it seems to be a big deal and somehow related. Makes no sense but, so far, that's the best information we've been able to piece together. Maybe he can make sense of it some. Do us all a favor and send him our best. Wythel is not the same without the Maynor's."

Holly nodded and thanked him for the information.

"Ben mentioned that many of you want to start a rebellion against the AMAN after the attack on the Maynor's," Milo interrupted. "Why don't you fill us in on that?"

For the next several hours, they discussed strategies and counted weapons, locations, and safe houses in great detail. Holly brought up other supplies, food, and resources necessary for self-sufficiency for the town. They needed to know the resources that AMAN provided and monitored. They knew if this went down, the AMAN would cut them off from all of that. The AMAN were smart and saw to it that they controlled the daily workings and resources of these small towns, making it nearly impossible to survive without them.

That's where the compound came into play. They had the resources and knowledge to get the town back on its feet after cutting ties with the AMAN.

Everyone knew this would be a fight for freedom, but the breaking point had come with Griffon being shot. They heralded him as their leader and the one that would stand before the AMAN and take Wythel back. The martyr status they were bestowing on him did not go unnoticed by Holly or Milo.

The town had secretly stored extra food in the old silo, and it was a source of enough wheat and corn to feed the town for a while if the AMAN cut off their food supply. Several families admitted to having secret gardens to help sustain their families and storing extras, should the need arise. Once they pulled together all the required food sources, they found there should be plenty to get them through for a full year, and, with the added plans for a community farm once the AMAN were defeated and removed from the area, they would be more than okay for many years to follow.

Weapons were in short supply. It was true that the compound had a great arsenal but they also were not going to share the full extent of those resources. They would protect their own first but would distribute a substantial amount of guns and ammo amongst the people of Wythel. Milo also had great knowledge of bow hunting. With a local mill able to provide the equipment, he would assist a group in the construction of bows and arrows that they could use for fighting and hunting. It would take some time to acquire enough for the rebellion planned against the AMAN, but they planted seeds and assigned tasks amongst the townspeople. They would begin work immediately and reconvene in one week's time.

Milo would stay down in the village to assist with the weaponry. Colton and Holly would take the news and plans for final approval to the compound. Colton would return with the first cache of promised weapons, and Holly would teach women the art of hiding things in plain sight so they could stock other necessary resources they would need when the rebellion commenced.

Many were anxious to attack immediately but they could not argue the need for preparation. They only had one chance to make their stance, and they needed it to make an impact big enough to keep the AMAN away from Wythel for good. There was great excitement in the air, and as Colton and Holly made their way back to the woods where Mike and Fred waited, they were surprised to find the sun low in the sky with sunset upon them.

It had been a long and grueling day. Griffon did not meet Holly on her arrival, and she stayed busy for several more hours, filling everyone in on the plans they had made. Charlie was not thrilled that Milo had taken it upon himself to stay in town, but he also understood the need for immediate action, as well.

Holly was exhausted as she headed back to her family's Pod. She showered and dressed for bed, but instead of bedding down for the night, she made her way back to Pod 7 to check on Griffon.

She saw the bolt removed from his door and carefully slipped in. She heard snoring coming from the back bedroom area. Lily was waiting for her, and before she entered the room, she motioned Holly over to her Pod across the hall.

"He's steaming mad that they locked him in like that. Doc drugged him with a strong sedative to calm him down. He planned to sneak out and follow you down, regardless of what the council decided."

Holly was not surprised at all. After all, she would have done the same for him.

"So, how did it really go? I know several people must have been furious when neither Griffon nor Charlie showed up."

"Yeah, they were but I handled it okay and made them understand. In the end, it all worked out okay, I think."

Lily could tell something more was bothering Holly. "What is it? What's wrong?"

"I dunno, Lily. It's just... it's just the way they talk about him. I feel like Griffon getting shot was the final straw for many, but it's not like a protective revenge kind of feeling. They are setting him up as a martyr. I'm not sure anyone could stand long on the pedestal on which they have put him. It made me very uncomfortable, but I don't exactly know how to explain it, either. I feel like they are doing all of this in the name of Griffon and not for themselves and Wythel."

Lily nodded, trying to digest what Holly was saying. She wasn't entirely surprised. So many people loved and respected her brother as well as her father and grandfather. They would have felt a great loss with them all moving to the compound. No one had thought of the repercussions to the town with that decision.

She hugged Holly and tried to assure her that everything would be okay... but would it?

* * * * *

Chapter 32

HOLLY LET herself into Pod 7 and decided to stay with Griffon. He looked so peaceful that she didn't want to wake him, so she pulled a chair up next to the bed and kept watch until she eventually drifted off to sleep.

He awoke, not knowing what time it was or even where he was. It took him a few moments for the memories of the day before to sink in. He jumped up, still mad, and ready to attack. *What did Doc give me?* He only knew he felt weak and groggy.

Holly. What happened to Holly? He shook his head to clear the fog and reached over to turn on the light. There she was, sleeping awkwardly in a chair next to him. For a moment, his anger and frustration disappeared. He picked her up, laid her carefully in his bed, and trying not to wake her, snuggled back down beside her. She was home. She was safe. The rest could wait until morning.

When she awoke, she stretched, expecting to feel cramps knowing the lack of logic in her decision to sleep in a chair. Instead, she felt soft sheets around her. She thought perhaps she had dreamed it all and was back in her room, in her own bed. She opened her eyes and took a moment to focus as reality set in. This was not her bedroom. This was not her bed. She sat up and saw Griffon lying next to her and watching her.

"Good morning, Sunshine." He smiled. "You know, I could really get used to waking up like this."

"My father will likely kill you first. We both know that's the truth."

She frowned, knowing that she wasn't exactly kidding. Two nights alone in his room and she was bound to get an earful when she returned to her family's pod.

Griffon laughed, "I'll take that chance."

Then his face changed and the memories of the day before sprung to mind.

"How did it go yesterday? You know, it was very stupid of you to go down there like that. They drugged me and locked me in here to keep me from coming after you." He was still angry, and it showed in his voice.

"I know," she said quietly. "Colton stopped a near riot when they realized you and Charlie weren't coming. Most figured you were dead, seeing as how I was there and you were not. But he set them straight, and they all got a good laugh over it." She smiled, trying to make light of the situation, but his face was serious. She knew what they had done was wrong.

"Holly, I can't have you running off to save the world like that. Do you have any idea what would happen if I lost you?" He shuddered. "I can't even think about it. Promise me you will never do something so stupid again." He held her tightly, willing her to agree.

"You know I can't promise that, Griffon." She sighed. "There's so much to do, and time is running out."

"Whatever needs to be done, we need to do it together."

She thought it over carefully and couldn't disagree. "I know, but..."

Before she could finish, there was a knock at the door. It flew open, and her dad and brother walked in.

Mike was not prepared for the sight of his baby girl lying in bed with a man, but a part of him breathed a sigh of relief to discover they were both fully clothed.

Charlie shut the door behind them, and both he and his father pulled up a chair and sat next to the bed. Charlie spoke first.

"Okay, so this is intervention time. Griffon, I like you, man, you know I do. But come on, you can't be disrespecting me by sleeping with my sister in our own house."

"Charlie!" Mike scolded. "He's not sleeping with your sister." He looked them both square on and spoke directly to Griffon... "Right? Please tell me that you are not having sex with my daughter under my own roof."

Griffon froze for a moment, not sure how to respond. He just shook his head no.

"Are you kidding me?" Holly was furious.

"You've not slept in your own bed for the past two nights, Hols, or on several other occasions since he's been here. Rumors spread quickly. You don't need that kind of reputation," Charlie said.

She laughed. "You're concerned about my reputation? Seriously? I mean, I've been practically living with him for half of every week for the last year, and now you're suddenly concerned about my reputation?"

Griffon looked terrified. Charlie's jaw dropped in shock, and her father's face turned red with anger. She hadn't meant to blurt that out but when they pushed her, she often had a hard time controlling her mouth and spilled out every thought that hit her brain.

"What?" her father boomed, and Charlie jumped in to intervene.

"Calm down, Dad, and hear her out first. You know she likes to poke the bear and often doesn't turn her brain on this early in the morning." He glared a warning at her but she pressed on.

"Dad, Charlie, I love you both but if I want to have sex with Griffon or any other man, you can't stop me. How dare you barge in here and check up on me like this. It's humiliating!"

She pointed a finger directly at her father. "Did you or did you not tell Griffon that he could move into MY Pod? Mine Dad, not his. I have every right to be here. You should have thought about that before you invited him to move in here with me."

"Move in with you, why I..."

"Why you what? I'm a grown woman and can handle my own love life just fine without the two of you." With that, she grabbed the blanket, yanked it over her head, and turned her back to them.

Both men now stared at Griffon. "I haven't touched her like that, I swear!" He held his hands up in a sign of good faith.

Charlie burst out laughing.

"Well Pops, you may never recover from this moment but I, for one, have all the information I need. Thanks Griff. I knew you were a stand up man, now shoo Holly back to her own bedroom at night so I know her virtue remains intact. If you want her to sleep in here, then you are welcome to room with me, or just put a ring on her finger and say I do, and then she's your problem."

Charlie was already making his way out of the room and dragging their father with him as he said it. Holly jumped up, cursing and yelling at the both of them. Charlie laughed as he dodged a pillow aimed for his head.

"What just happened?" Griffon asked.

"You finally got to meet the real, meddling, good for nothing men in my life who feel they need to control every second of it!"

Griffon thought it over for a moment. "They're right, you know." he told her.

"What? You're kidding me, right?"

"No really, this is a small group and rumors run rampant. I don't want to ruin your reputation or anything. It's important to them."

"It's not important to me."

"Well, it should be. You deserve better, plus, I'm pretty sure your brother just gave his blessing for me to marry you someday." He smiled and stroked her hair. "I've never allowed myself to even think it. We've always lived in the moment, not knowing if tomorrow would even come. Now we don't have to do that. We can make plans and talk about a future together. It's more than I ever dreamed possible."

He kissed her sweetly, and her heart soared. *The future. Could it really be possible?*

Her mind wandered, but not where Griffon expected it to go. "Griffon. A wedding!"

He grinned. "I know. We could actually do this, Holly."

"No, I'm sorry, not that, we can get back to that later. The wedding! I haven't had time to tell you everything I learned

from town.   They seem to think there's some correlation
between a wedding and you.   It doesn't make any sense,
does it? Even stranger, this wasn't an attack orchestrated
by Sarge.   It would appear that your attack came directly
from General Steinfeld himself and wasn't meant to be an
attack but a capture."

"Why would General Steinfeld want me?   That doesn't
even make sense. How would he even know who I am?"

Griffon frowned.

Holly thought about that.   None of it made sense.   She
remembered Griffon once telling her that the AMAN never
really married. She knew that she would have to go back to
the village to investigate further.

* * * * *

Chapter 33

THE COMPOUND opened once again over the next two weeks, and the people of the bunker joined the townsfolk of Wythel to prepare for independence. They built watch-towers alongside every road in and out of town and put a twenty-four-hour guard rotation in place.

Word of a rising rebellion circulated through the entire town. There were a few grumblings, but the majority were in favor. Milo established a leadership team and a planning committee to develop ideas for the long-term survival of Wythel without AMAN control or AMAN resources.

The town was coming alive. Everyone had a purpose. Main Street bustled with activity and excitement. Those assigned weapons or had weapons stashed from long ago, took to openly carrying them as a reminder that they could defend themselves. People felt safe for the first time in many years. The support and encouragement was infectious. Everyone felt the coming of a new era, a new beginning.

* * * * *

Holly spent nearly every day in town. During that first meeting with the town when she, Milo Weaver, and Colton Evers went down seeking information and offering assistance, something happened to her.

She had always been a bit of an outsider amongst her people... the princess who everyone wanted to protect, so she often chose solitude. She never felt considerably strong or authoritative, but the moment she stood up to speak at that initial meeting, she felt called to leadership.

She secretly formed her own small task force in the days following that meeting. In the room beneath the tavern, she set up maps of the area and of what used to be the state of Virginia that she brought down from the bunker. She worked closely with a number of men to establish the locations of AMAN camps in the nearby areas and gain intelligence on their whereabouts and plans. Then she sent scouts out to the north, east, west, and south to verify those locations.

She told no one of her work outside of the few men assisting her, and she swore them to secrecy. Jared Hastings was among them. He consistently encouraged her to fill Griffon in on her plans. He hated going behind his former super's back, but she didn't want Griffon involved.

She thought that he was still vulnerable and felt only a small stab of guilt, knowing how miserable and stir crazy he was up in the bunker at the top of the mountain. She considered telling Charlie but suspected that he would try to put a stop to her plans.

She couldn't shake the gut feeling that something bad was coming. She wanted to stay informed and know what they were facing. She had always been sneaky.

She was good at getting information from people and listening in when no one realized she was there. This had proven quite beneficial in the past. Now, however, she had a mound of information that still made little sense, just pieces to a puzzle she couldn't see clearly, yet, and it made her obsessive.

They found the location of nine small AMAN camps and two larger ones within a three-day walk of Wythel. The smaller camps appeared to be migratory and were heading southeast in the direction she knew as the old Virginia Tech campus, which was said to be the AMAN headquarters.

Her resources spoke to numerous other small towns in the area, and word was coming back that the AMAN had been scarce in a number of towns in the area. Many of those towns wanted to stand with Wythel and fight. Holly knew she would have to alert the others of that, and soon. For now, she sent word back, encouraging them to begin their own preparations for independence and resources, gather weapons, and store food, immediately.

She thought back to the fight that she had with Griffon the night before and tried to shake the heavy feeling that was weighing her down.

"I can't just sit here and do nothing, Holly," Griffon had said. "You are gone every day. I've asked Milo and Charlie to stop sending you so much, and they said that they hadn't sent you down there in well over a week. So where have you been? You told me they needed you down there but no one expects you to be there. So what, exactly, are you up to?"

She sighed, remembering how she told him that she was helping some of the ladies with preparations and just felt like that's where she needed to be right now.

Her chest ached with the knowledge that she was lying to the man she loved. She felt strongly that she was protecting him in the process and stood by her conviction, painting a quaint picture of happy days working in gardens and mending clothes for winter.

In reality, not three days earlier, she was scouting about five miles outside the next town to the west of Wythel when she came across three AMAN scouts who had set up a temporary camp. They discovered and detained her.

When one of the men dragged her into his tent and tried to attack her, she killed him with his own knife but not before he took a deep slice out of her leg. She stitched it up herself to stop the bleeding that she was certain the remaining two would use to track her. She concealed the injury from everyone and made up excuses for a number of bruises she was unable to hide on her arms.

Holly hated the deceit toward those she loved most, especially Griffon, but she felt energized and awakened, with a new purpose in life. She sighed and tried to concentrate on Devon Atley's report and the scouting reports her men had dropped off that morning, when word reached her.

* * * * *

It had been two weeks since the initial meeting Holly had arranged with Ben Hayes and eighteen days since the last

AMAN presence in Wythel. Spirits were high throughout the town until the horn blew from the tower to the north, alerting them all to the coming arrival of the AMAN.

The town was not ready. After all the preparations and growing excitement, the majority of the townspeople still panicked and ran back to their assigned AMAN jobs as quickly as possible. A few wanted to take a stand at this moment but others urged them to appear normal. They needed more time to stage a battle, especially given the reports of the number of AMAN heading their way. There was little time to react, so they hid their weapons and tried to appear as if everything was status quo.

Jared ran to the tavern to notify Holly the second the alarm descended upon the town. On the way, word spread that four vehicles full of AMAN were heading toward Main Street. Panic was rising as people ran toward their formerly assigned duties to appear to be working as usual in the AMAN ruled era.

"Four vehicles, Holly, at least twenty men! Some think that even more are on the way." Jared paced the dark room as he filled her in on the approaching convoy. "How is that possible? We've been monitoring those roads and area for weeks now. How did they slip past us?"

She swallowed hard before speaking. Her hand shook with the report still in it. "Devon returned from the northern route about twenty minutes ago, Jared."

She handed him the report. 'No signs of AMAN from the North. All Clear!'

Jared slammed the paper down on the table, which made her jump. He grabbed the maps off the walls and threw the reports in a box.

"Come on, we're getting out of here right now!"

* * * * *

She didn't have time to react before he pushed her down one of the tunnels she had never been in before. She went as quickly and quietly as she could while trying to digest it all. They turned a corner, and Jared stopped. It was nearly pitch black in that part of the tunnel but he seemed to know exactly where he was as he felt along the wall for a small latch and popped open a door no one would have known existed.

Her eyes were wide as she watched him closely. He pushed her through the door and closed it quietly. The room, inside, was partially lit. He signaled for her to stay put and be quiet as he did a quick recon of the place.

Then he grabbed her arm and led her further into a room furnished with old antiques. The light was natural, coming through the bottom of some grayed out windows that were barely noticeable toward the ceiling of the room. She couldn't make out the location. They had made a number of twists and turns in tunnels that she was not familiar with and had no idea how far they had gone. She made a mental note to learn the underground tunnel system herself, later.

Jared put his finger to his lips and motioned for her to move over to a large bookcase against the back wall. He moved a few books, pointed to a round metal hole toward the back of the bookcase, and motioned for her to lean in close. It was the end of some metal piping designed to amplify sounds from the other end. She could tell the other end must have been in the big room under the tavern because she could hear people talking and made out Devon Atley's voice.

"This is the place, I swear!" he said.

"Then where are the maps you told us about? Where's the girl?"

"They were all in here this morning! They couldn't have gone far. We need to check the tunnels, come on."

Holly's heart was pounding, and tears were stinging her eyes, threatening to spill over. He was talking about her. He was a spy working for the AMAN. How could she not have noticed or suspected or something? She strained to remember who had recommended Devon Atley to the team and couldn't recall.

"Forget the girl and whatever information she thinks she has. You've been manipulating it for weeks."

Anger flared in her as she listened.

"Just tell us where Griffon Maynor is hiding." Another voice demanded.

Holly's eyes flew to Jared's, who stood wide-eyed and stunned as he realized they were still going after Griffon.

Instinctively, he reached out and grabbed her arm just as she was about to turn and bolt. His finger flew to his lips to signal quiet as he capped the pipe, allowing them to speak without the others hearing on the other end. He tugged her close, and the unexpected motion left her clinging to him. *How am I going to get word to Griffon?*

It felt like hours, although it was only minutes that she stood there in his arms, crying. Jared was amazed as he watched her pull herself back together, take a deep breath, step back away from him, and ask if he had a plan, and she transitioned back into the soldier he knew her to be.

He was in awe of her strength and wisdom, even during times of great distress. He had to remind himself that this was Griffon's girl on more than one occasion over the last few weeks that they had worked so closely together. He reminded himself of that more than once.

"I don't know Holly. Do you have your field bag with you?"

"Yes, but Devon knows our frequencies. If I try to radio in word, he'll know it."

Jared nodded. It was true... but did it matter? "If we call up to the bunker, even if they hear it, there will be plenty of time for them to go into lock down before the AMAN get up there."

"True but we won't make it. Do you think it's worth the risk, Jared?"

He was amazed that she asked his opinion. He had never felt like a leader amongst this team. Never wanted to be one. He was a hard worker and loyal, but he did what they told him, nothing else, and he never offered suggestions. He never singled himself out nor did anything on his own until the moment he realized that Devon Atley was a traitor. That's when he grabbed Holly and led her to safety before the reality of the situation had registered, even to her.

"Jared?" her voice broke him from his thought process. "What should we do? Should I call up to the bunker or not?"

"If you do, they will lock it down, and you won't be able to get back until the threat has passed. You'll be stuck down here, Holly. The alternative is to try to make it up there and then have them lock down, but it's a big risk. You know that already."

She was nodding, deep in thought. Then she leaned down and opened the backpack she had shrugged off on arrival and picked up the two-way radio, dialing in to the bunker frequency. She hesitated only a second.

"Bunker, bunker, this is Holly, come in please."

"Hols? What's up? Why are you dialing in through this frequency?"

"Charlie! I can't explain right now but give the five-minute warning immediately, make absolute certain that Griffon is inside, and go into lockdown!" There was silence on the other end. "Do you hear me, Charlie? Do it! Do it now! They are coming for him, the AMAN are on their way."

"Where are you?"

"I'm in town. It's too late for me. I'm not going to make it back in time. You need to act fast! It's all my fault, Charlie! Don't let anything happen to him or to the group. Promise me!"

There was a long moment of silence before Charlie returned. "I promise," was all he said, and they could hear the siren going off through the radio.

Holly started to set the radio down, then grabbed it back up. "Charlie?" she whispered. "You let dad and Griffon know I'm safe. Tell Griffon I'm with the person that he trusts most, and everything's going to be okay."

Her words stunned Jared. She had to mean him. *Griffon trusted him the most?*

She turned off the radio. She couldn't risk it going off and someone hearing it. She looked distant when she spoke. "Griffon always told me that I could trust you above all others down here. That if anything ever happened and I was in trouble, to find you and you'd help. That's why I went to you first when we were setting up this task force."

Jared realized the praise in her words, but he felt a sudden stab of guilt. This was all his fault. He hadn't known Devon Atley well enough to bring him on board. He strained hard to remember exactly who had vouched for him.

He kept records and would have to go back and look soon. Could it be possible there was more than one traitor in their midst? The thought that he had let Holly down, let Griffon down, weighed heavily on him.

She noticed the weight he carried. "That was meant to be a compliment you know!"

She went back to the pipe and removed the cover to listen. At first, she heard nothing. Then she heard a whooshing noise, followed by a thud and groan; that pattern repeated several times.

"Where is this bunker? I'll blow the door right off," hissed a voice that she hadn't heard before, followed by another whoosh and groan.

She realized that the person talking was hitting someone and trying to get the location of the bunker.

"I-I don't know," came the slow, raspy voice of Devon Atley. He was in a great deal of pain as he said it.

She heard another whoosh, thud, and groan.

"Ya-you didn't give me enough time. I was trying to gain her confidence but you're a week early. It's up the mountain but I don't know where." Devon was crying this time as he spoke.

"The plans changed; we have to act now. General Steinfeld is growing impatient. The wedding is just two weeks away. We must have Griffon Maynor. Tell me how to get him."

Whoosh, thud, groan.

"The girl!" Devon cried out. "The girl that I've been working for. She's Griffon's girl. Get the girl, and you'll get him."

Holly had to stifle a scream. She heard a loud crash, followed by a "Get up!" She strained to hear more and signaled Jared over to listen.

"You said the girl would be here."

"She should have been; this is her office. All her stuff, it's gone, though. Someone must have tipped her off. I don't know where she would go. I just don't know, but the others might. Jared will for sure. They're all due back tonight. They'll know. We just have to wait for them to get back."

Jared capped the pipe.

"Oh crap! They'll know I'm with you. Tony and Jacob know how to get to this room. I don't know how to get word to them without alerting Devon to our location or putting them in more danger and us. They won't deliberately give us away, but I think Devon will persuade them that he's the victim here and seek their help in finding us for the safety of everyone."

He was pacing the room while he spoke.

Holly remained calm. "I do agree with that. Jared, where are we? In the town, I mean. Where in town are we right now?"

"We're under the old house near the dried up river bed. Do you know the place?"

"Yes, and that's perfect! Can you climb?"

"Um, yeah, I guess. What you got in mind?"

"I know a safe place, but we have to get up the mountain without being seen. Fortunately, we're in a good spot. I wish we had recon on where the AMAN are, but we'll have to make the best of it.

"Chances are, there will be some rebels anxious to fight the AMAN as soon as the sun goes down. We need to use that to our advantage to get away. We can monitor things a bit from there, once we're safe.

"Part of me says stay and fight; part of me says run. Unless you really want to stay and fight, running is the best idea I have. How about you?"

She was seeking his advice, again, and that threw him off. "You're too important for them to capture. I say we run." He nodded to himself as he said it.

* * * * *

It was late afternoon, and they spent the next several hours gathering everything they could use and preparing for the hike up the mountain. As soon as dark began to descend upon the town, Holly and Jared made their way up into the house and out the back door. Moving quickly and quietly, they made it to the edge of the woods with no issues. They walked in silence up the mountain at a steady pace.

A little over an hour later, Holly grabbed for his hand and pulled him around a large bush, which he saw at the last minute, was actually a concealed path. He wondered where she was taking him and did not at all envision the beautiful water hole, complete with waterfall. He saw a sign that read 'Holly's Hole' and smiled. He knew they must be close to the bunker.

They were both breathing hard, red faced, and sweaty. They made good time up the mountain, and Holly took a minute to strip down to a tank top and shorts. She dove into the cool water to freshen up before heading into the cave. Jared watched her quietly for a few moments before shedding his clothes down to his boxers and joining her. They splashed and laughed, and he had to remind himself of the danger they were in.

They hadn't spoken a word since they had left the hidden room under the house near the dried up river bed, and Holly broke that silence now.

"Okay, it's late. It's dark, and I'm exhausted. Grab your stuff and we'll head up."

"Head up where?" he asked, looking around and seeing a sheer rock cliff stretching high above, broken only by the waterfall.

"You'll see," she smiled and looked almost happy. "Just follow me."

He watched as she headed straight for the waterfall. He could tell she was trying to say something but he couldn't hear over the roar of the water. Finally, she stopped and motioned with her hands for him to follow. Then she stepped right through the waterfall and disappeared. He just stood there watching until she came back, took his hand, and urged him on, tugging him through the water.

Once on the other, side he saw a room with a second waterfall coming through the ceiling. She kept his hand and tugged him through that one, too. It was quieter on that side, and when she spoke again, he could hear her.

"I trusted you through the underground railroad tunnels. Now you're gonna have to trust me through mine. It's going to get very dark, so whatever you do, don't let go of my hand, okay?"

She watched as he nodded in acknowledgment.

It was still loud enough that she was yelling over the waterfall noise, and she laughed and said, "It's okay, the noise will die down in a bit. We're free to talk openly here. There is no one around to hear. No one even knows of this place except Griffon, and, well, Charlie and Amos know of it but have never actually been in here."

He walked quietly as she led him through twists and turns, often in pitch black, without ever stumbling. He was even more amazed by her than he had ever been and wasn't prepared when she stopped short and turned to him. There was a faint light up ahead, allowing him to see just enough to see the smile on her face.

"Okay, we're here." She sounded excited, but he still didn't know where they were. It looked just like any other tunnel they'd been through, so far. "Now close your eyes," she told him. "You can trust me."

He felt his heart leap into his throat and chastised himself for it. He did trust her, absolutely, but the sensations she evoked in him made him wonder if she should be trusting him quite so much.

When he closed his eyes, she reached out and took both his hands in hers. He was certain that she could hear his heart thudding in his chest and feel the acceleration in his pulse. He was not at all comfortable with the physical response he had to her. It seemed to be increasing throughout the day, which greatly disturbed him. He stepped forward at her urging and followed her with complete faith.

She stopped and looked around. Everything was just as she'd last left it in the cave. The moon was high and the stars were bright on this clear night. It looked magical and, for a moment, she just forgot herself and stood there, mesmerized by nature's beauty and holding on to Jared's hands.

They stopped, for what seemed like an eternity to him, and he cleared his throat. "Can I open them yet?" he whispered.

She laughed, which sounded loud next to his whisper. "Yes, sorry. I got a little lost in my head for a moment."

He opened his eyes and was visibly stunned at the picture before him. "Wow!" was all he could manage to say. He must have gotten a little lost in his own head because he had no idea how long he stood there staring at the beautiful night sky and the little lights twinkling down below in what he could only guess was Wythel.

He realized they were still standing close and holding hands. Holly looked more at peace and happier than he had ever seen her. It struck him hard just how beautiful she was.

He shook his head to clear that last thought, laughing to himself. What had gotten into him? He took a step back and let go of her hand.

* * * * *

Holly watched him closely in those first moments he opened his eyes, and she was acutely aware of just how handsome he was. He was tall and thin, yet strong and solid. His blue eyes looked almost purple in the night's light. His shaggy blonde hair nearly hung over them. She wondered why she had never noticed the tiny dimple in his right cheek when he smiled. Her trance broke as he stepped away and dropped her hand.

She shook off the thought and busied herself preparing the cave. Fortunately, it was a warm night but not too hot. They wouldn't need much more than sleeping bags and pillows, which she retrieved from a hole in the back of the cave. She and Griffon had stored them behind a stalactite.

He made himself comfortable on the large rock near the window that she claimed was a couch. When he turned around, the room had truly transformed. There were two sleeping mats rolled out with sleeping bags on top, complete with pillows and pillowcases. He hadn't seen a pillow case since he was a small boy, and his own pillow at home was barely more than shreds of what was probably once a pillow, though he wasn't sure. On the other side of the cave, she was setting up what appeared to be a kitchen.

Swinging some buckets, she asked if he was up for another walk through the tunnels or would prefer to rest. In light of the emotions that holding her hand had caused earlier, he thought it safer to stay put. She told him she was going for water and would be back in a little while.

After she left, he looked around. The first thing he noticed was how close she had arranged the beds. He had to remind himself that was probably what she was used to with Griffon and didn't think much about it. The kitchen had a nice camp stove and all sorts of pots, pans, and other utensils. He opened a large box and discovered enough food to feed a small army. He grinned. They definitely wouldn't go hungry up here.

She had also dragged out another box with books, games, and entertainment items that he hadn't seen since he was a small boy. The AMAN burned all the books so long ago that he couldn't help but wonder where she had gotten them all. There was also a box of assorted clothes... some were clearly hers, and some were clearly male. He assumed they belonged to Griffon, and a wave of guilt washed over him. He would have to pull himself together.

When Holly returned with the water, she went right to the little kitchen she had set up and got to work cooking something for the both of them. He noticed that she had changed into dry clothes. They looked like pajamas and, for the first time, he realized he still had on just his damp boxers, which suddenly seemed inappropriate. Holly must have sensed his uneasiness because she chose that moment to point to the box of clothes.

"I pulled a box of clothes out that we keep up here. There should be dry underwear, pajamas, and clothes of all sorts in there. Feel free to help yourself, unless you just like sitting around in wet underwear." She was laughing as she said it and went right back to cooking.

He rummaged through the box and found a pair of underwear, some gym shorts, and a tee-shirt that he thought would work. He moved into the cover of a tunnel and changed. He felt better in dry clothes and realized they smelled clean, like a memory of a past he couldn't quite place. He couldn't remember the last time he had worn truly clean clothes, and these looked brand new.

Holly made a simple soup for their first meal together, and he couldn't remember better tasting food, ever. He praised her for it and, even in the dim light of the moon and the two lanterns she had turned on, he could see pink flush her cheeks at his compliment.

"Do you think it would be safe to try to radio the bunker? Just to let them know we're okay?" she asked.

"Yes, but you can't tell them anything. You can say you're safe but that's it. Remember how you managed to send code to let Griff know who you were with without really saying it? That sorta thing, if it's only between the two of you, might be okay but that's it, no details. I have no weapons to protect you from the AMAN up here, should they come after us. So let's not draw their attention."

He was worried about her and knew that she was smart enough to know and do the things he said, but he still felt the need to say it.

She turned on the radio. "Bunker, bunker, this is Holly, over."

"Holly, thank God! Are you okay; where are you? I'm coming to get you right now!" Griffon had clearly been waiting for word.

"I'm fine; we both are. I'm positive this frequency is being monitored by the AMAN, so be careful what you say," she warned.

Smart girl, Jared thought. He knew Griffon would be too emotional to think of such a thing.

"I need to know... are you on lockdown?"

"Yes! But I'll bust out of this tin can the second I know where you are."

She laughed. "Not as easy as you think. Lord knows, I've tried in the past! I just need to know that you are okay, and I want you to know that I am fine. I'm with the one you trust the most in the place you love the most. We're safe."

A stab of pain hit Jared in the heart once again at her words.

Griffon sighed, "Can he hear this?"

"Yes"

"You promise me that you will take care of her and keep her safe until you're dying breath, if need be." It wasn't a question; it was more like a statement.

"You know I will, my friend," Jared said, and Holly noticed how serious his face was when he replied. She shivered, realizing that he absolutely meant it.

"I love you! Contact us in the days to come just to let me know you're still okay. I just hope this passes quickly."

"I love you, too, and I'll talk to you soon. We're gonna get through this okay; but be careful, they're coming for you."

* * * * *

Chapter 34

WHILE JARED lounged on the rock couch, Holly cleaned up from dinner and set about turning off each of the lanterns.

"I don't know how long we'll be stuck here, so we should conserve the lanterns as much as possible. I can't get to any more fuel during lockdown, and I don't have much stocked here. Since the sky is clear and the moon bright, we can still see. The full moon still looks a few days out, so we should be okay for the next several nights, at least," she told him.

He sensed that she just needed to talk. She joined him on the couch rock when she had completed her tasks. They sat in silence, just staring out into the night. Suddenly, there was a large flash of light from the valley below. He leaned forward and squinted to see better. He thought he made out flashes of bright light below, but they only lasted a second.

"Did you see that?" he asked, pointing to where the largest light was previously.

She didn't say a word but got up and fumbled around low against the wall to his left, then returned with two pairs of binoculars and handed him one.

He just shook his head, grinning to himself. *Was there anything that she didn't have in here,* he wondered. He put the binoculars to his eyes and, within moments, stood up.

"No, no, no, no! Holly do you see that? Something's on fire down there, and look over toward Main Street. Is that gunfire?"

Her heart sank as she turned to where he pointed. "Yes, Jared. It seems the rebellion has begun."

* * * * *

They both felt a sense of guilt for not being down there helping their friends, his family, and, perhaps, even some of hers. After all, how many from the bunker had been down in Wythel when she called in the five-minute lockdown alarm? They had prepared more than anyone for this battle and because of the deceit of that traitor, Devon Atley, they were stuck in hiding instead of fighting back for what they loved.

She couldn't watch for long.

"There's nothing we can do from here. Let's try and get some sleep."

He heard the sadness and guilt in her voice. He felt that he understood her well, as it matched his own feelings knowing the war had begun and they were missing it.

He followed her over to the sleeping bags and laid on the one next to her. He immediately regretted it and considered moving his over some to put physical space between them but didn't want to be too obvious. He knew instantly that he wouldn't sleep well that night, especially not if he couldn't control the crazy emotions she stirred in him.

They were quiet for a long time. A few times, he thought he could hear a muffled sound coming from her, and he wondered if she was crying but couldn't be sure until she rolled over and he saw the moon light glistening in the tears running down her cheeks. Without thinking, he reached over and dried them with his thumb, then opened his arms to offer her a safe place.

She lunged into his arms and cried openly as he held her. They didn't talk that night. He just held her close, smoothing her hair down her back with his hand until she finally gave a last shudder and drifted off to sleep in his arms. He didn't want to disturb her by moving, so he just held her and tried to clear his head of all thoughts. He suspected it was going to be a long night.

* * * * *

Jared did sleep that night. He slept hard and better than he had in a very long time. When he woke, the sun was already shining. He was groggy, and it took him a minute to adjust and get his bearings. All of his nerves stood on end as he realized that Holly was still cuddled up next to him, sound asleep.

He really looked at her. She appeared so peaceful and, so beautiful, as she slept. It was as if nothing had happened and life was perfect, but reality hit him like a brick. Stuff did happen. A war had begun. They were hiding for their lives, her life, and, more importantly, this wasn't his girl he was holding. As he stiffened at the thought, he felt her stir next to him.

She felt him next to her but continued to lay there. She knew he was watching her and wondered what he was thinking. She knew she had embarrassed herself by giving way to the stress and grief of the day before. She knew that she had no right to seek comfort from him, yet they felt like the last two people on earth, and she had clung to him. She felt too comfortable with him. As she thought about that, she knew she really didn't know that much about Jared Hastings.

She thought back to the night she and Griffon lay talking... *some time before, in another life,* she thought to herself. He had been worried about her going down to Wythel without him. He hadn't liked it at all and feared for her safety. Too many people knew how close they were, and he worried if the AMAN were still seeking him out specifically, she would become an easy target. He had been right to worry. She knew that, now.

Griffon had gone through a list of people he trusted would help her if the AMAN came and she found herself in trouble. The list was short but at the top was Jared Hastings. Griffon wasn't best friends with Jared. He was three years younger, so they didn't grow up together and had rarely hung out. They didn't really associate outside of work, but Jared was his backup at work, training to someday take his position. He trusted no one to watch over his men in his absence more than he trusted Jared. Griffon knew he was young for the job but he had heart and tenacity. He was hard working, loyal, and trustworthy, and Griffon could think of no one outside his family that he trusted more to watch after his men and now, Holly.

She knew that Jared was quiet and strong. He never offered his opinion, but when she asked for it, he would give it. She noticed right away that he was smart, quick-witted, and far more intelligent than he let on to others.

When she first approached him to discuss the task force that she wanted to put in place to begin recon and strategic purpose, he sat quietly and listened respectfully. When she asked his opinion after giving her rehearsed proposal, he sat quietly at first. With a little prodding, he opened up to her, and what he said shocked her.

Her plan was too narrow and would be ineffective. If she truly wanted to make a difference, they needed to move away from Wythel and begin mapping the surrounding areas. Perhaps even infiltrate the AMAN, itself. He was cunning and daring but not reckless. She liked him immediately.

The two had grown a kind of friendship during the weeks preparing and implementing the task force. He let her lead as she saw fit but, when prompted, would give her suggestions and was not afraid to tell her when he disagreed. He just never offered his opinion without being asked.

She often wondered what his story was. She wasn't even sure of his age. He looked rather young at times, especially when he relaxed and smiled, which was rarely. She briefly thought of the dimple she had noticed the night before. Most of the time, he seemed old and wise, hardened by years... but from what, she didn't know.

Jared had been watching in fascination the changes in Holly's face as she wondered about him. He couldn't begin to guess what was going in that pretty little head but certainly didn't expect her to speak before her eyes opened.

She knew that he was watching her and without much thought, she asked, "How old are you, anyway?"

He was stunned at first, then shook his head and laughed. "Good morning to you, too. That's a funny thing to ask."

"Well?" Holly said as she stretched, suddenly realizing just how close they were together.

"I'm nineteen. Why?"

"I was just wondering, that's all." She thought on that again and opened her eyes to look at him. He looked relaxed with his hair tousled from the night's sleep. In that moment, he did look young. "Just nineteen? Really? I thought you were much older. Mid to late twenties, maybe? You seem much older than nineteen."

She got up and headed for the water buckets. "I'm going to get water and clean up. You coming or not?"

He laughed and got up to follow.

As they migrated through the tunnels to the spring, she felt him relax. He usually seemed uptight, but she noticed him laughing and smiling more, despite the stress of the day before and all that was wrong in their world, right now.

As they headed into the pitch-black section, she stopped to get her bearings and put her hand out to touch the wall to feel her way through the turns. She didn't need light but stopped short, remembering that he probably did.

When she stopped suddenly, he walked right into her.

"Sorry, Holly."

He remained close behind her, and she noted again how relaxed he was. She realized that she was standing still but didn't move again until she asked, "Jared, we are in pitch black. You have absolutely no idea where you are going, yet you follow me with ease. Why, despite everything that's happened, do you seem so much more relaxed and almost your age even. You are normally so uptight. What gives?"

She was curious but didn't really expect an answer. He was still very close, almost pressing against her. He spoke softly in the dark.

"My dad wasn't a very good man," he admitted. "He used to beat me and my mom from the farthest back I can remember. When I was little, he locked me in a closet when he didn't want to deal with me. It was always dark in there. Instead of being scared, after a while, it became a safe place. He didn't hurt me when I was in there. Sometimes I'd just hide in there so he would leave me alone. It was the safest place in my life. I guess the dark just comforts me, now. I feel a bit at home here. Safe. I haven't felt that way in a long time."

Her heart ached for the boy she envisioned. What an awful way to live. It made her angry and sad at the same time. No wonder he always seemed so much older and so guarded. She surprised herself when her eyes welled up with tears.

"I'm so sorry, Jared," she said.

"Don't be. I have my baggage but everyone carries something with them. I'm okay, though. I got through it. When everything went to hell, my dad was out of town. He never made it back home, so, in some ways, the worst life imaginable for so many people was a welcome new beginning for me."

She was in awe of his strength, and while she knew that he most likely heard her crying, she was shedding tears for the man that she knew now and the boy he once was; she didn't care. She laughed through the tears and said, "Maybe that's why you always seem like an old man in a young man's body. You've lived through more than most of us."

He laughed with her and then grew serious. "I've never admitted that to anyone before Holly. There are people who suspected or knew something was going on at least, but I've never told another person. I'm not even sure why I told you. Sometimes I feel like you are so intuitive that you already know me better than I even know myself. You push me to do and say things that I might think of but would never act on, normally. You make me stronger."

She laughed, and he became defensive.

"That wasn't supposed to be funny!"

She laughed harder as they reached the light of the spring. She turned and watched the silhouette of his face.

"I was just thinking. I may make you stronger but most of the time, I feel like I am weaker or maybe I'm just more vulnerable with you. What is the irony in that?"

She became quiet as they entered the spring room and watched him take in the beauty. She was still contemplating what he had revealed of his past and what she told him. It was true.

"You should know that I'm actually not a crier. Never. Griffon's seen it once, maybe twice. Cassie and Chris get downright uneasy if I my eyes even start to tear up because it just doesn't happen. Most people think I'm pretty tough, hard as nails, and, sometimes, even without remorse but it's not really the case. I'm not really sure why I seem to cry all the time around you, but thanks for putting up with me."

He smiled, opened his arms and she went into the safety of them. He hugged her tightly, and she laughed, again.

"I'm not going to cry this time, I promise." A few tears trickled down her eyes when she said it.

"If it's any comfort, I'm about as familiar with close contact like this as you are with tears." He laughed. "We are quite the odd pair, Holly Jenkins, but I promise you, were going to get through this."

They walked back hand-in-hand, both feeling the new bond between them.

* * * * *

Chapter 35

L IFE IN the cave was happier than Jared could ever have imagined. Each night, they sat close together on the couch with heavy hearts, watching the lights flashing in the town below them.

On the third day, as he used the binoculars to scout out the town, he saw large plumes of smoke in several areas. From what he could see through the binoculars, it looked like a war zone down there.

Holly noticed how much time he was spending trying to observe, so she found the backpacks they had brought up with them, pulled the maps out, and spread them out across the cave floor. The maps had gotten wet when they came through the waterfall, and she was thankful that they were okay.

As the maps dried, she retrieved two notebooks and pencils from the entertainment box and brought them to him. She started to hand one to him, then thought maybe she should ask.

"Jared, can you read and write?"

She didn't want to sound arrogant but knew the stories of how the AMAN burned all the books, paper, pencils, and such.

He took the notebook and turned it over lovingly.

"Yes, I actually can read and write, although I'm sure that I'm a little rusty."

She nodded. She knew he was a survivor, so she didn't need to ask how he retained these skills.

"I think we should start writing down our observations, he said. I want to call the bunker, see what they know and ask if they've heard anything from Wythel. We should try different frequencies to see if we can tap into anything regarding the AMAN."

"Perhaps we should sneak down and check things out ourselves. We can't just sit here and let the world go to hell around us. That's my dad. That's not me."

He nodded. He understood and felt the same way. While hiding was comfortable for him, he had always chosen not to let it consume his life. He chose to face the world. Perhaps that's why Holly always said he looked and acted older than his age and why he always looked uptight and not easily approachable. He knew it was true. It was a defense mechanism that he found necessary when leaving the safety and comfort of his often all consuming darkness.

They got to work right away.

Jared called into the bunker. "Bunker, bunker, come in please."

"Identify yourself. Over."

"Jared Hastings with Holly Jenkins. Over."

"Jared, this is Charlie, Holly's brother. How are you two holding up?"

Holly could hear the stress in her brother's voice.

"She's safe. We're safe."

"Thanks man. I know we've never met, but I owe you everything for watching out for her."

Jared wanted to tell him that she didn't need his protection, that she could handle herself just fine. Instead, he said, "It's my honor. Any word from Wythel?"

Charlie relayed what news they had. Several fires had erupted throughout the town, but the rebels were standing their ground.

AMAN were more concerned with finding Griffon than fighting back, so most of the damage done was done by the rebels trying to flush out the AMAN.

Milo, Colton Evers, Pastor Weaver, Cassie, Lily, and, of course, Holly, were not accounted for but all others made it back to the bunker before lockdown, along with five additional people from Wythel.

As Jared signed off, Holly fought back hysterics. *Cassie and Lily were stuck down there while she was hiding out in the cave!* The thought was too much for her to handle.

He saw that she was barely holding it together, so he pulled her close to him and wrapped his arms around her, knowing the tears would come. He let her cry for a while, knowing she'd be stronger for it. When she calmed down a little, he spoke.

"So, what do you want to do?"

"I can't leave them down there! They aren't fighters. We have to find them and bring them back."

"Okay, boss, let's do this. Who and how many do you plan to extract? Will we bring them back here or have them open the bunker? What's the plan?"

"I don't have one yet. We need to think it through carefully. Please, don't make me force an opinion out of you. If you have something to say, please just say it. I need you right now!"

He grinned. She was always more observant than he gave her credit for.

"Okay then, what are our targets?"

"Cassie and Lily," she said without hesitation. "If we can get Milo out without compromising the girls, we should. I at least owe him that much."

He didn't know what she meant by that and didn't ask. He was a little surprised that she didn't say the Pastor. Pastor Weaver was perhaps in more danger than the ladies, with the AMAN around. He didn't say anything, however.

She could tell he was thinking something but not speaking up.

"Jared, you cannot hold back on me. Do you understand? I trust you, completely. You have to open up to me. I need to know what's going on in that head of yours."

He smiled, knowing that she'd blush and be sorry she asked if he told her everything that he had been thinking over the last several days.

Instead, he said, "It's nothing, Holly. I was just mildly curious about you not picking Pastor Weaver. He's in a lot of danger if he's down there with the AMAN around. They will kill him."

"I know. But he's not my concern." She hesitated before going on. "Lily and Cassie are two people I love most in this world. They are vulnerable down there, and I can't stand to think of them anywhere near the AMAN!"

Subconsciously, she rubbed her cut leg. It still throbbed, and she feared infection might be setting in. She'd have to remember to clean and redress it soon.

"Milo and I were to be married, you know."

He was shocked by her confession. Once the initial surprise receded, he laughed loudly. "You and Milo Weaver? I've met him a few times. Nice enough guy, but hardly your type."

He was so matter of fact that she was stunned for a minute. Did she even have a type, and what would he know about that? She pouted a bit.

"I just mean, I have a really hard time picturing you and Milo together." He tried to be nonchalant.

"It was a crazy time in my life." She decided to let him off the hook and changed the subject.

"If Colton wants out, then we should help him, too. He's ex-special forces, and my dad picked him for head of security for good reasons. He may have already established himself in the rebellion, so he may or may not decide to come back with us."

"Still no Pastor Weaver?" He couldn't fathom why she would not want to bring him along.

She hesitated for only a second. "No. I don't care what happens to him. He's not the man you think he is. He's more closely related to your father than our Heavenly Father." She didn't need to say anything more. He of all people would understand.

He was surprised to hear it but accepted it as truth. Holly wouldn't say such a thing without good reason. She was the only one who knew about his past, so he spared her from the gruesome details.

* * * * *

They ate lunch, talking easily with each other. He wanted to know more about her and Milo, and he wanted to know how she met Griffon. She told him more than she had ever said to anyone about the struggles of loving two men and how, ultimately, it was Griffon that she loved.

It pained him to hear her speak about her love for Griffon, but he needed to know. He was growing too comfortable and too close to her and needed the reminder that she could never be his.

After lunch, she told him she was going to clean up. She took her daypack with her and seemed a little under the weather. He felt she was hiding something but couldn't fathom what it could be. When she did not return for over an hour, he went searching for her. He was good with directions and had already memorized the path to the spring, finding his way there easily.

He found her sitting next to the spring crying, but it was not her normal cry. There were tears but she looked so pained. He noticed that she had her pants off, and he hesitated in approaching her.

He cleared his throat and watched her jump. She tried to pull her pants up quickly but not before he saw the blood trickling down her leg.

"Oh no, Holly! What happened? You're bleeding."

He ran to her side and pulled her pants back down around her ankles, ignoring the horrified look on her face. She had to know that he would never hurt her, but the wild look in her eyes stopped him, and he took a step back. He took her hands, which were shaking badly in his own, and looked into her eyes. He knew that look of terror and was disgusted that he was the cause of it.

"Holly, I'm here. It's okay. I'm not going to hurt you. Tell me what happened."

He spoke softly and reassuringly. He wanted a look at her leg to see where the bleeding was coming from and saw the fear on her face.

"I think it may be infected," was all she managed to say.

"I need to take a look." He wanted her to relax and let him look at it. "Are you okay with that?"

She hesitated, then nodded her head yes and turned to face him. He saw a large wound on her leg that looked as if it had stitches, but he wasn't completely sure, since it was swollen and red, with oozing green sores. He saw signs of infection on the bandages she had tossed on the ground.

"When Holly? How?"

She told him how it happened a week earlier. *What were we doing a week earlier? And how did I not notice this before? Man, that looks bad.*

"Were you trying to bleed some of the infection out on your own when I came in here?"

She nodded her head yes. She looked pale and still a little frightened.

"Good girl. Judging by that bandage, it looks like you've gotten the worst out but we have to keep a close eye on it and keep it clean."

He tore off a piece of the shirt he was wearing and dipped it into the cold spring water. Then he cleaned the area around the wound and washed away the blood that had run down her leg. He told her to leave her pants off until they got back to the main cave where the first aid kit was located. He helped her up, and they made their way back.

She was grateful that he hadn't made a big deal out of it. She knew he wanted to know what happened, but he hadn't pressed her about it, either. She saw the look of horror and regret on his face when she freaked out on him. She knew he blamed himself. She felt badly; she didn't mean to freak out like that.

When he pulled her pants down, she had a sudden flashback to the day that AMAN solider had dragged her into his tent, pulling her pants down while she kicked, screamed, and tried to get away. She had never felt so helpless, and the memory made her freeze like a coward.

She wanted to explain that it wasn't him or anything he had done, that she trusted him completely and was grateful for his friendship and company. She was just too humiliated to admit what had happened that day.

Once back in the cave, he bandaged her wounded leg as best he could.

"I need to know what caused the cut, Holly. You don't have to tell me what happened if you don't want. . . I'll accept that as your business, but I need to know the condition of whatever caused it to make sure we aren't dealing with something else or need to worry about tetanus or something. Do you understand?"

"It was a kn-knife," she stuttered.

"A knife?" he asked, not meaning to sound alarmed. "Was it clean?"

"I dunno; I guess."

She didn't want to think of the knife, the one that she used to kill that man. She didn't want to remember what it looked like or how it had sounded when she thrust it into his chest. She shivered and tried to block it all from her mind, but couldn't.

She knew he was waiting for her to tell him what happened. She didn't know where to begin or if she could even get it out, but this was Jared. If anyone would understand, it would be him.

"I killed him!"

He couldn't believe what she was saying. "You killed who?"

"The AMAN soldier that cut me." It was barely more than a whisper.

"What? When? How?" There were a thousand questions coming into his head at once.

"Three days before they arrived in Wythel. I was out scouting not far from that large town to the west. Three of them camping in the woods, and I stumbled upon their camp. It was stupid, I know."

She still couldn't bring herself to look at him. She didn't want to see the condemnation in his eyes as her words sunk in. She was a murderer.

He took her face into his hands and forced her to look at him. She saw neither disgust nor condemnation. She saw worry and maybe even love. He cared about her, she could tell, and it made her heart melt as tears welled up in her eyes.

"Did they hurt you?"

She understood what he was asking and shook her head. "No. I fought back when he tried. When I got hold of the knife, I just thrust it into his chest repeatedly, until I knew he was gone. I ran and never looked back. I'm a murderer!"

He hugged her tightly, and her tears flowed as he soothed her.

Anger raged in him. He was supposed to protect her. He had told her not to scout alone. He should have been there. It was all his fault. He couldn't stop accepting the blame, even knowing it wasn't really his fault. Mostly, he was angry that it happened to her.

"You're not a murderer. It was self-defense; there's a difference."

"Do you think God sees the difference?"

He thought about that for a moment. *The commandment reads 'thou shall not kill' but surely there must be exceptions for self-defense.* "Yes, I think God sees the difference. He knows what's in your heart and that it was not done in malice."

They spoke no more of it that day.

* * * * *

Chapter 36

HOLLY AND Jared set their plan in place. They would sneak down the mountain, find out where Cassie and Lily were staying, and get them back up to the cave as quickly as possible.

They sat at the edge of the woods at the spot where they could see clearly what little of the actual town they could and watched as people moved along as normal in the days of AMAN control. They spoke only when necessary. They saw a couple AMAN walking the streets with rifles pointed at the ready. They hadn't seen anything like this since the very early days of AMAN control.

She thought the laundry room would be the most likely place to find Lily and Cassie. She had dressed in layers, despite the heat, not knowing how long they would be gone. She stripped off her top shirt and dug out the extra set of clothes from her pack. Jared eyed her curiously.

She leaned in close to whisper her plan. She would gather the clothes and walk them right into the laundry room and hoped she wouldn't look out of place.

He nodded his agreement.

When the AMAN cleared from the road that led down to Main Street and the laundry room where her friends often sat and mended clothes together, Holly ran quickly out to the street, looking as if she had just come from one of the farmhouses. She headed for town with an armful of laundry that needed mending.

When she got to Main Street, she saw five AMAN soldiers patrolling the area. She feared they might see that her clothes were too new, smelled too clean, and were free of holes and damage. She said a quick prayer that they wouldn't look that closely. She could feel their eyes upon her, but no one stopped her or spoke to her as she hurried across the street and into the building.

Once inside, she closed the door behind her and sunk into the wall, breathing heavy as she looked around at the faces there. No Lily or Cassie! Rhoda Hayes was there and was at her side quickly.

"Holly, what are you doing here?! You're supposed to be in lockdown in the bunker. Has something happened up there?"

"No, I had to call for lockdown while I was still in town. We didn't make it."

Rhoda's eyes were big with surprise. "Lily, come out; it's Holly."

Relief washed over her as Lily ran out of the back room and hugged her. Holly couldn't believe she was actually there. They held the embrace for a long moment.

When Holly found her voice again, she asked, "Cassie?" She looked deeply into Lily's eyes for an answer.

"Cassie's fine. She's up the street, helping out in the bakery. Why are you here? You should be with Griffon in lockdown."

"They were coming for him, so I ordered the lockdown, myself. I was still in town and knew I couldn't make it back in time." She shook her head sadly as she spoke. "It's okay though. He's fine. When we found out that you and Cassie were not accounted for, however, we had to come down and get you out."

Rhoda spoke up. "Holly it's not safe for you, either. They're also looking for you. They believe you may be the key to get to Griffon and they're right, you know. That boy would do anything for you. Anything at all." Another lady nudged Rhoda to be quiet.

"It's okay Rhoda, I know that. That's why we ran and hid. But we can't hide forever, and when we found out Lily and Cassie were still down here, we had to come and get them both out."

"We. You keep saying we. Who else didn't make it? Who are you working with?"

"Miles, Colton, and Pastor Weaver also are unaccounted for, but Jared Hastings is the one helping me."

Rhoda gasped, "OH, not Jared Hastings, Holly! What have you gotten yourself into, now? That boy is damaged goods. You can't trust him."

Defensive rage flared within her. Of course she could trust him. She trusted him more than anyone else on earth. Before she could speak, Lily spoke up.

"Hush Rhoda. You don't really know anything about the boy. Besides, he is one of Griff's boys. He'll protect her. Any of those boys would. Griff always liked Jared. I think he'd be happy to know that she has him by her side."

Warmth and love filled the place of anger as Lily came to Jared's defense.

"I've spoken to Griffon by radio on several occasions. He's very happy to know that I'm working with Jared. He trusts him completely, and so do I."

"You can communicate with the bunker?" Rhoda asked.

Holly nodded.

"Ben was up at the bunker around the time of lockdown, and I haven't seen hide nor hair of him since. Is he there? Is he safe?" She sounded desperate for answers, and Holly's heart went out to her.

"I'm not sure, Rhoda. Charlie said there were five additional people from town in lockdown but didn't say who they were. I will ask him next time and try to get back to you."

"Bless you child, bless you! As much as that man drives me nuts, I just don't know what to do without him!"

Holly turned back to Lily. "Will you and Cassie come back with us?"

Lily's eyes widened. "Where, Holly? Can you get us into the bunker, even during lockdown?"

Holly was suddenly aware of the other women in the room, two of whom she didn't know. It wasn't safe to talk so openly with so much going on and so much hostility in the town.

Her first thought was to protect Jared, which unsettled her. He could take care of himself, she knew, but she was taken back when she realized how much she had come to care for him. He mattered to her, and she couldn't let him down. She also had to protect Cassie and Lily, which was the only reason she went into Wythel in the first place.

"No, they will not open the bunker during lockdown, not even for me, not for as long as the AMAN pose a serious threat to this area and to them."

She saw the questions in Lily's eyes and shook her head, hoping to convey the need to be quiet and not ask questions. She suddenly felt confined and uncomfortable. She had to keep moving.

"Out the back, come on, let's go get Cassie," was all she said.

Once outside, Lily began to question her quietly. "I saw that you look frightened in there, and I know you didn't want to talk in front of them. Why? Those are my friends; it's okay, I'd vouch for every one of them."

"Lily, I'm glad you can trust them, but I don't know them that well. Even those I do know, well right now, I trust you, I trust Cassie, and I absolutely trust Jared. Beyond that, I don't trust anyone down here. I have my reasons and you have yours, but you're going to have to just follow me on this one until I can get you both to safety."

She stopped walking and turned to face her friend, trying to convey the urgency for them to get out of there. "Do you understand what I'm saying Lily? Do not trust anyone!"

Lily looked frightened and a little ticked off but she indicated that she understood.

When they got to the back door of the bakers, Lily walked in first. She had a green shirt with her that she mentioned she was returning to Cassie. Holly smiled, remembering how a green shirt had become a sort of code amongst them.

Cassie responded immediately. Holly hid behind two large barrels of flour while the two women talked quietly. When the bell on the front door jingled, signifying that someone had entered the store, Holly took the opportunity to move back outside. As she rose, she saw two AMAN approach the baker. Instead of moving away, she moved closer, crouching behind the counter.

She strained to hear what they were saying.

"Yes, you heard correctly. We are to acquire the largest and most extravagant wedding cake ever seen." The date is in ten days. Are you or are you not the best baker around?"

Holly caught Cassie's movement in her peripheral vision and saw that she was signaling her to get out. She moved quickly, and no one spoke until they were back outside.

She whispered, "We're leaving now, do you need anything?" They both shook their heads no.

When they got back to the meeting point in the woods, Jared was not there. Holly's heart skipped a beat, and she fought back the panic that was building up inside of her.

While Cassie was often oblivious to her friend's true feelings, Lily was very perceptive. She laid a gentle hand on Holly's shoulder in attempts to calm her.

"I'm sure he's okay, Holly."

Lily worried for her friend and for her brother. She saw the frantic look in Holly's eyes as she searched for this other man.

"He should have been back by now. What if something happened to him? How will I find him or even know where to begin looking?"

As Holly's fears mounted, Jared ran quietly through the woods, and when she saw him, she ran right into his arms. He smoothed her hair down her back in a way they both found comforting. She fought back tears. She had been so worried. She just wanted to cry and melt into his arms, but she had to be strong for Lily and Cassie.

"You're okay?" she asked.

He took a step back and looked her over. "Yeah, you?"

"I'm fine. I got them. Let's get out of here."

* * * * *

The foursome made their way up to the cave. Cassie eyed her, suspiciously, as they entered through the waterfall and made their way up to the cave room with the big picture window that overlooked the valley and Wythel.

"So this is it?" her friend teased. "After all these years, you finally bring me here? I have to admit, it's nothing like I imagined."

Holly laughed at the disappointment in Cassie's voice.

"Seriously, what did you think it would be like?"

"I'm not sure, but a dirty cave wasn't it. I mean, the view's great, don't get me wrong but you've been hiding out in a cave all these years? I just expected something grander!"

As they looked around, Lily and Cassie made eye contact. Both took notice of the two sleeping bags lying side-by-side.

Holly hadn't prepared for more than two people to stay in the cave but thought maybe they could make it work with the extra blankets and stuff that she brought up the previous fall when the cold had started setting in. She set about unpacking what she had, putting the blankets beside her and Jared's bedding.

They made lunch, and the girls settled in. Holly had to make a water run, and Jared ran after her to help.

"Wait up, I'll help," he said.

He noticed the girls staring at the sleeping arrangements, and he saw the unasked questions in their eyes and the looks that passed between them. Although he had been careful to make sure nothing happened between him and Holly, he wasn't sure her friends would understand the friendship they had formed.

Not that he would complain if it was something more, but he respected Griffon too much to let that happen. Although he would never call Holly naïve, he suspected that she might be clueless in this regard.

He knew Holly trusted them completely but he had no reason to. They made him edgy being there, with their accusatory stares.

They didn't talk until they reached the spring. She looked happier and more alive than he'd seen her in days but she looked flushed, as well. Her cheeks were a little too bright, and her eyes were a tad bit dull. That worried him.

"We need to talk."

"What's up?" She sounded cheerful.

"I'm not real sure how to put this without it sounding bad." He cleared his throat. "I don't think your friends like me much."

"What?" She turned to him with a bizarre look on her face. "What are you talking about? Why wouldn't they like you?"

"Lily is Griffon's sister, and I don't think she's too happy to find you shacked up with me." He was trying to be serious but Holly laughed.

"We aren't 'shacking up.' That's crazy!"

She stopped laughing when she saw the look on his face. She could tell he was serious.

"I know nothing happened. You know nothing happened. But I'm telling you that they 'think' something happened."

He paused to think of how to explain and was slightly hurt that she found it funny that someone would think such a thing. That at least solidified to him that his feelings were definitely one-sided. They would only ever be friends. He could live with that, but he also couldn't imagine ever loving another woman the way he had grown to love her. It shocked him to admit it to himself. He loved her.

He sighed and started again. "Okay, picture this from their perspective. They know that you and I have been hiding out up here for several days... and nights... now. They walk in and see two sleeping bags lying on the ground together. You don't have to be a genius to figure out what's going through their heads with that alone. Then you hugged me and touched me spontaneously, and I could feel their glares.

I've lived with people staring at me my whole life. I don't have to turn and see it to know it's there. We are comfortable with each other, probably too comfortable by their standards. It's come out of necessity, but they don't know what all we've gone through together. Just try to see it from their perspective."

She was genuinely shocked. They both know how much she loves Griffon. They couldn't possibly think that about her. Could they?

She just stared at him. *He's just a little older than I am,* she thought. *Closer in age than Griffon. He may appear a little hard at first, but he's definitely just as handsome, especially when he relaxes and laughs. I always said I didn't want comfort and ease in life. Griffon is fire and excitement, but Jared is comfort. I can be myself with him. I can cry unashamedly. In some ways, he knows me better than anyone, even Griffon.* She gasped out loud.

"You see now, right? Maybe I should pack up some bedding and crash in here until things adjust. I think it may be for the best." He grinned a boyish, evil grin that she hadn't seen before. "Now that we've established you're friends think we're shacking up, and we both know we're not... drop your pants." He continued grinning at her, which made her heart beat faster. "Seriously, Hols, I need to check the cut on your leg."

He called her Hols, a nickname only those closest to her had ever used. Griffon never called her that. She couldn't stop comparing them. It was ridiculous.

* * * * *

She loved Griffon, absolutely, but she couldn't deny that she cared greatly for Jared. She hadn't allowed herself to think of him as anything more than a good friend. Now, hearing him voice the concerns that her friends had about their relationship made her wonder. *Was she being inappropriate with him? Did she care for him as more than just a friend? He had laughed at the absurdity of it all. Surely, he felt nothing more than friendship toward her.*

"No." she said aloud, without meaning to. *No, he couldn't possibly think anything more of her. No, she couldn't think about him in that way. No, her friends knew her well, and they wouldn't think such things. No, he couldn't leave her and move to another part of the cave. No, she couldn't, or rather didn't want to face this crazy, messed up world without him.*

"Come on, you look a little pale today, I just want to make sure the infection isn't getting worse."

"No, that's not what I meant." She removed her pants without a thought or care that she stood before him in her underwear. "I meant, no, you aren't moving out or sleeping in another part of the cave unless you plan to take me with you. We're a team, you, and me. We did what we had to do to get Lily and Cassie to a safe place. If I had anywhere else to take them I would have. This is my place, and even in the ten or more years that I've been coming here, I've never even brought Cassie here, and she's my oldest and dearest friend. Actually, I've never brought anyone here, besides you."

She didn't want to change things between them, but she needed him to know that he was special to her and that she cared.

His heart beat faster, and his hands faltered as he removed the bandages from her leg. He looked up into her eyes and asked, "What about Griffon?"

She wasn't sure if he was asking if Griffon would be concerned about the cave or them being together, and she didn't want to steer him in that direction. She still loved Griffon. She still planned to marry him someday and raise a family with him. *That's what I've wanted all along... isn't it?*

She decided to keep it light, so she laughed. "No, I didn't bring Griffon here. He found it on his own. I just stumbled across him one day while he was here in the big cave hoping to find a bear. He and Amos were out hunting on the mountain when he saw the opening and climbed up. He had some old rock-climbing gear he was using, and it scared the life out of me! I shot a rock at his head with my slingshot. That's how we met, more or less."

Jared grinned. "Is that the scar on his forehead right between his eyes?"

"Yup, that's the one!"

"Nice shot."

"Thank you." She half bowed and giggled.

He went back to work on the bandages, trying not to think too much about everything she had said. When he pulled back the last bandage, his body stiffened, and he frowned.

"Oh, no, no, no..."

"It's not good, is it?"

"You knew it was getting worse, and you didn't say anything!" It wasn't a question; it was an accusation.

"I knew you wouldn't let me go down to find them, if you knew."

"Damn right I wouldn't have let you go!"

He was pacing now. "We have to get you help! We have to convince them to open the bunker long enough to get you inside. You have a doctor there, right? He can help."

She took his hands in hers. "Shhh, stop. That's not going to happen, and we both know it. It doesn't matter whether they would or not. We both know I would never put them at risk like that. Do the best you can to clean it up and keep the infection down, and please, whatever you do, don't tell the others."

"Please, don't ask this of me." He was begging. "I don't give a damn about the safety of the others. I need you to get better. I only care about you!"

He was on his knees as she sat on the edge of the spring, and she pulled him close. He laid his head in her lap while she smoothed his hair and comforted him in the same way that he had comforted her so many times, and he cried. Jared was three years old the last time he shed a tear, but he wept openly now at the thought of losing her.

When the moment passed, he pulled himself back together, and cleaned and dressed her wound as best he could with the minimal supplies they had. He filled the buckets of water, and they made their way back to the main cave.

They were gone longer than should have been necessary, and Holly noticed the shared look between Lily and Cassie as they entered the room. She glanced at Jared, who gave her a quick, *I told you so* look.

"Just how far is the spring from here? You probably could have gone to the water hole a lot faster," Cassie accused.

Holly wondered why it took Jared to spell it out for her and how she had not noticed those looks earlier.

"It's a long, dark tunnel, Cassie. It's slow going, and we need to talk about our next move. You two are staying here, but we have some recon to do back in town, tomorrow."

She watched Jared as she said it and didn't miss the frustration and anger flare across his face.

What are you playing at, Holly? She could almost hear him asking her.

"You can't do that Holly. We aren't going to let you stroll back down there like that. You're in more danger than any of us are. If you want information, let me and Cassie go back down," Lily begged.

"Lily, I love you like the sister that I never had, and Cassie, you are my oldest and dearest friend but you both know I would never risk your lives like that. I didn't rush down to pull you out just to send you back. It's not going to happen, and since neither of you have any idea how to get out of this place, you're truly stuck."

They both looked at her, shocked.

"What makes you think you're so qualified then, Holly Jenkins?" Cassie was not happy.

"Oh please! Cassie, you know my extensive list of qualifications. How much food and supplies have I smuggled over the years? How many secret elders meetings have I listened in on by now?

I was born for this life. I've been running a small elite task force designed to gain intelligence and circumvent AMAN camps throughout the regions for weeks now. It wasn't by accident that Jared and I were together when everything went down. He's my second in command.

We wouldn't have run at all if one of our own hadn't betrayed us... we had no other choice. We're on to something. The puzzle isn't complete, but some of the pieces are falling into place. We have to get back down there and finish this."

Jared was furious with her, but would not say so in front of the others. She knew she'd get an earful the next day, but she couldn't just sit around and let the infection take over. She had to keep moving and do whatever she could to right this world while she still could.

* * * * *

Chapter 37

JARED SLEPT next to her that night, and she reached out to hold his hand as she fell asleep. He was still angry with her, she knew, but they couldn't openly discuss things until they were out of the cave the next day. When she awoke the next morning, she was laying across his chest with his arms wrapped around her. Clearly, she had reached out to him in her sleep as she had often done in their time alone.

But they weren't alone.

Her eyes met Lily's from across the room, and she looked sad. Holly sighed. She had to get out of there.

She got up, trying not to disturb Jared. The sun was just coming up. She reached for the water buckets, then turned back and signaled for Lily to follow her. When they were in the dark, but well out of the earshot of the cave, Holly started talking.

"Just say what's on your mind, Lily. I can't stand the looks you and Cassie keep giving me."

"Alright, so what's up? Really, Holly? You know that I love you as a sister, and that has nothing to do with Griffon. That wouldn't change, even if you weren't with him. You do know that, right? Just be honest with me. Is there something going on between you and Jared Hastings? Do you even know anything about him?"

"Yes, Lily, I know everything about him, and far more than I knew about Griffon when we first got together, I might add. Honestly, nothing's going on between Jared and me. I know what it look like, though part of why he followed me to the spring yesterday was to put it in perspective.

"I honestly didn't think about how it would look or what you and Cassie would think because it's nothing like that. We've gotten very close, yes. We rely on each other. We even finish each other's sentences. I look to him for comfort and guidance and well, everything. I depend on him for survival, but it's not a romantic kind of thing. I know it doesn't make sense. It just is what it is."

As they entered the spring room, Lily remained quiet. She looked around in awe before continuing the conversation. "Where does that leave Griffon, then?"

"I love Griffon more than anything! You have to know that. That hasn't changed because Jared's in my life, now. Chris has always been in my life and no one thinks anything about that."

"You don't reach out for him in your sleep, Holly."

"Actually, I have numerous times when we were little."

"Different."

"Not so much!"

"What about Milo? He's still in my life, and no one seems to be giving me the stink eye over him."

Lily laughed. "I don't mean to give you the stink eye. As for Milo, if you started hanging out with him twenty-four hours a day, snuggling up to him in your sleep at night, touching his arm subconsciously all the time in casual conversation, and running to hug him every chance you got, then yeah, I'd give you the stink eye for him, too. However, if memory serves me, you didn't go after Milo or even ask where he was when you came after us yesterday. That says a lot."

"It's still not like that, Lily."

Lily looked serious. "Do you really know him, Holly? I'm just asking because I'm not sure anyone truly does. Rumors say his dad used to beat him and his mom a lot. When Rhoda called him damaged, she wasn't kidding.

"We had an unsanctioned barn dance a few years ago. He would have been, maybe, sixteen at the time. I'm not sure exactly but he took my friend's little sister to it. People were shocked when he showed up. He was stiff and awkward all night long. He would flinch at her touch when they danced, even though you could tell he braced himself for it.

"Callie said she tried to kiss him, and he nearly freaked out. He said that he couldn't handle close proximity or physical contact at all, and that's not the same man I see by your side. He opens his arms to hug you when you need it, and he doesn't flinch when you touch his arm or leg. So yeah, I think there is more going on there, maybe even more than you're ready to admit to yourself."

Holly's heart broke for him as Lily recounted her story. Yes, she knew him. Yes, none of this surprised her but she hid that fact and, instead, just groaned. "You're completely incorrigible, you know! I love you but you drive me nuts sometimes. For the thousandth time, it's just not like that."

Lily shrugged. "Okay then. I believe you."

With that, the discussion was over.

* * * * *

When Lily and Holly returned with the water, Cassie and Jared were looking through a book together on the couch. They were sitting close with their heads together, talking about something. Holly felt a slight ping of envy and was quick to put it in check. Lily was wrong, she told herself. Jared may have been that scared little boy but he wasn't that person anymore, and she gave Lily a knowing glance as if to say, *See, I told you so.*

Holly and Lily started breakfast. When Jared heard them working in the little kitchen, he jumped up, kissed Cassie on the cheek, thanked her, and ran over to Holly.

"You got water without me?" He frowned but there was a smile in his eyes. He shrugged. "So much for that excuse, oh well, come along, anyway. I need to show you something."

Holly saw the confused looks on Lily and Cassie's faces, certain that it matched her own. She just laughed and let him pull her from the room. He was running through the tunnels, holding her hand tightly. Holly was amazed at how quickly he had learned his way around. He didn't slow until they arrived at the spring room. There, he let go and seemed to be looking around for something but Holly couldn't imagine what.

"Are you insane? I just spent half the morning convincing Lily that there was nothing going on with us, and you drag me out like a caveman or something." She laughed as she said it. "What are you looking for?"

He had somehow gotten to the back wall of the spring and was pulling himself up to a ledge near the top, which Holly knew led to the above ground spring they used for the bunker.

"Found it!" He yelled. "I actually found it! I knew that I saw this in here the other day."

She couldn't see what he found, so she waited for him to make his way back down. He was almost there when his foot slipped, and he tumbled backwards into the icy cold water.

"Great! Let me guess, you found pneumonia. I'll kill you myself before you get sick and die; now get out of there." She was still laughing as she attempted to help him out. He gave her a devilish smirk, and just before she had time to protest, he pulled her into the water with him. They were laughing and splashing when Cassie and Lily sneaked into the room to see what was going on.

As Holly and Jared got out of the water she said, "I could kill you for that! There will be payback, so you better find someone else to watch your back."

He was laughing too. "I couldn't resist. You were an easy target."

"You really dragged me out here just to dunk me in the cold spring water? You've lost your mind."

"Perhaps, but that wasn't all. I came for this." He held up some moss he had taken from the top of the spring. "According to the Nature's Medicine book that Cassie and I were looking through this morning, this moss will pull out infections in even the most severe wound. It's apparently quite rare but I could have sworn I saw it down here the other day, and I was right."

Holly hugged him tightly as her eyes swelled up with tears. She couldn't believe he had thought of that, that he cared enough to look.

"Hey, dry it up. No time for tears right now." He kissed her forehead before letting her go and noted it was a little warm, despite their dunk in the cold water. "Cassie was beginning to warm up to me, and I rather liked not being given death stares every five seconds, so we need to make this fast, before they start thinking the worst of me again."

She laughed, despite knowing that he was serious. "I'm pretty certain nothing's going to keep them from thinking that anyway, unless I killed you, which is tempting at the moment, or shooed you away and never spoke to you again, which isn't going to happen, either."

"Good to know!" He smiled, and then turned on his devilish smile, again. That always meant trouble. "All the same, I want to get you back within a normal time frame this time, so quick, drop your pants."

* * * * *

Lily and Cassie were watching and listening from the shadows. Lily seemed to come from nowhere, yelling, cursing, and getting up in Jared's face before she turned on Holly. "Pull your pants back up, Holly! You swore to me, swore it! What are you doing? What are you thinking?"

Holly, who was sitting on the spring room floor, folded over laughing. She laughed so hard it hurt. Cassie came over, too, and she couldn't help but laugh at Holly sprawled out on the ground with her pants down around her ankles, laughing. Despite Lily's anger, Jared joined in, which only made Lily madder.

"What the bloody hell is so funny?" Lily yelled, which made them laugh even louder. She sounded so much like her brother in that moment.

Gasping for breath, Holly tried to speak. "Not... what... you... think! I told you Lily, it's not what you think."

"Some strange man tells you to take off your pants, and you just do it? And that's not what I think?!"

"Not what you think, Lily, but yes, anytime Jared tells me to take off my pants, I do it." That sent her into hysterics again.

This time, Cassie and Jared just looked at each other. They both noticed how pale Holly was suddenly and how rosy red her cheeks were. It wasn't just from laughing so hard, either. Cassie might be naïve at times, but she was also very smart, and it didn't take her long to put it all together.

She looked at Jared, "How bad is it?"

"Bad enough. I think fever may be setting in."

"What's going on, really?" Lily asked, sensing the change in the room.

"Infection," Cassie said. "Am I right, Jared?"

"Yes; she has a cut on her upper thigh." He looked right at Lily, "Hence, why I told her to take her pants off."

Holly stopped laughing and was starting to cry for no apparent reason. Jared went to her and held her close. "It's going to be okay Holly," he told her as he smoothed her hair down her back and soothed her.

Holly didn't want the others to see her cry, so she buried her face in his chest and gave way to the comfort Jared provided. "It's okay. It's okay to cry." He continued talking in a soothing voice.

Cassie watched with wide eyes. "I've only ever seen Holly cry twice in her entire life, and no one was able to console her either time. She just does not cry. Not when she broke a bone, got a splinter, or suffered from a broken heart. You must be very special to her to let you console her like that, even when she is delirious with fever."

Cassie often spoke without thinking as she was doing now, and she saw in Jared's eyes that she was right. She suspected this wasn't the first time that he consoled her, and Cassie looked at them in wide-eyed amazement.

"Will you help me, Cassie?" he asked, not wanting to move away from Holly but knowing he couldn't continue to hold her and address her wounded leg.

As Lily calmed down, she watched and listened, and she knew with absolute conviction that she was right. Holly may not realize it, yet, but Jared meant far more to her than she was willing to admit.

Together, Lily and Cassie removed the bandage. Lily gasped when she saw how badly infected it was.

"Crap! It's a lot worse than it was just last night," Jared said.

Cassie remained unaffected and set about cleaning the wound before placing the moss on top of it. "This isn't a guarantee. If she's not improving in the next twenty-four hours, we need to alert the bunker and get her in there, somehow. Doc will be able to help but not from here. Let's just pray this works."

Jared noticed that Holly had stopped crying and was no longer clinging to him. She felt weightless. He looked down and saw her eyes close, and his heart stopped for a moment. He shook her lightly.

"I'm still here. I'm okay. Can we get out of here, now?"

* * * * *

After Holly stumbled a few times in the dark, Jared picked her up and carried her the remainder of the way back to the main cave. She felt as if she were floating. He kissed her forehead and felt his lips burn against her skin.

"Her fever's spiking fast, Cassie. Can we do anything?"

"Should be some Tylenol in the emergency kit in the box where we found that book. It'll be expired but it's better than nothing."

Lily was still unusually quiet, and she prayed repeatedly.

Holly was conscious of everything around her but couldn't bring herself to open her eyes. She felt Jared's cold lips when he kissed her on her forehead. He felt good, strong, and refreshing as she sunk into him when he carried her. She wished that he would come back and wrap his arms around her again but couldn't seem to find the words to say so. She could only moan softly.

He came back, soon, and supported her back as he lifted her to a sitting position.

"You have to open your mouth for us, Holly. We have to get this medicine in you."

She tried to do as she was told but nearly choked on the pills and the cold water sliding down her throat. She gasped for air. She transitioned quickly from very hot to very cold and started shivering.

Lily saw the transition and spoke up. "Last Thanksgiving, Griff was terribly sick with the flu. Holly said to wrap him in a heavy blanket, and she stayed with him, using her own body heat to help warm him. They sat next to the fire, and she had me give him hot tea. It helped break his fever, quickly. It's worth a try."

"There's a small room back over there that looks like it has a fire pit. The smoke should go up and out through the hole in the ceiling." Cassie told them. "We risk exposure, but it might be worth it."

Cassie looked at Lily with questioning eyes, and Lily nodded.

"Jared, I know you both say nothing is going on between you," Cassie was trying to phrase things as delicately as possible. But we all know she is most comfortable with you, um, physically." She blushed as she said it.

Lily stepped in. "Boy, strip down to your boxers. I'll get the fire started. Cassie, you get the tea. Is Holly wearing a bra?"

Jared wasn't sure who she was directing that question to, and he felt a bit uncomfortable with her commands.

Lily pulled her shirt to the side at the shoulder to confirm she was. "Okay, take her shirt off and grab a couple of the heavier blankets and move her in here."

He hesitated but did as she said. Lily dragged the bedding into the room where the fire would be and laid them out on the floor. She instructed him to lie down and pull Holly as close to his body as possible.

"What? This isn't right. I can't do that to her. It's not decent, it's wrong, and you know it. Plus, Griffon will kill me!"

Lily laughed. "I'll handle my baby brother. Besides, he'll kill you if you let this girl die. You have to do this. Judging by the way she likes to cuddle with you at night, I'd say she won't entirely hate the plan."

She was goading him but something had changed. She saw the way he cared for Holly, and she saw the hesitation to jump at the opportunity to be close to her, even though she suspected he wanted nothing more than to do just that. Begrudgingly, she had to admit that she really liked Jared Hastings.

At first, he was clumsy and awkward, trying to find a place to lay his hands that would be acceptable if she were awake. Then she rolled into him and groaned lightly but not quite in a sick and terrible way, and it set his every nerve on end. It was an emotional roller coaster for him, having her so close and exposed like that, even if all he could see was her face. After a while, it was hot and miserable but he continued to lay there because he felt completely helpless to do anything else.

Lily or Cassie would come in from time-to-time to check on her. He'd kiss her forehead and give a report but after a few hours, he was no longer a viable judge for her body temperature, certain his was about the same.

Most of the time, they were left alone. Lying next to the fire with the light flickering across her flushed face as she shivered next to him, sweat pouring off him, he felt on fire and realized it wasn't entirely from the heat.

They estimated it was about midnight when the ladies came in to stoke the fire one last time, and they agreed to let it die down for the night. Jared didn't think it was working anyway, but agreed to stay put until morning. He must have fallen asleep, and, after what seemed like only moments, he awoke when Holly stirred restlessly next to him. He leaned over and kissed her forehead, surprised to find it cool.

She was awaking from her long sleep. She slowly and lazily stretched, almost provocatively, from sleep. She didn't realize she was rubbing up against him in the process, nor did she recognize what it was doing to him physically and emotionally.

He could tell that she was having a very good dream. She moaned something that he couldn't quite make out. The little voice in his head knew that she was about to call out Griffon's name as she came out of her sexy slumber, and his heart nearly stopped as she moaned out his name instead. "Jared. Jared."

His heart was pumping faster than ever. He looked down at her face just in time to see her eyes open. She smiled and reached her hand out to his face.

"There you are." Her voice was deep and sexy. "Jared" she whispered again sending chills up his spine. "Where have you been? I've been waiting for you." She stretched up toward his face and before he knew what was happening, she kissed him on the lips. At first, he froze, then he couldn't stand it any longer and kissed her back with all the pent up passion he had tried to conceal.

His heart was pumping hard in his chest, and then she pulled back, smiled, and fell right back to sleep. He couldn't believe what had just happened. It was several more hours before he fell back to sleep with her snuggled against him.

* * * * *

When morning rose, so did Holly. Her fever had broken during the night. She was hot and sticky, and she tried to move some of the blankets, only to realize that he had her pinned down.

"Jared, wake up." She nudged him, softly at first, then harder.

He moaned next to her. "Go back to sleep."

"How long was I out?"

He groaned. He had gotten little sleep that night. "Not long enough. I'm tired. Go back to sleep. You kept me up half the night."

She opened her eyes and looked around, wondering why they were in the fire room and not in the main cave. It was then that she realized she was very nearly naked.

She gasped! "Where are my clothes?"

As she reached around, she realized that he, too, was naked.

"Jared! Where are your clothes?"

She tried to think. She had some crazy dreams that night, or thought they were dreams. Could they have been real? She gasped again, "Did we...?" She couldn't finish the sentence.

He was grumpy from the lack of sleep. "Did we what, Holly? Did we spend the night having amazing, hot sex? Really? If you couldn't remember THAT, do you really think it happened? Maybe you just kissed me and dragged me into your delirious fever half the night. Maybe I just laid here, sweating my balls off all night long because Lily told me it was the best way to get your fever to break. Now, please, let me go back to sleep. I'm exhausted."

She knew that he had a tendency to be cranky in the morning but never quite like this. She felt bad. He really must not have gotten much sleep the night before.

She knew they hadn't had sex. She hoped that she'd be able to tell if they had, at least. Something about the way he described that kiss, though, brought the memory of a dream she had, and that gave her goose bumps. *Nah,* she thought, *couldn't have. It must have been Lily's idea, and it seems to have worked.*

He reached over and pulled her close to him. She squealed when he caught her off guard by this sudden movement. She could feel him pressing next to her, and her eyes widened. Their faces were very close, and he watched her eyes carefully, seeing no recognition of the night before. He smiled and looked at her lips.

"You talk in your sleep. Do you know that?" He hesitated "You do other things, too." He gave her a devilish grin, rolled away from her, stealing the blanket, and left her exposed.

She was horrified and thrilled. There was something new in his eyes, and she wondered... *was that kiss really a dream?*

"Jared!" she fussed. "Give me another blanket, at least. It's cold."

"Not a chance. You're fever broke; fend for yourself."

"But, I'm nearly naked, here."

"Oh, I know! I had to sleep, or rather not sleep, next to you all night. Don't worry; I didn't peek... not yet, anyway!" He grinned and winked at her, then rolled back over and tried to go back to sleep.

* * * * *

When he awoke the next time, Holly was not in the room. His clothes lay neatly next to him. He dressed, quickly, and followed the smell of food into the main cave room. Holly was sitting on the couch talking with Cassie, and Lily was tending to something on the little camp stove.

"Good morning, er afternoon, sunshine." Lily greeted him.

"Hope you woke in a better mood this time," Holly chimed in.

He greedily accepted a cup of coffee Lily offered, before responding, "You try sleeping in a fire, literally in the fire, and see how much sleep you get."

Cassie laughed. "Yeah, we did kind of screw you over on that one... but hey, it worked!"

"So it would seem. I'm going to head to the spring to clean up. I don't think I've ever sweat so badly in all my life. It's kind of gross."

"You should use the waterfall, instead. It's not as cold," Holly told him.

He mumbled something about needing the cold, and then told her that he didn't know the way to the waterfall and didn't want to spend the rest of the day lost in the tunnels.

"Come on, I'll show the way."

Great, he thought! *Just what I need, another reason to take a very cold shower.* Instead, he said thanks as she jumped up, grabbed a towel and bar of soap, and led the way.

Cassie and Lily were so thankful for what he had done for Holly that they no longer gave him the stink eye or made comments about them sneaking off together.

"This is a good idea, thanks. A shower sounds heavenly. Now turn around, and no peaking," he told her, taking off his shirt and throwing it at her.

She laughed. "I slept naked next to you all night, and, now, you're going to be modest?"

"I told you, I didn't peak, so turn around."

She did as he said, but her heart beat faster than she expected when she saw the mounting pile of clothes he was discarding next to her.

As he stepped into the waterfall, he sighed. "This really is heavenly!"

With her so close by, he didn't waste much time savoring the luxury of his shower. Instead, he washed and redressed quickly.

"Your turn," he said.

"I'm not taking one."

"Yes you are. You were just as sweaty as I was last night, so get in," he told her with a smirk.

She huffed. "No peeking!"

"No promises this time, sweetheart." He glanced over his shoulder in her direction without really looking at her.

"Jared!"

She showered quickly. He had been right, she needed it, but she would not admit that to him. He seemed different and a bit cocky this morning. She was trying hard not to relive the kiss in her dreams.

She dreamed about him a lot, recently. It was disturbing how often he crept into her head. She should be dreaming of Griffon but no matter how many times she reminded herself of how much she loved him, when she dreamed, it was almost exclusively about Jared.

Jared disrupted her thoughts. "Don't put your pants back on just yet. I need to check your leg."

"Cassie checked it this morning. She said it looks a thousand times better, today."

"I don't really care. I need to see for myself. Please. It'll make me feel better." It was true; he was still very concerned about her.

She dressed, minus her pants. "Okay, see for yourself."

His face looked serious. She had removed the bandage and moss to shower, so the wound was exposed. Her shirt and underwear were on, her hair was parted and dripped down the front of her shirt, and, with the sunlight coming through the waterfall behind her, she looked like an angel. He couldn't help it, but it took his breath away, and he froze, just staring at her.

The heat rose in her cheeks as she became acutely aware that he was looking her up and down. He may not have peeked earlier but he sure seemed to be undressing her with his eyes, now. It disturbed her just slightly that she was not bothered by his intense look. She was rather enjoying it, actually. She felt empowered and didn't question or fret over every little thing the way she did with Griffon.

She sighed. She was committed to Griffon. She loved him. She told herself to stop comparing the two men. Jared had quickly become her best and more trusted friend. She needed him in her life but it wasn't the same as with Griffon.

He squatted down next to her and ran his hands up her leg to her upper thigh where the cut was, and it sent electric shocks up her spine. He examined it closely. She wondered... *if he's just a friend, could his simple touch really make me feel like that?*

"Yeah, it looks really good, today. I think the worst is behind us."

He got up smiling. He was almost taken back at just how relieved he felt. "You'll be good as new in no time."

"I love Griffon, you have to know that." She wasn't sure what made her say that at that moment.

He looked at her, and she wasn't able to read his expression.

"I know," he said, sounding sad. Then he smiled... but it wasn't a genuine smile.

"That's why we're here, right? This is all for him."

He looked sad again. "He's a really good man, Holly, and he's lucky to have you."

She knew she should be happy with his response but all she felt was disappointment.

He meant it. The fact that she felt the need to tell him that told him she must feel guilty. She either remembered their kiss the night before or was feeling something for him that she shouldn't.

A part of him wanted to hold on to that hope but she had made her decision, and telling him so solidified his need to keep his own emotions in check. She was Griffon's girl, and he would not get in the way of that.

He changed the subject to safer topics, and they chatted lightly on the way back to the main cave, discussing plans to move forward with leaving Lily and Cassie in the cave while they went back down to Wythel to find out what was happening. He felt that she would be strong enough in a few days to proceed.

* * * * *

Chapter 38

WHEN THEY returned to the main cave, Lily was talking on the radio. Holly knew immediately that it was Griffon. She didn't have to hear his voice; she could tell from Lily's face. She wasn't sure why she hesitated and just looked at Jared instead of rushing to the radio.

He saw her hesitation. Why was she watching him? Was she waiting for him to react? He wouldn't. He had been hurt physically more times than he could remember. He could handle the physical pain, but he had guarded himself against ever feeling emotional pain. He chastised himself for feeling something for her.

No matter what, it was going to hurt when she reunited with Griffon. He could only start building up a wall around his heart to protect himself as much as possible, if it was even possible at all. She gave up trying to figure Jared out and tuned in to the conversation via the radio. Lily was so lost in conversation that she hadn't heard them return.

"It's getting real bad, Lil." Holly heard Griffon say. "Don't tell Holly. I don't want to worry her... but the AMAN radioed us last night. They have Milo in captivity as well as his dad. Pastor Weaver is trying to negotiate for their safe release, but Mike won't hear of giving me up to save them. I don't know what to do Lil. I can't just sit here and let everyone else suffer because of me. All they want is me. I don't know why, and I don't know what to do. I think it's time to just give in and see what happens."

Holly was furious! "What does he mean 'see what happens next?' Has he lost his mind? He's not turning himself over to them. They are monsters! You tell him that Lily. 'Don't tell Holly.' Don't tell Holly?! Are you kidding me?"

Holly was pacing the room and talking loudly, causing her words to echo down the tunnels in both directions.

Lily looked at her friend, whom she loved like a sister. She didn't know what to do or what to say, so she did what she always did and followed her heart.

"Griffon, Holly's here. She heard everything."

He groaned before speaking, "You weren't supposed to hear all that, Holly." He paused then added, "I'm so sorry."

She grabbed the radio from Lily and yelled at him, "Do not give me that crap Griffon! You will not give yourself over to them. Jared and I will work on a plan to rescue Milo, but you have to stay put."

"Don't be ridiculous! How do you really expect to rescue him? You can't fight the AMAN. I just need you to stay put and stay safe. I'll be okay. They don't want to hurt me. I'm certain of that."

She was visibly shaking in rage and tears were prickling her eyes, but she would not cry, not this time, not in front of them. She took a deep breath, and, when she spoke again, her voice was deadly calm. "You don't know what I am capable of." Then she turned and started stuffing her daypack.

Jared just watched her at first, knowing that if she was stubborn enough to go down on a rescue mission for Milo Weaver, then he'd have her back, no matter what. He wouldn't let her go down that mountain without him. He sighed. *Caring about someone sucks,* he thought, and yet he knew there was comfort he had found in it's purpose.

Holly finished packing her bag, so Jared packed his, too. She looked at him long and hard, then nodded. He nodded back, and they started to leave.

Cassie cried through pleading eyes but did not beg them to stay.

Lily grabbed the radio. "Griffon, they're leaving. Holly and Jared are going after Milo. Stay put for a bit and see what happens, please!"

Griffon was furious. He couldn't let her just run down there; she'd get herself killed. "What is Jared thinking?"

Jared paused briefly, knowing that Holly would wait for him at the waterfall. He looked at Lily, then at Cassie, and sighed.

"You will both be just fine here. We'll be back, I promise," he reassured them.

Griffon was still grumbling across the radio. Jared just stared at it for a second, and then said, "She's going with or without me; you know that. She'll have a better chance with me."

"Take care of her," Cassie begged, as the tears spilled on.

Lily nodded, "She needs you. Go!"

"What's going on there Lily? Tie her down if you have to but do not let her leave!"

He heard Lily speak one last time. "It's too late Griffon; they're gone. Jared won't let anything happen to her."

Griffon yelled and cursed as Jared left the main cave. He ran through the tunnels to the waterfall. Holly was standing there with her back toward him. He smiled in spite of himself. He had known with certainty that she would wait for him.

Her heart beat faster when she heard his footsteps approaching. When she got to the waterfall, she turned and saw that he was not behind her. She panicked, thinking that he wasn't coming, that she had misunderstood what he was trying to communicate back in the main cave. She decided to wait to see if he would come, and here he was. She didn't even have to turn around to know he was there.

Jared approached, turned her around, and hugged her to him. He was surprised, and admiration flooded him when she did not cry. He couldn't tell how long they stood there holding on to each other, but he never wanted to let go.

Holly was the first to break the embrace. She looked up at him and smiled. She felt little pricks of electricity along her cheek as he rubbed his thumb there, almost absentmindedly.

"This is what you want, what you feel you need to do?"

She straightened herself up, held her head high, and stared right into his eyes. He felt that she was staring into his soul.

"Yes," was all she said, with absolute conviction.

He nodded. "Okay, but we're gonna need a plan... no running off blindly or doing anything crazy. We have to be smart about this."

"Agreed."

* * * * *

They left the safe cover of the cave, hidden behind the waterfall, and made their way into the woods. After a quick perimeter check, they stopped to talk.

Jared pulled out the sketchbook that Holly had brought down at the start of her recon group. She didn't know that he had sketched most of the town, along with maps and locations of where he found signs of AMAN activity in the surrounding areas. Holly looked at him in awe.

"What?" He felt her watching him.

"This is really amazing. You did all of this?"

She took the book from his hands and thumbed through it, impressed with what she saw.

He blushed. He'd never get used to receiving compliments. "It's nothing," he told her.

"Nothing? This is awesome, Jared."

They used the book to map out the possible locations of where in the city they could be holding Milo, if he was even still in the city. They determined they would have to go down blind, sneak into town, and find people they could trust to get detailed information.

As they came to the edge of the forest closest to town, Jared signaled her to get down, so they squatted, listened, and watched. Nothing.

He took out a pair of binoculars he had taken from the cave and looked thoroughly around the open area in front of them. Unfortunately, they couldn't see clearly down any of the streets in town from their vantage point, so when he was comfortable that there was no impending danger, they made their way out into the open slowly and quietly and ran to the closest building. They hugged the building, keeping aware of their surroundings, and made their way to a location that allowed them to see into town.

By this point, they could hear voices and noises coming from the street around the corner. He froze, but she urged him forward, and he continued. When he finally peeked around to see into the street, she noticed the confused look on his face. She felt him relax some, so she moved beside him to see what he saw, and the scene shocked her.

* * * * *

There were people in the streets armed with weapons. Not the AMAN, but people they knew from the town. Holly checked up and down the streets and saw no sign of an AMAN presence, so, she stood up and walked toward the group, many of whom she knew.

Jared didn't stop her, but he did stay in the shadows, watching her closely.

The crowd hushed as she approached. Then everyone hugged her. Jared couldn't continue to watch her safely from afar, with so many people surrounding her, so, he made his way out and joined her, careful to stay at arm's reach, always. He wasn't making sense of anything, since everyone was talking at once. He put his hand in the air, brought his other hand to his mouth, and whistled as loud as he could to quiet the group surrounding them.

"We appreciate the warm welcome but, with everyone talking at once, we have no idea what is going on or being said. Can someone just fill us in?"

Everyone began speaking again, at the same time. Holly laughed. "Okay, okay, just one at a time, please."

Jeb Little took control and painted a terrible story of AMAN attacks, fires set, animals slaughtered, and women attacked in their sleep. They all fought back and fought back hard. Milo led raids against all three AMAN camps surrounding Wythel. He had everyone move into Main Street, bringing all the supplies and food they could carry. They put up a barricade at the other end of Main Street and security checkpoints, coming and going. The AMAN attacked at night and tried to wear them down with no sleep and little food. . . but it didn't work. The townspeople were tougher, had more to lose, and held their ground.

As Jeb wrapped up his story, pride evident in his voice and on his face, he suddenly looked sad, stared at the ground, and kicked a stone around.

Ellie Parker spoke up next. "That Pastor Weaver of yours, Holly, he sneaked out two nights ago. He went out there and met with the AMAN leaders. He's trying to negotiate his and Milo's safe return to the bunker."

Jeb nodded and proceeded. "This morning, Pastor Weaver dragged Milo from his watch point in this section of town. There was a fire in one of the store backs, and everything just happened so quickly."

Holly had a knot in her throat as he spoke. She reached for Jared's hand without realizing it. She relished in the warmth and comfort of it. It gave her strength.

"Where's Milo now?"

"An AMAN party led by Pastor Weaver, dragged what looked like an unconscious Milo up the mountain and through the woods about two hours ago."

Holly screamed, "NO!"

"I'm sorry. I feel like we've let you down and let the Maynor's down. We were all trying to come up with a plan when you two showed up."

The crowd started talking all at once, again, and closed in around them.

Jared pulled her close to his side and put an arm around her. He could tell by the looks on a few faces that it did not go unnoticed, but he didn't care. He was there to protect her. He turned her to face him so she could see and hear him.

"They have a two hour lead, Holly. Even with a group unfamiliar with the area, they'll be closing in on the bunker soon, won't they?"

She stared at him in disbelief, then snapped out of it.

"Yes, Pastor Weaver doesn't know the woods as well as I do, but even he will find it within a three-hour window, so we'll have to be quick and quiet."

She knew what he was saying and what he was willing to do. He just smiled at that realization. He'd follow her anywhere, and she knew it. She trusted him, fully.

She turned back to Jeb and spoke loudly so he could hear her over the roar of the crowd.

"Which way did they go up?"

He pointed toward the south.

"Good! He picked the longest way possible but the easiest way to climb. You remember how to come up the middle from the Maynor's old house?"

She knew that he had been up to visit her dad and Milo a few times.

Jeb nodded.

"Good. Assemble a group, armed and ready to fight, up to the bunker from there. Be careful on approach. Send a scout ahead to watch for the AMAN camp. I'll bet anything that they'll set up camp to the south, right outside the main entrance. You know the one, Jeb. Jared and I will climb up the north side."

"The north side? It's too step and rocky; that's suicide."

"Not for us." She smiled and looked at Jared. "He's made the climb before. It's Griffon's favorite route and less chance of running into anyone. It's the fastest way, if you know what you're doing and where you're going. Now get moving; they already have a two-hour head start. My dad and brother won't open that door, not even for the Weavers!"

* * * * *

Chapter 39

HOLLY AND Jared made their way up the steep side of the mountain, helping each other over rocky terrain and over steep cliffs. It was a grueling climb but they continued to push forward as quickly as possible, feeling the importance of their journey. As they neared the top, she stopped. She listened closely and was certain that no one was around on this side of the mountain.

Jared wasn't sure why she stopped but he did, too, reaching for his water and offering her some. She accepted it and drank greedily. She was exhausted and not fully recovered from the fever and infection that had greatly weakened her. Pure adrenaline from the unknown and what might happen with the AMAN at her family's doorstep was all that kept her upright. She worried. If she sat too long, she might never get moving again. She wanted to chance a quick listen on the radio to see if there was any indication of what was happening.

She tuned into the frequency most used from the bunker for communication. Sure enough, voices flowed from the radio. She motioned to Jared to get closer to hear.

"Mike, me and Milo are in trouble. You have to help us! Us against them, right? Open the door, send Griffon out, and let us in. He's all they want. They promise not to hurt him."

Holly's heart sank, and she thought for a moment that she might throw up. It was Pastor Weaver, begging her father to turn Griffon over to the AMAN.

"I can't do that, Weaver; you know better. I'm sorry for you, and especially for Milo, but I have more than just the two of you to consider here. I have to protect our family, you know that."

"They have explosives, Mike, and they will fight their way in for him. You're not safe!" he sounded angry as he spat out the threat.

Charlie came across the radio, and Holly's eyes swelled with tears. It felt like ages since she heard her brother's voice, not just mere days.

"Pastor Weaver, we know you're bluffing. Our walls are impenetrable. They've been tested time and time again."

Jared raised an eyebrow to Holly, and she nodded to let him know that Charlie was speaking the truth. Her father and Colton Evers threw every amount of firepower they could get their hands on at that bunker in the early days to guarantee their absolute safety. The AMAN weren't getting in unless someone opened that door.

"Charlie," Pastor Weaver begged, "They're going to hurt Milo real bad if you don't open that door."

When his words met with silence, he spoke more aggressively, "You cannot possibly choose to protect that nobody your sister is whoring around with over my son! He's family, not those Maynors."

Jared reached over and turned the radio off. He understood why Holly was so adamant that they would not waste time on Pastor Weaver. Rage ran through him. *How dare he speak of Holly like that!*

He saw red and was ready to run in, with guns blazing.

She saw the effect of Pastor Weaver's words on him. She thought that he might bolt, so she took his hand in hers, which jolted him back to the present.

"They're only words said to goad them!"

"He basically called you a whore, Holly. He can't get away with it."

She laughed. "It's only words; who cares?"

He cared.

"Listen, he's just trying to start a fight in hopes that they'll open the door and come out after him. It's a stupid plan for a man who actually wants back into the bunker, but he's clearly not thinking rationally now. He's probably in over his head with the AMAN. Our focus is on Milo. I only care about getting him out of harm's way. Don't waste your time worrying about Pastor Weaver or anything he has to say."

"What's your plan? Cause I can see in your eyes that you have one."

She grinned with assurance. "We didn't exactly give the rebels much of a plan, so they should be up the mountain and stirring up whatever trouble they can by sunset. We need to get in position before that begins, if possible. There are a few tree stands in the area, and there is also a tree house. If we can get up high, we'll have a great vantage point."

"Holly, they'll trap us that way. It's suicide!"

"No, it isn't, because there will be so much chaos on the ground."

She turned the radio back on and changed the signal to one she knew that Colton Evers often used with special ops. "Mr. Evers, this is Holly. If you're out there, come in please. Over."

It was only a second later when his voice came across the radio. "'Bout time you remembered your training girl."

She laughed. "You out hunting on this fine evening?"

"Only grizzlies."

"Poke the bear," She told him.

"You got it. Shake and Bake, over and out!" He ended the transmission.

Jared looked at her skeptically. "That made no sense at all, Holly! What was the purpose of that?"

She laughed. "What? I just told him to cause chaos, so we can go in and get Milo." She looked at him innocently.

"That is not at all what was said. What the hell is Shake and Bake?"

"Just a line from some old movie that, I doubt, you've ever heard of. Basically, it means that we're working together. "Colton and I have spent hours with various phrases to communicate for 'just in case scenarios.' I loved hanging out at the armory and hearing his old war stories and all the crazy code names and stuff, so we came up with our own. I don't know why I didn't think to try and reach him sooner."

"So, we have a plan?"

"We definitely have a plan!"

She changed the radio frequency back to the bunker. "Big Brother. Come in, please."

"Please try again later."

"No can do. This little whore is lying low and flying high."

Jared shot her a look. "Not funny!"

She had to stifle her laughter.

Charlie did not return her call immediately. "Ten-four, little whore."

Jared was clearly not amused.

Holly laughed out loud as she reached over, hugged him, and kissed his cheek. "It's just a word, Jared. It's not one that I would normally use, and they know it. Lets them know that we are aware of the situation. Got it?"

"If they start calling you that, so help me..."

"Didn't you essentially tell me that Lily and Cassie thought the same thing when they thought that we were shacking up?"

He knew, now, that she was trying to push his buttons and pushed her away. "You are not nearly as funny as you think, Princess."

He was not at all amused with the whore remarks and rather content with calling her Princess to counter it. It was far more suitable to him.

She laughed even harder.

"Normally, the only people who call me Princess do so in replacement of a less than stellar name rhyming with Witch!"

He was horrified, and it showed, which made her laugh even harder.

"Hols, be serious! You're gonna get us killed, with all that laughter."

She warmed to her familiar nickname and settled down. "Hols; now that's a nickname only my most loved use." She thought fondly of her brother, Chris... Cassie... they always called her that.

"How about Griffon?" He blurted out.

Holly frowned and shook her head. "No, he never has."

Jared had no idea what had made him ask that, but he was curious now and couldn't stop himself. "So, does that mean it's approved or not, Hols, for me, that is?" He looked at her, shyly.

She wondered what he was really trying to ask. She felt as if they were skating on thin ice with this turn in the conversation, and when she turned to face him again, she noticed that they were very close.

"Approved." She almost whispered the words. Her heart was beating quickly.

He smiled, and she couldn't help but stare at his lips. They seemed far too familiar and inviting. She was quite certain that she was about to kiss him, without really deciding she wanted to, when the radio came alive again and jolted her back to reality.

* * * * *

"Holly Jenkins, you little whore, come out, come out, wherever you are."

The voice of Pastor Weaver sent chills up her spine.

Jared popped his head up over the brush they were sitting amongst and scanned the area. He saw an AMAN soldier about two hundred yards out and signaled for her to turn the radio off.

He leaned very close to her ear. "They're trying to flush us out with the radio; go silent." She turned the radio off.

They hadn't discussed this part. Jared scolded himself. He tried to signal to her and only hoped she'd understand. He put up one finger, then two, then none, then none again to signify the two hundred yards, then finally nine to signify they were at nine o'clock. He breathed a sigh of relief when she nodded that she understood. They lay on the ground behind the brush and tried to be very still.

They lay there for what seemed like a long time and didn't hear a sound. Then, suddenly, they heard footsteps approaching. Her eyes grew wide as they got closer. Jared rolled to his side, laying across Holly, who had already rolled to her back for better comfort. He squeezed them both under the brush as quietly as humanly possible, hoping they wouldn't be detected.

Her heart was beating too quickly. She couldn't decide if it was from the adrenaline of the AMAN nearby or the close, intimate proximity to this man she was growing to care for, perhaps, too much. She closed her eyes. She didn't know if she could face it and wasn't sure she'd ever be ready.

Before, she was so certain of her future with Griffon. He was exciting and passionate, and she loved that, but he also wanted to shelter and protect her almost as much as her father.

Jared, on the other hand, let her live. He stood by to comfort her when she needed it but supported her without question. He didn't try to hide her away or keep her safe all the time. She was free to be herself, with him.

She closed her eyes, and he saw the worry cross her face. He knew her well and could read most of her thoughts and emotions. She was very worried and a little nervous, and, with the AMAN so close, he couldn't blame her. He wanted to tell her it was okay, that they'd be okay but didn't dare speak. He would have stroked her hair and soothed her if he could, but not in this position, so he simply kissed her forehead.

Her eyes flew open. They were deep green, and they took his breath away. He felt like she was staring straight through him, reading every thought in his head, and it made him blush. Those eyes mesmerized him, and he couldn't look away. Those eyes held passion, fire, and something that he didn't understand.

She couldn't look away from him. She felt lost and confused, and his eyes were the only thing keeping her grounded. She loved Griffon. She reminded herself again that they were there to keep him safe. She had to remind herself of that more and more lately, and it left her feeling a little shaken. As she stared at Jared, she thought for a moment that she was going to kiss him. Nearby footsteps interrupted her thoughts.

He heard them, too, and they both froze. He lowered his hand to his jeans pocket and pulled out his knife. Then slowly, so as not to make noise, he moved his hand down her side until he found her holster and carefully removed hers, then worked his way back up and pressed it firmly in her hand. Content that she was locked and loaded and ready to fight, he nodded slightly to signal her to get ready.

Her body was on fire. He managed to set off every nerve within her, and then she heard the AMAN standing beside her. Their boots mere feet away, but she did not care in that moment.

She swore to herself. What was she doing? She had to get her head clear before she got them both killed. She desperately tried to push away the thoughts and focus on the situation before them. *Focus on Griffon. Focus on rescuing Milo. Anything but Jared,* she told herself, *if we're going to have a chance to survive this.*

When he signaled for them to move into action, she shook her head no. She wasn't ready or focused, and she couldn't risk his life with her distractions.

He just stared at her. He never saw her freeze in the face of danger, before. Normally, it sparked something amazing in her, and he had come to believe that she was fearless, but seeing the concern on her face, now so evident, he just lay there next to her, listened, and waited. It wasn't long before the footsteps moved on and grew silent. When he felt it safe to do so, he poked his head up from the brush and checked the area. They were alone once again.

* * * * *

"What was that all about, Hols? It was only one AMAN, and we could have taken him easily."

Too many emotions invaded her mind, and all of them were about Jared Hastings. She was acutely aware that she rarely thought about Griffon, unless it was to remind herself that she was supposed to be in love with him and protect him.

She dreaded seeing him in truth. She knew he was furious with her. He didn't understand why she insisted on the lockdown before getting there safely herself. He would never agree that what she had done was right.

She knew he would try to lock her away and keep her from ever doing something like this, again. *Is he really that much different from my father?*

She sighed loudly without meaning to. She had to pull herself together, stop thinking about her own problems, and face the task at hand. She mentally pushed aside her thoughts of Griffon and Jared. She tried hard to focus on Milo and what they had to do to get him to safety.

Jared spoke again. "What just happened? Cause it looked to me like you just froze." He looked hurt, and her heart ached, despite her silent reprimand to think of him only in terms of the job at hand. "I need to know that you have my back. I need to know that I can count on you."

She closed her eyes. She had been the one to force him to open up and speak his mind, after all. It served her right that he would want to discuss what just happened while she was trying desperately to just get a grasp on her emotions and think rationally. She wasn't even sure what had just happened, herself.

"I don't know. I didn't freeze; it just wasn't right. I'm not sure what happened. I need to focus. You're too distracting. Just stay over there and let me think. I can't concentrate with you so close."

She got up and distanced herself from him physically. He felt as if she slammed him in the chest. He had tried to build up walls to protect himself from her, knowing that his feelings for her were just one sided. *She was Griffon's girl. She IS Griffon's girl,* he reminded himself, but her rejection hurt just the same.

"What about Griffon?" He tried to get her to focus, to remember why they were here.

She cringed at Griffon's name. She never wanted to hurt him. She had already done that once and felt he was shot because of it. She didn't know what to do.

"I don't want to hurt him, Jared." She looked in pain. "I do love him, I do. It's just, I dunno, I don't know what's happening here." She looked at him for the first time since they began talking and smiled sadly.

He looked genuinely stunned and more than a little confused. He wasn't entirely sure what they were talking about anymore. He could usually read her thoughts, but he had no idea what was going through her pretty little head right now. "Okay, we usually seem to be on the same page with things, Hols, but I am not a mind reader, and I have no clue what we're talking about."

She was more than a little frustrated but mostly with herself, and she tried to shrug it off. "Don't worry about it. We need to put it aside and focus. Focus on Milo and how we're going to rescue him. That is what's most important, right now. We can't let them get into the bunker, and we can't let them sacrifice Milo trying."

Before Jared could respond, they were interrupted by a loud roaring that they couldn't place. She jumped. "What is that?!"

"I don't know." He stood up to look around the area. There was no one in sight.

As a shadow crossed the trees above them, they both looked up in time to see a plane flying low over head. Neither had seen a plane in the air since they were little kids, and they stood and watched it. Maybe four hundred yards away in the direction of the bunker, they saw the plane drop some sort of powder onto the area.

"Must be one of Jeb Little's crop dusters. I can't believe they got that thing in the air!" Jared exclaimed.

Holly dove for the radio and turned it back on to the channel where she knew she'd find Colton Evers.

"Queen to A4, Queen to A4," she called out into the radio. Jared gave her a crazy look, and she tried not to laugh.

"King to G6, I repeat, King to G6," Colton returned over the radio.

"Shake and Bake," Holly said.

"Mark 7," Colton replied.

"Ten Four, silent." She turned off the radio and looked at Jared, "Grab your gear, and lock and load. It's go time!"

"What exactly did he tell you this time?"

"Simple, it's like a chess board. The opposing King would be at Mark 7, that's the AMAN and where the crop duster painter is. We're to the left of that area, and Colton's team is to the right. They're a few yards ahead of us in position, though I'm sure there's more of them, so we'll probably have to cover the space faster. Thanks to Jeb, or whoever was flying his plane, we now have confirmation of their location, so let's go get Milo and end this once and for all."

He was amazed at how calm she seemed all of a sudden, and he had to calm his own nerves as the thought of what could go wrong crept in to his head. He had never worried over such things before. He was good at just shutting off his emotions in times of trouble. It had been a strong defense mechanism necessary to his survival from a very young age, but he couldn't seem to turn them off where Holly was concerned.

Without another word, she suited up and urged him on toward the battle awaiting them.

* * * * *

Chapter 40

THEY MOVED in perfect synchronization without ever having practiced or discussed it. After the first sprint across the open field, they took turns moving forward one at a time, watching each other's back.

Holly's blood was pumping hard, and her nerves were on edge. She moved quickly toward a full adrenaline rush, as the excitement grew stronger with forward progress.

As they raced closer to the painted target area, they slowed the pace and became even more vigilant about scouring the area when either of them was exposed. She was almost surprised when she found they were at the base of one of the tree houses. A sweep upwards showed no sign of immediate activity, although they could hear voices nearby.

She suspected the tree house would make a perfect watch for the impending battle, and with multiple escape routes in place, they would be safe there. She signaled up to Jared and started to climb, knowing well, the virtually undetectable footholds notched into the tree. Once at the top, she signaled for him to follow.

He struggled on the climb up but tried his best to follow the path he had observed her using. It took him several minutes longer, but he eventually made it to the top. He looked around and was amazed at what he saw. Only having heard rumors of the Jenkins's bunker, he never really understood what it was all about, until now. If the bunker was half as nice as this tree house, they were living it up pretty good in there, and he wondered, for a second, why they had ever come down to Wythel, at all.

After he had a chance to look around, Holly urged him to pay attention. She showed him three hidden spots that they could hide in, if necessary and two hidden safes. Opening a safe, she pulled out additional guns, with appropriate ammo. He smiled at her. With what they had carried up, they should have plenty of weapons, at least.

Next, she led him out the other side to a deck of sorts. There were two rope bridges connecting to platforms on the other side. In total, she showed him four zip lines, two of which would take them back down to the ground. Another three swinging ropes that he was unsure what to do with or where they would lead, and two rope ladders that could be lowered to climb back down to ground level.

It was a lot to take in. She went into one of the safe rooms and shut the door to give him time to take it all in. While inside, she used the time to contact Colton. He confirmed they were in place, with eyes on Milo, twenty-six AMAN soldiers, Pastor Weaver, and another man, who Holly knew must be Devon Atley.

She gave their location to Colton and told him they would be going silent but listening in. She retrieved two earpieces, one tuned to the radio frequency Colton was using, and the other set to the frequency which the bunker and AMAN were using as a bartering tool. She placed one earpiece from each radio in her ears. They would allow her to listen in to anything broadcast and simultaneously provide excellent hearing protection when shooting. She climbed out of the safe room and went to find Jared.

He was in awe of the tree house. She second-guessed bringing him here. It may have been too much for him, but she had faith that he would snap out of it and do what he needed to do.

She filled him in on the target sighting. Pointing out the best two spots to use for easy sight of the chaos that she knew was about to ensue.

As a last-second decision, she placed him in the safest place she knew that would still allow him to be effective in the cause.

There was one dead tree amongst all the others, and she pointed it out to him. He shook his head. She was crazy if she thought a dead stump of a tree would be his best bet. She shook her head at his protest and explained that it would be okay, and he could get to the ground quickly from inside. He hesitated only slightly before relinquishing. He knew he would never be able to tell her no. She showed him how to use one of the rope swings to get over to the dead tree.

He still wasn't sure about this plan, but he slung three rifles securely around him, filled his pockets with ammo, and consented to her plan. She pointed at a tree about seventy-five feet from his dead stump assignment to signify where she would be located. He didn't like this plan and was feeling very uneasy about it all when she stopped checking him over to make sure his gear was properly secured and just stared at him.

She was in a mode of action, thinking strategically, and not emotionally, after the emotional turmoil she had faced earlier in the day. At this moment, she hesitated, looked at him, and felt something that she knew only made her stronger. She smiled at him, took his face in her hands, and kissed him passionately on the lips. She felt a punch of emotion, excitement, and longing, and she had to pull back quickly before it began to consume her.

"For luck," she told him before pushing an earpiece in each ear and motioning him to get into place.

He was swinging toward the dead tree before the impact of what had just happened started sinking in. He couldn't believe what she had just done, and all he knew was that he wanted, no, he needed more.

He had tried so hard to convince himself that nothing could possibly happen between them, but that one kiss, for luck, gave him a hope that he hadn't dare feel before. He had to live through this day. They needed to talk. He tried desperately to shake off the kiss but knew it would stay with him always, so he channeled the energy and excitement surging through his body and landed with a quiet thud against the dead tree.

He hadn't braced himself for the impact and expected to find it soft and brittle, possibly not even sturdy enough to hold his weight. Instead, he landed hard against it, found a few notched footholds, and scurried to the top opening that Holly had pointed out. Once inside, he was totally shocked by what he saw.

* * * * *

The dead tree wasn't dead at all. It wasn't even a real tree, just designed to look like one. In reality, it was a fortress. There was a fireman's pole in the middle for a quick descent, if necessary. Otherwise, there was a narrow staircase wrapping around the inside of the fake, dead tree, with multiple landings. Looking out from the top allowed him to see from various vantage points, complete with gun holes through which to aim. He had never seen or imagined anything like this was possible.

He looked toward the tree that Holly was supposed to be on and saw her perched on what appeared to be a hunting stand placed too high up for good hunting. He frowned to himself, thinking that she should be in this fortress, not out in the open, exposed on her stand. He silently cursed the situation and made a note to discuss it when this was over.

She got into position just as Pastor Weaver led Sarge to the front of the bunker, and she watched as an AMAN pounded his fists against the door.

Jared watched from the second landing. He saw the pastor pound his fist against a knot of tree roots. He would have thought him crazy had he, himself, not been sitting inside a giant fake tree, and, so, suspected it was a hidden entrance to the bunker.

An arrow soared quietly through the air and clipped Pastor Weaver in the underside of his left arm. Jared and Holly both looked in the direction from which it came, as did all the AMAN soldiers. As one of them moved a few steps forward, Holly saw Milo tied to a tree and bound at the feet. Even from the distance, she thought his face looked swollen, and she silently cursed Pastor Weaver for allowing that to happen.

Chaos broke out quickly as about a dozen people from Wythel stormed the AMAN head on. Some wielded swords, while others carried guns. One had what looked like a baseball bat with spikes coming out of it. They moved in quickly and brutally attacked at full force. Holly was momentarily stunned at the apparent rage in which the people assaulted their enemies. They struck fast, they struck hard, and then they retreated back into the thick brush in the woods. Several AMAN were on the ground. Only one person from town was still in sight, and he appeared to be dead or, at the very least, lying very still on the ground.

She had never seen anyone die before she killed that AMAN soldier who tried to rape her, and she hadn't intended to kill him. It was a matter of life or death that left her with no other option. She struggled with the horror of it.

Although she practiced constantly, hunted regularly, and knew that she was capable of taking another person's life, she found it difficult to sight in and pull the trigger from a distance. In some ways, it seemed so much easier than the life she had to end. Here, her life was not immediately threatened, and it felt wrong to attack.

Jared watched her from his perch. The struggle was evident on her face, and his heart ached to shield her from this battle. He wondered what she would think of him when this was over.

* * * * *

As they both stood by, lost in their own thoughts, another team from Colton's group came out of the thick and struck again. The AMAN were more prepared this time, and gunfire rang out, shocking Holly back into reality. Pastor Weaver cowered in a corner, while Milo was left in the open, now awake, wide eyed, and struggling to free himself while caught in the crossfire.

One AMAN soldier was shaking badly and trying to aim at Colton's group, and Holly feared that he might shoot Milo instead of his intended target. She took a deep breath, sighted in, and shot him in the leg. He went down quickly and, amidst the chaos, no one noticed the trajectory of the shot or looked up.

Jared saw Holly's first shot. He knew she was capable of shooting center mass with ease from her position but she had chosen to disable instead. He took his cue from her and proceeded to do the same. He had five AMAN soldiers down before anyone even thought to look up. He was safe in the hollowed out, fake tree. No one would see him, and, even if they did, they couldn't get to him. He was certain of it and guessed that's why she set him up there. It was certainly something she would do... protect others before herself. He cursed himself for not thinking of it sooner. She had thrown him off with that kiss, and he didn't think things through. Now, she was exposed, out in the open.

He glanced her way. She was hiding behind the tree, now, just waiting. The people had retreated, and things were quieting down, for the moment, anyway. He did a quick head count. Only nine soldiers remained standing, and thirteen, total, remained armed.

Something in Holly's direction caught his attention. There was a gleam of something shining from the last remaining sun. It was the necklace she always wore around her neck, sparkling in the sunset, and it didn't catch just his attention. Gunfire rang out in her direction.

Jared's heart stopped. He watched her grab onto the zip line and disappear deeper into the woods. Fire continued to reign down in her direction, and he that knew she'd be on the ground soon.

He told himself to breathe. He put a fresh magazine into his gun and opened fire on the remaining soldiers, taking out as many as he could. When the magazine was empty, he left the gun, grabbed a fresh one, and secured it to his body. He grabbed the fireman's pole, wrapped his leg around it, and slid down.

Holly was already making her way, on foot, to the battle. She cursed herself for the necklace incident, pulled it off, and stashed it in the empty hollow of a tree, hoping she could remember which one when this fight was over. She flanked to the right, her heart pounding. A bullet grazed her in the calf on her descent, and it burned like hell as she ran, but it didn't stop her. She knew that she was leaving a trail of blood but, in a battle such as this, she didn't think it mattered.

She found Colton's group and was shocked at the number of people. They had two fresh groups about to go in from different angles. Gunfire was still ringing out, and she feared they had spotted Jared, as well.

As long as he stayed in the fake tree, he'd be fine, she knew, but she also knew from the sounds of the gunfire that he saw her flee and covered her. She knew he would come out and find her. He was probably already on the ground. Her calf throbbed, her heart pounded, and her breathing was coming faster. All she could think of, however, was getting to him and making sure that he was safe. Nothing else mattered. She grabbed her gun and led the group flanking the AMAN on the left into battle.

Her senses heightened as they reached the battle scene. Bullets were flying everywhere. Fists were flying in hand-to-hand combat. Milo was almost out of the ropes restraining him. Everything happened in slow motion around her, and she felt disconnected from the events. She just stood there in the middle of it all. She looked up and confirmed that Jared was no longer in the tree. As she ran toward the base of the fake tree, the bunker door flew open. Griffon came out first, in full surrender. Mike Jenkins and Don Maynor came out behind him, with guns blazing.

* * * * *

Holly was almost to the fake tree when she stopped in her tracks. She heard a loud "NO!" ringing out above the noise but was not aware that it was coming from her.

There were no lights at the bottom of the fake, dead tree. Jared felt trapped and groped around along the walls, looking for the way out. His heart pounded harder. He could hear the gunfire increasing from the other side, but he was trapped. He panicked. Then he heard Holly scream, and his heart, once again, stopped in his chest just as his hand came across the latch. He flung open the hidden door and stepped out into the darkening light, his gun at the ready.

A quick survey of the situation showed blood and bodies everywhere. Two AMAN soldiers led Griffon away. He didn't look bound, and he wasn't being dragged, like Milo. He simply walked along with them.

Jared started to run after him when a final shot rang out. He turned and saw Sarge grinning before he turned and ran after Griffon and the two soldiers hurrying into the cover of the thick underbrush of the woods.

He headed in their direction to go after Griffon when he heard the final shot, and the hair on his neck stood up. His heart was beating fast. He switched directions and ran back to the voice he knew so well, the one yelling "Daddy!" in a blood curdling scream.

Mike Jenkins was lying on the ground, and Holly was by his side. She talked softly to him and reassured him. She looked calm, too calm.

There was a new chaos around. People trickled out of the bunker and ran here and there. Holly just sat there, cradling her father in her arms. Jared approached quietly. He had to know that she was okay.

Charlie ran from the bunker and was now at his father's side, too. He yelled for someone to get the doctor and his mother.

"We need water and bandages!" Tears streaked down his face as he yelled one order after another.

From behind, Jared thought Holly was too still, too stoic. People gathered around them, and he had to push his way through. Charlie looked up at him and nodded, with a look of thanks in his swollen, crying eyes. Mike tried to sit up. Jared could hear the gurgling sounds as he tried to talk and knew it wasn't good. Charlie signaled him over, and Jared dropped to his knees next to Holly. She sat stiffly, cradling her father. He looked at her, but she would not look at him.

Mike Jenkins took Jared's hand. He was surprised at how strong the man's grip was. Mike pulled him down and Jared could hear the whispers from the people behind him. No doubt, people from town were afraid of how he might act at the touch of this stranger, but he did not flinch or recoil.

Mike looked right into his eyes and spoke. "Are you Jared Hastings?"

Jared could only nod. Mike closed his eyes. It was getting harder for him to speak. When he opened his eyes again, they were clear, wise, and strong, "Thank you for watching after my Holly, son."

Jared's heart fluttered. No one had ever called him son, at least not in a good way. No one except Holly had ever thanked him for anything. He was overwhelmed with emotions for this man he just met, and he closed his eyes and prayed. *God, please save this man. Please don't let him die.*

As he said that silent prayer, he felt the strength surrounding his hand disappear.

There was another round of tumultuous activity after that. Doc showed up and checked him but there was nothing he could do. Mike Jenkins was already dead. His wife collapsed across his body, crying loudly. As Jared looked around, there wasn't a dry eye to be seen, except Holly.

He could see from the side of her face that she had not shed a single tear. Charlie hugged and consoled their mother, and others did the same for each other throughout the on-looking group. No one moved to go after Griffon or Sarge. Who killed Holly's father?

Jared was aware that everyone consoled each other, broke off into smaller groups, and eventually dispersed but no one had spoken to Holly. She just sat there watching it all. She looked numb, emotionless. He realized that this was the Holly she showed the world. Everyone, except him.

She heard him speak. "Holly, are you okay?"

She knew he'd be waiting with arms open but she had to be strong. She couldn't break down in front of all these people. They expected her to be strong.

"Holly," he said. She shook her head NO.

"Holly," he said again and touched her shoulder lightly. She shook her head NO again. She couldn't look at him. She knew that she couldn't hold it together, if she did. There were too many people watching. She had to be strong for her dad, for her mom, for Charlie. They expected her to be strong.

He reached out, touched her cheek, and turned her face to his. "Holly," was all he said. He could hear the townspeople murmuring behind him, but he didn't care. He had to be sure she was okay.

He rubbed his thumb against her cheek to reassure her. After what seemed like a long while, she looked up at him. There was so much pain in her eyes that it broke his heart, and a single tear fell from his eye.

It was too much for her. She lunged forward into his arms and hugged him close, releasing the wall against the dam of tears that came, at last. She cried hysterically as he held her, smoothing her hair down her back and soothing her softly with reassuring words that it was going to be okay.

When he opened his eyes, people were staring at them awkwardly. Jaws dropped in shock. A couple of the ladies gasped aloud with apparent surprise. No one from town had ever seen him physically, or emotionally, connect with anyone, and no one from the bunker had ever seen Holly cry.

When their eyes met, Charlie nodded at him and smiled through his own grief. Their mother mouthed, "Thank you" to him and squeezed his arm reassuringly. All the while, Jared sat there next to Mike Jenkins' dead body, comforting the man's only daughter in his arms until the last tear ran down her cheek and she pulled back and looked up at him. They didn't speak.

Doc covered the body and told Charlie to help his mother up and escort her back to her Pod. He asked Jared to do the same with Holly. The remaining group dispersed with only a few remaining to assist with Mike's body.

Jared stood, pulling Holly up with him. He noticed Milo Weaver standing nearby. He was alive and safe but Jared knew that he was far from okay. There was no sign of Pastor Weaver.

Someone Jared hadn't met before came over and hugged Holly. It was a bit of an awkward hug and quite uncomfortable for Jared.

* * * * *

Holly felt exhausted and weak. She knew she was in shock and wasn't sure what to do. Her leg burned, and she feared another infection would set in as it had from the knife wound. When Chris came over and hugged her, she felt numb. The only thing she truly felt was overwhelming grief and Jared Hastings' touch. He was her lifeline, and she clung to him.

"I'm so sorry, Hols," Chris said through his own tears.

She turned and hugged him back. She closed her eyes, thinking that she would cry again but no more tears came. When Chris took a step back, she noticed that Jared was still right there next to her, and she quietly thanked God for his presence She wrapped her arms around his waist and hugged him close, tugging him along. She still couldn't find her voice.

Jared knew that he'd follow her anywhere she asked, but part of him was always surprised when she did. She hadn't said the words but he could feel her pulling him on toward the bunker. He stopped at the door and hesitated a moment. Not just anyone went into the bunker. You had to be invited, and very few outsiders were. He wasn't sure this would be okay, but Holly looked up at him with pain so raw in her eyes. She let go of his waist, took his hand, and walked him into the bunker.

He didn't know what to expect, and, certainly, nothing could have prepared him for what he saw as they walked through the common room, past the gym, and down a series of hallways to a door with a number 7 on it. When they entered the room, there was a masculine feel to it, and he knew that it must be Griffon's room. The pain that shot through his chest was almost too much to bear, but he didn't say a word. He simply walked in and shut the door behind them.

* * * * *

Chapter 41

HOLLY STILL didn't speak. Once inside, she let go of Jared's hand with a sudden urge to fix things. She grabbed a box and began shoving all kinds of stuff in it. She went in the bathroom and cleared out what appeared to be all of Griffon's things. She grabbed a laundry basket and threw all his clothes into it. Once all signs of him were gone, she put his few belongings into a closet and set about reconfiguring her room.

Jared had never seen anything like this place, and, despite his confusion over her behavior and curiosity over why she was throwing out all of Griffon's stuff, or at least what he thought was Griffon's stuff, he was totally fascinated with the room. With a couple of latches here and tugs and pushes there, she opened the living room space into a bigger area than it had originally been.

As she headed to the back room, which he had not seen yet, there was a knock at the door. Holly seemed not to notice or care, so he opened it. The guy who had come over to hug her outside walked in. Jared knew that he must be a friend, so he opened the door wider and invited him in.

Chris introduced himself and thanked Jared for watching after Holly, keeping her safe, and rescuing the girls. Jared learned that Chris was Cassie's boyfriend and was quick to assure him that she was safe and well.

"What's all that noise?" They heard bumps and curses come from Holly's room.

"I'm not sure what she's doing, but as long as she's not hurting herself, I don't have a problem with it. Should I stop her?" The two young men walked into the room together.

"What are you doing, Hols?" Chris asked her.

Jared couldn't help but smile at what he saw. She stood on what appeared to be a bed with a section of wall missing and was pushing against the missing section at a very awkward angle. He also noted that Chris called her "Hols" and knew he'd been right about him being special to her.

She hadn't spoken a word since her father died. Suddenly, she plopped down on the bed, looking exasperated. "Help me fix this bed, Chris."

"Fix it? What's wrong with it?"

"It's too small. I need a double bed."

"Why? You always sleep in a single bed. Why are you in here, anyway, and not in your own room?" He looked around the place and noted all of Griffon's stuff was missing. "Where's all of Griffon's stuff? He's usually a bit of a slob. This place is spotless."

She frowned at him.

"Pretty sure it's all been boxed up and shoved in the front closet." Jared whispered.

Chris frowned at her. "What's this all about Hols?"

"I don't want to talk about Griffon right now! I don't want his stuff in MY Pod. I am exhausted and just want to curl up and pretend for just a bit that this day never happened."

She looked so sad. It broke both Chris and Jared's hearts at the same time.

"And I can't go back to my room. It's too close to dad's Pod. I can't bear the reality of him not being there."

The guys looked at each other. Both were shocked that she opened up so easily in front of the other.

Chris got up and was able to release the bed to convert it from a single to a double. He teased her. "Suddenly a single isn't big enough for you? Maybe you have been living out in the open spaces too long."

She frowned at him. "We'd be okay in a single, but I'm going to either crash and not budge till morning or it'll be a restless sleep of tossing and turning. So, just in case, I wanted to give Jared a little extra room."

Chris's jaw nearly hit the floor. "Wait, you think he's sleeping in here with you?"

He shot daggers at Jared, who just stared blankly back and sighed. He thought for a second that, just maybe, he and Chris could develop some sort of friendship or common bond over Holly. At the very least, not the usual open hostility or awkwardness that he found so easily with others... but here it was, again.

Somewhere between being trapped in that stupid fake, dead tree and not knowing if she were alive or dead, and seeing her alive and suffering at the loss of her father, Jared had comes to terms with the fact that he loved her and didn't want to live in a world without her. He just stood by and let Chris think the worst.

* * * * *

While Chris argued with Holly over sleeping arrangements, Charlie walked in.

"Hey, hey, you two... calm down. What's going on here?" He noticed the absence of Griffon's stuff but didn't say anything. "What's all this about? You two never fight."

Chris spoke up first. "She threw out all Griffon's stuff and rearranged everything, most notably the bed. She thinks that he is going to sleep here, in that bed, with her." He pointed to the now double bed, then to Jared, then to Holly.

Charlie's brow furled as he looked at his sister. "Hols?"

He went to her and wrapped his arms around her in a big hug. "Tough day, huh?"

Jared mentally thanked him for not yelling at her like Chris was.

"What's this all about, sis?"

She looked up at her brother with obvious love, which moved Jared. He had never really seen sibling dynamics like this before, and it was beautiful. "I'm exhausted, and I'm overwhelmed. I don't want to think about anything tonight. I just want to sleep," she said.

Charlie pulled back and looked at her. "Okay, I get that. I think we're all feeling that way. Why don't you let me take Jared back to your room? He can get a good night's sleep there, and you can have some peace and quiet here."

Holly shook her head. "No! I need him here with me."

Charlie sighed deeply, concern evident on his face. Holly smiled at him and said, quietly, "He keeps the nightmares away."

Jared couldn't make out the last part of what she said but Chris's eyes got big as he glanced back but not with the hostility that he previously had. Jared didn't understand the looks passing between brother and sister. In the end, Charlie kissed her on the forehead, shook his head in approval, and helped make the bed for them.

Jared wasn't sure he'd ever understand people and didn't know what was going on.

Before leaving, Charlie turned to Holly. "You're sure about this? Doc could just give you a sedative for the night."

Holly smiled at her brother and then turned that smile toward Jared. His heart flipped over in his chest, and his cheeks reddened involuntarily. "I don't need it, Charlie."

Charlie wasn't entirely convinced; so on his way out, he put an arm around Jared and had him escort him to the door. "You should know that I love my sister more than just about anything."

He looked right into his eyes, and Jared fought not to break eye contact, although it was painfully uncomfortable. He nodded that he understood. "And," Charlie continued, "I have really big guns. Big ones. And lots of them. You'd do best to remember that."

He smiled when a pillow came flying toward his head from the other side of the room. Holly was laughing when she told him to get out.

"Seriously, if they get too bad, I'm just down the hall to the left, Pod 1. Come and get me if you need any help. The time doesn't matter, I'm used to it." He clapped his hand on Jared's shoulder and left.

Jared was not certain what they said and looked confused. As he turned to walk back to Holly, he realized that Chris was still there.

"Is it true?" Chris asked.

"Is what true?"

"The nightmares."

"What nightmares?"

"Holly said you keep them away. What does that really mean? How do you keep the nightmares away?"

Jared was getting flustered. "I really don't know what you guys are talking about. What nightmares?"

"Holly's nightmares. Charlie usually takes the brunt of them. I've sat up through my fair share over the years. She's always had them, especially in high stress situations, like now."

Jared frowned. "I've slept with her for weeks now, and she's never had one that I'm aware of."

Chris's eyes widened, and daggers surfaced. Jared was quick to reassure him, "Not like THAT! I mean beside her, not *with her* with her."

Chris laughed. "Well, that would be about a record for Holly then. Good luck. If she has one tonight and you need help, just remember, Charlie's in Pod 1, and I'm in Pod 10. Doc's in Pod 16 and can give her a sedative if it gets really bad. I'll check on you in the morning." Chris offered his hand, which Jared willingly accepted.

* * * * *

It's been a strange day, Jared thought to himself. After letting Chris out and locking the door behind him, he found the bathroom and took a quick shower. He was not prepared for hot water and wasn't sure how long he stood there, letting the warmth pour over his muscles. It was like heaven. He finally turned off the water, dried off with a towel, and put fresh underwear and gym shorts on from his bag. He even took a moment to brush his teeth thoroughly with the toothbrush Holly gave him in the cave.

He felt alive and rejuvenated when he headed to bed.

Holly, on the other hand, had fallen asleep right after they said good night to Charlie and Chris. While Jared was showering, her nightmares set in, quickly. He heard her cry out as he exited the bathroom and ran to see if she was okay.

She was sitting up. Her eyes were open, but they looked opaque and odd. He knew that she was still asleep. He had never seen anything like it, before, and it scared him a little. She was in a ball at the foot of the bed and shook badly as she yelled into the dark.

He felt helpless and didn't know what to do. At first, he thought he should run and get Chris and Charlie for help but, as he got up to leave, she called out to him.

"Where are you? I can't find you!"

She sounded so scared. He remembered how she had thrashed around the night of the fever and how she calmed instantly when she opened her eyes saying, "There you are."

He thought it worth a try, so sat next to her and gathered her up in his arms.

"I'm right here," he told her. Her entire body shuddered against him, her eyes closed, and she went so limp in his arms that it scared him.

"Holly! Holly! Wake up!"

She was sweaty and groggy, coming out of sleep. She couldn't remember where she was or how she'd gotten there. Before reality came crashing back down on her, Jared was there, kissing her forehead, her temple, and her cheeks.

"Oh God, you scared the life out me," he kept saying as she looked up at him to see what was wrong. Then he kissed her right on the lips. It was just a quick kiss and he hadn't meant to do it. She just turned her face up to him as he was about to kiss her cheek.

The shivers that shot through her, jolted her awake. Every bit of her was aware of every bit of him. She looked into his eyes and smiled.

"Morning already? I feel like I just fell asleep."

She yawned and stretched a bit. Her voice was deeper than usual and it was literally the sexiest thing he had ever heard.

"I'm sorry. You were having a nightmare, then you just went limp, and it scared me."

"Are you sure? I don't feel like I was having a nightmare." She tried hard to think for a minute. She was kissing him in her dreams, as she often did these days. She couldn't remember anything bad at all.

"You fell asleep when I was in the shower and were yelling and thrashing around when I got out. I hugged you, and you just went limp in my arms. I didn't know what to do!"

She looked sad. "Sorry, I didn't realize. Normally, I can tell, even if I can't remember the dream. Do I do that a lot? I only remember good dreams and wake up rested when you're with me." She sounded vulnerable as she admitted that.

"Never. I've never seen you like that."

He hugged her close and kissed her head.

"I can handle the nightmare part of it, but when you went limp like that, it scared me half to death!"

She smiled. "I'm fine, really. Think I'm going to jump in the shower, too, before going back to sleep."

* * * * *

After she got up and went to the other room, he lay there thinking through some of the events of the day. Griffon voluntarily left with the AMAN from best he could tell, and Holly hadn't once mentioned him.

She must have realized that Griffon was a traitor; otherwise, why would she have been mad enough to remove all his things from the room. She had cried over her father's death and wasn't ready to face the loneliness of her own room, since that served as a reminder that Mike was no longer with them.

She had kissed him twice that day, and they would need to address that, too, at some point. He felt closer to her than ever. She even convinced her brother, who was clearly very protective, that she needed Jared to stay with her. It was a lot to take in.

His stomach growled loudly. He suddenly realized they hadn't eaten since breakfast. It had been a long day.

"I'm hungry, too. Maybe we should find food before we attempt sleep again," Holly said from the doorway.

He jumped. He hadn't realized that she was standing there. He was lost in his own thoughts about the events of the day.

"Yeah, that's probably a good idea." He got up and followed her down to the kitchen.

* * * * *

When they arrived at the kitchen, they saw Holly's mom sitting and sipping coffee with Mrs. Worthington.

"Can't sleep, either?" She smiled, sadly, at her daughter.

"Apparently not. But mainly because his stomach won't stop growling," Holly said, a little too playfully.

The older women exchanged glances that Holly missed or ignored but Jared saw. In truth, Charlie had already spoken to their mother and told her that Holly needed privacy where Jared was concerned. He told her about the nightmares, and the two women speculated on what that meant.

"Let me make you some sandwiches. How does that sound?" Mrs. Worthington rose to prepare the food.

Holly nodded yes, and Jared thanked her.

"You look tired, sweetheart. Why don't you see if Jeanette needs help?"

Holly knew that her mom was dismissing her and frowned before turning sympathetic eyes on Jared.

"Is it, Jared?" she asked after Holly left the room.

"Yes ma'am, Jared Hastings."

She motioned for him to sit down next to her, which he did. She took both his hands in hers and looked at him, squarely.

He couldn't make eye contact with her. He was doing much better with people, in general, lately, but he couldn't bring himself to look at her.

"Don't worry. Charlie already made it very clear to lay off and not discuss the current sleeping arrangements," she said awkwardly, stating her opinion, yet not really going against her son's wishes.

She saw him flinch, uncomfortably, and was satisfied with that.

"But, I do want to thank you for taking such good care of my girl. You can't begin to know how worried her father and I were. Just knowing that she had someone to help her and be with her made a world of difference for us."

He felt guilty. She reached up and, with two fingers under his chin, brought his face to eye level. He couldn't just avoid it and looked at her with such pain. A tear slid down his cheek, and he moved a hand to wipe it away. "I couldn't save him," he said softly.

"Oh Jared!" Her heart went out to this stranger. "That was not your fault. No one expected you to save him. He was doing what he felt he needed to do. I'm still not even sure why they opened the door, but he must have thought it very important to do so. None of this is your fault!"

He realized that Holly's inner strength came from this woman. He couldn't help but like her.

"If I could have traded places with him and taken that pain from, Holly I would have. I just couldn't get there fast enough." He looked so sad, she couldn't resist hugging him to her as she had done with her own kids, so many times.

"That's quite admirable but I'm very certain that our Holly would be grieving just as much." She gave him one last squeeze and then sat down to her tea before Holly and Mrs. Worthington came back with the sandwiches.

Holly looked from her mother to Jared and back but couldn't read the look on either of their faces. They ate in silence and said their good nights. Holly held his hand and hugged his arm as they walked back to Pod 7 together.

Jared felt something change between them that day, which created a slight awkwardness for him, but Holly didn't seem to notice. She pulled him down into bed with her. He laid on his back and she was on her side, snuggled up next to him with her head resting on his chest. It was only minutes before he heard her snoring softly and knew that she was sleeping soundly. He watched her for some time to be sure the nightmares didn't return. When he was convinced that she was at peace, he followed her into sleep.

* * * * *

Chapter 42

HOLLY DIDN'T want to see anyone the next day. She mostly stayed in bed and let the grief consume her. She asked Jared not to let anyone in, not even Charlie or Chris. He agreed. They slept in late, so, by lunchtime, they were both hungry again. She did not want to go to the kitchen where she knew she would have to face people, so he made his way to the kitchen, alone.

Several people were in there eating, and everyone stopped and stared at him when he entered. He was used to people going quiet and staring at him, but this was almost too much. Chris jumped up from the table and came to his rescue.

"Hey, man," Chris greeted him with a handshake. "Come on, I'll show you around; the food's back here."

"Thanks," Jared said when they were away from the prying eyes.

"No problem. That was pretty uncomfortable, all around. I can't imagine how much worse it must be for you. They'll come around, though. They're good people, just a bit leery of outsiders, especially you, seeing as how the Maynor's are part of us now. It's a small place, and everyone knows you're sleeping with Griffon's girl," he told him, unashamedly.

Jared winced visibly, which made Chris laugh.

"I'm not sleeping with her like THAT. I would never do that to Griffon. He's one of the only people on this planet that has ever given me the time of day. I owe him a lot, including taking care of Holly."

Chris grinned at him, "You keep telling yourself that, man. But, I've known Holly a long time, and I can tell you, when she sets her mind to something, there's not much you can do about it."

Then he turned serious and dropped his voice. "She and Griffon were fighting a lot before the lockdown. From what I heard and saw, Griff ran out of here and turned himself over to the AMAN, voluntarily. If Holly saw that, she's going to be very angry with him. Just be careful that she's not using you. I love her, but..." Mrs. Worthington came into the kitchen just then, and Chris never finished that sentence.

But, what? Jared couldn't help but wonder.

"Hello, Jared, can I get you something?"

"You don't need to go to any trouble. Chris was just showing me around the place."

Mrs. Worthington shot Chris a look that made him turn to Jared.

"Do you think Holly would take me to the cave to bring Cassie and Lily home today? I know it's a lot to ask, but we're," he looked at Cassie's mom, "pretty anxious to get them home."

Jared sighed. "Holly doesn't want to talk or see anyone today; that's why I'm down here looking for something for her to eat."

"Lunch is still out, so help yourself."

"Thanks. I'll talk to her."

They nodded as he got a plate and filled it up with things he thought Holly would like. He nodded to them both and started to leave.

"That's it?"

"I'm sorry Chris... I will talk to her. She's hurting badly today, as everything sinks in. I'm not sure she'll be up for it but I'll ask."

"No, not that... I mean the food, dude. No way that's enough for the both of you." Chris proceeded to pile food high on a plate and passed it to him.

Jared stared at the plate of food, not sure that he'd ever seen so much on one plate. "I couldn't possibly."

"Don't be ridiculous. You're Holly's guest, and you're welcome to whatever food we have. No one's going to starve you or expect you to run out and hunt your own food," Mrs. Worthington said, warmly.

He was so overwhelmed that he just nodded, took the plate, and headed back to Pod 7.

"Wait up a sec," Chris called. He was carrying a basket. "Cassie's mom threw some snacks together. You can keep them in the pod in case she's not feeling up to coming out."

"Thanks," was all he could manage.

Chris nodded and walked him back to Pod 7 but was careful not to go in, no matter how badly he wanted to run in and beg Holly to bring Cassie home.

Jared managed to get her to eat. The rest of the afternoon went by uneventfully. A few people stopped by to check on her, but he had no problem turning them away. It was almost early evening before he finally mentioned Chris's request. She looked visibly pained.

"I never even thought about it! I'm a terrible person! I just don't think I can face them, yet."

"Would Chris be able to get me to Holly's Hole? I could go up and bring them back from there. You could stay here and rest."

"Would you mind terribly?"

"Of course not!"

She snuggled up to him, and he kissed her forehead, which was becoming normal for them.

"I should get moving. I'd like to be back by dark. Do you want me to get your mom or brother to come sit with you?"

"Absolutely not! If I wanted to be fussed over, I'd walk down to the common room." She laughed. "I'll be fine. Go. Hurry back!"

* * * * *

Jared made his way back to the kitchen. He noticed that most people seemed to be hanging out in the common room, and they all stared, quietly, as he passed by. He tried to ignore it and walked through quickly after seeing Chris was not there. He wasn't in the dining room area, either. In the kitchen, he found Holly's mom.

"Hi Jared, can I help you with something?"

He looked around. "I'm trying to find Chris. Would you know where he might be?"

"Did you check his Pod?"

"No, I can't remember the number."

She laughed. "No worries, come on, we'll check the greenhouse first."

She led him through the kitchen and into a pantry, which led to a hallway and into the greenhouse. It was huge. There was more fresh food in that one room than he thought all the people in the town saw in six months, maybe a year. He was, once again, astounded at everything he saw in the bunker.

"Jeanette, have you seen Chris?" Holly's mom asked Mrs. Worthington.

"He's on watch this evening; check the camera room," she offered, looking at Jared, hopefully. He just smiled back at her.

Holly's mom escorted him to the surveillance room, introducing him to various people along the way. It was more than a little uncomfortable, but they eventually made it to the room and found Chris looking through some old footage taken around the time of the battle. He looked apologetically at Mrs. Jenkins.

"Jared's been looking for you."

She turned to Jared, "If you need anything at all, I'm in Pod 1."

"Thanks so much, Mrs. Jenkins." He didn't know why, but he reached out and hugged her goodbye before she left.

"So what's up?" Chris asked.

"Holly's not up for going to the cave today, but, if you can take a break from this place and get me to Holly's Hole, I can get you up to the cave where the girls are staying."

Chris's eyes grew wide. "From Holly's Hole? You're sure? You know the way? I talked to Cassie, and she said the tunnels are dark and twisty, and they were scared they would get lost. You really think you can find them?"

"Yeah, I know the way. I'm just not sure where Holly's Hole is from here."

Chris immediately ran to find his brother, Eric, to sit watch for him so they could head out. Amos was waiting at the back door.

He looked Jared over, once. "I hear right, you going to get my girl?"

Jared knew who he was, knew that he was Lily's husband and Griffon's best friend, which made him feel uncomfortable. He shook his head yes. "Yeah, we're heading out now."

"Not without me, you're not!"

They set off for Holly's Hole as quite the awkward trio.

On the way, Jared held back behind Amos and Chris, who were busy talking.

"You figure it out yet?"

"Nah. Mrs. Jenkins brought Jared in just as I was pulling up the footage."

"Gotta be something, the way Griff just hauled ass out of here and gave himself up so easily. I mean we knew that Holly was there. He'd have done it to save her, but she weren't in no danger. Ain't that right, Jared?"

"She was too close to danger, if you ask me," he mumbled.

"Chances are, Griffon thought the same thing," Chris said optimistically. "Think they were serious and won't hurt him?"

"I don't know nothing, and I sure don't trust no AMAN to keep their word." Amos nearly spit the word, AMAN. "Ain't no one making a move to go rescue him, neither. Can't blame them, with Mike gone and the whole place in mourning. And Holly ain't said a word about it. We can't bring ourselves to ask Charlie to step in and help. His poor mama is absolutely beside herself, but I dunno what to do 'bout it."

"I'll track him just as soon as I know Holly is okay, I'll put a small crew together from town. Let the bunker grieve. There are enough trustworthy people to pull together a team. They'll do it for Holly," Jared told them.

"Funeral's in three days. Think the trail will be too cold by then? I really think she's going to need you to get through that," Chris told him honestly.

"It should be okay. I already have an idea of where they're headed, and we've made enough contacts throughout the valley that we can confirm that."

Amos and Chris both looked at each other. "So that's a yes?" Amos asked.

Jared laughed. They didn't know about Holly's task force team. How would they? "Yes, I'll get the team together, and we'll head out after the funeral... four days from now." As he confirmed the plan, they arrived at Holly's Hole.

Amos shook his hand, and Jared wasn't sure he'd ever get used to that. "Thanks, Jared. You aren't like I thought you'd be. I owe ya. Taking care of Lily and Holly, now going after Griff. Not sure how we'll ever be able to repay you."

Jared didn't know what to say, so he just turned and headed for the waterfall. "Follow me, and stay close so you don't get lost. It's going to be loud on the other side, then very dark in the tunnels," he warned.

They made their way quickly through, with no issues. When they came into the main cave, there was no sign of the girls. Jared checked the smoke room and laughed at the sight. Lily and Cassie huddled back into the side of the wall, trying desperately not to be seen.

When they saw Jared, they relaxed. "Jared Hastings! You announce yourself next time, you hear me! You about scared us half to death!" Lily fussed, while Cassie ran to hug him.

"Is Holly here?"

Jared shook his head solemnly.

"Is she okay?" Panic rose in her voice.

"She will be," he told her. "Brought you guys a surprise, though," he said more cheerfully, leading them back into the main cave.

Squeals and laughter washed out the normal, quiet calm of the cave as Lily and Cassie ran to their men. Jared stood by the window, as Holly always referred to it, thinking of how nice it would be to have a woman, or anyone for that matter, that was excited to see him. He could live or die and really, no one would care. That's just how it was for him.

Holly was the closest thing to a friend he ever had, and he knew, despite the rumors and accusations, that is all he'd ever have because he knew in his heart that he would never be good enough for her.

When the noise and excitement of their reunion started to die down, Jared led them out of the cave and back to the bunker. Along the way, they brought the girls up on all that had happened.

* * * * *

Chapter 43

HOLLY WAS anxious and had paced for what seemed like
hours when they finally returned. Cassie and Lily both
wanted to rush to her and console her, but the guys asked
them to hold off until the next day, giving her the space she
needed. Lily wasn't entirely comfortable with Jared sleeping
in the same room, much less the bed, and she let them know
it. He sighed and promised to talk to her about it.

When he walked into Pod 7, Holly was in his arms before
he even had the door closed. She was borderline hysterical.

"Hey, calm down. I'm back, and we're all fine. Cassie and
Lily are home safe and sound," he reassured her.

"You were gone a lot longer than I thought. It scared me!"
She looked at him seriously. "I can't lose you, too!"

He worried about all that she implied with her eyes. *How
could he tell her that he was leaving shortly after her father's
funeral?* The thought weighed heavily on him.

"You sure you don't want to ditch this place for a while?
It's getting late, probably not too many people still hanging
out. I could scout ahead and check for you."

"No, thanks. Charlie brought me a couple movies and
some dinner. Yours is in the fridge. If you're hungry, I
can heat it up. Maybe a quiet night, watch a movie, or
something?"

"Sure, whatever you want."

She heated up his dinner and a bag of popcorn, and they
settled onto the couch to watch the movie. They didn't talk.

When he finished eating, they readjusted. She wanted to stretch out, so they laid on the couch with her in front him, his arms around her, and a blanket over them. Not even halfway through the movie, there was a knock on the door, and before he could move to answer it, the door flew open and Chris and Cassie walked in.

"Oh!" Cassie was stunned at the sight of them intimately snuggled up on the couch together.

"I told her that you didn't want to be bothered today, but she wasn't going to sleep or shut her mouth until she saw you for herself." Chris apologized as he closed the door behind them.

Jared was trying to sit up, feeling very awkward with the situation. But Holly didn't move, leaving Jared pinned behind her.

"I'm fine, Cass, really. I'm sorry I didn't come up to get you myself. I've just been wallowing a bit, today. Sorry." She sounded pained, and Jared had the urge to console her but bit back the words and tried to keep his hands to himself, not wanting to make the situation worse.

"You are allowed to wallow. You are just not allowed to shut your friends out."

"I know, I know. I just didn't want everyone fussing over me today. It's all so surreal, you know, still sinking in. I didn't think I could handle it, especially without my besties here for support."

Cassie hugged her and cried. Holly cried, too. She hadn't done that since the moments after her father died. When the two girls broke their embrace, they both laughed, nervously. "We're a mess!" Cassie proclaimed.

Since Cassie was already on the floor, she turned around to face to the TV. Leaning back against the couch, she asked what they were watching. "Got any popcorn?" she asked.

Jared handed her the bowl. Chris rolled his eyes and moved to sit beside her.

The movie wasn't very good and within a short time, they were back to talking again.

"This reminds me of all those make-out movie dates we used to have when you and Milo were still dating," Cassie announced. "You aren't going to start making out with Jared, now, are you? Cause that would just be weird since I just mentioned Milo, and you two keep insisting that nothing is going on between you. Even though you look mighty cozy all snuggled up here, tonight."

Jared's face was bright red. Holly just laughed. Chris shook his head apologetically.

"I'm sorry, man; she has no filter after dark! I don't even know what to say about that."

"Awkward," Jared agreed.

The girls just laughed. It lifted a weight in Jared's chest to hear Holly truly laugh again, and he silently thanked Cassie for it. Jared tried to sit up, but Holly grabbed his arm and wrapped it around her waist, refusing to let him move. He lay like that for a long time, just listening to the girls talk, until he drifted off to sleep.

When he awoke, he wasn't sure how long he had been out but his body felt stiff and needed to stretch. He knew immediately that Holly was still there next to him, and, before his eyes were open, he could hear the girls still talking away.

"I can't believe they both fell asleep on us." Cassie giggled. "So come on, fill me in. What's really going on with you and Jared? Or you and Griffon?"

Jared froze and just laid there trying to control his breathing. He, too, wanted to hear the answer to these questions.

Holly absentmindedly stroked his arm while she spoke. "Griffon opened the door and just left with them, Cassie. Why would he do that? We had things under control at that point. The AMAN were outnumbered three to one by the time he did that. I can't understand it." She sounded so sad, confirming what he thought. She still loved Griffon, and he vowed to get him back for her.

"Chris has been going over tapes to see what could have triggered that. Amos thinks he saw something that made him react. Apparently, he started fighting to get out just moments before the fight really began. When you started getting shot at and headed for ground level, your dad agreed they needed to get you to safety at all costs and that's when he opened the door."

Holly sighed. That made her angry. "Neither of them truly knew me at all. I was never in any real danger. Even while they were trying to shoot me down from that perch, Jared was busy taking them out one-by-one. He wouldn't have let them get to me. We make a good team," she told her friend, and he could hear the pride and happiness in her voice.

"So, spill it. What is going on between you two?"

Jared stiffened just a bit and listened closer.

"Honestly, nothing."

"Nothing?"

"Yup, nothing." She sounded a bit exasperated. "I've tried to talk to him but I don't think he hears me. Not even sure he gets it. You kind of have to just spell things out with this one."

"Men, sheesh! They can be so stupid sometimes."

The two girls laughed.

"Seriously, Holly. I've watched that man take care of you when we thought you might die. I see how he's protecting you through all this, but on your terms, not locking you away for your own good like all the other men in your life. He's good for you. I didn't want to like him but I do, and he loves you. You do know that, right?"

"I really don't think it's like that for him, Cassie." She sighed. "But it's okay. I'll take him however I can get him." She smiled, knowingly, at her friend.

What does that mean? he wondered. He tried not to be too distracted by the soft movements of her hand up and down his arm that were sending tingles of sensations throughout his body.

"So what about Griffon? Are you going after him?"

"Yeah, I think I need to. Don't get me wrong, I'm beyond pissed at him for doing something so stupid and a little hurt that he didn't trust that I could take care of myself, especially if it turns out that he did that thinking he was protecting me or something. We were already fighting so much. I was lying to him. It wasn't a good situation, even before all this happened. I shouldn't have to lie to someone I supposedly love, should I?"

Cassie shook her head no, so Jared didn't actually know the answer.

Holly continued talking. "I have to do it for his family, though. I love them all so much, and he'll always be special to me, but I don't see him as I once did, Cassie. Maybe it'll be different when I actually find him, but I doubt it. I know that I deserve someone who will support me and not just protect me, and I don't think he can. I didn't really know how desperately I needed that until I met this one." Holly smiled at her friend while squeezing Jared's arm tighter around her.

His heart felt like it would pound out of his chest. He had never really followed girl talk before. He scolded himself to get control of his feelings, that he wasn't really hearing what he thought. Holly said that she needed someone like him, not him. She couldn't possibly love someone like him. A small voice in the back of his head kept hearing, *Don't be another stupid man; of course she loves you.* He twisted and felt cramped, then sighed.

When he opened his eyes, they were both staring at him wide-eyed, like they'd been caught with their hands in the cookie jar.

"How long have you been awake?" Holly asked.

He looked at them with an innocent face. "Long enough to know you two aren't going to stop yapping anytime soon." He tried to sound grumpy, as if they just woke him up, but he was too happy to pull it off right. "I'm going to bed. See you guys in the morning." With that, he got up, headed into the other room, and climbed in bed.

* * * * *

Soon after Chris and Cassie left, Holly joined him. "Wanna talk?" she asked, before climbing into bed.

He didn't answer, just pulled back the covers to let her climb in and snuggle up against him. He was having a harder time controlling his physical responses to her lately, and it was becoming almost uncomfortable sleeping with her in his arms now.

She lay there, quietly, for a few moments. "Okay, how much did you hear, really?"

He sighed, knowing she wasn't going to sleep or let him sleep until they were past this.

"Let's see, you're angry at Griffon but going after him because it's the right thing to do."

He hadn't yet told her that he was already working on the details of that and, while he'd prefer her not to go marching into AMAN territory after him, he also knew that she'd never let him leave without her. "And all men are stupid, especially me." He was grinning while he said that.

She gasped and punched him lightly. "You were listening in on our conversation!"

She was somehow relieved. They really needed to talk things out, but she had a tough time getting through to him. Perhaps Cassie had somehow helped that along. "Wanna talk about it?"

"Not really. I want to sleep. But, I suspect you aren't going to let that happen until we do." He rolled on his side and faced her. He told himself that no matter how much it hurt, he would not run away.

She was all he had in this world, and he wasn't willing to walk away from it because he feared rejection. He knew she didn't love him as a woman loves a man, but there was love there and whatever it amounted to, what she needed him to be for her, he was okay with that. It was so much better than not having her at all.

"What are you thinking about?" She suddenly wasn't so confident, with him looking at her so intensely.

He shook his head slowly. "I'm not very good at the personal stuff. You know that, Holly." He preferred to keep his thoughts and feelings locked away where they were safer in his mind.

She looked sad and then reached up and brushed his hair from his eyes. "Cassie is convinced that you love me."

There wasn't a question there, just a statement, but she felt relieved to have it out there.

He wanted to run and hide. It was too much, but he was determined not to. He took her hand and stroked it with his thumb, absentmindedly. He spoke very deliberately.

"You are the only person who has ever given a damn about me. The only person in this entire world that I care about. Of course, I love you." He went on, knowing that he was truly in love with her.

He had to let her know that he understood there was a difference between loving someone and being in love. She didn't need to know that he was both.

"You have so many people that love you; you can't possibly know how much it means to me. You have many friends, and I know that your best friend spot is more than full. But, you have to know that you are my best friend." *My only friend*, he added silently.

She teared up. It nearly broke her heart. He was right. She couldn't know how that felt. All that happened in the last forty-eight hours came crashing in on her, and she couldn't stop the tears.

Jared felt terrible. He hugged her close and tried to console her. *What did I say?* He didn't understand. He was trying to be honest and sincere. *Why is she crying?* He just held her and tried to be there for her.

Holly nearly cried herself to sleep, but she couldn't without finishing this. She saw the pain her tears caused him. She knew he blamed himself for them. They weren't about him. He had to know that. She sniffed loudly and tried to get a grasp on her emotions.

"I'm not crying because of anything you said; you have to know that. Sometimes, these waves just hit me, and I can't get a grip on it. Feeling anything right now seems to make me feel everything." She knew that he wasn't following but she had to tell him.

She looked at him seriously, with her puffy red eyes and tear streaked face. "You mean more to me than anyone, too, Jared. You are my best friend, and I love you."

She watched his face and saw the shock in his eyes. She expected him to kiss her but he did not. She watched him closely and saw the battle of what she meant in his eyes and, finally, the resolution of what he thought she meant. *How much clearer can I be?* She loved him, not as a friend, but as a woman should love a man.

* * * * *

Jared rolled onto his back and pulled her close. She laid her head on his chest, and he sighed. He could deal with best friend status. It was more than he ever hoped for, and she loved him, too, at least, in that way.

"You really are an idiot," she mumbled to herself.

He looked at her and grinned. "Probably," he admitted. He had a best friend. She cared about him; his heart soared. He didn't know what came over him but it was all too much to take in. He didn't think; he just felt.

He looked at her in a way that made her entire body feel like a pool of jelly. Her heart was beating faster, and she smiled at him as he leaned down and kissed her softly on the lips.

It wasn't the quick peck they had shared a few times before. His lips felt like velvet against hers, like a new beginning. As he started to back away, she pushed forward and met him with all the passion and frustration she felt. She loved him. Truly loved him.

That kiss was nearly blinding, blocking out everything else in the world. All that mattered was Jared. Their kiss seemed to last forever. There was fire and excitement mixed with comfort and understanding.

When she finally pulled away, he was more than a little shaky. He had always been scared of intimate contact, but, in this moment, he couldn't remember why. It was better than anything he ever imagined.

She was everything to him, and she was kissing him, loving him. He didn't want to get his hopes up entirely but the walls he had tried to build around his heart to protect himself from her were destroyed in that moment.

They slept in each other's arms that night, and it felt like a new beginning for them both.

* * * * *

Chapter 44

THE NEXT morning, Holly was still sleeping soundly in his arms. He had a list of things that he had to do, so he kissed her forehead, smiling at the memories of their kiss the night before.

He got up, showered, and changed. Seeing that she had still not budged, he left her a note telling her that he'd be back in the evening and that he'd have Cassie and Charlie check in on her. He signed it, "Love, Jared."

He set off for the kitchen, first, to get some breakfast. Amos and the Maynor's were all there, eating together. As usual, the room grew quiet when he entered, but nothing could dampen his spirits today.

He held his head high and walked past them into the kitchen to make a plate of food. When he returned to the dining room, contemplating going back to the pod to eat, Amos motioned him over. He hesitated a moment, then walked over to them.

Amos shook his hand and clapped him on the back, telling him to sit down and join them. He introduced him around the table, even though he had known them for many years. He politely said hello to everyone.

Fred Maynor spoke first. "I can't tell you how relieved we are that you are willing to set up a rescue mission for my son. It means a lot to us, Jared."

He nodded. "I'm just grabbing a bite to eat, then heading down to town to round up a few of Holly's boys to help out.

Most of them are Griff's men. I'm sure they'll be happy to volunteer."

Lily spoke up. "What do you mean by 'Holly's boys?'"

He blushed. He didn't think it was important that it remain such a secret, at this point, but it probably wasn't his story to tell, either. He felt trapped and continued on.

"Holly and I headed up a small intelligence task force out of Wythel, have for a while now. We monitored AMAN traffic and locations throughout the region within a two-day radius of Wythel." He tried to sound official and matter-of-fact.

"Holly's been doing that?!" Don Maynor asked sounding surprised.

Jared nodded. "Yeah... her idea, her team. She just brought me on to help her set things up and recruit the right people." Anger flooded him as he thought of how Devon Atley had betrayed them, and he knew it was his fault, but he didn't mention that.

"Did Griffon know about this?" Griffon's mom asked, sounding disapproving.

"I really don't know, ma'am. With Griffon injured and held close to the bunker, I haven't seen him since before the original shooting. Talked to him a few times on the radio but that's about it, and the conversation was not about our team."

He tried to sound apologetic. He tried to think of how he would feel if the AMAN took Holly like that, and he shuttered at the thought.

"I don't mean to sound harsh," his mom continued. "I'm just really surprised to hear it. Griffon never mentioned anything about it to us."

Jared thought from what he heard about Griffon and Holly the last few days; he seriously doubted that he knew anything about it. Wasn't sure he really even knew Holly, for that matter.

"So what's your plan, then?" Don questioned.

"We'll start with getting the team together. Some of them probably have continued scouting without us and may have reports of camp sightings in the area. They certainly weren't trying to cover their tracks, so I'm hoping I can pick it up easily. Already have a good idea in what direction they headed. I'm hoping my guys can confirm that, today. Holly's by far our best tracker, so if she chooses to stay behind, we'll have to compensate for that some, but we'll manage."

"Holly? You can't take Holly on a suicide mission to rescue Griffon; that's ridiculous!" Lily was furious.

"Lily, you know Holly better than that," he said, seriously, and saw the impact of his words register on her face. "I'm not telling her to go. I'm not even asking her to go. But, if she decides that's what she needs to do, it's not my place to stop her."

Fred Maynor turned to his wife, who was begging him to do something. "We'll have her put on lockdown after the funeral. We'll keep her safe; don't worry. She's far too emotional after the death of her father to go running into AMAN country on a suicide mission."

Jared did not say a single word. They really didn't understand her at all, and it made him sad. He appreciated that so many people loved her enough to want to protect her, but they didn't seem to understand that they were smothering her in the process. She needs to be free to live her life the way she wants.

After breakfast, he went back to the Pod to grab his daypack. Holly was still sleeping peacefully. He kissed her forehead and headed out. He passed Cassie in the hallway.

"Just the girl I wanted to see." He grinned at her.

She laughed, enjoying this upbeat Jared. "What's up?"

"I need a favor. I have to run into town to take care of a few things today. Keep an eye on our girl for me?"

"Certainly! What are you up to in town?"

"A Griffon rescue mission. I need to find our boys and get a small team together. Don't tell Holly," he added, with a wink, knowing that she absolutely would tell her.

* * * * *

Milo was waiting at the door for him.

"You're Jared Hastings, right?" Milo extended his hand.

Jared smiled, thinking how strange it was that everyone here wanted to shake his hand. No one had ever offered that to him outside this odd group.

"I'm kind of in a hurry; what's up?"

"Mind if I join you?"

"Uh, sure. I'm heading down to town for the day."

"I know," Milo said.

When they were safely out of the bunker, Milo seemed to relax. "I want in."

"In what?"

"Griffon's rescue mission. I want in on it."

"Why? Seriously, why? From everything I know, you're more politician and talker than rescue team. No offense, but it takes every kind to make a village."

"No offense taken. It's mostly true, and you may need that along the way. I'm strong and capable. Better than most. Holly will tell you she's the best shot in the bunker, but, I can hold my own against her as long as she doesn't bring out that blasted slingshot." He laughed and so did Jared. "I can keep up and pull my own weight. I won't let you down." He was practically begging.

"Aren't you engaged, and aren't you one of the elders in the bunker? Won't they need you? I have no idea how long we'll be gone." Jared would have to discuss it with Holly to make sure she was okay with him going, but he didn't mention that part.

"I have to do this! It's my father's fault that all this happened. He fled like a coward, after the battle. No one has seen him, since. It's up to me to right my family's wrongs!"

Jared felt sorry for the man.

"I know that feeling better than most, but, you have to remember that you are not your father, Milo. His wrong doings are not yours. They are not representative of who or what you are. It took me a long time to understand that. Probably still not the greatest at it, but, you need to really think about that."

Milo nodded. He liked this guy. "Think about it?"

"Sure. Want to tag along and see what we can put together today?"

Milo was quick to accept and thanked him for giving him a chance.

By the end of the day, they had five guys on board who would leave from Wythel and meet them at a designated location in three days. Milo proved himself invaluable by convincing the guys and sorting out the details.

He was precise and questioned everything, and Jared knew the team was all the stronger for it. He still needed to discuss him actually going with Holly, but, as far as Jared was concerned, he thought it would be okay.

On the way back, Jared shared the Maynor's concerns about Holly going.

"They'll never let her go, Jared. You're going to have to come to terms with that and keep her there, safe and sound, until we return. Let her know that we have this under control. She'll be safe there; I promise."

Jared shook his head. "How is it that no one in that bunker seems to know her at all? I already told them that I wouldn't ask her to go, but I know Holly. She'll want to go, and, if she sets her mind to it, why does anyone think they can change her mind or even have a right to do so?"

Milo rolled his eyes. "No wonder she's crazy about you! Holly doesn't know fear; it's not even in her vocabulary. She doesn't always think straight and gets herself in trouble more often than not. She doesn't always know what's best for her. She acts emotionally, and not always rationally. I've seen how depressed she gets locked away, but it's really for her own good."

Jared shook his head, no. "You're wrong about her, Milo." He didn't bother to try to explain.

* * * * *

The door to Pod 7 was open when he arrived back at the bunker. It was standing room only inside, as everyone was dropping in to check on Holly. Her mother and brother were both there, going over the funeral arrangements for her father the next day. Jared watched her for a moment. She looked exhausted, trapped, and overwhelmed. His desire to protect her was strong, and he finally pushed his way forward.

When she saw him making his way into the room, she felt like she could breathe for the first time. She saw him stop and fuss at Cassie for allowing so many people in. It made her smile.

Charlie noticed Holly's spirits lift when Jared walked into the room. The stress of the day seemed to melt away with his presence. It worried him a little. He had spoken with the Maynor's earlier in the day and knew Jared was planning a rescue mission for Griffon. He would have to talk to him and make sure he understood the importance of not discussing the plans with Holly. He knew that she would try to follow them, and he couldn't allow that to happen.

Jared made his way over to Holly and knelt beside her. "Decided to throw a party while I was away?" He smiled, wanting to touch her, to kiss her, to reassure her. She smiled back, and the relief on her face melted his heart. "You okay with all this?"

She shook her head no, and then spoke. "It's important to mom, though, so I'll survive."

He nodded, then leaned in and whispered, "If you change your mind, just let me know. I'm good at being a jerk!"

She smiled gratefully at him. Charlie and their mother both noticed the encounter.

Charlie got up to stretch and talk to Jared.

"Is all this really necessary, Charlie?"

Charlie winced. "There are a lot of people who care about her, Jared, not just you. Everyone just wanted to make sure she was okay."

"I get that, but, don't you think this is a bit much?"

"Yeah, I'll clear them out."

"Thanks," Jared said. He offered his hand. Charlie smiled and shook it.

Charlie didn't make a big scene about it like Jared would have. Instead, he went from person to person and said a few words. Jared saw them nod and say their goodbyes. As the crowd dwindled to Charlie, Holly's mother, Chris, and Cassie, Holly felt she could finally breathe. She stood up, stretched, and walked over to hug Jared.

"Don't leave me like that again. These fools let just about anyone in." She was only half joking. She loved her family and the people in the bunker, but it had been a long stressful day.

He kissed her forehead and smiled. "It's over now; you can relax."

"You should have gone to the common room, like I told you this morning. Then you could have left when it got to be too much, and everyone would have been okay with it," Chris chimed in.

Holly sighed. "You're probably right."

Her mom got up to go. "I'm getting hungry, and I think we have everything settled for tomorrow."

Jared looked down at Holly. "Want to go down for dinner tonight?" He was hungry, too, and thought it would be good for her.

"Not really, but I will. Just promise that we don't have to stay and socialize. We'll just eat and come back here to relax."

He nodded and rubbed her shoulders while shooting a look at Cassie, who lowered her head, knowing that she failed to take care of her friend.

The six of them headed down to the kitchen. Holly had to admit that she enjoyed herself. The food was good. People spoke with her but didn't smother her as they had in her Pod. They stayed longer than they had planned before heading back to their Pod.

* * * * *

It was the first time they were alone since the kiss they shared the night before, and she suddenly felt shy. He had kissed her passionately, but they didn't really settle anything or talk about it, yet. She was so disappointed when she awoke to an empty bed this morning and thought maybe he freaked out and left. If he hadn't left that note, she would have been certain of it.

Jared settled easily onto the couch, and Holly sat on the opposite end. She didn't snuggle up to him as she normally did. He felt pain in his heart. Something was wrong.

"Are we okay, Holly?" He tried to keep the sadness and desperation out of his voice.

She turned, smiled at him, and jumped into his arms, tackling him against the back of the couch. She hugged him tightly and just held him close. It was a while before she spoke.

When she looked up at him, he tucked a stray hair behind her ear, and it sent shivers down her body from that simple touch. He wanted to kiss her but wasn't sure it was okay. She must have read his mind because she kissed him, relishing in the velvet warmth that surrounded them.

He breathed deeply and looked into her eyes. "We have a lot to talk about."

She nodded.

"Charlie doesn't want me to tell you this. Most of the bunker doesn't want me to tell you this... but you need to know. I have a group of five men... our guys, but only those I trust the most. We're going to get Griffon back." He watched her closely.

"I know. Cassie told me. When do we leave?"

He cringed. "They aren't going to let you go with me, Holly. They'll be watching you closely and are prepared to put you on lock down if they need to do that."

She sat, away from him. "You agreed to that?" The pain of betrayal tore through her.

"Of course not; don't be ridiculous! This is your decision to make, only yours," he assured her.

"I'm going. I want to be with you. I need to see this through. We need to see this through. We're stronger together, you and I, you have to know that."

"I do," he said simply. "You're certain? This is what you want?"

"I'm positive!"

"Okay then, you cannot tell anyone. We'll have to move quickly. Right now, everyone thinks I'm pulling out in two days. We have to pull together everything we need and get it out of the bunker tonight.

"How important is your father's life celebration tomorrow? Because honestly, the actual funeral will be outdoors and our best chance of getting away with little notice, but it's your decision. I don't want you to have any regrets, and I don't want you to feel like you missed out on your final goodbye. We'll come up with another plan, if that's the case." He squeezed her hand for encouragement.

She thought about it. Her mom and brother would need to lean on her through the funeral, which was the bad part.

The Life Celebration would just be a party, of sorts, where people recount stories of her father throughout his years of life. The spotlight would be on her at the party, and getting away afterward would be tough, especially since they were locking the doors at night, now. She knew all the stories. She carried them with her. She could relive them another day. Jared was right; this was her best chance.

She looked up at him. "I'm in. After the funeral, while everyone is heading inside, we go."

Charlie may never forgive her for it, but it was something she felt she had to do.

"Alright, so next question. Milo Weaver?"

She rolled her eyes, not getting what he was asking. "Milo? Really? What do you want to know? We dated briefly because our families more or less insisted. We were engaged for a short time. He's currently engaged to Emma Grace." She was about to go on when Jared laughed.

"I'm not quizzing you on ex-boyfriends, Holly. Milo wants to go with us. He feels terrible that his father instigated the whole thing and wants to make it right. So, is Milo in or out? He claims to be almost as good a shot as you are and able to handle himself in combat. Plus, he's really smart and good with talking. He already convinced the boys to join us."

"Yeah, sure, whatever. He can handle himself, I think. Emma Grace already hates me, so no harm there."

They finalized their plans and packed supplies for the long trip ahead. They worked side-by-side, talking little. By midnight, they managed to smuggle out both their packs, with upgraded supplies, and two small tents. Holly gathered enough emergency food bars to sustain them for a few weeks. Even if hunting was bad and they couldn't eat off the trail, they wouldn't starve.

By one o'clock, they collapsed in bed, exhausted, and fell fast asleep.

* * * * *

Holly woke first, still lying in Jared's arms. She looked at him sleeping soundly and smiled. He often appeared a bit rough around the edges, but, when he relaxed, as he did now in sleep, it hit her how insanely handsome he really was. She looked him over, thoroughly memorizing the cut of his jaw, the shape of his nose, everything about him. She knew it would embarrass him to have her look at him like that, so she tried not to often; but while he slept, she could look all she wanted.

He woke and opened his eyes to find her staring at him. He smiled at her. "Good morning," he told her, reveling in the sensation of waking with her in his arms. He snuggled her closer and kissed her forehead. She turned her face to him and kissed him. He wasn't sure he'd ever get used to that feeling. "Mmm, definitely a good morning."

He stroked her hair down her back. "You ready for today?"

"I'm ready; are you?"

"Ready."

As they got up, got dressed, and got ready to start the day, things moved quickly. Holly went to be with her mom, and Jared met up with Milo and told him the plan. Milo nodded. He would help shuffle everyone into the bunker so Jared could get Holly away, and then he would meet up with them.

It seemed like only moments later, they were all standing outside in their best suits and dresses, saying goodbye to the father and founder of the compound. Mrs. Sawyer, who often played music for their Sunday services, played a haunting tune on her violin that echoed off the mountain. They sung a couple of old hymns that Jared didn't know. Several people came up and told of memories or special moments in Mike Jenkins life. Everyone cried.

Jared didn't even know the man, and he, too, cried for Holly's pain and the man that had called him son and thanked him for caring for his daughter. Holly fought back tears as Charlie spoke and then her mother.

They lowered Mike Jenkins' body into the freshly dug grave, and then Holly took the stand to say a few words.

"My father always said that no matter what happens in this world, our job is to protect and love one another. To continue on past the despair and ugliness of this life. To find hope in a hopeless situation and pursue a better future for tomorrow. His life was a testament to these ideals. He died by example; now we must continue on for the common good."

She gave Jared a knowing look. People came forward, one-by-one, and shoveled dirt into the hole containing her father's body as she, Charlie, and their mother stood by, thanking everyone for coming and accepting their condolences. Jared was at the end of the line.

"I'm so sorry for your loss," he told her mother, who hugged him and thanked him.

"Sorry, " he told Charlie. They shook hands, and Charlie clapped him on the shoulder.

Lastly, he turned to Holly with open arms. She hugged him tightly and buried her head into his chest. She was crying. Her mother and brother looked on and then squeezed Jared's arm as they passed by, silently thanking him for taking care of her. They let the two of them have their moment and headed inside with the others.

"You okay?" Jared asked.

Holly turned to look one last time at the now filled hole and said her final goodbye to her father.

"Let's go!"

They ran.

* * * * *

To be continued...

Get a sneak peek at
Julie Trettel's anticipated
sequel...

COMPOUNDERS:
DISSENSION

BOOK TWO
THE COMPOUNDER SERIES

JULIE TRETTEL

Coming in 2016

Sneak Peek

HOLLY COULD see her mountain on the horizon and it gave her strength she didn't know she still had.

"Look!" She pointed with excitement. Her voice was hoarse against the bitter cold. "Up there, that's my mountain."

The others looked up, and a spark of excitement grew, fueling them onward. They were too close to give up now. Holly examined their sunken faces and tired eyes. They were too skinny, all of them. Looking down at the clothes swimming around her, she knew this last week weighed heavily on her as well. The knowledge that they would all be safe and sound, warm, and fed when they reached the compound lifted her spirits and gave her hope.

They pressed on through the cold wind. Snow was falling again, and the ground was dusted white. No one knew what day it was for sure, but it would all be behind them soon.

As they neared Wythel, Holly stopped.

"What is it?" Milo asked.

"I'm not sure," she admitted. "But come on; let's check it out."

There was something not quite right off in the distance. She couldn't put her finger on it, but from where she stood, she could see that something had changed.

As they neared, they saw what appeared to be a large fence. As they approached, they were perplexed and confused. They backed up and looked for a way over or around it. It was too high to climb over, and there was no end in sight to go around it. So they followed it west towards one of the main roads into Wythel.

When they finally arrived at the road, they found a large blockade and a locked gate.

"Hey, you up there." Holly shouted to someone in a tower above. "What is all this?"

"Ma'am, you are coming upon Compounder territory, you'll have to redirect around the town limits. If you seek admission into Wythel, you'll need to proceed west about half a mile to the newcomer processing center and tell them you are seeking conversion. If you're just passing through, you need to continue on around our walls."

"What's your name?" Jared shouted up.

"Eric, sir, Eric Weaver and I'm sorry, but that's as much as I'm at liberty to say. Good day to you all and best of luck."

He turned and started to walk away.

"Eric, get back here." Milo yelled.

They all watched as he froze and turned slowly back to the group below.

"Milo? Is that really you?"

"Yes little brother, now let us in; we're freezing and we're starving."

"Holy crap! I gotta call this in. Is Holly with you?"

"I'm right here Eric."

"Charlie's never gonna believe this. We thought you were all dead!"

* * * * *

About the Author

JULIE TRETTEL is a full time Systems Administrator, Wife, Mother of four, and part time Musician and Writer. She resides in Richmond, VA and can often be found writing on the sidelines of a football field or swimming pool. She comes from a long line of story tellers and has a thousand stories running through her mind.

Writing has always been a stress reliever and escape for her to manage the crazy demands of juggling time and schedules between work and an active family of six. In her "free time," she enjoys traveling, reading, outdoor activities, and spending time with family and friends. Her husband, James, challenged her to write a book in one year, and she took on and mastered that challenge. This is her first published work.

* * * * *

Visit
www.JulieTrettel.com
for more information

CPSIA information can be obtained
at www.ICGtesting.com
Printed in the USA
FFOW02n0501050716
25585FF

9 781624 870804